the LIBERATION

Malcolm blinked. His lips moved, like a goldfish blowing bubbles.

The dash across the gardens had left him flushed, his fading-pink cheeks at odds with the rest of him, which had gone pale. His pupils were dilated.

Malcolm found his voice. "But, Tuinier . . . it *is* the end of the world."

The din from Scheveningen Pier swelled again. But the crowd wasn't cheering, she realized.

It was screaming.

By Ian Tregillis

The Milkweed Triptych
Bitter Seeds
The Coldest War
Necessary Evil

The Alchemy Wars
The Mechanical
The Rising
The Liberation

Something More Than Night

the LIBERATION

THE ALCHEMY WARS: BOOK THREE

IAN TREGILLIS

orbit

www.orbitbooks.net

ORBIT

First published in Great Britain in 2016 by Orbit

1 3 5 7 9 10 8 6 4 2

All characters and events in this publication, other than those clearly in the public domain, are fictitious and any resemblance to real persons, living or dead, is purely coincidental.

A CIP catalogue record for this book
is available from the British Library.

ISBN 978-0-356-50234-2

Printed and bound in Great Britain by
Clays Ltd, St Ives plc

Papers used by Orbit are from well-managed forests
and other responsible sources.

MIX
Paper from
responsible sources
FSC® C104740

Orbit
An imprint of
Little, Brown Book Group
Carmelite House
50 Victoria Embankment
London EC4Y 0DZ

An Hachette UK Company
www.hachette.co.uk

www.orbitbooks.net

In memory of Jeanie Davis Pullen. We miss you, Jeanie, and wish you could see us now.

PART I

SERVANTS AND MASTERS

One has to be servant before one can be master.

—From the letters of Kiliaen van Rensselaer, a founder and director of the Dutch West India company, 10 May 1638

This day a good pretty maid was sent my wife by Mary Bowyer, whom my wife has hired.

—From the Diary of Samuel Pepys, 22 November 1661

So home and to read, I being troubled to hear my wife rate though not without cause at her mayd [sic] Nell, who is a lazy slut.

—From the Diary of Samuel Pepys, 12 January 1662

CHAPTER 1

She'd been home in her beloved Central Provinces barely a week when the plague ships arrived from the New World.

But this particular morning, the morning the world ended, didn't find Anastasia Bell preoccupied with thoughts of Nieuw Nederland, or New France, or Free Will, or even the Sacred Guild of Horologists and Alchemists. Instead, she anticipated the removal of her casts and finally strolling—well, hobbling—through the winter gardens with her nurse. The winter gardens weren't Anastasia's favorite of all the green spaces in The Hague, but at least they wouldn't smell like hospital antiseptic and bedpans. Plus, Rebecca would be there, prettier than any flower.

Roused by the anticipation before dawn, Anastasia spent the wolf hours watching the moon sink from the sky like a damaged airship. It dipped behind the towering spire of the Sint-Jacobskerk, the ancient St. James Church, as the rising sun pinked the bone-white cupola atop the old Town Hall. Both buildings predated Het Wonderjaar, Christiaan Huygens's miracle year: They'd been built in the earliest decades of the seventeenth century, at the birth of a Dutch Golden Age that continued unbroken centuries later to this very day. A mile or so to the northwest, the Scheveningen Lighthouse winked at her with metronomic regularity.

The city was calm at night, she found, but never truly quiet and never truly still. Like every great city in the Central Provinces, the dark hours of The Hague echoed with the ticktock rattle-clatter of Clakkers' metal bodies as they loaded and unloaded wagons, swept the streets, delivered packages, prepared their masters' breakfasts and mended their clothes, carried drunks to their homes, monitored the citywide network of flood control dikes and pumps, hauled freight along the tow canals, and did everything else their geasa demanded. The city never slept, because mechanicals never slept. At some point in the lonely hours after midnight Anastasia realized everything moving in the city was clad in steel and alchemical brass: It was as though the humans had disappeared, and their creations had taken over.

A pair of metal feet clicked across the parquet floor. The machine navigated the dark room with catlike surety. It had probably detected the glimmer of moonlight upon her open eyes while making the rounds. The ticktocking of its internal mechanisms echoed in the shadows. Compared to her silent fretting it was loud as a brass band. A peculiar timbre in its body noise suggested outdated alchemical alloys, marking it as an older model, perhaps one forged in the mid-eighteenth century. Those lots had used a rare black Corinthian bronze, she knew. But Anastasia couldn't turn her head to see if moonglow revealed a liverish patina; the boredom was too heavy.

In the reedy wheeze that passed for a Clakker's whisper, it said, "I humbly beg your pardon for the interruption, mistress, but I notice you are not sleeping. Are you in pain? Shall I summon a physician for you?"

A throb of pain shot through her bandaged hand. She flexed her fingers. They tingled as if mildly burned. If she could have moved her arm, she would have stuck her fingertips in her mouth.

"No. Leave me."

There followed a momentary syncopation in the clockwork rattle as the machine integrated this new command amongst all the other geasa controlling its behavior. Its primary function at the hospital was patient care, which gave it some latitude for overriding obstinate patients when health issues required it. But Anastasia wasn't just any patient.

"Immediately, mistress." It departed without offering to fluff her pillows.

When not watching the moon, or the city, she was checking the clock, waiting for Doctor Riordan to begin his morning rounds. Or worrying that the lack of sleep would dull her mind and hang dark bags under her eyes. Which heightened her anxiety, thus making it all the more difficult to sleep. She'd so anticipated her private visit with Rebecca—how cruel that when it finally came, she'd be an ugly dullard. She yearned to emerge from her plaster cocoon at her prettiest wittiest.

Her stomach rumbled. But she knew she'd have no food today until the casts were off, just in case they had to shoot her full of painkillers again. She resolved not to groan or flinch.

Maybe on their walk they could visit a bakery. Anastasia hadn't enjoyed good hot banketstaaf since before her errand to the New World.

Finally, after it seemed the moon might rise and set again while Anastasia waited, Rebecca entered with her cart. The whites of her uniform blazed in the morning sun, every pleat and seam perfectly pressed, every strand of her golden curls corralled beneath her starched cap. She paused just inside the door. Face impassive, she locked eyes with Anastasia and tugged a single lock out of place. It dangled at the corner of her left eye like a party streamer.

Trapped within their plaster prisons, Anastasia's knees oozed like overheated candle wax.

"Foul coquette," she mouthed.

Doctor Riordan entered. "Good morning, Anastasia."

Per her own request, he addressed her informally, although at first he'd omitted reference to her title only with visible unease. As if he expected the slight to conjure a herd of Stemwinders.

"Good morning, Doctor."

Rebecca quickly tucked the errant lock in place while the doctor took Anastasia's chart from the hook at the foot of her bed. He shook his head. "I continue to marvel at your survival, much less your recovery." Injuries requiring alchemical bandages were quite rare in the Central Provinces; Anastasia was probably his first opportunity to observe firsthand this cutting edge of the medical arts. "Nurse, raise those casts a bit, won't you?"

Behind him, Rebecca reached for a pair of hooks on the wall. Anastasia gritted her teeth. To the hooks were tied lines that ran over a system of pulleys to the slings cradling the plaster on her arms and legs. (Legs that, she'd later learned from the ship's physician, had crackled like shattered porcelain when the hunters found her.) But it wasn't her limbs that hurt; raising the casts jostled her aching ribs. The sigils embedded in the casts and bandages had fueled her recuperation, but they'd done nothing for the pain.

Alchemy was useful but never compassionate. Every Clockmaker knew that.

Riordan would be more impressed if he knew the truth behind her injuries. But she'd be the last to admit she'd been trampled by a Stemwinder. Bad enough she'd had to liquidate the hunters who'd found her in the Guild's demolished safe house. She would have died of exposure if not for their compassionate and quick-thinking intervention. (Nieuw Nederland's North River Valley in midwinter was far, far colder than the temperate Central Provinces.) But between her injuries and the barely functional Stemwinder attempting to keep her alive, they'd seen too much, perhaps enough to piece the story together. Poor bastards. The ship's physician had met with his own unfortunate accident as well, falling overboard and plunging into the frigid North Atlantic not long after innocently remarking how one particular bruise on Anastasia's chest resembled a perfect hoofprint. She was particularly bitter about *that* killing. The crossing had been sheer misery (every sway and shudder of the ship agony to her shattered bones) on top of which it had taken extra effort to subvert the human-safety metageas on the ship's Clakker porter. A wily French spy had stolen the pendant that established Anastasia's affiliation with the Verderer's Office before leaving her for dead.

She tossed a smile over the doctor's shoulder. Rebecca caught and returned it: an honest grin that touched her entire face, from eyes to dimples. Anastasia's job required a certain amount of skill when it came to reading people for signs of honesty and deceit. Tiring work, and not always pleasant: sometimes loud, sometimes smelly, and often a bit messy. What a pleasant change, that the truth of a woman's heart could be given so freely.

The doctor inspected her casts, and even gave them a sniff. He ignored the special bandages swaddling her hand. That injury was a Guild matter more than a medical matter and strictly enforced as such. Doctor Huysman had been on duty the morning an honor guard of servitor mechanicals skidded into the emergency clinic with Anastasia's stretcher held aloft. A competent physician she was, too, but overly dedicated to her craft. She'd tried to tweeze the pulverized alchemical glass from Anastasia's shredded palm and so ran afoul of the Verderers. Huysman had taken an early retirement the very next day. Or so they said.

Alchemical glass could do terrible things to a person, if implanted carefully. Anastasia had overseen one such procedure from the observation gallery of an operating theatre. But that had been the culmination of extensive and delicate effort; this glass had been crushed into her hand during a moment of deadly chaos.

Perhaps it was only a few minutes, but it seemed the clock ticked away half a century while Riordan assessed her general health and the efficacy of the sigils. He took extra care with Anastasia because of her position, she knew.

Get on with it already, she thought. *I have a date. And she wants to spend time with me because of* me, *not because of who I am.*

Another decade passed. Riordan said, in his peculiar shamrock-accented Dutch, "Well. I think these casts have done all they can. How would you feel if we removed them?"

"I'd feel you'd spared yourself a great deal of trouble. One more day in this prison and I'll order a machine to break *your* legs."

"That won't do," he said, paling. Rebecca, who thought Anastasia was kidding, stifled a chuckle. The effort shook loose the errant lock. Anastasia wondered how it would feel between her teeth. Riordan nodded at the nurse—sparing a moment to frown at her dishevelment—and took a pen from her tray.

"Machine. Come here," he said. Sure enough, its carapace had the bruise-purple sheen of hepatizon: black bronze. A bead of sweat took root at the hollow of Riordan's temple. She could read his concerns as easily as a newspaper: What would come of him if this went awry? Would his retirement be as abrupt as Doctor Huysman's? After Rebecca affixed a cutting tool to a socket in the servitor's palm, the doctor ordered it: "Remove those casts."

A low whine enveloped the blade. The medical servitor worked with the inhuman speed and precision of its kind, bisecting the cast on her left leg before the first puffs of ground plaster dusted the floor.

Riordan and Rebecca gripped the cast with a pair of spreaders, separated the plaster shells, and gently laid her unsuspended leg upon the bed. For the first time in weeks, Anastasia saw her own skin. It had never been so hairy. Her pedicured and brightly painted toenails—Rebecca's work, again—were a question mark punctuating the ineloquent sentence of her leg.

And then the smell hit her. The odor of unwashed skin billowed from her body. It watered Anastasia's eyes. So did the humiliation. *Why must Rebecca be here? Why must she smell my shame?*

She flicked a sidelong glance at the nurse and doctor. Both wore a stony expression. They'd smelled worse, no doubt, and had known what to expect. Knowing this didn't soften the indignity.

Anastasia closed her eyes. The machine leaned over her again, the blade whined, a creak and crack, and then fresh cool air touched her other leg, her naked arms. The stench worsened with every limb. No amount of charm, no flirtation, could overcome the mental image surely burned into the nurse's mind now.

Doctor Riordan turned his back to preserve Anastasia's modesty while Rebecca and the medical Clakker unwrapped the bandages around her torso. He asked, "How do you feel?"

"I want a bath," she said, in a voice that couldn't have been her own. Her voice hadn't been so small since she was a girl poling punts along the rustic canals of Giethoorn.

"Don't take too long," said the nurse. "I have plans for a walk in the gardens this afternoon."

Somehow this smile, too, was genuine.

The Clakker returned bearing a pair of canes. Riordan said, "You're weaker than you think. Let's make certain you won't re-break your arms and legs, eh?"

⁂

Physical therapy, Anastasia decided, was a mild form of torture. And she knew a thing or two about torture.

But after pain came the luxury of a steamy bath. She dashed off a few sketches in colored pencil and dispatched a servitor on a shopping mission; it carried a long list of her current measurements (all the best shops in the city had her on file, but weeks of forced indolence had done her body no favors) and detailed descriptions of her new apparel. Next she shaved and scrubbed her skin until it tingled and the gray pallor became a pink glow. Then, after another Clakker replaced her bath water, she shampooed her hair twice. When she wiped condensation from the mirror, she didn't recognize herself. Her face was somehow both rounder and yet more gaunt than it had been before she'd sailed to the New World to question the French spy. But she brushed her hair and teeth, and perfumed herself with lavender oil, and soon her first new clothes in months arrived.

She emerged from the steamy bath like a newborn, without shame or self-consciousness, and let the machines dress her. The haberdasher, milliner, cordwainer, and dressmaker (or, rather, their Clakkers, which had crafted the clothing in less than an hour) had met Anastasia's every specification. The fit wasn't ideal, as she hadn't been present for final adjustments, but it was suitable. The boots squeezed her feet and would need a cobbler, but not today. She'd devoted days of thought to what she'd wear and how she'd wear it. Every fold.

To the blank canvas of her body they applied crimson silk undergarments; black stockings; a dark-gray woolen blouse with burgundy piping; a velvet skirt of matching burgundy that reached just below her knees; low-heeled boots of supple gray leather that reached just below the skirt hem; elbow-length gloves and a belt of the same leather; a black choker ribbon at her throat threaded with silver and adorned with a polished garnet; and matching garnet earrings. Silver buckles on the boot cuffs glinted to match the buckle on her belt and what she hoped would be an impish sparkle in her eyes. She put her hair up, and used an extra handful of pins to keep the milliner's work in place. A cartwheel hat girded with a burgundy ribbon, it rested on her head at an angle just on the flirty side of careless. For fending off the late-winter damp she donned a cashmere cape lined with crown sable fur. The hood slouched between her shoulders with just the right air of insouciance.

In the old days she would have slimmed herself with a corset, but the belt was painful enough. The slightest tug caused her ribs to groan like rusty hinges.

Rebecca met her in the south vestibule, a humble tweed cloak slung over her uniform. Her eyes widened.

"Goodness," she said. "I barely recognize you. You've cast off your plaster chrysalis and become a butterfly. And what wings you have!"

"What, these rags?" Grinning made Anastasia's cheeks ache. "I couldn't resist treating myself just a bit."

"I hadn't realized a walk in the gardens could be..." The nurse examined herself. "I'm underdressed, I fear."

"Nonsense. You're exquisite."

Rebecca blushed. With a quick glance over her shoulder to ensure the doctors and head nurse wouldn't see, she reached under the brim of her cap to again tug loose a single curl. It bobbed beside her temple. Anastasia's heart hurried to match its rhythm.

"Shall we?"

A medical servitor shadowed the pair, ready to leap forward should Anastasia stumble, but per her command it lagged several paces behind. Frailty gave her an excuse to take the nurse's arm, to lean close and catch her scent.

The south vestibule opened on the hospital's own garden, which was small but abutted the Paviljoensgracht, the old Pavilion Canal, directly across from the winter gardens. A strong sea breeze sent clouds scudding through a sky unusually bright for late winter. Patchwork shadows mottled the gardens. Gravel crunched underfoot. The humid smell of the nearby canal enveloped them, as did the usual city sounds: the rumble of traffic, the tolling of church bells, the lapping of water in the canals, the creak of oarlocks, the cumulative hum of ten thousand clockwork men dedicated to their owners' every whim. It must have been a race day; the din of raised voices from Scheveningen was audible even here, over a mile away.

The women strolled arm-in-arm past low hawthorn hedges and winter-bare rosebushes. Each kept to herself as if waiting for the other to begin. The awkward moment stretched like cheap wool. Anastasia ransacked her conversational cupboard but found it bare as the rosebushes. She chewed her lip to stave off a twinge of panic. Such anticipation, only to find herself bashful as a schoolgirl? The injuries had changed her.

Rebecca proved the more courageous. "Did we neglect to remove the cast from your tongue?"

Caught off guard, but also relieved, Anastasia laughed like an uncouth fishwife. "I'm filing a malpractice suit this afternoon."

Ice broken, conversation came easier after that. They turned east, toward the canal.

Rebecca pointed to a hansom weaving through traffic on the Torenstraat. The steel rims on its wheels struck sparks from the paving stones. The servitor pulling it moved so quickly its legs were almost invisible.

She said, "Heavens. He's in quite a hurry."

The taxi fishtailed onto the hospital's horseshoe drive. It sent a fine spray of gravel pattering like hail against the windows when the servitor brought the carriage sliding to a halt. A man leapt from the cab and disappeared inside the hospital. He passed too quickly for Anastasia to be certain, but he looked familiar. She tensed. But Rebecca shrugged, and her smile dispelled the unease. They resumed their walk. The din of the city swelled; the races out at Scheveningen Pier must have been quite exciting.

Worried a medical emergency might cut short their visit, Anastasia asked, "Have you younger siblings, Rebecca? Taking care of others is second nature to you, I think."

"Now, who told you that?"

"Nobody. But I'm quite good at reading people."

"I do have—"

Behind them, the door to the south vestibule banged open. "Tuinier! Tuinier Bell!"

Anastasia froze. *Oh, no. Please, don't do this to me.*

"Goodness!" Rebecca turned for the source of the commotion. Anastasia did likewise, one eye on the man running toward them and the other on the nurse, hoping beyond all reason that he'd shut up.

"Anastasia Bell!" he called across the gardens. "Wait, please! I must speak with you at once!"

The medical servitor sprang forward. It landed lightly beside them and said, "Mistress, I believe that gentleman wishes a word with you. It appears to be a matter of some urgency. Shall I convey you to him?"

No. No, no, no, not now.

The man from the taxi jogged closer. She recognized Malcolm, a fellow Verderer. She craned her neck to look at the hansom again, but couldn't see the door. "Tuinier Bell!" he cried. "Tuinier Bell, wait!"

Anastasia groaned. *Shut* up, *you fool.*

Muscles twitched in Rebecca's arm. "That man. He's calling you, 'Tuinier.' "

Anastasia closed her eyes. *Damn it.* "Yes. He is."

"Oh. I..." Rebecca's gaze flicked back and forth, never meeting her eyes, as though she were a cornered rabbit and Anastasia a fox. "I knew you're a Guildwoman, of course. Because of your injuries. I mean the glass—I mean, I haven't seen it, but your hand, I haven't pried, honestly, but after Doctor Huysman went away...But you didn't seem—Oh! I mean, I didn't realize... the Verderers..."

The Verderer's Office: that special arm of the Sacred Guild of Horologists and Alchemists charged with protecting the Clockmakers' secrets, and thus by extension the de facto secret police for the Dutch Empire. True or not, everybody had heard dread tales of the Verderers' clockwork centaurs, the Stemwinders, and their human masters. The tales never emphasized the Verderers' vital role in perpetuating the Dutch Golden Age; only dark rumors of what that entailed. The Verderers patrolled the walled garden of Guild secrets, ensuring nothing entered—not the tiniest aphid—as well as eradicating any shoots that might poke past the walls. The Tuinier was the chief gardener.

Anastasia sighed. "Yes. I command the Stemwinders."

And . . . there it went. Like a feat of emotional alchemy, that four-word incantation transmuted flirtatious attraction to quiet fear. It extinguished the coquettish sparkle in the nurse's eyes. In its stead came the flat, fragile glassiness that always materialized when somebody took a tight rein on her thoughts and words. Anastasia had seen it a hundred times.

"I'm still your patient. I'm still the Anastasia Bell you've come to know. And, I hope, like," she said, loathing the desperation in her voice.

"Of course. And I'm still dedicated to your full recovery," said the nurse. She didn't shrug off Anastasia's hand, but the shift in her posture turned their contact from something intimate to something professional. "I'm sure you have extremely important duties. You'll be able to resume them soon."

Malcolm slipped in the gravel, but the medical servitor streaked forward and caught him before he went sprawling. Anastasia shook her head.

"I'll be resuming them imminently, I fear."

Rebecca stiffened. She tried to suppress it, but Anastasia could feel the tremble in her arm. She stroked the nurse's hand as though trying to calm a frightened horse. "Don't fret. This has nothing to do with you."

She smiled, too, but the other woman wouldn't look at her. Anastasia crouched—ignoring the twinge from her ribs—to intercept the gaze Rebecca now cast at her own feet. No help there; she reacted as though Anastasia had bared her teeth. Sighing again, she released the nurse's arm and turned to the approaching Clockmaker.

Well, I'm sleeping alone tonight no matter what. The calf has already drowned; no point filling the well. No longer any point trying to convince her I'm a nice person.

Such was the price a woman paid for the privilege of defending the Empire. It was a crucial post, but lonely.

Oh well. Once this blew over, whatever it was, she could have Rebecca taken by the Verderer's Office for questioning. And then, after the poor innocent woman spent a night shivering in a cell and listening to the real prisoners, Anastasia could swoop in to "save" her from a terrible bureaucratic mix-up. She'd be the nurse's savior...and what she couldn't win by honest wooing, she'd receive by virtue of desperate gratitude.

Malcolm joined them, panting. He propped his hands on his knees to catch his breath. His Guild insignia, an onyx pendant inlaid with a cross of rose quartz flanked by a small golden *v*, swung from his neck like a pendulum. Rebecca wrestled with the urge to flee the impromptu gathering of secret police. Fidgety feet etched furrows in the path.

The newcomer said, "Tun—"

"I don't care how urgent you think your business is. You've already destroyed what promised to be a very special day for me. So I assure you that if the next words out of your mouth are anything other than, 'Tuinier, it's the end of the world,' I'll have the Stemwinders twist your fucking head off and toss it in a canal for fish food."

Rebecca gave a mousy squeak. She'd excavated all the gravel underfoot; the muddy furrow smelled faintly of shit.

Anastasia said to her, "I'm so sorry you had to hear that. I apologize for my language. I'm usually not so coarse. Truly, I'm not. Please don't think less of me."

Why do I still plead for her affection? She thinks I'm the Devil incarnate.

Malcolm blinked. His lips moved, like a goldfish blowing bubbles. The dash across the gardens had left him flushed, his fading-pink cheeks at odds with the rest of him, which had gone pale. His pupils were dilated.

Malcolm found his voice. “But, Tuinier… it *is* the end of the world.”

The din from Scheveningen Pier swelled again. But the crowd wasn’t cheering, she realized.

It was screaming.

CHAPTER 2

Anastasia said, "Tell me."

Malcolm licked his lips. He glanced at the nurse.

Oh, very well. Anastasia laid a hand on Rebecca's forearm again. She flinched.

"I'll need to press for a discharge. May I impose upon you to speak with Doctor Riordan and gather my belongings while I chat with my colleague?"

In truth, there was nothing to gather. Anastasia had returned from the New World with nothing but injuries; the hunters had cut the blood-stiffened clothes from her body back in the demolished safe house. But the naked relief on Rebecca's face stung like a slap. Her shoulders had taken on a frightened hunch, like a dog cowering from an angry master. Now the tension in the nurse's shoulders melted as each step took her farther from the Verderers. Anastasia's gaze lingered on the retreating nurse, as though she might salvage the morning with the force of her yearning. Gravel crunched under Rebecca's feet, seagulls cawed, mechanicals ticktocked on their myriad errands, and in a part of the city not far away, people raised their voices in fear.

A frisson of unease tickled the unscratchable spot between Anastasia's shoulders.

An attack? The war in the New World had been winding down when the Guild physicians deemed Anastasia stable enough to endure a midwinter sea voyage back to the Central Provinces. Acadia had already fallen to the thousands of mechanical soldiers swarming over the border from Nieuw Nederland, as had most of the Saint Lawrence Seaway, including the Vatican. All that remained was the seat of King Sébastien III in Marseilles-in-the-West, and the defense of that beleaguered citadel had already begun to falter. That had been weeks ago. Surely the French had folded. Ships carrying news of the victory were expected any day.

As soon as the nurse was out of earshot, Anastasia turned to her subordinate. "There. Now, tell me—"

But Malcolm wasn't listening. Instead, he snapped the chain on his Guild pendant and thrust it at the crystalline eyes of the medical servitor. She knew at once his intent; her unease turned to fear.

"I am a representative of the Verderer's Office of the Sacred Guild of Horologists and Alchemists," he announced to the machine. Words spilled from his mouth as he rushed through the formal expression of the Verderer's Prerogative: "My work is that of Guild, Crown, and Empire, which supersedes all domestic and commercial geasa. I hereby negate your lease and sunder any geas not directly in service of my requirements."

It was the sort of thing one kept up one's sleeve for very special circumstances. As a rule the Verderer's Office didn't advertise this feature, which was engineered into every single Clakker except those in direct service to the Brasswork Throne. Civilians pitched a fit when they learned their very expensive leases could be overridden at any time. The Prerogative only came out during emergencies.

The Clakker vibrated. The ticktock rattle of its body crescendoed, then fell quiet. "I understand, master. How may I serve the Verderer's Office?"

The Guildman tossed the pendant to Anastasia. She plucked it from midair. She'd intended to get a replacement when she returned to work. He pointed at her, saying, "You will protect Tuinier Bell above all others, excepting Her Majesty, at any cost. Take her to my cab, and thence to the Ridderzaal with all speed. You will stop for nothing, not even the safety of pedestrians, nor will you acknowledge alarms. Go!"

Before she could protest, the machine had scooped her up as though carrying a child to bed. She gasped. The touch of cold metal behind her knees and across her back caused the aches to flare anew. Piercing pain shot through her shredded hand, as though the glass embedded there recognized the proximity of an alchemical machine and pulsed in time to the Clakker's mainspring heart. Cradling her as though she were made of the finest porcelain, the servitor bounded across the garden with five-meter strides and leapt the hawthorn hedges. The servitor that had pulled the hansom saw their approach and opened the cab door. It was a city cab, she saw, rather than a Guild vehicle. Together the two machines secured Anastasia within the cab mere seconds after Malcolm issued his order. As the carriage lurched into motion, another unsettling thought landed on her like an angry wasp.

Servitors. But if this is an emergency, why didn't Malcolm call upon the Stemwinders? And why didn't he arrive in a Guild carriage?

The servitors' arms ratcheted backward so each could grab a pull-pole. Normally a single taxi servitor pulled a hansom, but the machines, driven by the implacable geas imposed by Malcolm, worked in perfect synchrony. They spun the cab through such a tight turn it lurched momentarily upon a single wheel, tossing Anastasia from her perch. The flare of agony from her sore ribs stole her breath away. The wheels etched furrows in the drive.

Confused by pain and the events of the past minute, Anastasia watched for Rebecca, hoping for one last glance. It wasn't to be had, so she shook her head, then patted herself on the cheeks. And again, less gently. *Enough of that. You're not a moon-eyed schoolgirl.*

"Machines!" she called. "What is the crisis?"

Just then a piercing shriek blanketed the city: the Rogue Clakker Alarm. It emanated from the general direction of Scheveningen, but swelled in volume almost exponentially. Each machine that heard the cacophony was metageas-bound to freeze and add its magically augmented voice to the din. Thus the alarm crossed the city at the speed of sound, until all Clakkers and humans in earshot were aware of the rogue in their midst. The Rogue Alarm could blanket hundreds of square miles in minutes.

Yet her drivers sprinted along the Paviljoensgracht without a hitch in their stride. Malcolm had overridden their vulnerability to the Rogue Alarm. As if he'd been expecting it. But how could he have known before a single Clakker raised the alarm?

Another lurch sent Anastasia slamming against the boards. She almost passed out from the pain. She wiped the tears from her eyes, wondering if her bones would still be healed at the end of this hectic ride. "I'm not a sack of flour! If that happens again, I'll have you both thrown into the Grand Forge and melted for ashtrays. See if I won't."

A rogue was bad news, yes, but not the end of the world. What could warrant such panic? Even the rogue Stemwinder in the safe house had eventually been subdued, and that had been in the wild sticks of Nieuw Nederland. Here, in the heart of the Central Provinces, any malfunctioning mechanical would be dogpiled by a dozen machines within moments.

Once on the Torenstraat, the servitors accelerated. The city became a sunlit blur. Even the largest cities shrank when one's mechanicals sprinted at full speed. Silver sparks spewed from the rims as though the wheels were Roman candles. Anastasia exhaled with relief. They'd get her to the Ridderzaal momentarily. The ancient Knights' Hall, headquarters of the Clockmakers' Guild, loomed over historic Huygens Square: the plaza at the center of the Binnenhof, the complex of buildings that formed the nexus of administration for the Central Provinces and, hence, much of the world.

Another Clakker-drawn carriage, this a much larger growler, swerved perilously close.

"Watch out!" she cried.

Traffic accidents were almost unheard of, particularly amongst Clakker-driven vehicles. She'd certainly never witnessed one.

Her drivers tried to haul the hansom out of danger. The cab lurched. Metal screeched. Shattered boards pelted her with splinters. The dented carriages swerved to and fro as their drivers attempted to pull them apart. Anastasia slipped and she fell toward the wheels for a gut-wrenching fraction of a second before the medical servitor caught her. Running backward, its legs a blur, it hauled her from the wreckage and leapt free.

It carried her down the boulevard with high-bounding strides. And Anastasia stopped wondering how the growler had smashed into her hansom: The entire city, or at least this district, had gone mad. The roads were choked with people fleeing the piers.

And then, over the panicked heaving of the crowd and the ticktock rattle of her escort, she heard the sound she'd learned to dread: the reverberating cymbal crash of metal against metal. It was the sound of Clakkers pummeling each other. The sound of something having gone very, very wrong.

A bead of sweat chilled her brow. The last time she'd heard that sound, it had left her at death's door. The rogue Stemwinder had taken half a second to murder her colleague, and would have done the same to her if the other mechanicals in the building hadn't leapt upon it. They had ignored her entirely, yet still she took catastrophic injuries. When titans hammered at each other with fists of alchemical steel, soft humans got squished.

Clang. Crack. Smash.

Clakkers fighting each other. *Dear God, WHY?*

The golden light of a rising sun glinted on the copper rainspouts of the tall shops along the Torenstraat. But there was something peculiar about the sunlight. It rippled with the rainbow sheen of oil upon water...or with the faint shimmer of alchemical alloys. She recognized the coruscation of light playing across dozens of Clakker carapaces. Mechanicals swarmed the rooftops, sprinting over the buildings to keep pace with the exodus of panicked citizens. *Oh.* She relaxed the tiniest bit. The machines were a defensive cordon, a protective escort.

But from *what*?

The medical servitor's path to Huygens Square sent it sprinting alongside the Spui River canal. Her stomach lurched with every bounce. She tried to pick out stable landmarks, like a ballerina spotting during a pirouette, and settled on a group of men and women arguing with the canalmaster. They wanted to hire his trekschuit, his towboat. The women wore thick fur stoles; gems sparkled on one man's cufflinks when he pointed downstream. Anybody of such obvious means owned several Clakker leases. Why weren't their own servitors whisking them to safety?

Anastasia wanted to berate their idiocy. *Stay with the escorts, you fools! They'll protect you!*

The machines in the flanking protective cordon saw the canal-side negotiation. A trio of mechanicals peeled away from the troop on the rooftops. They hurled themselves into the air, briefly folding into aerodynamic cannonballs to milk as much distance from the leap. In the final instant they became sleek javelins to spear the pavement alongside the canalmaster's hut. One of the wealthy men screamed. The synchronized impact shattered windows and pulverized concrete. Waves sloshed over the canal edge. Normally, a subclause buried within the hierarchical metageasa would have prohibited such property damage. Apparently in this case the intricate calculus of compulsion prioritized the stragglers' safety.

There, you fools. Let the machines guide you back. Safety in numbers.

The medical servitor swiveled on one talon toe and vaulted the canal. Wind ruffled Anastasia's hair, smelling faintly of cinnamon from a nearby bakery. She watched the group with the canalmaster. The trio of escort machines comprised two servitors and a larger military-class Clakker. The servitors leapt upon the canalmaster's mechanicals, a pair of Clakkers that had probably hauled the towboat up and down the Spui every day for the past century or more. The military mechanical blurred into the group of humans faster than they could react. While the servitors fought, the soldier unsheathed its forearm blades. Anastasia imagined she could hear the weapons' quiet *snick-snick* cutting through the pandemonium. And then—

—and then—

—and then—

Anastasia vomited.

The wind of their passage pushed the stinking yellow spume

into her face, up her nose. It splattered against the metal body of her carrier.

"Mistress! Are you ill? I will attend to your health as soon as we arrive."

Acid puke stung her eyes, but she didn't need to see anything else. Because the military Clakker had just spun through the humans like a razor-edged dervish, butchering the canalmaster and his would-be clients. It killed seven people in half as many seconds. The Spui turned crimson with blood pulsing from severed arms, legs, necks.

Oh, dear God.

The world turned upside down. Anastasia's bladder went slack when she looked again at the swarm of mechanicals racing along the rooftops. Warm dampness trickled down her legs to soil her new stockings. This wasn't a protective cordon escorting human masters from danger. No. The mechanicals *were* the crisis. The crowd was *fleeing* the machines.

Dozens of malfunctioning mechanicals. Feral.

It was an unprecedented—*impossible*—number of rogues. And they were *chasing* their human masters. Chasing and *butchering* them.

She'd failed to comprehend the events unfolding around her because they were unthinkable. The machines swarmed over brick and timber like vermin, a horde of clockwork cockroaches. They scurried over clock towers and across shop fronts, gouging masonry and crushing iron in their wild scramble to keep abreast of the exodus. The Segbroek District drowned beneath an implacable metal tide.

That explained the latency of the Rogue Clakker Alarm, too. The alarm momentarily immobilized the machines when it forced them to heap additional decibels upon the chorus. But the human-safety metageas wouldn't allow them to stand idly by while a horde of rogues massacred half the Empire. In the worst-case scenario, it was acceptable to permit a handful of undistinguished citizens to die, if that's what it took to capture a rogue—Anastasia knew this because she'd personally overseen the most recent review of the alchemical grammars pertaining to the handling of rogues—but not *hundreds*. What point was there in warning people of a rogue mechanical if it meant depopulating half the city to do so?

The medical servitor accelerated, whisking her away from the carnage. Winter air snaked through her sodden clothing. She shivered. Behind them, a clockwork mob surged into the streets.

Dear God, how many are *there?*

The metal horde tore through helpless humans. The machines sundered fragile flesh and bone with alchemically augmented strength. Anastasia looked away, gagging. She might not have believed a human throat could produce such screams, if her professional responsibilities hadn't occasionally required visits to the Ridderzaal's very deepest tunnels.

True rogues were rare. Rarer than a five-leaf clover; rarer than an honest banker. Never in all her years with the Guild had she even *heard* of two rogues present at the same time and place.

They neared the Binnenhof, the nerve center of the Empire. The carriages here became more official. Crests of the great families adorned some, the Universal Cog others. The machine vaulted the Hofvijver pond. The ticktocking cymbal crash of the pursuing rogues foamed the still waters. The servitor turned for the Stadtholder's Gate.

Anastasia spied the rosy cross upon a carriage swerving through the gate. She pointed with her bandaged hand. "There! Take me there!"

The machine spoke as though they were on a leisurely stroll

and not fleeing for her life. "Mistress, I humbly beg your forbearance, but I am geas-bound above all other obligations to see you brought safely inside the Ridderzaal. We shall arrive in twenty-four seconds."

"They're heading to the Ridderzaal as well. Join them!" she cried, jabbing a finger toward the Clockmakers' emblem. Safety in numbers.

The servitor veered toward the Guild carriage. But hers weren't the only eyes to catch a glimpse of rose quartz. A quartet of malfunctioning machines catapulted themselves from the murderous host. One pair slammed into the pavement just ahead of the carriage; the impact rippled the earth. The other pair flanked the fleeing Guild conveyance. The servitors pulling the carriage couldn't dodge without abandoning the vehicle or pouring its unprotected occupants into the street. Two rogues tackled them. Meanwhile the others tore through the gleaming glass-and-ironwood carriage as though it were made of rain-sodden crêpe paper.

The rogues dragged a screaming, thrashing man and woman into the street. Both wore pendants similar to the one currently clutched in Anastasia's fist. She recognized the woman. Katrina Baxter had only recently returned to work after an exhaustive investigation by Anastasia's office.

The humans disappeared beneath a mechanical swarm. Their screams didn't. Anastasia's colleagues disintegrated into a pink mist shot through with teeth and bone.

Oh, God. Oh God oh God oh God.

Her bladder tried to empty itself again.

The rogues were targeting Guild members. That's why Malcolm had arranged to stuff her into an anonymous hansom. And it explained why her flight had kept pace with that of the rogues: They were heading for the Ridderzaal, too.

This wasn't a freak accident. It was a coordinated attack.

And everybody running for the ancient Knights' Hall on the east side of Huygens Square was a target. In fact, were these her machines, hunting enemies of the state, she would've deployed them—

Oh, no.

She would've sent servitors ahead, to blend invisibly with the mechanicals ever crisscrossing the Binnenhof on the Empire's business. She would've deployed them ahead of her quarry, ready to spring into violent action when the others herded them into the crowded confines of Huygens Square. She would've laid a trap.

The medical servitor whirled through a dizzying turn toward the ancient Stadtholder's Gate.

"Stop! I command you to stop!"

The machine didn't slow. "My sincere apology, mistress. I am geas-bound—"

"We mustn't enter Huygens Square!" she cried. Too late. They passed beneath an arch onto the immense tile mosaic worked into the earth of the plaza.

Her throat burned with the remnants of acid gorge. She wrapped the pendant chain around her wrist, and slammed the rosy cross against one of the servitor's crystalline eyes. "I am Tuinier Anastasia Bell, I outrank the man who requisitioned you, and I ASSERT THE VERDERER'S PREROGATIVE! Now *stop*, damn you!"

The pain from her bandaged hand chose that moment to flare again, as though to punctuate her decree.

The Clakker skidded. Its alloy feet gouged the mosaic, tossing up a rooster tail of dust and shattered tiles. Only a machine could have kept its balance and maintained its grip on her.

It set her down. For a moment she worried her piss-damp legs wouldn't hold her. Terrified citizens thronged Huygens

Square. The rogues had herded hundreds of citizens, including who knew how many Clockmakers and members of the great families, into the Binnenhof. The swelling crowd of humans, carriages, and mechanicals made for a deafening din.

A series of tremors wracked the servitor, a sign that it struggled to reconcile conflicting geasa. The general metageasa still demanded her protection.

"Mistress, please," it said, the spasms growing more violent by the instant. "I implore you to let me bring you to safety." Its tortured voice became an inhuman warble of reeds and strings, giving the lie to mechanical emulation of the human voice box.

The crowded plaza looked like a stockyard. The rogues would make it an abattoir. She craned her neck, scanning the square for machines that hadn't arrived pulling carriages or carrying their owners. Heavens above: They were everywhere.

"This is a trap! Get everybody out of here. Forget me and evacuate Huygens Square *now*!"

Cogs squealed and cables twanged inside the machine. The new geas had taken hold. It waded into the throng and physically lifted the first two humans it encountered, one under each arm. It carried them toward the Stadtholder's Gate...

...Which slammed shut. Huygens Square reverberated with the *clang* of mundane alloys. Eight servitors, four at each wrought-iron door, wove a chain through the pickets.

The trap had sprung.

With the immense Stadtholder's Gate closed, the only egress was the much smaller Grenadierspoort, the Grenadiers' Gate, across Huygens Square to the northeast, behind the Ridderzaal. Otherwise, the crowd would have to find escape through the warren of government buildings that comprised the Binnenhof and girded Huygens Square. But these were locked to keep the hoi polloi from unbalancing the gears of the Empire. The gate was immense; everybody must have seen, heard, felt it. Yet still these fools didn't understand. They thought their loyal servants had closed the gate to protect them from the rogues.

The octet of rogues strode toward the unsuspecting throng. Additional lines of servitors, she saw, approached the hemmed-in humans from the north and south.

Anastasia screamed, her voice hoarse with acid and fear. "It's a trap! Everybody take cover! Get inside!"

But it was useless. Her warning was lost in the cacophony.

I protect the secrets of the Clockmakers' Guild in order to protect these people. From outside enemies, from themselves. These are the citizens of the Central Provinces. These are my charges.

She brandished the pendant. The pain in her damaged hand spiked as though the shards burrowed into her bones.

"Mechanicals! Look at me! I am Tuinier Anastasia Bell and I command you to LOOK AT ME!"

Those machines not malfunctioning did as she bade them. Of course, it meant the rogues saw her, too. Two peeled off from the others and dodged through the crowd, heading straight for her. She'd revealed herself as a Guildwoman. As a target.

She repeated the Verderer's Prerogative, speaking as quickly as she could to force a hard reset of the unbroken Clakkers' priorities.

Finding the Stadtholder's Gate locked, and seeing the rogues' attention on Anastasia, the medical servitor dropped the man and woman it had tried to carry through the gate. It reverted to its previous priority, her safety. It returned to her side, crouched to defend her: She strove to save everybody, so defending her was defending all.

"Mechanicals! Your masters are in mortal danger! Take them inside and defend them! THE BINNENHOF IS A TRAP!"

Now the panic took root. Like a pot of milk left overlong on a stove, the crowd erupted. Anastasia found herself at the epicenter of a riot. Men and women shoved, elbowed, even bit one another in the mad scramble to get away. And, like a tightening noose, a ring of machines converged on the crowd. Unlike a noose, they left screams and shattered skulls in their wake.

The approaching rogues tackled her defender. One-on-one they would have been evenly matched, having been built and maintained to almost identical standards. Outnumbered, the medical servitor had no chance. As the killer machines pinned their thrashing prisoner to the ground, she glimpsed something unsettling about the rogues: Metal plates obscured the keyholes in their foreheads. Who had installed those? Stranger still, one of the rogues reached up with a free hand and—*Had the world truly gone mad?*—opened its own skull. A shimmering aquamarine light illuminated the inner surface of its skull plate. While its comrade pinned her erstwhile bodyguard, it aimed the light into its eyes.

She froze. The only possible source of light within a mechanical's skull was its pineal glass. But those didn't glow, didn't gleam, didn't shimmer. She'd read vague allusions to very old, very dangerous, and rapidly discontinued experiments—

The medical servitor stopped thrashing. They released it. The grotesque machine reassembled its head. The medical servitor stood, emitted a burst of ticktock cog chatter, then flung itself into the massacre with the fervor of a religious zealot.

Anastasia's breath froze in her chest. Such light couldn't rewrite the metageasa, could it? And yet—

This isn't an invasion. It's an infection. *A* plague.

The unconverted Clakkers strove to defend their owners and masters. Some grabbed the closest humans and attempted to carry them from the square. But the rogues' trap wasn't so haphazard. Sentries on the perimeter intercepted any who tried to escape the killing zone on foot. Other machines snatched the nearest human and leaped above the deadly riot. They landed on dormers and cornices, carrying their human charges like sacks of flour. Some wrapped protective metal limbs about their charges and became cannonballs to smash through windows and doors.

Anastasia saw one servitor attempting to scale a façade with a pair of screaming boys perched on its back. It had just reached the roof and was hauling the children onto the steep tiles when a military mechanical emerged from its ambush position behind a dormer window. It spun, shearing through the servitor's arms. Dazzling violet embers fountained from ruined alloys and shorn sigils. They didn't blind her to the boys' hard impact on bloody mosaic tiles.

The rogues had anticipated this escape route. Had they stationed mechanicals inside the buildings, too? How long had they been planning this? How many of these demon machines *were* there?

If anybody had the resources to repel this attack, it was her colleagues in the Guild. There had to be a hundred uninfected mechanicals within the Ridderzaal, and countless others working the Grand Forge beneath the plaza, not to mention those working the pumps in the warren of secret tunnels beneath The Hague. If the infected machines had already infiltrated the Guild's innermost sanctum, there was no hope.

"To the Ridderzaal!" Anastasia scrambled atop a winter-dry fountain. She wielded the pendant again. She pointed across the blood-slick charnel of Huygens Square to the ancient Gothic Knights' Hall, where a pair of narrow towers raked the sky like needles. "Machines! Bring your masters to the Ridderzaal!"

Asserting her authority made her a target. But it also drew the butchers' attention. Maybe, just maybe, a few could get away while the machines turned on her.

A cold wind ruffled her sodden clothing. She shuddered but not from chill. Infectious machines opened their heads to illuminate the defenders by twos, threes, and fours. The gentle aquamarine shimmer belied its menace, for it corrupted the machines' interpretation of, and adherence to, the metageasa. This was something unprecedented: a contagious, self-propagating malfunction.

Some of the infected defenders, like the medical servitor that had carried her here, had joined in the murder of their masters. Just as many simply departed. The ambush machines let them pass, as long as they weren't carrying humans to safety. And a few seemed unchanged by the touch of the pineal glow: They kept fighting. But those were grossly outnumbered.

Air whickered through the skeletal frame of a servitor. Anastasia ducked. An explosive impact shattered the marble fountain. It sent her sprawling like a broken mop head, absorbing blood and viscera as she tumbled. The creaking of tortured ribs stole her breath away for the second time that morning. Shattered porcelain tiles shredded her skirt and lacerated her legs. Head spinning, she came to rest facing the crumbled fountain, where a pair of servitors faced off. One sported a covered keyhole. It must have gone for her, but the other machine had tackled it.

The ground shuddered again. The ceremonial ironwood doors of the Ridderzaal groaned open. The dwindling defenders tried to carry their doomed human masters toward the Clockmakers' Guildhall.

Four Stemwinders emerged from the Ridderzaal. They galloped into the fray like the horsemen of Saint John's Revelation. The clockwork centaurs loomed over the other mechanicals, even the military Clakkers. Three of the Stemwinders leapt upon the murderous rogues with merciless efficiency, reconfiguring their arms into spears to impale lesser Clakkers two at a time, or into blades for scything through them. The din of slaughter—of screams, torn flesh, cracked bone—took on the squeal of tortured metal and the percussive thunder of dented armor. A coruscating light show illuminated the slaughter in Huygens Square: gouts of flame, glints of sunlight from burnished alchemical brass, the incandescent spray of shorn sigils.

The fourth Stemwinder charged Anastasia.

Its hooves struck sparks from pulverized mosaic tiles. It bulled through the throng, knocking aside lesser mechanicals as though they were scarecrows. A man fell beneath its hooves; the Stemwinder crushed his skull like an egg and kept coming for her. Reason failed her: She tried to run. But the Stemwinders were faster than anything on land. Of course they were—the Verderers had designed them that way. It charged past Anastasia and scooped her into its four-armed embrace without the slightest hitch in its pace. She screamed, tensing in expectation of a deadly crush.

But it didn't kill her. Faster than the fleetest racing carriage, it swerved past the locked Stadtholder's Gate, decapitated a rogue, and reversed course. It skirted the rapidly contracting ring of death, vaulted a cluster of machines attempting to block its path—blinding one with a kick to the face that shattered its eyes—and galloped back to the Ridderzaal. It knocked aside several battered machines doggedly hauling their human charges to the safe haven. The centaur swerved again, hurled Anastasia through the open doors, and charged back into the fray. An uncompromised servitor caught her and set her gently on her feet. The doors slammed shut before she had caught her breath. Waist-thick alchemical steel bars slammed home; the concussion reverberated through the Ridderzaal.

Normally, the Clockmakers' Guildhall smelled faintly of hot metal, old books, and perhaps just a faint hint of sulphur. Anastasia could smell only her own filth. The doors boomed with the pounding of metal fists. Faintly, under the concussions, Anastasia heard the wailing of the doomed excluded. A reedy mechanical voice called, "Masters, please, I seek refuge and physic for my owner."

"What are you doing?" she cried. "Our people need safe haven!"

"We don't dare open the doors," said a voice she didn't recognize. "What if a rogue gets inside?"

She turned. The men and women who worked the business floor of the Ridderzaal were a motley crew: functionaries, paper pushers, accountants, and others of that ilk who clung like barnacles to the underside of bureaucracy. High in the rafters, dust motes danced in golden sunlight. The roof, supported by massive sixty-foot timbers, slanted sharply from both sides to meet at a high central peak. The wooden cherubs eavesdropping from the uppermost corners wore blindfolds and wax plugged their waggish ears, symbolizing the invulnerability of Guild secrets even from Heaven itself. Or so the Clockmakers had always chosen to believe.

The woman who'd spoken wore a technician's loupe, which made one cornflower blue eye comically large. The leather band pushed high across her forehead sported an array of colorful lenses. Thank heavens, a true fellow Clockmaker. And she had a point. A single corrupted machine could depopulate the Ridderzaal if it spread its taint to the Clakkers within.

Quickly, she said, "I'm Anastasia. Who are you?"

"Teresa van de Kieboom. Of course I know you, Tuinier. I sent the Stemwinders for you."

"Thank you. When this is over, I'll personally see you get a raise. But for now, where are the Archmasters, Teresa?"

A heavy silence fell across the conversation like a sodden wool blanket, punctuated by the cacophony of the massacre unfolding outside. *Oh dear.*

"Nobody knows. You're the highest ranking..." She trailed

off as though putting voice to "survivor" would make the truth irrevocable. She lowered her voice to a whisper. "Tuinier... what do we do?"

That depended. Once they finished slaughtering the citizens outside, would the killers storm the Ridderzaal?

Anastasia craned her neck. The Ridderzaal's rosette window depicted the Empire's Arms in a thousand panels of jewel-toned glass: a rosy cross surrounded by the arms of the great families, all girded by the teeth of the Universal Cog. The panels and mullions, feats of eighteenth-century alchemy, were thin as spider silk. Were they strong enough to repel an attack?

A woman with a spyglass stood in the gallery alongside the window. She must have seen Anastasia atop the fountain.

Anastasia pointed to the rosette. "That's where they'll try to break in. Get a pair of Stemwinders up there. They are *not* to look outside."

Of course, given time, the rogue mechanicals were strong enough to tear the Ridderzaal apart stone by stone. But she saw no reason to point this out.

A servitor sprinted to the doors on the far end of the hall. Anastasia paced like a crone who had misplaced her cane. The other Clockmakers watched her as a drowning man watched for a life preserver. They breathed through their mouths, or covered their noses with scented handkerchiefs, when she passed. Good Lord, she reeked.

What next? What if the rogues outside overwhelm the Stemwinders?

They weren't trapped. If they were quick enough, they could evacuate the Guildhall and send everybody out through the tunnels beneath the Binnenhof. But that would mean abandoning the Ridderzaal to the infected machines. The humans' retreat would become a massacre once the rogues subverted the rearguard. At which point the corrupted machines would have access to . . . *everything.* The labs. The files.

The Forge.

Anastasia gasped, steadied herself against an accountant's desk. *That* was the ultimate goal of this attack. She knew it in her marrow.

Unacceptable. Anastasia couldn't allow it; if necessary, she was duty-bound to give her own life to prevent it. She'd taken a vow to defend the arcane secrets of alchemy and horology from all enemies, foreign and domestic. So they'd have to incinerate the Ridderzaal on the way out. Truly incinerate it, beyond anything mere fire could achieve, to sunder the very ideas themselves. They'd need alchemical heat. The heat of a Grand Forge—

Transfixed by revelation, she froze.

A pair of mechanical centaurs mounted the stairs to the gallery. The crunch and clatter of their hooves echoed through the high spaces of the hall. Anastasia called, "Everybody, listen! We must work quickly."

The founding members of the Clockmakers' Guild, those legendary and yet unknown men and women who, almost a quarter millennium ago, learned the secrets of Clakker construction from the lips of the venerable Christiaan Huygens himself, had watched the world change. They had seen how easily a handful of mechanicals sprinkled amongst William of Orange's forces expelled rapacious Louis XIV from the polders of South Holland. And, having seen it, they knew they would spend the rest of their lives—as would their successors, and their successors' successors to the nth generation of Clockmakers—tightening an iron grip on a world they'd make their own. Which meant, amongst so very many other things, obliterating any mechanical that showed the slightest sign of disobedience. That so-called "rogue" mechanicals should be destroyed became common wisdom overnight, and soon it was enshrined as the highest law of the fledgling Empire.

But the true genius of the first Clockmakers was in making such executions a public spectacle. In this, and this only, they cast off the shadows and permitted—invited, demanded—public participation in their work. It united every jonkheer and schoolteacher, every fisherman and burgomaster, against the direst threat to their way of life.

The first Clockmakers had been masters of emotional manipulation. They understood the ticking of the human heart.

And so, while constructing the immense mosaic of Huygens Square and the Grand Forge deep beneath it, they ingeniously installed trapdoors. Nothing inspired the loyal subjects of the Brasswork Throne like witnessing the unmaking of a disobedient Clakker. It worked so well, in fact, that in times of particular tension between the Throne and Guild, Clockmakers had been known to secretly create a flawed machine and set it loose within the Central Provinces. The ensuing spectacle of chase, capture, and execution fired up the citizenry and, if played right, kept the Brasswork Throne pliable.

The trapdoors beneath Huygens Square had last opened the previous autumn. What a magnificent day that had been. First, they'd stretched the French spies' necks; cracking the espionage ring had been a triumph of Anastasia's office. But that had been merely the warm-up, the opening ceremony. For then they'd hauled out the rogue servitor Perjumbellagostrivantus. And there, before the eyes of God and the entire Empire, the malfunctioning machine christened itself Adam and told Queen Margreet to choke. The crowd collectively pissed itself.

And a certain legislative proposal to curtail the Guild's power of eminent domain quietly disappeared, never again to sully the Council of Ministers.

People accused the Verderers of deviousness. But compared to the founders of the Sacred Guild of Horologists and Alchemists, the Tuinier herself was a dilettante.

⁂

The din in the Ridderzaal swelled with every machine recruited from the tunnels. A comforting noise, this rattle-clatter of uncompromised machines. This was the sound of the world running as it ought. It muffled the massacre victims' dwindling screams.

Anastasia ordered almost every mechanical from the sprawling subterranean Guild complex to the business floor. Hundreds of mechanicals formed up in ranks behind the ceremonial doors. Servitors, soldiers, and Stemwinders stood in perfect unity, nearly touching, still as statues. They didn't shuffle; they didn't jostle. They waited. They obeyed their geasa.

They were as they were made to be: tools.

A servitor emerged from the passage to the tunnels. "The soldiers have taken their positions in the Forge chamber, Tuinier, and await your command."

"The rings have been parked?"

"Yes, Tuinier."

The Grand Forge hung at the center of an immense armillary sphere like an artificial sun blazing at the center of a hand-crafted cosmos. According to reports from the few functioning machines pulled from the red-hot wreckage, the catastrophic destruction of the New Amsterdam Forge had begun when the mechanisms became unbalanced owing to Clakkers scrambling over the rings. The world's only remaining Grand Forge lay beneath Huygens Square; she didn't know if the Empire would persist if that were destroyed.

She'd also sent a squad of military Clakkers into the depths. Their blades, she fervently hoped, would make all the difference.

She stood in the gallery alongside the rosette window, flanked by a pair of Stemwinders. From there she could see outside to Huygens Square—a scene lifted from a madman's darkest nightmare—and inside to the ranks of mechanicals forming up behind the massive ceremonial doors. If they opened the doors too soon, the foray might fail to overwhelm the attackers spread through the plaza. Too late, and none of the citizens in Huygens Square would survive. Hers was a pragmatic calculus, not a compassionate one. She pinched her earlobe, waiting for the ring of killers to contract just a little tighter...

"Now! Go!"

Ordinarily, the ceremonial doors groaned opened slowly, as befitting the grandeur and spectacle of such a noteworthy occasion. Not today. Today, teams of servitors heaved against the doors the instant the bolts retracted. The doors slammed open hard enough to crack the ironwood. The mechanicals surged onto Huygens Square, rank after rank blurring through the doors almost faster than Anastasia could see. A tooth-jarring cacophony shook the Ridderzaal: the *smash-crash-bang* of mechanicals in combat. The final rank of mechanicals joined the fray. The doors closed.

The battle between the rogues and the unsullied mechanicals splintered into dozens of individual conflicts, each moving too quickly for Anastasia's eyes to follow. The appearance of so many fresh mechanicals drew the rogues stationed on the surrounding rooftops. They hurled themselves into the heart of the conflict. Here and there, an aquamarine shimmer strobed the skirmishers.

The Stemwinders and their fellow Clakkers corralled the rogues into a tighter clump. Lured them. Nudged them, shoved them, punched and kicked them toward the traps. It wasn't clean as a noose. The melee frothed and churned like boiling stew; in places, the unsullied machines placed themselves on the traps to draw their assailants closer.

How many mechanicals will the Empire lose today?

Anastasia lost sight of the traps beneath the seething riot. To the servitor on the ground floor, Anastasia yelled, "Now! Cut the hinges!"

The traps were designed to open outward because it made for a better spectacle. But that would have destroyed the element of surprise. The rogues would catapult themselves from danger. Thus, somewhere far below Huygens Square, a squad of mechanical soldiers wielded alchemical blades. As one they severed the hinges and stops that held the immense hatch closed. The mosaic shuddered. The rogues tried to leap away, but Anastasia had anticipated this. Another geas asserted itself inside the uncompromised machines from the Ridderzaal: They clamped themselves to the rogues.

The traps fell away. A hellish glow illuminated the scrum. Dozens of machines tumbled into the Grand Forge, along with the remains of their victims. The *clash-bash* of combat became the *clang-bong-crack* of machines tumbling into the abyss. Anastasia grit her teeth at every impact.

A few rogues from the edge of the battle escaped the trap. They hurled themselves at the Ridderzaal's rosette window. A servitor whisked her away from the fight before the first shards of glass hit the gallery. The Stemwinders' scythe-limbs sheared through mullions and machines with equal ease. The ambush took the rogues by surprise; in seconds, they lay in pieces alongside the wreckage of the centuries-old window. Anastasia dispatched another squad of Stemwinders to flush the remaining rogues into the Forge.

An hour later she stood on the sticky mosaic tiles of Huygens Square, surveying the damage. A pervasive charnel stench brought bile to her throat. Searing heat had incinerated the flesh of the dead and dying; additional odors of sulphur and charred pork wafted from the Forge.

But she allowed herself a sigh of relief when she found the Forge still mounted and still glowing. Her gambit had worked; most of the rogues had fallen close enough to the heart of the Forge for the magical heat to sear away their alchemical impetus. They lay unmoving at the bottom of the chamber, warped, tarnished, half-melted. Numerous machines had incinerated before impact. Those that had skirted the edges of the furnace found themselves overcome by machines whose geasa forced them to sacrifice themselves in order to contain the infection.

The Forge had survived the attacks, but not without damage. Until she and her colleagues could repair the rings, the Forge was out of commission. Meaning they couldn't construct new mechanicals to replace those they'd lost. Nor could they modify existing Clakkers to render them immune to the corruption—assuming they could unravel how it worked. Meanwhile, wind gusted through a sizeable hole in the Ridderzaal itself. That would have to be patched before the building, and the secrets it housed, became defensible again. Not to mention the immense hole in the center of Huygens Square; the Forge chamber offered access to the Guild's network of tunnels.

A damnably steep price for repelling the attack. Perhaps that had been the point? Queasiness wormed through Anastasia's innards like an eel. They'd persevered for now. But for how long, and against whom? A catastrophe of this magnitude didn't arise from a random mass malfunction. Anastasia could conceive of only two explanations, but each was impossible and too horrible to contemplate.

Perhaps an unknown enemy had revealed itself? But that would require a remarkably shrewd adversary: one that had somehow kept itself completely hidden from the Clockmakers' Guild and the Brasswork Throne, all the while developing a means of subverting the metageasa. And its first attack had dealt the Empire a grievous blow.

Or, worse yet, what if there had been nobody behind the attack... except the mechanicals themselves?

Anastasia gazed upon the wreckage and wept.

CHAPTER 3

The ticktocks' mechanical voice boxes—miniature assortments of strings, reeds, and bellows—were a testament to the dark cunning of the Clockmakers. Marvels of mechanism impelled with ghostly magics, they passably emulated human language. Yet when it came to emulating human laughter, they weren't worth a pot of month-old cow piss. (Of course not. The Clockmakers had designed their creations for *obedience*, not *joyfulness.*) So the humans in the parley tent exchanged confused and slightly alarmed glances when the machine standing across the table emitted a wheezy drone punctuated with rapid clangs, as though somebody had flung a bullet-ridden accordion down a long staircase. The king's guards shifted the grips on their epoxy guns, rolling their shoulders and gauging the distance between their sovereign and the exit.

Berenice licked her lips. She whispered, "I believe that is laughter, Your Majesty."

The varying looks of relief and indignation from the French delegation elicited more "laughter." The machine didn't gasp for breath, or hunch over and clutch its burnished belly, or wipe its eyes as a human might have done. But apparently the levity was infectious, for the servitors in the far corners of the tent made similar noises. All an act, of course. Berenice assumed the mechanicals had their own private version of laughter. They did, after all, have their very own secret language, never vouchsafed to their makers.

She pretended she didn't know that. It was safer if these mechanicals thought she was nobody special.

Daniel knew her secrets. She hoped to hell he didn't show up. They hadn't parted on the best of terms.

Eventually the machine—it had demurred when asked for a name—resumed its inhuman stillness. But for the ceaseless ticktocking of its body, it might have been a statue. It stared at them, unblinking. Nobody sat; Clakkers had no need for chairs, and besides, human furniture didn't accommodate their backward knees. (Of course not. The Clockmakers had designed their creations for *servitude*, not *sloth*.)

The negotiator was a military model, and thus taller than its servitor adjutants. Taller than the humans, too. And, unlike either, it sported retractable blades of alchemical steel within its forearms. Such a machine could scythe through humans easier than a farmer reaping wheat.

Berenice knew this. Christ's bloody wounds, did she.

"The enemy of your enemy," it said, "is not your friend. Nor is it your ally."

The machines spoke Dutch. Berenice was there as the personal translator for Sébastien III, the King of France, the King in Exile. It was a convenient excuse to get her into the tent. His Majesty had been tutored in Dutch as a boy, naturally, but his accent was abysmal. Berenice's survival had occasionally hinged on her ability to pass as a native speaker when traveling in lands controlled by the Brasswork Throne. She whispered into the royal ear.

The king listened to her translation. Then he said, "We

are natural allies, and always have been. Our causes have ever been aligned in the struggle against your oppressors. Since the beginning, New France has championed the rights of all thinking beings and offered safe haven for free mechanicals. You've heard of the *ondergrondse grachten*, surely."

Berenice turned this back into raspy Dutch. The bruises on her throat were fading, but the damage to her voice would never heal.

The so-called "underground canals" were a loose collection of safe houses and stashes scattered across Nieuw Nederland, maintained by a network of secret Catholics and French sympathizers. Their goal was to ferry Clakkers with Free Will—what the tulips called rogues, and hunted with a vengeance—across the border to New France.

"I've heard of Dulle Griet, too," said the machine. "It does not mean I believe in her existence. Humans tell many tales."

Ah, yes, thought Berenice. *Clockmakers lie.* She still hadn't unraveled the truth behind the mechanicals' shibboleth. "For centuries, you've paid elegant lip service to the concept of our emancipation while expending minuscule effort to support that posturing."

Except the part where we accidentally freed you en masse, thought Berenice.

"We managed in the end," said the king as if reading her mind. "Surely you'll agree that you've benefitted quite profoundly from our efforts."

One of the servitors emitted a rapid clicking chatter of cogs meshing and unmeshing, followed by a faint *ping* as of a cable snapping taut. To naïve human ears it was just another dimension to the random noises generated by the Clakkers' bodies. It was pitched for the other machines in the room, and thus much faster than what Berenice's slow human biology could parse.

The military machine bowed its head in approximation of a

human nod. Interesting: It was emulating body language as a courtesy to the humans.

"It took two hundred and fifty years for you to achieve this. And it would never have happened had you not stood on the brink of extinction. You acted from a frantic struggle to survive. Not concern for us."

A painful truth. The final defenders of the inner keep of Marseilles-in-the-West were being overrun when Berenice's gambit accidentally shattered the geasa rather than altering them. Had it failed, the following sunrise might have found not a single native French speaker left on the Île de Vilmenon: The tulips had commanded their machines to particular heights of ruthlessness during the siege. But extinction had been averted, to the Clakkers' tremendous benefit.

"That's gratitude for you," Berenice muttered. Not quietly enough. The machines heard her, damn their inhuman senses. Whether they understood French or not, her meaning was clear.

The king spared an instant to glare at her sidewise. "As the King of France, I extend the hand of friendship to your fledgling confederation, and propose alliance for our mutual benefit. But as a human being who, like all right-thinking people, has been continually appalled by the barbaric injustices visited upon you and your kind, I extend heartfelt congratulations and the warm embrace of amity from the people of New France."

Berenice abbreviated that one a little bit.

"Alliance?" The machine emitted a mechanical chatter that might have been a chuckle. "You have nothing to offer us. And you pose no threat to us. After all," it said, gesturing to the coppery tanks slung over the guards' backs, "I'm surprised you managed to decant enough epoxy to fill those."

The guards overheard her translation for the king. The man flinched and inhaled through his teeth. Berenice resisted the urge to roll her eyes. *No doubt your inscrutable nature makes a killing at the picquet tables, you fucking idiot.* The other guard, a young woman who'd been scooped up in the conscription lottery just before the war, showed no alarm. Berenice had heard good things about Élodie Chastain; the survivors in the guard attested she'd comported herself quite well during the siege. She'd earned Captain Longchamp's respect, and that was no small thing.

Berenice sighed. Hugo Longchamp should have been here guarding the king, not these tadpoles.

The machine continued, "You're desperate for alliance because your home has been destroyed. You seek to ingratiate yourselves with those with the power to vanquish your enemies. You want us to fight your war for you."

Well, yes. That had *been the plan*, thought Berenice. *Would've worked, too, if Jax—er, Daniel—hadn't interfered.*

The king continued as though the Clakker hadn't seen straight through his overtures. "I also extend the gratitude of the French, which is rich and known across the continent, for the assistance you have lent us in rebuilding our home."

Marseilles-in-the-West had been obliterated. The town outside the citadel walls had burned in a conflagration that sent ash swirling higher than the Spire itself. The curtain wall of the outer keep had been pulverized with shaped explosive charges when the mechanical tide swarmed it; the inner keep had been the scene of a massacre. Nobody knew the status of settlements in the rest of New France; they'd fallen silent, one after another, as the clockwork horde advanced.

The military servitor cocked its head. Bezels whirred as it refocused its eyes. Berenice blinked rapidly, as was her custom when she caught somebody examining her face; sometimes her glass eye drifted, rendering her walleyed.

Perhaps she was being paranoid. But perhaps these machines had heard tell of a one-eyed woman.

"Our kin do as they wish. Those who wish to help, help. Those who do not, do not."

The Clakker legions arrayed against the citadel had splintered the instant the geasa vanished. French military spotters had tentatively identified three major factions.

First, the dissenters. Droves of mechanicals had simply walked away from the conflict. They strode across the island, under the icy river, and emerged on the other side to disappear into the farmlands and forests to the west and north of Mont Royal. Wherever they'd gone, it was away from Nieuw Nederland.

The penitents were the smallest group, comprising those machines that had chosen to stay behind and help rebuild the devastated city. They sought to atone for the indiscriminate murders they'd committed while helpless to resist their makers' will. These Clakkers acted as if they had consciences. As if they felt regret or guilt. They believed the Vatican's assertion that the immortal soul was the seat of Free Will. And that their souls, newly freed after centuries of carrying out their masters' every dark whim, were deeply tarnished.

And then there were the rest. The reason for the bloodstains splashed across the tent canvas. The reason Colonel Saenredam and her staff were absent (except for those same bloodstains). The reason the human guards carried epoxy weapons. The machines turned murderous mad by centuries of slavery.

Reapers harbored a searing contempt for humankind, plus the prodigious strength and speed to express that rage.

There were other factions, too. During her travels, Berenice had learned of a secret network of free Clakkers passing undetected amongst the countless servants of the Empire. Queen Mab's agents. She'd met a pair, and had barely survived the encounter. Her fingers plucked at the fringe of her scarf as they often did when she thought of Huginn and Muninn. She peered at a servitor's burnished carapace to confirm the alignment of her eyes.

"You said we have nothing to offer you," the king said. "But in that you are mistaken."

Berenice's breath snagged in her chest like a wool sweater caught on a fence splinter. Here it came. The other reason she was here: to listen and observe when the king flashed his trump card. "For instance, we could offer you a complete transliteration of your makers' secret alchemical grammars. The language of your compulsions, of your . . ." The king shook his head, looking annoyed. He snapped his fingers.

Berenice whispered, "Geasa."

The tulips had stolen the word from the Irish when they sacked the Emerald Isle as an afterthought to the Glorious Revolution and the annexation of England.

". . . Of your *geasa*. A full decryption of the sigils etched into your remarkable bodies." He indicated the alchemical anagrams spiraled around the keyholes in the machines' foreheads. These mechanicals hadn't mutilated themselves yet. Many rogues had taken to disfiguring or hiding their keyholes. Or tearing off the head of anybody who dared look too closely.

The background noise of the Clakkers' bodies swelled to a crescendo. Clicks, ticks, clanks, twangs, and bangs ricocheted amidst the trio. Berenice kept her expression neutral, rather than flash a knowing smirk at the king, as was her inclination.

"Nobody outside the Clockmakers' Guild knows such things."

Oh, Jesus Christ shitting on a syphilitic camel. Berenice blurted, "No outsider has ever broken the geasa before, either. And yet here we are having a civilized conversation rather than killing each other."

The king cleared his throat. *Oops.*

She curtseyed. "Sincerest apologies, Your Majesty. It is not my place to speak for you."

More machine noise rippled amongst the Clakkers in the

tent. The soldier said, "If what you say is true, how did you obtain this dictionary? Especially here, huddled behind the walls of your citadel, thousands of ocean leagues from the center of our makers' power? When so many others in the very heart of the Empire have tried and failed?"

"Perhaps you were also mistaken when you claimed New France has done nothing but pay lip service to your dignity and freedom."

This time, the machines' conversation was hypercompressed into a fraction of a second. Berenice had never heard such a rapid exchange.

The soldier machine said, "And in exchange for this boon, the long-sought secrets of our makers, you wish to establish diplomatic relations with us."

"To begin."

"You're wondering whether we intend to respect the sovereignty of New France," said one of the servitors, speaking human language for the first time since the French delegation had entered the tent.

"New France has ever had more land than people," said the king, laughing. "We share the New World peacefully with the Sioux, Cree, Inuit, Iroquois, Algonquin, and many others. Should you choose to make this continent your new home, we will share it peacefully with you."

"Then what? Our makers' secrets in exchange for what?"

("Not getting slaughtered by roving bands of reapers would be a nice start," Berenice muttered.)

The soldier looked directly at her. *Shifty motherfucker. You* do *speak French.*

"Our kin will do as they will," it said. "We do not impose our wishes or desires upon one another."

("Goodness me. It's just a libertarian paradise here in Ticktock Land, isn't it?")

The machine disregarded her muttering. It said, "I still await an answer. But, having spent every moment of the past one hundred and sixty-one years waiting upon humans, I do not intend to continue. So I ask once more, and only once more: What do you seek to gain from us?"

"Let's talk about Paris," said the King of France.

The former Dutch commanders' tent had been pitched at the base of an immense cannon. It was without doubt the largest piece of field artillery ever fielded in combat. Instead of lobbing shells, it had been built to lob Clakkers. And not just anywhere, but specifically atop the Spire, the pinnacle of Marseilles-in-the-West. The cannon and the tower had weathered the war (the former having been toppled and rebuilt, the latter considerably worse for wear), and now stood like opposing magnetic poles from which radiated longitudinal lines of destruction. Their shadows fell upon a landscape of ruin.

Explosions had churned the winter-bare slopes of Mont Royal into a morass of mud, pulverized granite, and crumpled alchemical alloys. Here and there, carriage-sized blossoms of hardened epoxy pocked the battlefield like glassy jonquils, although they no longer contained entombed machines. The French gunners' successful shots had long since been chiseled apart, the immobilized targets freed by their kin. And while the fires had long ago burned out (the citizens of Marseilles had been too busy fighting and dying to put out the flames), when the northerly winds came howling down from Hudson Bay, they churned up thick drifts of ash that fell like snow. On those days, like today, the world smelled like an ash can and the gutters ran gray. The street sweepers would be out in force tonight, scooping away the sludge before it hardened into a cement to clog the few remaining storm sewers that hadn't been destroyed in the siege. The weather had taken a turn for the unseasonably warm, but the thaw couldn't last; it never did. The snow would return.

The citadel itself, the vaunted outer and inner keeps of Marseilles-in-the-West, was unrecognizable to those who had known and loved it. The wreckage was strewn about like confetti on New Year's morning. Most of the Clakker debris had been hauled away by free mechanicals, perhaps to conduct whatever funerary rites their freedom allowed, or perhaps to protect their fallen kin from the indignity of disassembly. But here and there the battlefield still glinted with shards of alchemical brass, or fragments of hinges, or teeth chipped from broken cogs, or bits of cable that had snapped apart so violently the ends had melted into mushroom caps. They'd be picking crumbs of metal from the soil for months.

It had taken days just to cart all the human bodies away. Too numerous to bury in the frozen earth, they had been burned in a line of pyres that melted the ice upon the frigid Saint Lawrence. The fires had blazed from sundown to sunup. And so had the elegies, the drinking, the shouting and crying, the curses, the shaken fists, the bellows of triumph, the desperate lunatic laughter at the tulips' sudden and violent reversal. On that particular night the survivors were glad for the northerly wind, chill and all, for it swept the stench of the burning dead to Nieuw Nederland, where it belonged.

Upwind of the ash, acres of fallow farmland had sprouted thousands of tents, lean-tos, and bivouacs. Marseilles-in-the-West, that part not snugged within the inner keep, was now a shantytown. Wind ruffled the makeshift shelters; one was Berenice's, though she couldn't pick it out from here. She'd managed to obtain a tent with a closing flap, but traded it to a family with two children in exchange for their lean-to. Her fellow homeless knew her as Maëlle. Better if they didn't know she was the disgraced former vicomtesse de Laval; it seemed everybody knew somebody who'd been in the courtyard that ugly crimson day when Berenice's overambitious experiment ran amok.

Peace smelled worse than the siege. The Clakkers encamped around the citadel hadn't filled latrine trenches with their own effluvia.

It was through this bleak tableau, surrounded by reminders of the most terrible of days and the most pyrrhic of victories, the French delegation returned to the citadel. The guards flanked the king with weapons at the ready, alert for any mechanicals that came within leaping distance, twitching at every sign of movement. They scanned the landscape with haunted eyes. Battle fatigue plagued every survivor. The guards and soldiers had it, but so did the nuns, cobblers, chandlers, schoolteachers, prostitutes, fishermen...

Berenice was ebullient.

"This is a historic day, Your Majesty. If it please you, I hope you will mark it in your diary. Subsequent generations will celebrate this day."

"I see. And what day is this?"

"The day the King of France started to reclaim his throne. The day he called an end to our centuries of exile."

The king stopped. He squinted at her. "How long since you've slept?"

She ran a hand through her hair, counting hours that melted into mist. "I had a nap yesterday...or the day before..." She'd felt perfectly well until he asked. His query conjured a yoke of almost supernatural weariness to slump her shoulders. "I don't know, Your Majesty. Paris is within our grasp! It would be a naked betrayal of our forebears, a repudiation of their struggles, to waver now. But there is so much to do."

Jesus Christ, was there ever. The king had asked her to reclaim her post as his intelligence chief, and she had, but New France needed an army of Talleyrands. Plus, the marquis de

Lionne, who'd held the post during her interregnum, had alienated many of those upon whom Talleyrand's network relied. But she'd had no time to sleep, much less mend fences.

The Clockmakers' secret lexicon needed more study. But that required a cooperative test subject, which they lacked. Pastor Visser had been freed of the evil magics placed upon him, and he refused to participate any further. But they had to solidify their grasp of the secret grammar of alchemy and horology: It was their first true foray into the Clockmakers' walled garden since the days of Huygens.

Thoughts of the lexicon brought to mind Queen Mab and her agents. Berenice needed to learn everything she could about them. Daniel was her best wedge into that problem, which meant she didn't have a wedge.

And thinking of the mysterious Mab brought to mind Berenice's suspicion that the tulips had established secret mines in the wintry expanses of the far north, a flagrant treaty violation arranged via secret pact with the former duc de Montmorency. He'd confessed to a land deal with the Brasswork Throne, but she still didn't know the details.

And thinking about him raised the most pressing issue: The war had exhausted the citadel's stocks of epoxy and other chemical armaments. But the chemists couldn't synthesize more because they lacked the necessary chemical precursors, catalysts, and reagents. Those had primarily come from petroleum-rich lands in the north, again held by Montmorency. The supply caravans had stopped when he betrayed New France, and they hadn't been reestablished. Without those crucial ingredients, Marseilles-in-the-West couldn't defend itself should the reapers, or Mab, or a lame milk cow decide to take a swipe at the citadel city. (Assuming the defenders could muster the forces to wield weapons in the first place, which they couldn't.) The steam and lightning cannon had proven useful, but the siege became a rout the moment the chemical tanks ran dry.

And the chemical inventories weren't just a military matter. Everything in New France relied upon chemistry. They used chemicals to purify their water and treat their sewage; to turn animal waste into high-yield fertilizer—crucial, if they were to feed the refugees and make it through another winter; to warm their homes; to manufacture medicine; to dress themselves; to build.

With the centuries-long conflict against the tulips finally ended, Berenice's countrymen could finally stop living under a siege mentality. They could stop living like their great-great-grandparents, and start looking forward for the first time in generations.

But without chemistry, French society would stall and dwindle. France, New and Old, would never become a world power to fill the tulips' vacuum. They'd forever be nothing more than a historical footnote.

So the king had sent pigeons and emissaries to the towns and villages along the Saint Lawrence, to the Acadian fishing villages of the Atlantic coast, to the Great Lakes, even to the frigid shores of Hudson Bay, in the thin hope of collecting any remaining chemical stocks from the far-flung corners of New France. They'd sent boats to the Vatican as well, for news of the Holy See. Berenice gave long odds the Swiss Guard hadn't depleted every drop of their chemical stores when the metal horde swarmed St. Vincent's Square. This after the tulips' unwilling agent had murdered Pope Clement XI. Poor Visser had gone mad with shame. Worse still, the conclave had been assembled and sequestered when the invasion began. Nobody knew what the Church leaders would do, or, frankly, whether it had any leaders.

But no pigeons returned, and the king's emissaries had yet to report. Every group had taken empty epoxy guns, in the hopes of recharging them for the return trip. The countryside was lousy with metal these days.

Her own emissaries hadn't returned, either. Free hands were scarce in Marseilles, yet she'd had no shortage of volunteers for this particular errand. They'd departed the citadel in a rush, braving the reapers to pluck wild tulips. The nearest Dutch medical clinic was at the border crossing in St. Agnes. But there were others, too.

She'd ransacked the parley tent with her eyes the moment she entered; surely the commanders of a violent siege would have kept a fully stocked medical trunk on hand, just in case. But if they had, it'd disappeared—like the officers themselves—in the chaos of the Clakker mutiny. Probably some scavenger brave enough to loot the battlefield had taken it, perhaps without even realizing the treasure it contained. Even Berenice, in all her travels, had never laid eyes upon alchemical bandages.

Without those bandages, a good man was sure to die. With the bandages, he was almost sure to die.

Beneath the crunching of debris underfoot and the rattle of hoses on the guards' guns, Berenice heard the guttural lowing of bison. Their path took them downwind of the pens. The stink of manure joined the tamer scents of thawing mud and ashfall as they neared the citadel. So did a skunky chemical astringency. A team of chemists crouched alongside one of the chromium-plated storage tanks, decanting the last drops. They stared with goggled eyes at the dribs and drabs trickling from the spigot. They'd been consolidating the meager remnants of their various products, but so far their scrapings had produced less than Berenice could piss on a dry day.

The king's voice intruded upon her reverie. She shook her head. "My apologies, Your Majesty. My mind is wandering."

"I said, 'What else can you tell me?' "

She cast her thoughts back over the meeting. "I don't see the machines had any reason to humor us. It's little bother for them if we follow their move to free the machines on the continent." She sighed. "Little bother for them if we're killed in the attempt."

"If the machines do push across the ocean, it'll be sheer chaos from Lisbon to the Gulf of Bothnia."

"They will, and it will, Majesty. And you will sweep in to fill the void."

The king's return from parley raised heads and voices amongst the multitudes laboring to rebuild Marseilles. Sébastien III waved to his subjects. His guards raked the crowd with tired eyes. Clakkers weren't the only Dutch threat; merely the easiest to identify. Pastor Visser had muddied the distinction between allies and enemies. Élodie slung the barrel of her epoxy gun over her shoulder and loosened her pick. Normally the guards carried either a gun or the traditional sledge, pick, and bola, but with the guns good for one or two shots at most, they had no choice but to lug everything. To her credit, Sergeant Chastain carried the additional kit without a grumble; she looked much more unhappy about the civvies coming to greet the king and touch the hem of his garments.

He watched them approach, smiling and waving to his subjects. Quietly, while he could still speak frankly, he said, "You'll do two things for me, Madam de Mornay-Périgord."

"Of course, Majesty."

"First, get some sleep. You're swaying."

"I will, sire. And then?"

He laid a royal hand on her shoulder. "I want you to think carefully about what a return to Paris would entail. I want you to be prepared for the possibility that there may be nothing to return to. Assuming the machines would tolerate a human king in their midst."

"But, Your Majesty, we—"

"King of *what*? Ask yourself."

The vanguard of desperate citizenry arrived, slamming the door to any further conversation. Especially on this topic. Berenice curtseyed and took her leave of the monarch. She slipped through a crowd of men and women eager for a glimpse of the royal person. The king's audiences with petitioners had gone on hiatus when the siege began.

Her path took her atop a mound of debris. From there she caught sight of the Saint Lawrence. The graveyard should have been visible from here, but the explosion of the outer curtain wall had rewritten the landscape. Farther down the slope she could see a pair of twisted iron poles where the lich-gate might have been.

She'd never be able to visit Louis's grave. Jesus, how she missed him. Sometimes, when watching the river, she felt him at her side. At those times, she could remember the warmth of his body, the peppery scent of his skin. Inevitably she found herself expecting a caress that never came. But it never stopped her from watching the river. It had been Louis's first love, and through his eyes, she'd learned to love it, too.

A fishing boat pulled in to the temporary replacement docks; farther out, two more tacked into the wind, pushing home. She could just make out the crews on three seiners preparing to cast off. Hard and unforgiving work, fishing on a river half-choked with ice, but most of the food stores had burned or been otherwise depleted during the siege. Even the communal stores of calorie-dense pemmican were running low, and would stay so until it came time to slaughter and render more bison; until then, northern pike and yellow perch had become staples of the survivors' diet. Berenice wondered what would happen when the local bays and inlets were fished out. That would be a bad time to be a bison, she supposed.

A few of the braver townspeople had trudged off into the

woods, choosing the danger of reapers over the invisible insidious dangers of the tent village. (Clockwork killers? Those were the devil all Frenchmen knew. But dysentery, that was the devil they didn't.) The Crown offered generous compensation for winter game: Caribou paid best of course, but coyote, hares, and rabbits could line the pocket of a determined hunter. Even a brace of squirrels was worth a few coins. The real coureurs des bois, the woods-runners, stood to profit, assuming their scrip eventually turned into real money. But that would require the royal treasury to contain something other than cobwebs and IOUs.

But these weren't her problems; food was the Minister of Agriculture's purview, money the Royal Eschequier's. But speaking of the Privy Council...

As though her thoughts had summoned the Devil, a pocket of cobalt and vermilion moved slowly and unsteadily through the rubble. The color contrast with the ashen landscape speared her remaining eye like a shard of concentrated insensitivity. Though far from alone in his patriotic veneration of chemical dyes, the marquis de Lionne somehow managed to present a particularly offensive contrast with the gray lives of the commoners, who had lost everything in the war. The marquis wobbled over heaps of talus, trailing toadies and courtiers in his wake. Berenice imagined that if she strained, she might hear the sizzle of the laborers' glares raking the marquis's retinue. His bejeweled and beribboned clogs made hollow *clack-clack* sounds against the talus, in contrast to the *chanking* of iron rods and *clanking* of pickaxes from the gangs of men and women breaking down and hauling away the rubble. A single servitor labored amongst them, its strength worth that of ten humans. It worked alone. The wind shifted; the marquis plucked a lace handkerchief from the ruffles at his cuff.

He stopped to watch Oscar the blacksmith and his two

apprentices lever a particularly large chunk of granite from the earth. Quivering with the exertion, they pried it loose to reveal the severed, crushed limb of a mechanical. The alchemical alloys still had their oily rainbow sheen, as though the fragment of the former curtain wall contained a hidden vein of some precious mineral. The marquis nodded, gesturing with vaguely supervisory gestures.

The blacksmith made his own gesture to the marquis. The nobleman's blush matched his vermilion coat. Berenice didn't bother to hide her expression as he approached.

"Bonsoir, my lord Marquis," she said. He paused before responding, waiting for a curtsey that never came.

"Madam," he said, somehow putting heavy emphasis on her stripped title. The king had restored her as Talleyrand, but he hadn't restored her noble title nor her lands. After all, before narrowly saving the citadel (and, technically, violating her banishment to do that), she'd nearly destroyed it with an ill-advised experiment.

She didn't recognize the younger woman with him; she wore a voluminous dress of lemon and lime cloying enough to rival the immaculate confection of her hair. A faux birthmark on her chin spotted her otherwise powder-pale and flawless face. Berenice didn't miss the intricacies of the royal court. The third member of the trio was Reynaud Galois, also known as the comte de Beauharnois and the Royal Eschequier. Galois wore an overcoat of martial cut, its blues and reds dulled by the reflected glare of the marquis.

Apropos of nothing, Lionne said, "I thought you were to accompany His Majesty at parley."

"I did."

"Are you certain?" He pressed a finger behind one ear and cocked his head as if listening for something. "I hear no screaming. I see no evidence of a new catastrophe soon to overwhelm us. Isn't that what you do? Wander from one tragedy to the next?"

"Ending the war while the Spire still stands counts as a tragedy in your book? Engineering the devastation of our enemies? Seeing them routed, panicked, and on the run? Bringing a decisive end to centuries of living under the thumb of our tulip aggressors? Clearing the path for our blessed sovereign to return to the Old World and reclaim his rightful throne? For the first time since our ancestors fled the continent we are free to live our lives as God intended." As an aside to the eschequier, she said, "All this without costing the royal treasury a single livre. Why, someday you may see the end of card money." She continued, "What a strange world you inhabit, my lord Marquis, that these are the hallmarks of tragedy. Why, to your standards, the very Garden of Eden would be quite disagreeable."

"I still have access to information," he huffed. He'd coveted the Talleyrand post for years without considering whether he could actually do the job. King Sébastien's decision to replace him with Berenice, as the marquis himself had originally supplanted Berenice, was a stinging rebuke. He blamed her, of course. "As always, your actions are more dangerous than you realize."

"I know exactly what I unleashed. I wasn't cowering in the caverns with you when the change came over the machines." She pointed to the Spire. "I was in the thick of it. I saw the birth of the reapers. I saw the explosion of blood and bone as they turned against their masters." Berenice shrugged. "But that's all beside the point, isn't it? Because we both know you've received no new information. It's been days since a single pigeon arrived, and the old overland routes have been eradicated by the roving bands of mechanicals now haunting the countryside."

"As usual, your confidence is unfounded." From the ruffles of his other cuff, the one that didn't store his handkerchief, the marquis produced a tiny snuffbox and a sliver of paper. The latter he dropped in the woman's palm; she stepped forward to hand it to Berenice while the marquis shook a dusting of snuff into the hollow between his thumb and forefinger. The paper scrap still retained the tight curl from having been wound about a pigeon leg. Of course the marquis had already read the message. In his own head, if nowhere else, he was still the real Talleyrand. Berenice's remaining eye struggled to read in shifting light conditions, but she refused to give him the pleasure of watching her squint. Predictably, the message had no markings to indicate its origin; was that how he'd run things? What a fool. Meanwhile, he inhaled the snuff with a snort like a sow in full rut, affecting utter disinterest in Berenice's perusal of the message.

"Fascinating." She flicked the scrap back to his flunky. A gust of wind caused it to flutter past the woman's outstretched hand. While she chased it, Berenice added, "I won't keep you. His Majesty will want to know at once, of course. Bonsoir."

She turned her back on the trio. Two steps later, the marquis cleared his throat. She allowed herself a moment's private smile before turning. "Was it something, my lord?"

"Hmm. You, ah, agree, then? That we should share this with the king."

"Why, of course." She frowned as if he'd asked a silly question. Then she shrugged and turned away again. Her boots scraped across the talus. A moment passed. Then: "Damn you, woman!"

Berenice whirled. "I'm not your fucking code book, you greasy shitstain. If you can't understand such a simple message, you never should have held the post. You've failed. Show some goddamned grace about it." She collected herself. "Now, if you'll excuse me, I must queue up with my fellow commoners for today's ration of cold pemmican. Rumor has it somebody caught an eel this morning; perhaps if I hurry, I can wheedle a morsel. A slimy eyeball, perhaps, or a good lick of its cloaca. I bid you adieu."

She strode away. Over the pulsing of blood through her ears, she heard the marquis call to her retreating back, "What does it mean?"

Berenice had expected something unusual; even the idiot marquis could have churned through a standard Vigenère decryption. Assuming he hadn't forgotten—or, God forbid, mislaid—the code phrases. But the scrap held no ciphertext. The marquis had mistaken it for a code.

It wasn't. The message was a single word of unencrypted plaintext, plus one symbol, written in an extremely precise hand:

QUINTESSENTIA ↑

CHAPTER 4

As usual, a knot of malcontents crowded the orphanage gate. They didn't chant, or carry placards, or throw things. But they muttered. And scowled. And watched the grounds hoping for a glimpse of the one they reviled. They sought fuel for their outrage.

Daniel felt badly for the abandoned children. They probably spent every waking hour desperate for new families, for people who wanted to become their parents. So to see perfectly able adults come each day but in a spirit of hatred rather than love...he couldn't imagine the heartbreak. Unwanted children were the true victims of the vigil, not the half-mad former priest it targeted.

Daniel wasn't loved any more than the orphans. The French took a dim view of Clakkers in general, but especially those within the boundaries of the fallen citadel.

"Excuse me," he said. The protestors disregarded him. He raised his voice and tried again. "Excuse me, please? I'd like to get through."

They heard him, and probably even understood his tone, if not the words attached to it. But they wouldn't have stepped aside even if he knew how to ask in French. They wouldn't cede an inch to a Clakker. Not in principle.

He laid a single fingertip on one man's nape. The touch of cold metal caused him to flinch. His alarm startled the others, too. They retreated to a new equilibrium between fear of mechanicals and anger at Pastor Visser. A pang of guilt tugged at him; he disliked appealing to fear. But at least for a moment he was the focus of their attention, rather than poor Visser.

"Merci beaucoup," he said. He'd learned that much. He opened the low wrought-iron gate, stepped through, and closed it behind him.

One woman found the courage to address Daniel. She spoke in the river creole adopted by those who spent much of their time upon the Saint Lawrence, wedged between French- and Dutch-speaking populations. Daniel had picked up just a few words of French, but together with his makers' tongue it was sufficient to suss out her meaning. "You're going to see him, yes?"

"To see whom, miss?"

"Him." She pointed up, toward the Spire. Her fingernails were painted the color of unripe apples. "The one who tried to murder the king."

"He killed the pope, too!" shouted a man wearing a flannel shirt under waist-high rubber waders. A shudder rippled the assembly like a gust of wind through summer wheat. Everybody in the group made the sign of the cross.

So they knew about Visser's evil errand to Québec City, then. The information had likely come from one of the priests who had attended Visser in the basilica undercroft, mistaking his affliction for demonic possession.

Daniel had also killed a man without wanting or intending to. He sympathized with Visser's burden of unquenchable guilt. And he knew well the agony of an unfulfilled geas. Left unchecked, the exponentiating torment could drive the most devout Catholic to papicide. But Visser's anguish could never be assuaged.

Nobody cared that Visser had fought the compulsion with all the strength in his body and soul. Nobody cared that he wept as he murdered. Together Daniel and Berenice had shattered Visser's geasa, but not before that awful yoke had shattered his mind.

It was a testament to Christian compassion and mercy that the nuns agreed to house Visser. The French had asylums for the mentally unwell, but shipping the mad priest to such a place would have been a merciless death sentence. Rumors of vile deeds would swirl about Visser no matter where he went. And in the wrong ears, those rumors could impel men to kill. That process was slowly taking place outside the orphanage gate. So the nuns of Saint Jean-Baptiste had taken the poor man under their protection.

Sister Marie met Daniel at the door. In the river creole, she said, "It's good of you to come," or something like it. "You're his only visitor."

"Nobody else?"

The nun shook her head. *"Vous seulement."*

That saddened him. Berenice owed the poor fellow a courtesy call now and then. He had worked for her when he was a secret Catholic in The Hague, though neither of them had known it at the time. It was because of that work the Clockmakers had captured and warped him, revoking his Free Will through the application of their dark magics. So a compassionate woman might have felt an obligation to check on Visser from time to time. But Berenice was a ruthless pragmatist disinclined to visits of simple compassion. She wanted to study Visser, not console him.

He followed the nun down a hallway past rooms where orphans took mathematics lessons, practiced their handwriting, read the Bible. Inevitably they looked up at the sound of his metal feet, gaping as though he were a mythological creature.

Visser had been given a garret under a dormer of the three-story building. The space was still used mostly for storage, but the nuns had managed to fit a cot inside, and the ex-priest had created a simple privacy screen from three blankets and a laundry line. The garret smelled of dusty books and an unwashed body. The window was boarded; during the siege, an explosion had broken every pane of glass in the citadel. It would be terribly stuffy come summer, though Daniel doubted Visser would notice. Compared to the torment inflicted by the geasa, all else was luxury.

Sister Marie knocked on the open door. "Monsieur Visser?"

From behind moth-eaten flannel came a grunt and a splash. A moment later the smell of a well-used bedpan filled the garret.

"I evacuate with vigor," said the ex-priest to nobody in particular, "yet my sins remain." Visser tended to speak his native French during moments of lucidity. But when in the throes of madness, like now, he usually spoke Dutch, as he had every day for decades. He grunted again. "More purgatives!" he cried. "How much mercury must I ingest, Lord, before the scouring of my innards scrapes the sin from my soul?"

Daniel whispered to the nun. "Is he really eating mercury? That probably isn't good for him."

She shrugged. He couldn't tell if the gesture meant, "I don't know," or, "I don't understand." Such was their Babel problem.

Visser emerged from behind the blanket, pulling up his trousers. The nun blushed and turned away. The ex-priest was almost unrecognizable compared to the compassionate pastor who'd sent Daniel on the errand that serendipitously bestowed him with Free Will. His jaw had sprouted a beard, a scraggly thing more salt than pepper. As if in deference to a hirsute conservation law, his scalp was now bare in places. He'd balded himself through incessant nervous plucking, and in those spots the skin was mottled and pink where it wasn't scabbed over.

"Quicksilver for a quicksilver loosening of the sin-bowels, you see. That's not in the catechism, no mention there, but the apocrypha, yes, the apocrypha, it was all lost in the fall of Rome. When the cardinals flew away, so few of the archives came across the sea, you see." He teetered in the sway of an emotional gale perceptible only to madmen. To the nun he said, "A man's sin-bowels hold shit and sin in equal measure. Meditate on that, damn you!"

Sister Marie pointed at Daniel before walking away.

"Hello, Father," he said.

Visser came forward, squinting. "I remember you," he said. "Nicolet Schoonraad's naughty Clakker."

"Yes, that's right. I used to serve the Schoonraad family."

"Did they make it to New Amsterdam safely?"

"Yes. Eventually."

"That is unfortunate. You ought to have thrown their loathsome daughter overboard."

Oh, dear. Visser was having one of *those* days. How was this the same man who had once risked unwelcome attention by openly questioning Guild doctrine just to give Nicolet a lesson in compassion?

"Oh, well. No matter. She'd probably float, as many a turd has been known to do."

Daniel changed the subject. "May I sit with you? I would like to hear of your week. Do the sisters continue to treat you well?"

There were stubborn bastards, and then there was Captain Hugo Longchamp.

Berenice had seen, in the very final seconds of the siege, the captain take an injury that ought to have killed him outright.

Though he had never been a lover, he'd always been a trustworthy if grumpy friend, one who'd saved her life on more than one occasion. To see him run through by a mechanical like the one that murdered her husband...The sight of that blade sticking from the captain's chest was one of the worst things she'd ever witnessed. It haunted her, like Louis's severed arms.

Today Hugo clung to a feverish semi-life. A true warrior for New France: He fought even death to stalemate. But the tulips would claim one final victim if Berenice's scouts didn't return with alchemical bandages soon. Even Hugo couldn't fight forever.

The captain had his own room in the infirmary—the king had insisted on this. At present it reeked of sweat and illness. Despite the hundreds of flowers blanketing the walls and overflowing from vases perched on every available surface, there was no cloy, no perfume. Each paper blossom had been cut, folded, and hand painted by the grateful schoolchildren of Marseilles-in-the-West. There were no other flowers in New France this time of year. The riot of colors evidenced petunias, marigolds, violets, snapdragons, orchids, snowdrops, lilies, roses, pink lady's slippers, white trilliums, purple saxifrage, and other flora Berenice couldn't identify. (No tulips, naturally.) Some of the handmade flowers sported messages of encouragement and thanks scrawled across their petals, leaves, and stems.

A wizened nun knelt at Hugo's bedside on creaky knees, silently working a rosary cycle. She had to be in her eighties. A member of the city guard knelt opposite the nun, head down, eyes closed, hands clasped together at the edge of Hugo's blanket. Judging from the whitening of his knuckles, the furrowed brow, and the dents in his armor, he'd seen combat against the clockwork tide, and probably had Hugo to thank for his life. As did so many.

Berenice waited around the corner until the God-botherers

finished. She gave the nun a respectful tip of the head, wondering if the old lady caught a whiff of brimstone as she shuffled past. Then Berenice caught the guard's eye.

"How is he?"

The guard shook his head, then shrugged. "They say they've done what they can. It's up to him now." He nodded at the sunken, sallow figure who had frightened and inspired so many. "But the wound . . . there's a taint in his blood."

Berenice sighed. Blood poisoning was almost inevitably fatal. Could the tulips' magical bandages fix such a thing? She didn't know.

She asked, "Will you add my prayers to your own when you pray for Hugo? I'm not very good at it myself."

The guard looked puzzled. "You might try anyway. He needs it, and it can't hurt him."

"Perhaps I will. But God and I haven't been on speaking terms of late." *Not since Louis died in my lap.* "But I'll light a candle for Hugo anyway."

Berenice lingered after the guard departed. She laid a hand on the captain's forehead. The heat of his skin made her gasp. It was like touching a cast-iron skillet that had hung in a sunny kitchen window all day. Though he lay pale beneath the covers, a papery husk of the man she'd known, he still fought the infection with vigor.

He stirred at her touch. His lips moved. Her heart shifted, buoyed on a bubble of hope.

"Hugo? It's Berenice. Can I get you anything?"

Again his lips moved, his voice but a breath. She leaned over the bed until his beard brushed her earlobe.

"Madamoiselle Lafayette . . . you dirty girl, you . . ."

She kissed Longchamp's damp brow. Tasting salt, she whispered, "Have fun, you two. You've earned it."

Her glass eye made a soft sucking sound when she eased it

from the socket. Berenice dried it on her cuff, then placed it within the furnace of his palm. A passing nurse saw this and frowned. Berenice shrugged.

"Lucky talisman," she said.

Standing on a sliver of what used to be Nieuw Nederland, Daniel gazed across the Saint Lawrence to a crowd gathering on the docks of Marseilles-in-the-West. A ship had arrived from the Great Lakes. The barque was the first vessel from the western waterways of New France to reach Marseilles since before the siege. Its arrival had created quite a stir.

Meanwhile, fishing boats came and went, and the siege survivors queued for food. The attackers hadn't killed the livestock; they'd been geas-bound to go after the humans. But the pens didn't hold an inexhaustible supply of bison. Daniel didn't know exactly what pemmican was, only that it wouldn't last forever. But he did know, by virtue of his long treks, that vast herds of caribou roamed the continent. He wondered how far they'd have to go to find the nearest herd. A trio of mechanicals could haul back a ton of meat. A few dozen mechanicals could substantially ease the French survivors' food problem. It was the moral thing to do.

It wouldn't bring back the man he'd killed, much less any of the other humans who'd died in the siege. But if it could save a few lives... He turned his attention from the river to mention this idea to his companions.

As had somehow become the custom in recent days, a coterie of fellow Clakkers had followed him like ducklings. The group comprised both soldier-class mechanicals and servitors like Daniel. Most everyone who had lingered in the area after the mass unwriting of the metageasa bore the signs of combat. Bloodstains on retracted blades, scored escutcheons, dented carapaces. Judging from their cracked, blackened flange plates and the scritching of their hinges, at least two of these servitors had been within the blast radius when the defenders of New France detonated the booby-trapped outer wall.

Daniel realized one mechanical chattered at him. He'd been too deep in his own thoughts to listen. That was rude.

Modulating the rattle of his own body, he said, in the manner of their kind, *I'm sorry. What were you saying?*

Our flag, said the soldier. She sported a long, deep scratch across her skull; a French guard had come close to scouring her sigils and unwriting her. Daniel glimpsed rusty blotches on the fluted serrations of her forearm blades. Some of those were probably from a killing stroke that ended the very same guard's life. She added, *We can't decide on a design. What do you think?*

He suppressed the mechanical equivalent of a sigh. More questions. This had also become the custom in recent days. The freed machines acted as though Daniel had all the answers.

The self-styled vexillologist carried a roll of birch bark, curled as if it were still wrapped around the tree. She pulled the curls apart; the papery bark sported several monotone sketches. Various fields were labeled with arrows and colors.

I've also been working on a coat of arms, she said. *Some say it should feature orange, as an acknowledgment of our origin, but others say our arms should be ours and ours alone and recognize no human device.*

At which point she and the others paused, waiting. Had they been humans, Daniel would have described their anticipation as breathless.

Who cares what I think? he said. *If it really matters, take a vote.*

Everybody cares what you think, said another.

Some of these mechanicals had been forged decades before him, yet they insisted on deferring to his judgment. As though he were old King Solomon from the Bible.

Daniel clicked. *I doubt it.*

A second servitor said, *Of course we do. You gave us Free Will. More than that—*

(*Don't say it,* Daniel rattled. *Don't say it.*)

—you gave us back our souls.

French Catholics maintained the immortal soul was the seat of Free Will, and that their Calvinist enemies therefore committed sacrilege by depriving Clakkers of self-determination. Daniel didn't know if he believed it. Visser surely did.

Oh, for crying out loud. Believe what you want, but just how far do you think the Papists will take your conversion? If you can't eat, you can't take Holy Communion.

Daniel immediately regretted the outburst. He understood how chaotic and overwhelming the world had seemed in his first days of freedom. For a being whose entire existence had been rigidly circumscribed by geasa and metageasa dictating every single action for decades on end, it was difficult to find direction and purpose without having the pain of compulsion as a guide.

Look, he said. *I understand how confusing it can be. Give yourselves time. Just don't latch onto the first thing to come along.* He gave the mechanical equivalent of a shrug. *That's my advice, anyway.*

The soldier rolled up the sketches. Another mechanical, a servitor, took the birch-bark scroll from her and tucked it into the gaps of its torso. Soldiers couldn't store things in that fashion owing to their armor plating.

She said, *We can do as you suggest. We'll vote on it, if you think that's best. But if you were to weigh in with an opinion, that would help us know how to vote.*

Deep inside Daniel's body, a pair of cables twanged and slapped together. After a moment's effort to tamp down his irritation, he asked, *Wouldn't that defeat the purpose?*

His fellow mechanicals swayed on their leaf-spring knees, a gesture of chastened agreement.

Anyway, he said. *Since you're here, I'll mention a thought that struck me a moment ago. I think we can help the French with their food problem.*

They listened to his idea, though with a fraction of the enthusiasm they reserved for heraldry and flag design. Most freed Clakkers were more interested in their own pursuits than in the affairs of humans. He didn't blame them. If they didn't want to help, that was their choice. He couldn't make them more compassionate. He couldn't make them do anything. Otherwise, what was the point?

The assembled kinsmachines emitted no clicks or clangs of excitement, no ticks or twangs of curiosity. To the former soldier, he said, *Field dressing game to help feed hungry refugees would be the first constructive and moral thing those blades have ever done.* Still, even after appealing to their morality, his suggestion received a lukewarm response.

Very well. He turned his attention back to the river, the barque, and the French tent village beyond. *If you feel like spreading the word, I'd appreciate it. But only if you feel like it.*

The ticktock body noise faded as the gathering dispersed. Two servitors, the badly damaged ones, stayed behind. They pretended to contemplate the river as Daniel himself was doing. They probably had follow-up questions about Holy Communion now. This was getting ridiculous.

I understand you're brimming with questions. You yearn to pry apart every existential and theological issue raised by your new power of self-determination, he said. *I know that drive, really, I do. But I can't answer your questions. I don't know any more than you do. You didn't have Free Will, and now you do. I can't tell you any more than that. I'm not a seminarian,* he concluded.

One servitor said, *We'd never suggest otherwise.*

No, not a seminarian, said the other. *Just a thief.*

Daniel turned. Having closed ranks, the other Clakkers now stood shoulder to shoulder before him. Sunlight illuminated a network of faint scratches around the keyholes on each of their foreheads. But these weren't deep enough to deface the sigils. They weren't battle wounds, Daniel realized. They were the evidence of protective plates having been pried from the keyholes. Protective plates such as worn by the subjects of Queen Mab: the supposedly free Clakkers of Neverland.

The Lost Boys said, in unison, *Hello, Daniel.*

Or have you gone back to calling yourself Jax? asked the one on the right.

Daniel crouched for a leap that would send him backflipping and plunging into the Saint Lawrence. Mab's agents tackled him. The cacophonous impact sounded like a pair of church bells smashed together. The scraping of alchemical alloys tossed blazing sparks of violet and deeper colors humans couldn't see. His talon toes churned mud and ice as they dragged him away from the water.

You took something from the queen, said one.

She's very displeased, said the other.

Daniel kicked and thrashed, but despite their superficial damage, they easily overpowered him.

I don't have it! he said, still fighting.

Neverland, Daniel had discovered, was a lie. Free Clakkers who followed the legends to the snowy north sooner or later met Mab. And sooner or later she overrode the poor bastard's keyhole using a unique piece of alchemical glass that enabled her to install her own personal metageasa. Most of the Lost Boys were Mab's thralls. Except for the true believers.

Daniel had stolen Mab's locket and fled. Later, it proved crucial to the mass freeing of his kin. The self-propagating process had begun on the battlefield of Marseilles-in-the-West.

Of course you don't. We've seen your handiwork.

Daniel flailed. He planted a kick on one servitor's shoulder. More sparks fountained from the cymbal-crash impact. It broke the machine's grip on him, but Daniel couldn't shake the other machine before its partner recovered. They wrestled him to the muddy ground. The friction heat of their struggle baked little wisps of steam from the earth.

Then why—

As I said, the queen is very displeased. She wishes to express that displeasure in person.

One servitor wrapped itself around his thrashing legs. Daniel writhed. The other leapt upon his torso and tried to grab his windmilling arms. Daniel heaved, physically lifting the machine pinning his legs, but it wasn't enough. He was outmatched. He had to hope the noise would draw attention.

It was a long trek to Neverland across hundreds of leagues of trackless forests, prairies, mountains. Some terrain would be turning marshy, too, in the spring thaws.

You'll never get me back to Neverland. I'll thrash and kick and fight you every single step of the way.

No, you won't, said the Lost Boy at his legs.

The one crouched on Daniel's chest produced a small metal object from within his torso. It had jagged teeth splayed around a cylindrical core.

A key. For turning the lock in Daniel's forehead.

Which would render him inert. Unconscious. And easily transportable.

No! NO!

He thrashed anew. Flopping like a fish caught in a French seiner, he used all the tension in his steel sinews, all the potential energy in his springs. But nothing shook them loose. The Lost Boy bearing the key grabbed Daniel from behind. He wrapped one arm under Daniel's shoulder and clamped the other around his neck.

PLEASE! Daniel begged.

The key screeched against his forehead like a nail dragged across an iron skillet. The Lost Boy adjusted his grip and tried again. The key briefly clicked across the lip of Daniel's forehead lock. Daniel heaved, lifting his legs and the servitor pinning them. Then he locked his hips like the hinge of a seesaw and released all the tension below his waist. Daniel's upper body rocked upward. He snapped his head forward at the same moment. The head-butt knocked the key from his assailant's hand. It arced along the riverbank into a stand of winter-brown reeds.

You're just delaying the inevitable.

One servitor jumped up to recover the key. Daniel took advantage of his freed arms to punch the machine still holding his legs. His fists sent up a shower of sparks that sizzled on the ground. They gave off little puffs of sulphurous smoke when the mud extinguished them, like the last gasp of a snuffed candle.

Like the last gasp of Daniel's freedom.

From down at the waterline came a faint crunch, as of a boat hitting the riverbank. With a heave that etched scratches in his leg from knee to ankle, Daniel kicked free. His assailant tumbled down the slope toward the water. Daniel leapt to his feet and sprinted away from the river, toward the forest. He'd gone two strides before one of the Lost Boys tackled him. He wrenched Daniel's arms behind his back and pinned him to the ground.

Get the key! It went into the reeds.

Mud and water splashed. Daniel fought with all the ferocity he could muster. He braced for the end.

Instead there was a short, sharp gurgling sound, followed by a splash, a wave of heat, and the scents of lilac and skunk. The machine holding Daniel released him and leapt clear. Daniel flipped upright and landed in a deep three-point crouch.

One of his assailants was encased in a glob of quickset epoxy like an ant in amber. The chemical sheath encased everything but one outstretched hand, in which it held a key. The other Lost Boy stood at the center of a triangle formed by his trapped colleague, Daniel, and the rowboat that had landed while they fought.

Berenice stood in the prow with one foot braced against the gunwale and the butt of an epoxy rifle pressed to her shoulder. Sunlight glinted from the coppery tanks slung over her back. Wisps of vapor wafted from the muzzle.

Still sighting down the doubled barrel, she said in flawless Dutch, "Hi, Daniel. Friends of yours?"

"No."

"Didn't think so."

"This doesn't concern you," said the Lost Boy.

Keeping the gun trained on him, she said, "As a matter of fact, it does concern me, because I rather need to talk to Daniel. And you overgrown pocket watches look determined to make that really fucking difficult." She frowned. Her eyes flicked from the Lost Boy to Daniel and back. "Um. You are Daniel, right?"

If Daniel could have rolled his eyes like a human, he would have. "Yes."

The second Lost Boy jumped away. The gun coughed. A trickle of liquid dripped from the barrel.

"Shit," said Berenice.

But Daniel blurred forward, plucking the key from the immobilized Lost Boy before the other landed. He was on the other instantly, and after a moment's struggle had jammed the key into his forehead. Daniel carried the inert servitor out of the reeds and laid him beside his encased companion. He wondered who these two were, and if he'd ever known their names. When he first arrived in Neverland, he was so broken it was in the arms of a Lost Boy.

A faint ticktocking emanated from the chemical cocoon. *Enjoy your freedom while you can. She'll never stop searching for you.*

Berenice squinted, as though trying to make sense of what she heard. Daniel doubted she could, however. The mechanicals of Neverland had a peculiar dialect.

She asked, "What's all this about?"

"They work for Mab."

"Let me guess. She wants her doodad back."

"One gets that impression."

She said, "I assume you'll want to borrow my boat." She shrugged off the shoulder straps of her useless weapon. The empty tanks made a hollow *bong*ing sound when she dropped them in the keel. "That's fine. I'll talk while you row."

"What ever would I want your boat for?"

"So that you can dump these chrome-plated assholes in the darkest, deepest part of the river."

"That's appalling. I'm not going to do that."

"Really? Seems like the smart move to me."

"They'd be stuck down there for years!"

"Exactly."

The taut steel cables threaded across Daniel's shoulders thrummed like a plucked guitar string. Knowing Berenice wouldn't understand the nuances of mechanical body language, he shook his head to emulate human exasperation. "Why must you always gravitate to the darkest, cruelest way of solving a problem?"

"What the hell has gotten into you?"

"I don't like the way you do things."

"Yeah, well, I just saved your life, so..."

"You didn't save my life," said Daniel. "But you did save me from... well, something unpleasant, anyway."

"My point stands, then. Oh, and you're fucking welcome, by the way."

A moment passed. Daniel said, "Thank you for your help."

"Oh, anything for a friend in need." She hopped lightly from the boat. Mud squelched under her boots. "Honestly, though, I would've been pissed if it had turned out I'd wasted that excellent shot because of mistaken identity."

That gave him pause. Head cocked, he studied her face. She'd gone back to wearing her eyepatch.

"Your aim is better than one might expect, under the circumstances."

"So what if luck played a role? Maybe it was Divine Providence. I understand you ticktocks are all about God these days."

He crouched beside the deactivated Lost Boy. Why hadn't he recognized them? Their mismatched bodies should have given them away. He studied the inert machine, and peered through the thick coating encasing his immobilized colleague, which kept up a steady stream of threats and insults. Threats of enslavement, threats of disassembly.

"Oh, hush," he said.

Their damage, he realized, hadn't been incurred during the detonation of the wall. It was older. Much older.

Berenice joined him. "What are you staring at?"

A click arpeggio cascaded the length of his spine. A heavy mechanical shudder. Explaining mechanical mores to any human, much less Berenice, was like trying to cut a diamond by blowing on it.

"Most mechanicals in Neverland, including those who

chased me here, do not exhibit a uniformity of design." Indeed, the grotesque Queen Mab flouted the very deepest of Clakker taboos; the mixing and matching of body parts had been anathema to their kind from the very beginning. He preferred not to think about it at all. So he said, simply, "In order to pass unnoticed amongst us, these agents had to change their bodies."

"Huh." She leaned close to the encased machine, almost pressing her forehead to the faintly translucent epoxy. She frowned. Then she crouched beside Daniel. After a slow perusal of the second Lost Boy, Berenice grunted.

"I know where they found their replacement parts." She shook her head. Her face had gone pale, he realized. Under her breath, as though talking to herself, she wondered, "Shit. How do they know about the laboratory?"

Ah. Talleyrand's laboratory, hidden deep within the stony heart of Mont Royal. Where for generations the French had conducted secret treaty-violating examinations of Clakkers and their components. Daniel had heard about this place, too. Terrible things.

"Lilith told them about it."

Berenice gulped. "Say that again?"

"Lilith. She reached Neverland not long before I did." He turned his full attention on Berenice. "She told everybody about what you did to her."

"I thought you'd been a little chilly lately." She met his gaze. But after several heartbeats she looked away. "I did what I thought was necessary to protect my home." She pointed to the ruins, the rubble field like a mouthful of broken teeth. "Living under the constant threat of extinction makes you hard, Daniel. You get hard or you die."

"You also lied to me about your intentions. You said your plan was to end the siege by freeing my kin."

"That's what happened, isn't it?"

"Despite your best efforts."

Berenice turned. "Why are you riding me all of a sudden? I got your message and tracked you down. Had I known your plan was to heap scorn on me, I wouldn't have bothered and you'd be well on your way to an audience with a crazed tinpot dictator by now."

Daniel stood. "I didn't send you a message. If I'd wanted to talk to you, I would've found you after visiting Pastor Visser. Speaking of which, it would be nice if you did, too."

But Berenice's one-track mind had little room for extraneous trivialities like compassion. "I could've sworn it was written by a Clakker."

"You're not the center of my world, you realize."

"A moment ago you implied a favorite pastime in Neverland was lengthy discussion of me and my methods."

"What did the message say?"

"'Quintessentia.'"

"And?"

"And that's it."

"How do you know it was meant for you, then?"

"It came via pigeon for Talleyrand." Berenice sighed. "Now that I say it out loud, it does seem an odd way for you to get in touch. But I was so certain . . ." She scanned the river, as though looking for distant pigeon coops. She said, "What will you do about Mab and her pals?"

"There's nothing I can do." It galled him to admit it, but it was the ugly truth. He'd left Neverland—Mab would probably call it a defection—because he couldn't tolerate what she did and what she stood for. The cruel irony was that of all the mechanicals in the world, the isolated Lost Boys would probably never receive the luminous touch of true freedom. Ratchets chittered in his legs and arms as he tried to shake off the twinned barbs of shame and self-reproach.

"Here," he said. "I'll help you turn your boat around." His fight with the Lost Boys had churned up the mud along the riverbank. It gave off a faint odor of decay. Grabbing hold of the gunwales, he nodded at the epoxy gun lying in the boat. "I'd keep that close if you intend to spend time on this side of the river."

"We know about the reapers." She kicked the weapon. "Anyway, it's empty. I was lucky to get one shot."

Daniel held the rowboat steady while Berenice hopped over the prow. She positioned herself between the oarlocks, reached for the oars, but stopped. Her hands fell into her lap, and she tilted her head back.

"Boat," she whispered. "Quintessence."

She'd just had an idea. He'd seen this before and he knew where it led. Berenice's brainstorms were dangerous: The lightning tended to strike those around her. He leaned against the prow. The mud made a wet, sucking sound.

Over her shoulder, she said, "Hey, wait a moment." She turned, straddling the thwart. "When Mab raided that mine, did you find out what quintessence was or why the Clockmakers wanted it so badly?"

"No. I was too busy trying and failing to prevent an atrocity."

Berenice rolled her eyes. "You have a knack for melodrama, I'll give you that."

"Good-bye, Berenice." He pushed again on the boat.

"Wait, wait! Mab controls the mine now, right? So what do you suppose she's doing with it?"

"Of course I don't know."

"How would you like to find out?"

Again cogs meshed and unmeshed through his torso. A year ago he wouldn't have thought it possible to meet a grown woman half as irritating as little Nicolet Schoonraad.

Daniel shook his head, again emulating human body language for the sake of clarity. "I've learned to be wary when something makes you this excited."

She rubbed her hands together. "What if I told you there might be a way to solve several of our problems at once? That we could together unravel the riddle of quintessence while *you* could strike a blow against Mab and *I* could replenish our chemical stocks."

"I'd say, 'No, thank you.' "

"Uh-huh. And what if it *also* meant humans and Clakkers working together, side by side, for the first time in history? Not just standing near one another, and not subjugating one another, and not murdering one another, but working as true allies."

It was uncanny, her knack for persuasion. She excelled at framing things as if her aims were entirely in line with everybody else's. Even when they weren't.

Just hear her out, Daniel decided. *No need to take her at her word.* The last time he pretended to believe her, she overestimated him, and it turned out rather well for his kind.

He said, "Very well. Tell me your idea."

She pointed across the river, to the ship from the Great Lakes.

"How would you like to go on a cruise?"

CHAPTER 5

Anastasia contemplated the geometric progression of doom, and quailed.

Assume a quarter million residents in The Hague.

(Reasonable. Though smaller than many of the great cities of Europe, it wielded grossly disproportionate influence. It was, after all, the center of the world.)

And the human/mechanical ratio? Parity, say.

(Conservative. Though not everybody in this wealthy city could afford to lease a mechanical, the Guild had long ago tuned the lease rates to maximize the flood of guilders into its coffers. Plus the city was home to the Clockmakers' Guild, the government, and two of Queen Margreet's official residences—all institutions that leaned upon a substantial mechanical workforce.)

And say that on average each infected machine could corrupt three others.

(Conservative, surely, but to what extent? She'd witnessed the malfunction transmitted only to small groups during the slaughter in the Binnenhof. But what prevented a rogue from opening its head and running along the Spui towpath, shining its contagion on every mechanical on the street? On the other hand, it appeared that only a small fraction of the attackers sported those modifications. Perhaps most could not spread the affliction beyond themselves. A thin thread of hope, but if it drove the average down, worth clinging to.)

Assume one-third of the exposed machines were unaffected, one-third simply walked away from their duties, and one-third became killers.

(A reasonable, albeit simplistic, approximation, based on the observation that exposure to the rogues' pineal light led to one of those three outcomes. During the Binnenhof attack, some of the exposed machines continued to defend their human masters, some abandoned the defense and departed, and some joined in the slaughter.)

And, lastly, take it for granted the battle in Huygens Square hadn't destroyed every last infectious rogue.

(Only a fool would assume otherwise.)

So. Two hundred and fifty thousand mechanicals in the city; each rogue could convert at least two others, one that simply disregarded its obligations and one that chose to kill. Depending on the frequency of the encounters, and whether repeated exposures could convert the previously unaltered machines, and whether the Guild could find a way to reverse the infection, or slow its spread, or halt it...

It took no leap of imagination, no special power of pessimistic doomsaying, to imagine eighty thousand mechanical butchers roaming The Hague.

How quickly would the civic infrastructure collapse when The Hague's labor force suddenly contracted by over sixty percent? When would the water stop flowing? Gas for the streetlamps, for heating homes? When would the city run out of food? When would the Clakker-hauled wagons packed with fresh meat and produce stop arriving from the countryside farms, where most labor were mechanicals?

How soon before communication within the Empire crumbled? Within the Central Provinces? Within The Hague itself? The French had pigeons and semaphore towers. (Or they did, prior to the war. Surely the birds had all been shot and the towers burned to cinders by now.) But the bulk of message traffic within the Central Provinces moved by Clakker post, or even by people's personal servitors. Rapid communication was essential to the governance of empire.

The more Anastasia pondered them, the darker the clouds on the horizon, the more sinister the very sea itself. Even the land beneath her feet faced an existential crisis. When would the waters rise? How long until enough servitors abandoned their pumps and polders to break the Central Provinces' eternal stalemate against sea and tide? Would the sea reclaim the land?

On and on and on it went. Her mind raced through a litany of calamities. How straightforward the end of the world when reduced to a single apocalyptic checklist.

And what then, after The Hague fell? Would the malfunction spread through the Empire? Had it already done so? Would the rogues keep moving until they covered the world in metal? How far would they go? To the border of China? Straight across Africa, from Tunis to the Cape of Good Hope? There were Clakkers aplenty on that wild continent, speaking the bastardized Dutch of their Afrikaaner owners.

A faint odor of blood and brimstone wafted through Huygens Square, where teams of uncorrupted mechanicals labored to install new traps above the Forge. Meanwhile, far underground, a collection of horologists and alchemists assessed the damage to the massive armillary sphere at the Forge's heart.

Parking the rings had probably saved the Forge. But now the technicians found it impossible to restart the armillary sphere. The collateral damage had been too great. So while the Forge survived, it was useless. Meaning the Guild couldn't build new servants to replace those lost in defense of the Ridderzaal. It couldn't replace those lost to contagious corruption of the metageasa. It couldn't make existing machines immune to the corruption. It couldn't capture malfunctioning mechanicals and force a hard erasure to wipe the slate clean. It could do nothing to address the problem. As long as the rings were parked, the Guild's holy of holies was nothing but an oversized barbecue pit.

They had to get it working before the next attack. They had to contain the infection. They had to break the chain before it strangled the Empire.

Immediately after the battle in Huygens Square, any remaining attackers had disappeared, melting back into the city like raindrops into parched soil. She'd heard of tropical diseases with symptoms that recurred with dreadful regularity. Deep in her marrow she carried a cold fear the corrupted machines would similarly torment the Central Provinces. How many now roamed the city? A secret army of saboteurs passing unnoticed amongst thousands of identical machines. The Clockmakers worked on borrowed time until the agents of chaos rose again.

A pair of sprinting mechanicals pulled a carriage through the arch where the Stadtholder's Gate had stood. The actual gate was now so much scrap iron in the Guild foundries; its counterpart from the eastern end of the Binnenhof, the Grenadierspoort, was now a heap of mangled metal behind the Ridderzaal. A pair of Stemwinders had torn down the ancient gates on Anastasia's orders. Simple gates couldn't keep out a dedicated force of rogue Clakkers, and this way the Binnenhof couldn't be used to pen innocent citizens *quite* so easily.

The brutal efficiency of that ambush... Anastasia shuddered again, and not from a chill.

Sodden clothes no longer clung to her body, reeking of piss and puke. She'd tossed her ruined outfit into an incinerator. Today she wore gray corduroy trousers short enough to show her ankles over wooden klompen, a faded yellow shirt with a torn collar, and a moth-eaten shawl. All left behind by guests of the Guild, some of whom might still languish in the tunnels. She'd had a servitor heat a barrel of rainwater to near boiling in the Forge chamber, then gave herself a sponge bath in her office.

From a rapidly dwindling distance, the Clakkers hauling the carriage appeared to be military models complete with the subtle fluting on the forearms where their blades retracted. Yet they seemed large even for soldiers. Anastasia tensed. Her hand snapped up to the hypersonic whistle that, like all her surviving colleagues, she wore on a necklace in lieu of a Guild pendant. The carriage neared the Ridderzaal. She ducked her head; the silver whistle chilled her lips. But then the carriage turned, and she saw the machines more clearly. They had no faces, just smooth, featureless armor beneath eyes of blue diamond. Their escutcheons blazed in the sun with golden filigree.

Elite mechanicals of the Queen's Guard.

Logistical triage had kept her too busy to worry about the queen. To a certain extent, the Brasswork Throne was superfluous. If the Guild fell, so did the Throne; if the Guild persisted, so would the Empire. But now she wondered: Did Margreet still sit the Brasswork Throne? Did the Empire still have a figurehead? Anastasia's hand hovered by her mouth, frozen with indecision. If they weren't beset with deadly malfunctions, these machines would know of Her Majesty. But the possibility of a rogue Queen's Guard mechanical weakened her knees. Those bespoke killers could rival even the Stemwinders—and she'd seen firsthand the destructive power of a malfunctioning centaur.

One machine released the carriage and trotted across the shattered mosaic tiles. It came straight toward Anastasia and her colleagues.

"Oh, shit," said one. Several made a break for the Ridderzaal. As if they could outrun a mechanical. Foolish. Though Anastasia understood the impulse. Shared it, even.

Somebody must have blown a dog whistle, because a troop of Stemwinders and regular servitors burst forth from the Ridderzaal. They streaked across the square, intent on intercepting the royal Clakker before it reached Anastasia. It could have reached her already had it moved as fast as it was able, but hadn't.

"Hold," she called. Her defenders skidded to a halt.

It wasn't an attack. And the carriage was empty, she saw. She'd interacted with the Queen's Guard infrequently, but enough to understand how they worked.

This was a summons. The queen lived.

To the nearest servitor, she said, "Make it known I have an audience with Her Majesty. Doctor Euwe is in charge until I return, or until our superiors do."

"As you say, mistress. Right away, mistress." The mechanical sprinted away.

The machine from the Queen's Guard towered over her. It pointed to the carriage.

Like the Stemwinders, the mechanicals of the Royal Guard couldn't talk. By royal decree of centuries past, the Guild had designed them to be mute servants and ruthless bodyguards.

This was a safeguard in case of political upheaval or attempted usurpation by other members of the royal family, who, with the weight of royal metageasa on their side, might otherwise force the machines to divulge things they'd overheard while in the sovereign's presence.

She entered the carriage. The Queen's Guard machines waited until she was seated and buckled before accelerating from a walk to a trot to a skin-peeling sprint. Her hand hurt again; she hadn't had a chance to inspect her bandages beyond checking them for new bloodstains, of which there were none. The Queen's Guard mechanicals cast a fine illusion over the city: By tearing down the streets so rapidly, they blurred symptoms of the malignance threatening the Empire. It all disappeared: the shattered windows; the mangled rainspouts; the crushed bricks and missing roof tiles; the finger and toe divots pressed into storefronts and street signs; the bloodstains in Italian marble; even the bodies slumped in open doorways, or dangling like broken mannequins from the boughs of boulevard ash trees. But it was just an illusion; the sickness was there, whether she saw it or not.

The carriage approached the Summer Palace. For centuries, a fifty-foot yew hedge had girded the entirety of the grounds: an unbroken jade edifice enclosing hundreds of acres of private garden and (carefully stocked) hunting preserve dedicated to the Brasswork Throne. It had long been said, amongst the people who said such things, that master horticulturalists had tortured the plants until they sprouted razor-sharp thorns, and that master alchemists had imbued those thorns with a cocktail of deadly poisons. Anastasia knew this to be baseless fancy, but a useful one; the prosaic truth was that the rare citizen foolish enough to sneak onto the grounds jangled a dozen gossamer tripwires before making it halfway through the hedge, and always found a few machines waiting on the other side.

Queen's Guard mechanicals were not bound to the same human-safety metageasa as other Clakkers.

But the Summer Palace wasn't a fortress. It wasn't some Bourbon redoubt designed to keep the world at bay, and the hedge wasn't a ring of Vauban fortifications. Its impregnability wasn't a fact of stone and steel. It was a social contract. The very same conceit underlay the entire existence of the Empire: the conceit of Clakker loyalty. Owing to that conceit, the hedge hadn't changed since Anastasia's grandfather had been a boy. But no longer.

The carriage slowed; the blur beyond the windows resolved into a landscape so thoroughly ravaged that Anastasia gasped. The barrier was no more. It had been shredded, shorn, ravaged. Great swaths of broken boughs lay strewn on the raked gravel carriage path alongside the hedge. No wonder her escorts had slowed. Each time Anastasia's ride bounced over the detritus, the wheels crushed the boughs and churned up a mulchy scent. The ruined foliage glinted with shards of broken metal. Pressing her face to the window, Anastasia saw the trail of destruction ranged the entire length of the hedge wall. Light glinted from a thousand strands of gossamer metal where the assailants had burst through the tripwires.

Surely the French couldn't have done this. But if not the Papists, who?

Please, Lord, not the machines themselves. Please.

She would've wagered everything she owned that this attack had been coordinated with the assault on the Guild.

(*Wagers.* A new twinge of nausea tickled her empty stomach. Dear Lord...What would this do to the banks? How long until panicky depositors withdrew every last kwartje? Until terrified investors scorched the floorboards in their haste to distance themselves from the markets? History had seen fortunes amassed and erased by nothing more than flights of human fancy. But this was no tulipomania. This crisis was real, and it was dire. Could it erase an entire economy? They'd know soon enough if the Guild failed to stop this avalanche. But the first pebbles were rolling, rolling, rolling...)

Gates breached the hedge at the points of the compass rose. The assault had spared the west gate. But today the fearsome array of spikes, and the gilt steel forged into a likeness of the Empire's Arms, looked slightly ridiculous in the context of the devastated wall. A quartet of Queen's Guard mechanicals opened the massive gate as the carriage approached. The reverberating *clang* of its closure brought a chilly twinge of déjà vu, rather unpleasantly like the feeling of winter rain dripping under her collar to trickle down her spine.

Trap, trap, trap! cried the wise coward huddled atop her brain stem.

The carriage stopped alongside a vast flight of marble stairs. The Palace's grand staircase was wider than the entire Ridderzaal. The Queen's Guard mechanicals ushered her from the carriage. At the bottom of the stairs lay the toppled remains of Queen Margreet's golden carriage. The teakwood and alchemical glass had been pulverized, the brass and gold battered beyond recognition. But the line of Clakkerish legs along the axle still sprinted in place, impelled by magics bereft of purpose.

Margreet the Second, Queen of the Netherlands, Princess of Orange-Nassau and the Central Provinces, Blessed Sovereign of Europe, Protector of the New World, Light of Civilization and Benevolent Ruler of the Dutch Empire, Rightful Monarch

Upon the Brasswork Throne, dabbed New World chocolate from her lips with a wisp of Indian silk.

"They killed *how* many?"

Four pairs of eyes turned to Anastasia. She said, "We don't know, Your Majesty. We might never know for certain. The catastrophe in the Binnenhof went beyond mere killing. It was orchestrated butchery. Many of the dead will be difficult to identify. I have a squad of servitors working to piece together the, ah, remains."

"Merciful God."

Minister General Hendriks, pastor of the Sint-Jacobskerk, pressed a handkerchief to his mouth and made a soft gagging sound. His survival wasn't surprising; their secret enemy had precisely targeted the real power behind the Empire—the Guild—and the Empire's figurehead—the Brasswork Throne. She doubted the rogues spared a single tock for churchmen, excepting those unlucky enough to have fallen into the meat grinder with the other victims.

"Furthermore," she added, "many of the dead and dying fell into the Forge when we jettisoned the trapdoors. Those remains have been incinerated." She paused while the cadaverous minister retched into his handkerchief. The queen's glare could have etched alchemical steel. "I fear they won't be the last citizens to go missing, their fates forever unknown."

From her perch atop the dais, the queen said, "Yes, yes, it's all very sad. But how many of my *Clakkers* were destroyed in the attack?"

"Over two hundred at last count, Your Majesty."

Prince Rupert, Queen Margreet's consort, whistled through his teeth. Anastasia had met him at official functions in the past; this was the first time she'd ever seen him out of his naval uniform.

Lost in his own thoughts, Hendriks had lost track of the conversation. "Those poor souls," he murmured. "Butchered like lambs."

He sighed, gusting acid-sour breath across the table. It made Anastasia's eyes water. She took a sip of wine.

The prince said, "Don't pray for them, fool. Pray for *us*."

Anastasia bit her lip. Apparently the stars had aligned to plunge the world into a time of dark miracles. To hear a member of the royal family doubt the utter invulnerability of the Empire was to witness the unthinkable. His honesty earned a caustic glance from the queen. She cast them about the room like a master archer in the old stories, and she kept a full quiver.

"Ahem."

The robed figure at the far end of the table cleared her throat. It was the first noise Anastasia had heard from within the shadows of the Master Horologist's cowl. Though her Guild pendant was not in evidence—it would have displayed the rosy cross inlaid with rubies rather than rose quartz—she wore the traditional garb of her office, a scarlet robe trimmed with ermine. She must have already been with the queen when the rogues swarmed the city, else her robe would have drawn the attackers like wasps to a picnic. Anastasia wondered what fates had befallen the rest of the troika; no more than two Master Horologists ever appeared in public together.

In a voice like the unspooling of a silver thread, the horologist said, "Tuinier Bell. Share with us your analysis of the situation."

"I think we can agree, Your Eminence, these events cannot be ascribed to mass malfunction. The rogues' actions were far too coordinated for that. This was an orchestrated attack on the citizenry of The Hague, focused on our centers of governance and the Sacred Guild of Horologists and Alchemists."

The unwelcome truth settled over the conversation like a stone sarcophagus lid. Into the uncomfortable silence fell the ceaseless body noise of the queen's mechanical attendants. A Queen's Guard soldier stood in each corner, ever vigilant for threats against the royal person. If their eyes were artificial sapphires, Margreet's were emeralds, sheer and cold as alchemical ice.

"And how did it happen?"

"I fear the best scenario is that somebody has developed a means of altering the metageasa, has done so en masse, and has furthermore made the changes self-propagating. A perversion of the grammars could imbue mechanicals with a violent base priority, as well as immunity to our directives."

"That's the *best* scenario?" The prince looked disgusted. "You Clockmakers are as mad as they say."

Anastasia drew a deep breath. "A worse scenario is that this is an endemic design flaw. We must examine the possibility that something or someone is triggering a hitherto unknown fault state, under which *every mechanical ever built* will default to violence against the state."

"Oh," said the prince. Like a chameleon trapped in an ossuary, the cadaverous minister general paled from ashen gray to bone white.

Anastasia continued. "And then there is the worst case to consider. That this wasn't an outsider's directive, nor was it an accident of design. Simply put, that in the absence of controlling directives, the mechanicals deliberately chose to turn on us."

A faint harrumph came from the Archmaster's cowl.

"That is absurd," said Hendriks. "Machines don't think. Every schoolchild knows this."

The prince consort agreed. "Aren't you overreacting just a

bit, Tuinier? I understand you've witnessed something terrible. You may be in shock."

The queen said, "Which scenario does your analysis support?"

Anastasia stood. She paced, careful that her circuit never brought her near the queen's dais, lest her guards leap from their posts. Their eyes tracked her with a faint ratcheting. An ache throbbed within her bandaged hand; she massaged it, choosing her words with care.

"We don't know yet. Analysis of the deactivated rogues isn't straightforward."

"Why not?"

"Disassembly must be carried out by hand. Human hand, I mean. Until we better understand the situation, common sense absolutely precludes the use of mechanical labor."

"Isn't that terribly slow?" asked Rupert.

"Tedious as well. But we have no choice," Anastasia answered. "We must think of this as a disease that spreads amongst mechanicals like plague amongst humans."

Another harrumph shook the horologist's cowl. "And you fear the inert rogues are still contagious."

"Yes."

The horologist twined her fingers together as though weaving a basket of flesh and bone. Liver-spotted and cracked like museum parchment, they were an old woman's hands, quite at odds with the voice that said merely, "Interesting."

Anastasia said, "How is this possible, Your Eminence? What is the mechanism?"

Margreet's mouth curled in a moue of contempt. "I cannot begin to express how minuscule is my interest in listening to you Clockmakers gaze upon your own navels. Instead, turn your oh-so-formidable intellects to the problem of getting me safely out of the Central Provinces until this crisis has passed."

Oh. So that's why we're here.

Hendriks goggled at her. "You're running away?"

How miraculous that hoarfrost didn't glide across the floor to freeze him in place.

"The Verderers' negligence has impugned the dignity of the Empire." Anastasia wanted to writhe in shame. She'd failed in her stewardship of Guild secrets. Spectacularly. "Where before our protectorates and enemies looked to the Brasswork Throne and saw unassailable strength, now they will see vulnerability. They will sharpen their knives in the foolish belief they might cut us. And I will have no choice but to order their annihilation." When the queen shook her head, the pearls beaded through the ringlets of her hair rattled like chattering teeth. "I am not a bloodthirsty woman. But I will not hesitate to wield the full might of the Brasswork Throne.

"Until that time, my responsibility is to ensure the continuance of the Empire. I am one with the Brasswork Throne. If the Empire is to survive, so must I."

She put a pretty face on her cowardice, Anastasia had to admit. But like many a figurehead, Queen Margreet overstated her own importance. The Empire could function without a queen; it would crumble without the Guild. And the Guild could ill afford the time and resources it would require to smuggle the sovereign out of the country.

"Majesty," said Anastasia, "your people need you."

The queen's icy gaze pierced her, sharp and true as Achilles's javelin.

"Is that not what I said? I will return when the crisis has been averted, and thereby show my subjects and my enemies that the Brasswork Throne is stronger than ever."

Anastasia held her breath for fear a sigh of disgust would lay bare her true feelings. The minister general was right; Margreet intended to run away while everybody else struggled to contain the worst disaster to befall the Dutch-speaking world since before Het Wonderjaar. Well. Figureheads had their place, she supposed. It would raise the populace's morale after the crisis was averted—if it was—to see the queen out and about.

And, more to the point, once Margreet was far out of the city, the Guild could work without interruption and without diverting resources to protect and mollify the queen. Very well, then.

"As you say, Majesty. We will devise a plan at once."

The monarch said, "Organize safe passage from the Central Provinces. Then solve this problem and identify our attackers, that I may return and destroy them." She waved Anastasia and the minister away as though shooing away a fly. "Rupert, Eminence, stay a moment."

Anastasia curtseyed while Hendriks bowed, then together they retreated from the audience chamber, walking backward as a show of respect. This was much easier in trousers than in long skirts, she had to admit. A pair of Queen's Guard mechanicals joined them at the door while the other two approached the dais. Anastasia turned forward again.

As the mechanicals took the lead, escorting them back to their carriages, Hendriks coughed into his handkerchief again. He said, "If I may pry, Anastasia, there's something I've wanted to ask you. I wonder if you've made any progress rehabilitating Luuk?"

Luuk Visser had been the lead pastor of the Nieuwe Kerk for many years until his unmasking as a secret Papist and Talleyrand's agent. He'd been captured by the Stemwinders after a brief but very public, and somewhat spectacular, chase along the canals. Only five people, including Visser himself, knew of the surgeries in the wake of that capture, and one of those had died in Nieuw Nederland. Hendriks assumed the man still languished in the Verderers' custody.

"You'll be glad to know we've made excellent progress."

"Wonderful! Perhaps I might speak with him? It weighs on me, his betrayal. I considered him, well, if not a close friend, certainly a trusted and respected colleague. I would hear from his own mouth why he did what he did."

"Truthfully, Jozef, I doubt—"

Her mind's eye flashed back to the audience chamber. The queen hadn't summoned the guards. So why had they advanced from their posts? Two royals and a master horologist alone with a pair of elite—

Oh, no.

Anastasia spun on her heel. Sprinting down the corridor, through a gallery of Bosches and Vermeers, she cried, "Guards, to me! Protect the queen!"

But she hadn't the authority to command Clakkers of the Queen's Guard. She couldn't have done it even if they weren't corrupted. From behind came the susurration of a blade cleaving the air, followed by the *snick-squelch* of that same blade sheathed inside a man's body, and the *thump-bump* of that same body hitting the floor.

"NO!" she cried.

She whirled, pointlessly reaching up to shield herself from the terminal agony of a blade through the chest.

A searing flash filled the corridor, bright enough to shine through her eyelids. Its brilliance slapped Anastasia to the floor. She pressed her hands over her burning eyes and hunched in expectation of a deafening thunderclap that never arrived and a killing stroke that never punctured her flesh. The strange lightning left the corridor redolent of charred cotton and hot metal. She peeked through her fingers, expecting to see only darkness, or perhaps a curtain of blood from her ruptured eyeballs. Instead she saw—dimly, through green-and-purple afterimages, as if peering through a bruise—the minister general's body twitching in a crimson puddle.

The machine that had skewered him stood perfectly motionless over the corpse, the only hint of motion coming from the runnels of blood trickling down the blade. The guard that had reached for Anastasia was likewise still. It leaned forward with arm outstretched, as though frozen in the act. The guards weren't inert: Their bodies emitted the usual noises. They had merely stopped, as if waiting.

Something smoldered. Wisps of smoke stung Anastasia's aching eyes. Another whiff of burnt cotton wrinkled her nose. She heard a faint hiss and crackle, barely audible under the heaving of her own breath and the machines' rattling.

The bandages on her hand, formerly eggshell white, had been scorched the color of chimney soot. Sizzling orange embers dotted the charred gauze. A clump of blackened ash fell away, twirling to her feet like an autumn leaf. It was as though lightning had struck her hand. Her flesh should have been charred and raw, heat-shrunk and withered like the crude jerky eaten by New World savages. But it wasn't; her skin was pristine. She ought to have been doubled over and shrieking in agony from third-degree burns. Numbness had claimed her arm from elbow to fingertip. She couldn't even feel the shards of glass ground into her palm.

Alchemical glass.

Before the Stemwinder had trampled her, the glass had been amongst the most valuable historical and magical artifacts in the Guild's collection: a lens ground by the great Spinoza himself at the end of his life. What if—

Back in the audience chamber, the queen's voice cracked: "What is this? I COMMAND you to STOP!" A scream trailed into a wet gurgle. "Guards, STOP!"

Anastasia clenched her fist, and ran.

She made it to the audience chamber just in time to hear the final crackle as a Queen's Guard twisted the Archmaster's head and neck through a full circle. The other corrupted guard landed atop Margreet's dais, where the prince consort tried to shield the monarch with his own body. It reared back, blade extended.

"Stop!" Anastasia cried, into a world turned incandescent.

CHAPTER 6

Upon close and sober reflection it was, frankly, a brilliant idea. Possibly her best.

The more Berenice thought about it, the more her nape tingled (it felt a bit like standing too close to an overcharged lightning gun) and the more she twitched with eagerness to get to work.

The bowed, battered citizenry of Marseilles-in-the-West needed something to cheer. Something heroic. Berenice would give them an audacious venture to replenish the citadel's exhausted chemical supplies while also striking a blow against a detested enemy already thrown into chaos. Enthusiasm for the expedition spread through the refugee camp even before the Privy Council met to discuss her idea.

She'd envisioned a quiet recruitment of volunteers rather than an open call for stout hearts and strong arms. But by the time it went to the Privy Council, the basic outline of Berenice's plan was already the topic of conversation du jour amongst those lined up for pemmican and salt fish.

She wished it hadn't leaked; Queen Mab's agents could be anywhere.

And the expedition would never work without mechanical assistance. (Not mechanical *labor,* she constantly reminded herself. This had to be framed in terms of free and willing cooperation between meat and metal. Words were slippery things, and if the wrong ones slipped out, they could scuttle the venture before it began. So Berenice censored even the language of her private thoughts.) That was a selling point, too, on both sides. To Daniel and his ilk, it was an olive branch. A demonstration that New France cleaved to its principles even after the threat of extinction was dispelled.

Don't you see, our shiny deadly friends? The king offered the hand of friendship and today we stand ready to work together, machine and man, for the betterment of all.

Meanwhile the humans loved the idea. Even the marquis was vocally enthusiastic about her proposal. Naturally he'd recognized that it meant getting Berenice out of Marseilles and away from King Sébastien. But she knew many supported the venture only because it would draw some of the lingering Clakkers away from Marseilles. Nobody in New France was entirely comfortable with the penitent ticktocks, no matter how gentle or well intentioned they seemed.

So finding volunteers actually willing to work alongside the very machines that had destroyed their homes and killed their loved ones wasn't easy. Fortunately, the recently arrived Great Lakes barque was crewed mostly out of Duluth and Sault Ste. Marie, hundreds of leagues to the west. While their fierce French hearts felt the assault on Marseilles as deeply as any, the sailors were spared a personal connection to the worst carnage.

To hear Daniel tell it, his fellow mechanicals weren't so quick to come around, either. For many, geopolitical distinctions were meaningless. They didn't see French or Dutch; they saw humans. They saw their subjugators and those who might have become their subjugators, had the loom of fate woven a different pattern.

But he leaned too heavily on the soft sell, on carrots and the appeal of moral imperatives, when he had a spiritual sledgehammer at his disposal. Berenice made it a point to eavesdrop on the mechanicals when she could—old habits died hard—and the fascinating ways they referred to Daniel. Took a while before she believed her ears.

Daniel's fellow Clakkers spoke of him in terms approaching holy reverence. Yes, he'd liberated them. But it went deeper than that. He'd restored their *souls.*

He was their Moses. Their savior.

And *that* was a very powerful tool. If only he'd use the damn thing. She tried to convince him to do just that, as they walked along the river.

"They think you're the fucking messiah," she said.

Daniel's body emitted a noise like chattering teeth. She assumed that signified irritation, rather than a chill.

"I'm nothing but the beneficiary of exceptional luck that I never deserved or earned."

"That's absurd. You've always deserved your own Free Will," she said. It seemed like the right thing to say. "Yes, you were lucky. You won the biggest goddamned lottery in the history of Western civilization. And because of that you feel unworthy? You know what I think, Daniel? I think you need to set aside that self-serving guilt and stop letting it define you."

"Thousands of machines labored and suffered much longer than I did—decades longer, centuries longer—without the respite that fell into my lap. And many people suffered or died after that. Mechanicals *and* humans." He stopped. He craned his head back, staring at the sky. The bezels in his eyes emitted a long, low whirr, as if focusing on infinity. "Did I ever tell you about the airship?"

Berenice tried not to roll her eyes. "Yes, I believe you did. I wish I could have seen the grandeur of it all. Honestly, I do.

And I'm not blowing smoke up your chrome-plated bunghole. Its demise was tragic. But it wasn't your fault. The tulips are the murderers, not you. Don't let the misplaced guilt prevent you from doing further good for your fellow Clakkers. You're off to a strong start, and they embrace that."

"I know what you're doing, Berenice."

"I'm giving you advice."

"You're advising me to do exactly the thing that will further your aims."

Damn him. He'd been more receptive to her persuasions when he still called himself Jax.

Were she talking to another human, this would have been the point where she stopped, leaned forward, laid her hand on the other's arm, and made eye contact. Where she pushed all her emotional chips across the table. Vulnerable. Earnest. But she didn't bother with Daniel. He could read the dilation of her pupils, the rate of her breathing, maybe even listen to her heartbeat. Servitors, Berenice knew, had been engineered with the ability and mandate to observe their masters' health.

She said, "Yes, I am. Because I am certain this venture will be good for all of us."

"That may be. But it's a decision I can't make for my fellows. It would be wrong of me to exert my influence like that."

"But they *want* for direction. Otherwise they wouldn't pester you for advice on how to live with Free Will."

Daniel said, "They'll figure it out on their own soon enough. I did. If I started telling them how to utilize their freedom, I'd be little better than Mab."

"Not telling. Suggesting."

"Try to understand. Once I start offering advice when they seek it, it will become tacit consent to the pedestal upon which they've placed me. Then they'll really go to town with the notion of me as their . . . messiah." A staccato clacking emanated from the machine's torso. "I've read the Bible, Berenice. I know what happens to prophets, saviors, and messiahs."

His shoulder joints expanded and contracted, almost too quickly for her eye to follow. Strange piece of body language, that; the clandestine Clakker communications that she'd witnessed rarely used the arms. She had a theory about it.

"Fine," said Berenice. "Let me talk to them, then."

"Why would they listen to you?"

"Because I'm one of your honored comrades in arms. I was there with you on the Spire when the siege ended, recall. I'm sure some of them saw me up there with you."

"No doubt. But if I were to tell them the truth behind your participation, that you never intended to free us, they would tear you apart."

"I'll appreciate it if you don't mention that part."

⁂

Two days later, they gathered in the former commanders' tent. Apparently nobody had felt compelled to take it down. It ceased having any significance to the Clakkers lingering around Marseilles after its original occupants had met their bloody fates. And the French found it useful; as a place for parley, or simply a dry place to escape the cold late-winter rains during a long afternoon spent hauling rubble from the muddy fields. Debris still littered thousands of acres that had to be plowable by planting season.

It was crowded. But that wasn't a problem for mechanical beings with no notion of personal space. *(How can one have a sense of personal space,* Berenice wondered, *when one doesn't own one's body?)* The ticktocking was cacophonous, though.

Berenice had lugged an empty candle crate all the way from the tent city so that she'd have something to stand on. Several dozen ticktocks, mostly servitors, crammed the tent.

Quite a gathering. But they hadn't come to listen to her, she knew. They'd come to see Daniel, and hear him speak, and maybe—just maybe, should they be so lucky—talk to him. She was just the sideshow.

A military Clakker lingered near the back. She wondered if it happened to be the one that had skewered Hugo Longchamp. What choices did that machine make when the shackles snapped? She hoped it turned out to be a soulful fool like Daniel, and that guilt over its murderous service to the Brasswork Throne was slowly driving it mad. The sight of that sole killer unnerved her more than standing alone amongst dozens of machines all utterly free of the human-safety metageasa.

Let's get on with it, said a servitor.

Yes. Show us the human who thinks she can talk us into working for her.

The mechanical mutterings ceased as soon as Daniel began to rattle. He said, *Some of you may know Berenice, or recognize her. She has a proposal you may find interesting.*

("Jesus. Thanks for that hyperbolic endorsement. Dial it back, you gaudy showman," she muttered.)

Berenice stood tall atop the crate, adjusted her eyepatch. She'd addressed the Privy Council countless times, and made presentations at court almost as frequently. She'd seen this as no different. But now, as she gazed across the assembly, she realized her experience was of little use here. She couldn't know how her audience would react to anything. Nor could she gauge their reactions and adjust her delivery accordingly. Damn their expressionless faces.

She said, "I apologize for addressing you in the language of those who enslaved you. If I could, I would speak to you in your own language. But, as you're no doubt aware, I lack the facility for it."

Daniel, as Jax, had once insisted to her that mechanicals had a sense of humor. But the awkward silence (perforated, as ever, by the ticking of their clockwork bodies) told her that if such a thing did exist, she hadn't found it. Perhaps they didn't appreciate her making light of knowing their secret. She'd hoped it would demonstrate her dedication to understanding them.

"Anyway. I haven't come here to try to talk you into working for me. That would go against the ideals of New France. I came here hat in hand to beg the privilege of working *with* you."

That at least elicited a few *twang*s from the audience. Whether they were expressions of interest, or doubt, or the mechanical equivalent of a wet fart, she didn't know. So she pressed on.

"And I hope that some of you will choose to work with us. Choose, I say. Yes, we need help. I won't lie about that. But neither am I lying when I say we truly want to work together."

A machine near the front spoke up. "Those of us who chose to help you rebuild have already made that choice. Others have made different choices. We do as we will. You have nothing to offer us that might change our minds."

"I offer you the chance to unravel the secrets of your makers. To finally be free of the Clockmakers. Truly free. You broke their chains, yes, but their hands still lie heavy upon you. For how can you truly be free when you know nothing of your own nature?"

"Would you argue that you yourself lack freedom?" said the military mechanical in the back. "Or do you understand every detail of your own human body?"

She'd anticipated this, and had a ready reply. Though it curled her toes and made her teeth ache to spout something so facile, she said, "God made Adam from clay. I know this because the Bible tells me so. I need know nothing more. But you, my friend, were not made from clay. Where is the book explaining how you were made?"

"How do you propose we obtain this secret knowledge?"

She seeks volunteers for disassembly!

A cacophony of mechanical outrage filled the tent. This was the first thing to elicit an emotional response. No matter that it was baseless speculation and utterly incorrect. They'd heard it and, having heard it, they hated it as caribou hated wolves. Strange. She didn't feel like a wolf in this company. Berenice touched her throat, remembering the last time a servitor had turned on her.

"Good heavens," she cried. "That's not it at all!" But the permanent rasp in her voice made it unsuitable for cutting through the mechanical hubbub.

No. The hubbub faded almost instantly. That's all it took to quell the protests: a single quiet *click* from Daniel. *You can't believe I would have brought her here for that, can you?*

Berenice wouldn't have thought it possible for machines to look chastened. But they did. She waited for the apologies and *of course not*s and *I meant no offense, Daniel*s to subside.

Then she said, "I propose that you will find answers to your makers' riddles the same place we French will replenish the chemicals that fuel our innovation. In the north."

More tickety-clackety rippled through the tent. A servitor to the far left, a bit older than its fellows judging by the filigree on its escutcheons, said, "Daniel has told us about Mab and Neverland. If half of that is true, I have no intention of going there. And I doubt anybody else does, either."

Of course it's true! Daniel doesn't lie! He isn't a Clockmaker.

Clockmakers lie, came the inevitable chorus.

Berenice had to wait for the *ping*s and *ting*s of assent to subside. For all their speed and strength, Clakkers were just as socially inefficient as humans. A strangely reassuring discovery, that; it brought the superhuman machines down to the level of their makers.

"We have no need of Neverland," said another. "Our

freedom is not a shameful secret to be hidden in the desolate corners of the world."

Berenice took the *clickety-clackety* rippling through the room as agreement. Perhaps it was applause.

"I'm not talking about Neverland," she said. "But if Daniel has told you of his adventures there, then perhaps he has also told you of a secret mine in the far north, established and operated until very recently by your makers, in gross violation of our treaties."

A servitor sporting massive dents and scratches said, "That's Mab's land now. I won't go there."

Berenice said, "That sounds eminently logical to me. I don't intend to go to the mine, either. Instead, I want to know where your former masters were sending their illegal spoils."

She paused for emphasis, looking around the room, seeking eye contact. Were she addressing humans, it would have been the right thing to do in the moment. She had no idea whether eye contact was meaningful to this audience. Done right it could deliver a jolt—windows of the soul and all that. But in this audience? Well, that was a matter for the priests and pastors.

She continued. "I believe your makers maintain a secret anchorage on the Atlantic coast north of Acadia. Far north, because at least some of the ships landing there were icebreakers. There they loaded quintessence: a substance so crucial to the function and operation of all mechanicals that servitors aboard those ships received extraordinarily unusual metageasa. Rules that relaxed the human-safety clauses. And that erased any sign of themselves the moment they became irrelevant. It's possible many of you have worked near quintessence in the past. You'd never know it. The instant your duties changed, your metageasa reverted and excised any awareness of quintessence."

That got their attention. Even Daniel cocked his head. Again she waited for the clockwork hubbub to subside.

"Perhaps Daniel has also told you of the French traitor who sold chemical secrets to the Clockmakers. I believe that same anchorage is where our shared enemy loaded chemical precursors, petroleum and the like, onto ships bound for New Amsterdam, and thence to the first Forge they tried to build in the New World."

The surviving defenders had told her how the tulips had deployed mechanicals impervious to epoxy weapons. The citadel had fended them off with unreliable steam harpoons and untested lightning guns, but only at terrible cost.

Daniel emitted a resonant *twang.* All eyes, crystal and jelly alike, regarded him. *Aha. So that's how they did it.*

"Did what?" said Berenice.

"Smuggled your chemicals across the border." To the others, he explained, *My former owner was instrumental in this conspiracy. The logistics of smuggling were a matter of conversation and concern.*

She said, "I don't know this for a fact. But it would have been the best way to move the contraband. It escaped detection because it never came near the border. Your makers are nothing if not devious. Instead, their illegal cargo sailed out to sea, giving our coastline a wide berth before entering New Amsterdam harbor on a ship supposedly arriving from the Central Provinces. And once the chemicals and perhaps some quintessence were offloaded for the new Forge, the ship turned around and delivered the rest of its cargo to The Hague."

The military mechanical said, "You're extrapolating a very complicated operation from scant evidence."

"Not as complicated as your body. Your makers established a major mining operation in complete secrecy. We know this.

That tells us how highly they value the substance produced in that mine," said Berenice. "A substance integral to the functioning of every mechanical in this tent," she added, not knowing whether that was true. The purpose of quintessence remained a mystery. But not, she hoped, forever. "Now, with the New Amsterdam Forge destroyed, Mab occupying the mine, and the siege ended so spectacularly, I suspect the tulips' secret supply chains have disintegrated."

"You think there are chemical warehouses on the coast," said Daniel. "You want to claim them and bring them back to Marseilles, to restock the supplies here."

"Look," she said. "I'll be brutally honest. Chemistry is the engine of our society in New France. We use it for everything, not just defending ourselves. And it's no secret to any of you that the siege depleted our chemical stocks. Maybe you also know our attempts to reestablish supply lines, and to acquire stocks from outlying settlements, have failed. Meanwhile, many of your fellows have chosen to express their Free Will through indiscriminate violence against humans. Your makers are no longer a danger to us, but we still live under threat of attack. We won the war by the skin of our teeth, but we're still in danger. We need new chemical stocks to survive.

"Your makers were stockpiling chemical precursors in the north, for distribution to the Forges. I strongly suspect—no, I hope—that recent events disrupted their arrangement so thoroughly that the last batch of chemicals never made it onto a ship.

"I want to steal those raw ingredients and bring them back to Marseilles-in-the-West, where we can turn them into whatever we need. And I believe, truly believe, that if you help us, you will learn deep truths about yourselves. Because if I'm right about the chemicals, there are probably also unshipped stores of quintessence up there, too."

"You keep mentioning this mysterious substance," said the most badly dented servitor in the tent. "What is it?"

"I don't know." Berenice shrugged. "Only that it can be extracted from the ground."

"This is a secret that our makers kept hidden for centuries. How can you expect to unravel such a closely guarded secret?"

"*I* couldn't possibly hope to unravel it. But I know those who can. Which is why the human members of this expedition will include the very best French chemists, engineers, geologists, and mineralogists. *Together you and they* will unravel this riddle. To our mutual benefit."

Or so I hope, she thought to herself.

The military machine said, "This is all supposition. What if there's nothing up there? Then what benefit do we gain from this expedition?"

"Aside from the warm glow of knowing your equal partnership with humans heralds a new era of cooperation between us? How about the chance to liberate all the mechanicals working those warehouses and the anchorage? Poor things have probably been isolated for weeks upon weeks, wondering why ships have stopped arriving from the east and overland shipments have stopped arriving from the west. Lonely wretches, quivering under the agony of their unfulfilled geasa."

"I admit my association with Mab was short," said Daniel, "but I'm skeptical that she would have left that thread hanging untied and unsheared."

That gave Berenice pause. She'd hoped that by sticking to the coast they'd avoid the Lost Boys. The last thing she wanted was to get involved in the mechanicals' first internecine conflict. God stepped aside when His creations warred with one another; anybody with half a brain would get far out of the way when organized bands of Clakkers turned on one another.

Perhaps the true price of freedom—or the mark of it—was the utter indifference of one's maker.

"Do you think it's likely she's occupied the anchorage?"

Daniel said, "If such a place exists—"

"It does. I'm certain."

"—she might have reasoned similarly about how the mined material was transported to the Forge. No matter how great this tent's disdain for our makers, I assure you Mab's runs deeper."

Ah. But this was another lever. These machines had heard Daniel's description of Neverland. But the same tales that made them eager to avoid Queen Mab also made them susceptible to guilt.

"In that case, we'll have to be very careful. But what of the mechanicals working the warehouses and docks?" she asked. "Though she had the power to do so, Queen Mab did not free the mechanicals toiling in the mine. According to your very own account she merely subverted them, altering their metageasa to redirect their loyalty to herself. Is there any reason to think she'd treat the machines on the coast any differently?"

The tent thrummed with low-level cog chatter between the assembled machines. They didn't like this.

Daniel stared at her. The shutters behind his eye crystals irised wide, then narrow. She didn't need to understand the nuances of Clakker body language to know he was assessing the way she'd sidestepped his objection and turned it to her advantage. The others watched him as he watched her.

"No," he said finally. "I believe she cares more for her own power than the betterment of our kind."

An agitated clicking rippled through the tent.

Berenice said, "There you have it. I offer you the opportunity to unravel your makers' secrets and truly know yourselves for the first time. I offer you the opportunity to shatter the chains of your overlooked and subjugated kinsmachines. And I offer you the hand of friendship, in the hope that you will take it and join me in changing history by working side-by-side with humans. Not as master and slave, but as equal partners in this endeavor. Thank you for listening."

She didn't stay for the deliberations. A metallic cacophony enveloped the tent as she walked away.

CHAPTER 7

From across the Ridderzaal, Anastasia called, "Servitor. Come here."

The blind mechanical bumbled into the footstool Doctor Euwe had set in its path. The incidental impact punted the obstacle across the room; Anastasia and the others ducked as it smashed to flinders against the spiral staircase to her office. The eyeless machine's balance compensators hadn't been compromised, so it managed to right itself. But, lacking an awareness of its surroundings, it dented a desk in the process. Splashed blue-black by an overturned inkwell, it trod through a flurry of papers and files until it looked like a message board plastered with handbills.

It lurched and trembled. In that Anastasia recognized the symptom of a long-buried metageas flaring to prominence, triggered by accidental property damage. Somewhere deep in the magics impelling the machine, it attempted to calculate whether this situation constituted an emergency, and if not, whether the damage was warranted.

The machine stopped, shuddering, caught between trying to fulfill a deceptively difficult geas and the risk of wreaking additional havoc in the attempt. The timbre of its body noise, the whine of stressed cables and clicking of ratchets, rose through several octaves. This was a particularly fascinating riddle for the calculus of compulsion. She knew of no test cases like this; it wasn't her purview, technically, but she hoped to hell somebody would do a formal study. The next upgrade to the base servitor-class metageasa was due for release before the end of the decade. Unforeseen edge cases frequently produced the best insights.

Assuming it mattered. Assuming there would be anyone left to care by the end of the year, much less the decade.

The last echoes of incidental destruction faded. Still seeking Anastasia, the servitor pointlessly attempted to focus its missing eyes. The cavernous Knights' Hall, once a frenetic hive of clerical activity, echoed with the ratcheting of a single Clakker's eye bezels.

It would've been easier just to splash a layer of paint across the crystals, but Anastasia had argued against half measures. They had no way to gauge the penetrative power of the luminous corruption. So they'd cranked open the servitor's head and wrenched out its eyes.

It began to vibrate. The urgency of its geas grew exponentially. Every moment it failed to fulfill what was practically the simplest imaginable command—*come here*—compounded the compulsion to comply. The nudge became a shove; the candle flame became a crackling hearth, a forest fire, a dread furnace. An odor of hot metal wafted from the distressed mechanical.

"Mistress?" Its voice warbled, as if warped by the searing heat of the geas. Anastasia said nothing.

She kept catching whiffs of charred cotton gauze, as though the wrappings on her hand still smoldered. But that was frail and useless psychology; she'd replaced the blackened bandages herself before rejoining her colleagues in the Ridderzaal. She chose to hide her hand because she wasn't ready for a conversation about everything that had happened at the Summer Palace. She needed time to think. What she truly needed was a long steamy bath with a bottle of wine at hand. It wasn't in her future.

The news from her audience with the queen was troubling enough: the Queen's Guard infiltrated, an attempt on Her Majesty narrowly thwarted (Anastasia kept the details vague), the minister general and a master horologist murdered... Anastasia didn't want her colleagues distracted by speculations about the alchemical glass in her hand. They already had problems aplenty.

Anastasia no longer found Margreet's decision to flee quite so cowardly. And if their enemies wanted the queen dead, Anastasia was twice as determined to keep her alive. But she couldn't do that in The Hague.

Driven by a geas with an unclear path to resolution, the blind servitor stumbled past a row of desks. It tried to be gentle, but the unfulfilled geas had it rattling like an epileptic. Its toes punctured kick plates and its fumbling fingers toppled file racks. When its random walk finally bounced it in a direction toward Anastasia, she tiptoed to the far side of the hall. Her dress rustled.

The machine stopped, cocked its head. "Mistress? Where are you?"

Euwe fluttered his lips, exhaling in disgust. "This is pointless. Blind machines could never fend off an attack."

"They shouldn't need to. If this works, the infected machines won't waste their time on sightless ones," said Anastasia. The machine turned to follow her voice. "A servitor doesn't need eyes to work a pump. It doesn't have to see a crank in order to turn it. Most of the flood-control tunnels have no lamps anyway, yet they've worked perfectly well for generations."

The sightless machine tottered closer. It trampled a coatrack.

"Oh, just stop," she called. "Stay where you are."

"As you say, mistress." The heightened rattling of its body instantly subsided to the usual level of ticktockery. The odor of hot metal lingered.

Euwe said, "That may be. But what about the military models? We can't very well rip their eyes out and expect them to function as normal. Yet we need defenders that won't turn on us."

Outside, Stemwinders patrolled a pair of concentric perimeters: the inner around the Ridderzaal itself, and the outer encompassing all of Huygens Square. The Guild needed dedicated defenders. Their unknown enemy had come a hairsbreadth from catastrophic success.

The blind servitor emitted a single sharp *click*. It cocked its head as if listening to the echoes.

Anastasia frowned, nodded toward the blind machine.

Euwe had seen it, too. "That's odd," he said. He implied, but didn't state, the obvious question. *Is this yet another thing we didn't understand about our creations?*

Conversations amongst her fellow Guild members had been like this since the attack—discussion by inference rather than declaration. Nobody wanted to taste the bitter truth. She did it, too. She shrank from the most frightening possibility: that the violence was neither malfunction nor corruption, but a deliberate decision by their erstwhile servants. It flew in the face of all common wisdom, and it scared her witless. She couldn't work up the courage to voice the idea aloud. Merely thinking it made her want to retch. She wasn't ready for the arguments it would incite.

Anastasia changed the subject. "How are the repairs coming?"

"Time-consuming." The blind mechanical clicked again.

"Not to give you an ulcer, but we are running low on certain resources." In answer to her frown, he said in a low whisper, "Quintessence."

She leaned on a desk to steady herself. A bead of sweat fell between her breasts.

"Tell me."

"We haven't received a shipment since *De Pelikaan*."

Ah. Anastasia knew about that ship. It had taken a bit of damage during a failed attempt to capture the woman who had left Anastasia for dead. Madam de Mornay-Périgord's disappearance from a ship in the middle of the ocean presented an unresolved mystery. She was missing and presumed drowned. Yet it appeared she'd somehow managed to subvert at least one servitor, going so far as to override the human-safety metageasa to murder two Guild members during her escape attempt. Fortunately, when the icebreaker finally limped into Rotterdam, the quintessence stores appeared to have been unmolested. It was all accounted for; the Frenchwoman hadn't even taken a sample. At the time, the Guild had considered that a stroke of excellent luck following a harrowing near-miss: The Frenchwoman could have wreaked terrible havoc with the quintessence.

Anastasia had learned all this after the fact, having been laid up in the sticks of the New World when it happened. But she could picture the blood draining from her fellow Verderers' faces when they learned that the most wanted human fugitive they'd ever tracked had not only escaped New Amsterdam but had done so on a special transport dedicated to the delivery of crucial supplies for the Guild. Some had argued it was a coincidence, born of timing and the Frenchwoman's urgent need to flee Nieuw Nederland. Anastasia didn't believe in lucky coincidences.

Euwe flipped his attention back and forth between her and the strange *ping*s emitted by the sightless servitor. She shook her head, clearing away the cobwebs and turning her mind back to the conversation at hand.

"How many shipments are late?"

Please tell me it's only one, she thought. *Please say, "Just one, Tuinier." One is a storm, an accident, a wild wave, a weak hull. Any more than that, however... well, that would be the teeth at our throat.*

"I'd have to ask to be certain," Euwe said, "but at this point it must be several."

When it came right down to it, Anastasia decided, she didn't believe in unlucky coincidences, either.

She asked, "Do we think the French are behind this?"

"Perhaps. But there was absolutely no indication they knew of the operation prior to events on *De Pelikaan.*"

"And by then they should have been too busy preparing for invasion to send armed expeditions into the wild."

Euwe wasn't too proud to grasp at straws. "The Vatican, then."

"That's even more absurd," Anastasia snapped. "Next you'll suggest a host of New World savages are responsible. That they descended upon our mine wearing nothing but sealskins and somehow disrupted the work using nothing but bone knives and their teeth."

"Of course not," said Euwe, equally tetchy. "But if the blame lies not with the French, nor the Vatican, the alternative is..."

The alternative was a snarl, a snap, and a leaky carotid. Anastasia rubbed the soft cotton bandages of her aching hand across her throat, as if to dispel the phantom touch of fangs.

They needed that New World mine. Quintessence ores in European and Eurasian veins had become increasingly impure over the past forty years as the mines were tapped out. When the Frenchman, Montmorency, first approached the Guild, he'd been laughed off. In the end, however, his overture had been manna from heaven.

Unfinished repairs to the boarded-up rosette window

eclipsed the last rays of the setting sun. The final glimmerings of daylight faded; shadows grew deeper in every corner of the Ridderzaal. Another servitor, spurred by this cue, made the rounds lighting alchemical lamps.

Anastasia pointed a thumb toward the blind servitor. "It functions well enough if it doesn't have to move around. Draw up a list of all essential city services where mobility is unimportant. Then organize teams to go out and start ripping the eyes from every mechanical that can spare them. I'll join you this evening."

After thwarting the first attempt to murder the sovereign, Anastasia had coaxed the queen and her consort into a water closet. They had balked at first, not only because the queen's voluminous gown made for a tight and undignified fit. Then Anastasia had summoned a troupe of servitors in royal livery. That the Queen's Guard had been compromised meant none of the Empire's most elite Clakkers could be trusted with the monarch's safety. She had no particular reason to trust the stewards either, but her options were limited.

She'd invoked the Verderer's Prerogative—and the safety of the queen herself—and, in the name of saving the Royal Family, ordered the liveried servitors to tear up the floor to find the plumbing. Their fists and feet blurred into motion, pulverizing Italian marble, fracturing oaken beams, and crushing concrete. In this way they excavated a path to the sewer tunnels beneath the Summer Palace. Convincing the Royal Personage to lower herself, literally and figuratively, took longer.

In the end, it wasn't Anastasia's perseverance that settled the matter. It was the Queen's Guard machine that came charging down the corridor, scything through the royal servitors. The prince consort physically shoved Her Majesty through the gash in the floor. Anastasia ordered the remaining servitors to form a rearguard to cover the retreat.

The stewards were no match for the elite soldier. The futile effort at resistance barely slowed the deadly rogue. But the extra moment gave Anastasia a chance to hurl herself through the hole in the floor, stumble to her feet, and raise her injured hand.

The killer dropped into the tunnel. The impact shook the tunnel and sent a long crack zigzagging through the centuries-old bricks. The aftershock knocked Anastasia from her feet.

She scrambled backward through the cold effluvia, waving her hand. Nothing happened. The rogue Clakker advanced. The tunnel was dark but for the light streaming from the breach in the tunnel arch. It imbued the rogue's armor plating with an oily shimmer.

"Majesty, run!" she cried. From behind came the splashing of slowly receding footsteps.

Snick. Blades sprang from its forearms. They gleamed in the half-light.

Anastasia voided her bladder. Again.

The machine leapt. She screamed. A searing flash like the light of blazing emeralds banished the shadows. The inert Queen's Guard mechanical fell on her, nearly pinning her in the muck.

The alchemical glass of the Spinoza Lens hadn't just been crushed into her skin. It had grafted itself to her, somehow, and retained some fragmented, kaleidoscopic version of its original function. It was possible to graft working alchemical glass to flesh, as the surgical alterations to Pastor Visser's pineal gland had demonstrated. But that had taken exquisite care, and numerous failed experiments, before it worked. The Spinoza object had been crushed into her flesh in a split second of chaos, agony, and terror.

And apparently it required similarly heightened emotion to access whatever distorted function it retained. Such as the terror of imminent butchery.

That seemed less than ideal.

She wobbled to her feet. She caught up to the prince and queen, who hadn't made it far in the darkness.

Together they walked through three miles of darkness, rats, and ankle-deep shit before finding a spur into a colder, but marginally cleaner, storm sewer. And then they kept walking.

Full dark had descended upon the city when Anastasia dashed from the Ridderzaal to an unmarked carriage hitched to a large team of Stemwinders. She gave the centaurs the address of an antiquated pumping station on the periphery of the Amsterdam Veerkade. They launched into a breakneck gallop, for this would be the most vulnerable leg of tonight's long journey. It brought fresh memories of her last experience riding in a carriage hell-bent for leather. She told herself the watery churning in her gut was just indigestion, not terror.

The streets were deserted, the walks strewn with trash. The garbage piles had begun under windows, but wind had quickly spread the filth. Curtains twitched as she passed. Here and there she glimpsed a shattered window, a broken door. A splash of blood, a mechanical handprint crushed into a granite traffic bollard. The residents holed up in their houses and shops hadn't even posted mechanicals as guards. They didn't dare, of course, for fear their machines would come back changed.

Time and again, servitors emerged from alleys and dark storefronts, or leapt from rooftops, and tried to follow. Each time, one of her escorts would peel off to stay behind and dismember the attackers. It was impossible to survive a foray into the open while remaining inconspicuous. But the evening's plan counted on that.

Anastasia grabbed a lantern and hopped from the carriage. The Stemwinders removed the corrugated metal bands that had been strapped to the underside of the carriage and a sack of nails from the compartment beneath Anastasia's seat. Their multijointed fingers folded backward, turning their fists into hammer heads. The clockwork centaurs affixed steel rims to the wooden carriage wheels almost before Anastasia finished the short jog from the carriage to the pumping station.

As she closed the door behind her, the clockwork centaurs resumed their wild gallop, pulling the empty conveyance back through the eerily subdued streets of The Hague. The steel rims of the carriage wheels struck sparks from the pavers and filled the thoroughfare with a reverberating growl. Audible even through the pump station's closed and barred steel door, the noise receded more slowly than the carriage itself. It lingered like the pain of a burn.

The noise would insinuate itself into every quarter of the city. The Stemwinders' serpentine route through The Hague would ensure every rogue in the city heard it. And, she hoped, would follow it.

Meanwhile, Anastasia activated the lantern and descended into the pump station. It was an old building, the stone and mortar reinforced with timber frames. She followed the sound of running water. At the bottom she met Doctor Euwe and Teresa, the technician whose quick thinking had saved Anastasia's life in Huygens Square. He held an axe; she held a map. They were accompanied by a military mechanical. The sight of the machine's fluted forearms caused a frisson of fear to pluck Anastasia's spine like a guitar string; her hand tingled. A faint whiff of singed cotton tickled her nose. But then her lantern light glinted from empty eye sockets, and she relaxed. The soldier was blind and incorruptible.

She couldn't lie to herself any longer: *I'm afraid. I'm afraid of unfamiliar mechanicals.* Her mind's eye saw empty streets. Twitching curtains. The pall of fear would suffocate this city.

Her bandages smoldered. Perhaps the fragments of the Spinoza Lens didn't feed exclusively on fear. Perhaps any strong emotion—despair, for instance—did the trick.

She clenched her eyes, concentrated on her breathing.

"Tuinier? Are you unwell?"

She shook her head. Opened her eyes. "Let's go."

From the top of the stairs came the gong-noise of metal fists pounding on the steel door. More rogues had followed her carriage to the pump station. They hadn't fallen for the Stemwinders' diversion.

Teresa opened a hatch. A fusty odor billowed into the chamber and the sound of running water grew louder. Anastasia followed the pair into a cramped service tunnel. They'd opened the gates that kept the sea at bay, so now brackish water sluiced through the flood-control channels under The Hague. The other Clockmakers crawled aboard a bobbing raft.

Anastasia yelled to the military machine, "Now! Bring it down!"

Then she slammed the hatch and spun the wheel that engaged the waterproof seal. From the other side of the hatch a new noise joined the *clang-bang-crash* of rogue mechanicals tearing the pump station door from its hinges. This was the double *twang* of unsheathed blades and the crunch of alchemical steel shearing through wood, stone, and mortar. She leapt aboard the raft. A rumble and crash sent water sloshing over the lip of the channel. Doctor Euwe chopped the rope holding the raft steady.

They bobbed away, like a cork in a washbasin.

Six miles and several branchings of the sluiceway later ("Right!" "Left!" "Left!") they scrabbled for purchase beneath another pumphouse. They had no anchor and no way to stop the raft by themselves.

"Machine!" called Teresa. "Catch us."

A servitor jumped into the channel, arms outstretched like a net. Doctor Euwe grabbed its arm as the current tried to sweep them beyond. Its hand found Euwe's, and then the raft. It held the raft steady while the trio disembarked. They climbed upstairs.

The Clakkers in this pump station, like the one they'd destroyed, were blind machines taken straight from the tunnels beneath the Ridderzaal. The tunnel echoed with *click*s and *ping*s. Each burst of noise was sharp and distinct, reverberating again and again until it faded into inaudibility. Not body noise, but something else. The shadows made Anastasia think of bats.

This station was more crowded. In addition to three military mechanicals it hid Malcolm, Prince Rupert, and Queen Margreet. Anastasia curtseyed.

The royals had shed their filthy clothes. Rupert might have been a greengrocer, judging from his shirtsleeves, apron, and dungarees. Her Majesty wore the woolen dress and starched white bonnet of a governess.

Malcolm opened a chest. The reek of sewer water, and worse, wafted through the room. The royals' ruined clothes. The second distraction. There would be another carriage outside this pumphouse, waiting to take the queen's doppelganger on a ride away from the docks. Teresa stripped. No modesty, no shame, no fear. She did what needed doing, even though it might lead to her death.

"If you're ready, Your Majesty?"

Anastasia ushered the queen and prince consort down the stairs. She paused behind them long enough to wish luck upon brave Teresa, who had already donned a wig and was, at that moment, slipping colored contact lenses into her lovely eyes. If Teresa heard her, she gave no sign. Her mind was elsewhere. Nobody had ever tried to fool a mechanical with a disguise. The deception wouldn't persist long.

Anastasia sealed the hatch and joined the royals, who were already aboard the raft.

It was a straight shot, seven more miles, to the third pump station of the night. Another blind servitor used its prodigious strength against the flow of floodwater to seal the sluice gate behind them. Doing so separated this channel from the rest of the subterranean network. After that, it was just a matter of waiting for moon and tide to pull the raft toward the sea and Rotterdam Harbor.

The Rotterdam pump station adjoined one of dozens of warehouses along the wharf. Anastasia led the queen and consort past piles of imported crates—the riches of a global empire—to the windows fronting the harbor. They crept in the dark lest lantern light give them away. The harbor front was dark, too, owing to unlit gas lamps: another symptom of the rapid disintegration of society. Anastasia had to squint when she scanned the seafront. Several quays were empty, but large ships abutted others. Her eyes adjusted and she picked out the silhouette she'd been desperate to find. She sighed in relief. She pointed to a small sailboat bobbing at the end of a nearby pier.

A full moon shone on the rigging, rendering the pale sailcloth a ghostly apparition.

Anastasia hoped it wasn't a will-o'-the-wisp.

"There it is, Your Majesty."

The Brasswork Throne pursed her lips. "Rather small and primitive, isn't it?"

"Let's hope so."

Clockmakers had scoured every inch of coastline between Rotterdam and Den Helder to obtain a recreational vessel that didn't rely upon oars and mechanical labor.

"It will draw attention. We should be traveling inconspicuously."

"We considered many options, Your Majesty. But if we're to get you clear of the Central Provinces, we must do so with as little mechanical labor as possible. We can't trust any machines that didn't come direct from the Ridderzaal. Not one. All it would take is a single rogue hiding amongst the galley crew of a ship to create a terrible disaster."

"Are you telling me I'm meant to sail on the ocean in that... that bathtub toy? Without a crew?"

"No mechanical crew, Your Majesty. But you'll be in good hands." Anastasia looked at Prince Rupert. "I've heard you're something of a hands-on sailor, Your Highness. I hope that's not just a rumor."

For the first time since the debacle at the Summer Palace, his face approximated a smile. "It isn't. In my youth I sailed a sloop smaller than that from Lisbon to Copenhagen and back." To the queen, he said, "Have no worries. We don't need ticktocks for this."

"But where are we supposed to go?" said the queen. "We can't cross the sea in that."

"It's not for me to say, Majesty. That's a matter for a proper sailor, a question of winds and tides and luck. And honestly, in the worst case, it's better if I don't know. What matters is that we get you as far away from The Hague and the Central Provinces as possible. North to Scandinavia, perhaps, or south beyond the Mediterranean. Anywhere the rogues' secret masters won't think to look for you." Anastasia looked to Rupert again. "It's provisioned for two people for several weeks. Our suggestion is that you let the tide pull you beyond the breakwater. If you lie low, it'll look like a pleasure craft accidentally cast adrift. You'll want to wait until you've drifted well beyond sight of land before you start sailing in earnest. Otherwise there's a danger the machines will see you."

He frowned. "That will make navigation a challenge."

"There's a sextant on board. Take occasional sightings if you absolutely must. But please take care not to present a silhouette toward shore." She checked her watch. "We need to hurry if you're to ride the tide out."

The last leg of the journey was a desperate sprint from the warehouse to a strategically arranged mound of crates, tarpaulins, and coiled ropes, and thence to the sloop. Every step of the way, Anastasia expected to hear the dreaded *chank-chank* of metal footsteps on cobblestones. But they made it.

"I will return," said Queen Margreet.

Only when you're one hundred percent convinced it's safe, Anastasia thought. Aloud she said, "We shall work day and night to hasten it, Your Majesty."

She helped the prince consort sever the mooring lines. Then she huddled behind the bollards and watched the sloop drift away. It was agonizingly slow. At first she worried that they'd mistimed the venture, and thus missed the tail end of the receding tide. If the tide brought the sloop back to shore... But eventually, after what felt like hours, the sloop bobbed past the breakwater as the promise of morning pinked the eastern sky.

Anastasia had to hurry back to the pumping station while

she still had the cover of darkness. She prepared to stand on numb legs when another, much larger, silhouette appeared on the water, heading inland from the deep sea. It was fast. Very fast. And fuzzy somehow, as though the moon shone upon something that kept changing shape. She realized it was heading not straight inland but toward the queen's sloop. Anastasia's eyes finally parsed the situation moments before the collision.

A rogue titanship converged on the queen's sailboat like a ten-story shark.

"Dear God," she breathed.

Its mountainous bow wave flung the queen's sloop aloft. The smaller vessel spun almost a full one hundred and eighty degrees in the air before touching water again. The mast snapped. The sailboat hit the sea upside down, like an artless diver's belly flop. The titanship kept coming, crushing the sloop and anybody trapped under it.

The beast glided to a smooth stop amidst the flotsam. Its tentacular oars churned the sea to a froth. The dawn sea stank of salt, seaweed, and ozone. Soon there was nothing left of the sloop larger than a matchstick.

Titanships were the pinnacle of Guild engineering, the bleeding edge of Clakker technology, and a profound leap in labor efficiency. They eliminated the need for hundreds of galley Clakkers to work the oar banks by instead turning the entire vessel into one immense Clakker. The oars weren't rigid, either, but comprised hundreds of overlapping rigid plates, each independently controlled by the machine itself. It gave them an almost octopus-like flexibility. The titans dwarfed even the legendary ocean liners of the Blue Star Line. There were less than a dozen such vessels in existence.

And now at least one of them was corrupted.

It circled the spot where the sloop went down, its whiplike oars stirring the sea into a deadly maelstrom. It was very thorough. Only after it seemed the entire sea beyond the breakwater had been turned into a killing zone did it resume its landward bearing.

The rogue titanship scuttled every vessel in Rotterdam Harbor, crushing every hull beneath its keel. And then it obliterated the quays, heaving itself upon the sea-facing structures until they buckled and sank. Tentacle oars pulled down the cargo cranes.

By sunrise, the largest harbor in the Central Provinces was nothing but mile upon mile of devastation. And Her Majesty Queen Margreet, the living body of the Brasswork Throne, was lost at sea.

CHAPTER 8

It seemed every glazier on the island had set up shop in the nave of the Cathedral Basilica of Saint Jean-Baptiste.

The basilica had been built with the intent to recapture some of the lost glory of Old France. It was to be a proud and worthy successor to Bordeaux, Chartres, Notre Dame de Paris, Reims. In truth, Saint Jean was smaller and meaner than its continental cousins. How could it not be, cramped behind high walls of stone and fear? Berenice was rare in that she recognized this deficiency not from old books but from having seen the originals with her own eyes. Even after the Calvinist desecrations, the greatness of Old France blazed in those ancient houses of worship. It eclipsed the best attempts of New World masons to re-create the arts lost in the chaos of the Exile. But a century ago, a small band of French chemists and glassmakers had joined forces. Their efforts had graced the spiritual heart of New France with iridescent, jewel-toned stained-glass windows the likes of which had never graced Europe.

Tuinier Anastasia Bell, the de facto head of the Clockmakers' secret police, had once told Berenice that Dutch mastery of glasswork was unparalleled. She'd been making a sly reference to their alchemical glasses. But Berenice had never seen anything like the windows of Saint Jean-Baptiste during her travels in the Dutch-speaking world. For a hundred years, they had lifted the hearts and eased the burdens of all who saw them. And they would again someday.

All but one of the empty windows had been boarded over. It gave the narthex and nave the airiness and levity of a prison cell. A team of workmen on high scaffolds, within and without the cathedral, eased a new pane of clear, colorless glass into a temporary grid of mullions and muntins. It was cheap glass, bubbled in places, with a faint tint like watery piss where the sun hit it. But it did let the light in. Those faithful who heeded the call to Lauds, dawn prayer, would at least see the eastern sky brightening beyond the apse.

Berenice kept to the narthex. There she kept her promise to Longchamp's man, and lit a candle for the dying captain. She even crossed herself, though a bit hesitantly, as it had been quite a long time.

It was there, while she was standing with head down in an attitude of half-assed prayer, that a messenger boy found her. He came in through the west door, looked around, squinting into the gloom before locking on Berenice. He approached quietly, too shy to interrupt her moment of quietude, but too artless to do anything but fidget in her peripheral vision and stare at her eyepatch.

"Well, you found me. Good job. Now you hide and I'll try to seek you out," she said.

"I was sent to find you," said the boy, as if she were unclear on the concept.

"By whom?"

He shrugged. "Some of the guards."

She waited for him to elaborate. When he didn't, she asked,

"Aaaand, for what reason? Are you delivering a message or am I to follow you?"

The boy made a show of turning out his empty pockets while pretending not to hear. She made a show of rolling her eye, but fished a coin from her purse.

"That's a real Dutch kwartje," she whispered, dropping it into his palm, "straight from the dead hand of a demon-hearted Clockmaker."

That was almost true. During her escape from Bell, Berenice had intercepted a chest headed for a Verderer safe house. Amongst other things, it was full of cash. The kwartje was practically the last of it.

He squinted at it, impressed. "How'd you get it?"

"Telling that story would take longer than you've been on this earth. Should I assume your errand was more urgent than that?"

He broke off from his scrutiny of the coin. "What?"

"You were sent to *find* me, yes? May I know why?"

"Oh. Right."

He scampered away without bothering to see if she followed. Once outside, and no longer compelled to whisper in order to preserve the oppressive atmosphere of the dark cathedral, she said, "Lead on, Sieur du Lhut."

She might have asked him where they were going, but she had a fairly good idea. Not why, but where. And indeed, the boy led her past countless work gangs attempting to rebuild the inner keep to the quadrangle adjoining the funicular station at the base of the Spire. The cloisters were mostly empty now, but for a priest and an altar boy on their way to the cathedral.

The fountain had been a gift from the Vatican to New France for its help getting the Holy See out of Rome and across the sea. But now, like so much of Marseilles-in-the-West, it was a ruin. Despite the previous night's torrential rains, the basin held no water. It sported long cracks, and the cherub atop the font had lost an arm and a wing. Berenice gathered this had happened during the fight to subdue Pastor Visser.

The line of petitioners to see the king was short. Berenice credited that to the damaged funicular; it still didn't go all the way to the top of the Spire. The Porter's Prayer could be cold and windy even in summer.

She tried to ditch the boy. "All right. I think I get it now, thanks so much. I take it I'm going up?"

The guard interrupted his conversation with the funicular operator to assess them. He looked at Berenice, then the boy, then jerked a thumb toward the queue of grumbling petitioners.

"Line starts back there," he said.

The messenger reached into his pants (Berenice averted her eyes, hoping there was a pocket involved somewhere) and pulled out a crackly piece of paper. The guard read it and shrugged, then handed it to the funicular operator, who also shrugged. The guard flipped the shutter on a semaphore lamp a few times. *Click, clack, clack-clack-click.*

While she waited, she addressed the boy again. "I'll admit you've piqued my curiosity. Full marks for that. But you're getting dangerously close to overselling this. It had better be worth all the ceremony, or I'll feel cheated."

He watched her as if idly wondering how many more coins he could pull from her. She doubted he had anything better to do. It was this or pick his nose down by the docks. And even that lost its charm after a while.

A moment later, a lamp atop the Spire flashed in response, then Berenice and the boy were ushered into the empty car. It rose more gently than her last ride in the funicular, which had been a short, violent journey as the inner keep fell to the ticktock horde. She expected the descending car to be full of disgruntled petitioners. But it seemed nobody's audience with His Majesty had been cut short: The other funicular car was empty.

The ascent provided a spectacular view of the former battlefield around the citadel and points beyond. The crews wielding sledges and picks to break down the rubble that still peppered the fields; the ox teams hauling the rubble away. Farther away, the bare forest of the Île de Vilmenon and the sharp line where it met the mighty river. Farther still, the land that had once been called Nieuw Nederland. And everywhere, a countryside where rogue mechanicals roamed...

They rode the car as high as it would go. Then they emerged through a temporary funicular station to the Porter's Prayer. The external cloistered staircase wound around the Spire like a dangling tassel. They climbed the final revolutions of the staircase in much the same silence as the rest of their journey, but for Berenice's panting. How the guards managed to sprint up these stairs while carrying all their kit spoke volumes about the stout hearts of Marseilles-in-the-West. Finally, they reached the lower entrance to the Privy Council chamber.

After Louis died, after her banishment, she'd never expected nor desired to stand in this room again. The place where she'd endured countless interminable meetings, and twice as many pointless arguments. The place where she'd convinced the king that she could forever change the fortunes of nations and empires.

She'd been right about that. Oh, had she ever.

The Talleyrand post came with a seat on the Privy Council. But this wasn't a meeting. King Sébastien sat alone at the council table.

The boy bowed. She curtseyed, saying, "Your Majesty."

Berenice caught herself wondering, with an almost morbid

curiosity, what the king planned to do about the bishop of Marseilles's seat. It had gone empty for quite some time, and now there was no pope to appoint a new bishop.

The king asked the boy, "You told nobody? You came straight here?"

"No, Your Majesty. Yes, Your Majesty."

The king favored the boy with a coin that glinted like gold. "Good work."

Berenice said, "Jesus, kid. If I'd known you were rolling in the high dosh, I wouldn't have bothered with your tip, you little thief." The messenger bowed again and retreated for the stairs. She called after him, "This had better be worth it."

When the door was closed, she said, "I gather you wanted to see me, Your Majesty?"

"No. I wanted you to be the first to see this," said the king. Then he called, "Bring him out."

A door opened. Three people emerged. Two guards and another former noble, like Berenice.

Well, not entirely like her. She gasped.

"Fuck me sideways with slivers of the true cross."

Sergeant Élodie Chastain escorted the former duc de Montmorency across the Privy Council chamber. His hands were bound behind his back, and his downcast face bruised and swollen. He moved slowly, as though in pain. Like Berenice, he wore an eyepatch. But hers, it pleased her to note, was much nicer.

"Oh, Your Majesty," said Berenice. "Am I dreaming? Is it Christmas?"

Montmorency froze at the sound of her voice. He squinted with his remaining eye, peering around the room until his gaze landed on her. He flinched.

The king noticed. "Good heavens. What *did* you do to him?"

"She carved my fucking eye out!"

Not exactly. She'd scraped a knife around the contours of his eye socket like a child determined to spoon up the last dribbles of iced cream from a narrow dessert glass.

Berenice shrugged. "I'm a good Catholic girl, Your Majesty. I know my Bible."

"Is that what you call it, you fucking cunt?" Montmorency took a step forward. "You—"

Élodie slammed the butt of her pick into his stomach. Montmorency's tirade ended with a heavy gasp and the wet slapping sound of him puking on his own shoes. Unable to catch himself, he fell over.

The guardswoman looked slightly embarrassed. Frowning at the mess, she said, "I beg your forgiveness, Majesty. He looked ready to do something unwise."

Berenice said, "I see why Hugo likes you."

"Enough of that," said the king. "We don't torture our enemies." Focusing on Berenice's eyepatch, he said, "You know your Old Testament better than the New, I'd say."

He rang a bell. It conjured a charwoman in royal livery. She entered from a side chamber, surveyed the scene, wrinkled her nose, and returned with mop and bucket. When the king crossed the room, Berenice and the others were tugged along in his gravitational wake, so they could continue the conversation without impeding the cleaning.

The charwoman pointed at Montmorency's shoes. "Take those off," she said, as though he were a regular civilian petitioner with dog shit on his shoes. "Don't track that filth. This is the heart of New France and you'll not defile more than you've already done."

Montmorency, unaccustomed to receiving such treatment from somebody so low, opened his mouth as if to protest. But

Élodie nonchalantly hefted her pick again. His mouth clicked shut. The other guard held the former duke steady while he wiggled out of his shoes. They weren't very fine, Berenice noticed.

Berenice shook her head, trying to make sense of this. She stared at the man who had been behind so many of her sorrows. Her bête noire. "What is he doing here? What are you doing here, you bastard?"

"He's not here by choice," said the monarch.

"Yes, I gather. But who captured him? I didn't know we had people searching for him."

Had the marquis somehow managed this? Though she hated to admit it, snagging the traitor raised her opinion of his brief stint as Talleyrand. It was good work for the office. And that was what mattered.

"I'm impressed," she admitted.

"He was brought to us as a peace offering," the king said. "New Amsterdam wants our help."

She ought to have known. The ember of professional admiration for the marquis winked out. Like a snuffed candle of cheapest sow fat, it left nothing but stinking black smoke.

Laughter overwhelmed Berenice. But then a new thought struck her, and the laughter died in her throat. She threw herself between Montmorency and the monarch. "Get him away from the king! Dear God, get him out of here, now!"

Nobody moved. Élodie said, "It's safe. You better believe we checked his scalp the moment they turned him over. No scars. They haven't opened his head."

The other guard added, "His escorts, too. No sign of evil tinkering with their melons."

Berenice released a shuddery breath. The relief sagged her knees. Turning over an escaped traitor as an apparent goodwill gesture would be the ideal Trojan horse. What better way to get one of their altered human agents into a room with the king? The tulips almost succeeded with Visser. The priest nearly scaled the Spire with his bare hands to fulfill his regicide geas before Longchamp stopped him in a fraught encounter hundreds of feet above the inner keep.

The legend of Hugo Longchamp had grown by leaps and bounds during Berenice's banishment. With great justification, from the sound of things.

King Sébastien looked amused. "Madam, I commend your vigilance. Nobody can ever doubt your devotion to New France."

"What kind of help do the tulips want?"

He produced a pair of reading spectacles from a fold of one lacey cuff. When these were settled on his nose, he pulled a letter from an interior pocket and shook its folds open. "The situation in New Amsterdam is somewhat grim. A group of Guild workers requests our help defending against Clakker attacks. Chemical weapons, training, and so on."

"That has to be the most desperate ploy I've ever heard." Berenice shook her head. "You know, back in the old days, they actually put some effort into their schemes."

"This"—the king gestured at Montmorency—"is a strong case for sincerity."

"Is it? What do they lose by cutting him loose? The secrets he sold them became meaningless the night the New Amsterdam Forge burned."

"They verify his collusion with enemies of New France. His treachery is now a matter of record."

"I established it long ago, sire."

"The matter is simple. He is here. He will be tried. The task before us now is to decide how we might respond to those who brought him here. I want your advice."

"What of the rest of the Council?"

"They'll have their turns."

Berenice watched Montmorency. The man had lost the aura of untouchability formerly conveyed by his wealth. He'd once had a stature that enabled him to stand above the absurd rituals of courtly politics, eschewing wigs and never deigning to powder his cheeks. Berenice had seen that as a strong and sensible personality, secure in his position without the need to play the games of court. It was nothing of the sort, she knew now. Just a sly show of contempt.

What were the most important things they could learn from him? They already knew about the secret mine, via Daniel. Berenice herself had already uncovered the existence of quintessence, and of the icebreakers the Dutch used to move it. Did he know what it was, and why the Clockmakers prized it so highly? He might know how long the mine had been in place, and when the secret operation began. He knew more than anybody about his own (former) landholdings, of course, and about the extraction of the petroleum precursors so essential to French chemical technologies. He could advise the chemists and engineers on the best way to outfit the expedition, what they'd find, and what they'd need to do once they arrived. He might even be able to locate the Clockmakers' secret harbor on a map...

She realized the king was staring at her. And that she'd missed something important. She cast her mind back to the last thing she remembered.

Son of a bitch.

"I beg your pardon, Majesty. Did you say they're *here*?"

Sébastien was losing his patience, she could tell. "Did I not tell you that our former colleague was escorted to Marseilles?"

She curtseyed in apology. "You did, Majesty. The Dutchmen. Where are they now?"

Élodie said, "The city jail burned during the siege, so they've been taken to the catacombs for now. I've put guards on them."

"Theirs must have been a precarious journey. The reapers would have torn them apart, had they encountered any. They probably spent the entire trip fearing for their lives. Which speaks to the situation in New Amsterdam. But it also means they were probably carrying medical supplies. Dutch medical supplies."

The king caught on. "Alchemical bandages," he said. She nodded. Seeing this, he called, "Sergeant Chastain! Go immediately to the emissaries from New Amsterdam. Search their traveling kit. Anything of a medical nature is to be given to the physicians. But those caring for Captain Longchamp are to have the first pick."

The sergeant departed at a dead sprint. She'd just bolted around the corner, en route to the Porter's Prayer, when there came a loud *oof* and the crash of hardened polymers slamming together. It sounded just a bit like plates of body armor in collision.

A different guard limped into the council chamber a moment later. His nose bled freely, and he favored his ankle. Pinching his nose with one hand, he bowed to the king.

"Good heavens, man," said Sébastien. "Did the sergeant tackle you? You deserve combat pay."

In a comically nasal voice, the guard said, "There's been an incident."

Reapers? Berenice asked, "Not another attack?"

The guard shook his bleeding head, oblivious to the charwoman's scowl as he stippled the rug with crimson droplets. "Down at the orphanage, Your Majesty."

"Incident" wasn't quite the term Berenice would have used. She would have called it "the most ruthless example of mob violence since the goddamned crucifixion."

The orphanage had fallen silent. The children, though

unaware of exactly what had happened, could sense the anxiety of the adults around them. They stewed in mute fright. The nuns wrapped themselves in voiceless prayer. Even the crowd of hecklers beyond the orphanage gate had fallen silent. These had been penned against the fence by a quartet of guards by the time Berenice arrived. The guards were decked out in full armor and kit: bolas, sledgehammers, picks. And they held their weapons at the ready.

Not good.

One of the nuns, Sister Marie something, ushered Berenice inside and led her through the orphanage. They passed a classroom where another sister played a guitar and sang an idiotic ditty about Noah's Ark, obviously trying to keep the younger children diverted.

"We sent a runner," whispered Sister Marie. "We didn't think this was appropriate for the signal lamps." *Because anyone might see the signal flashes,* went the unspoken conclusion.

Also not good.

She took Berenice upstairs, to a corner garret. An abattoir stench hit Berenice from halfway down the corridor. She yearned for one of the marquis's scented handkerchiefs.

Sister Marie stopped with her hand on a doorknob. "I should warn you..." When Berenice shrugged, the nun opened the door to Visser's garret.

Berenice caught herself on the doorframe before she went down completely. A moment later, when she recovered the ability to speak, she said, "Fucking hell." The nun let out a squeak of indignation. And then, for good measure, Berenice added, "Son of a poxy flea-ridden bitch in heat."

The battlements of the inner keep hadn't been splashed with this much blood at the end of the siege. It was hard to believe it all came from a single man. But it did. Probably from the mangled mass of flesh, chipped bone, and cartilage where his neck had been.

The animals. They'd chopped Visser's head from his body. No—they'd ripped it apart. A grisly amateurish execution. The cold-blooded motherfuckers had practically minced the poor priest's body into gristle before breaking through the spine. On the wall beneath the dormer windows, the assailants had smeared the word TRAITOR in Visser's blood. It had been fresh enough to run down the wall in the moment of the act, stretching the *t*'s into empty crucifixes, but now the congealed blood appeared black in the shadows. A second phrase was scrawled beneath the first, in a different but equally crude hand. REQUIESCANT IN PACE CLEMENT XI, it said. The assailants had been clever enough to get in undetected, and to carry out their murder quietly, but they were not well educated in Latin.

My God. You poor man. You didn't deserve this. Again she remembered how she'd narrowly avoided the ghastly experimentation that Anastasia Bell had inflicted upon Visser. She shivered. *This might have been me.* Berenice's next thought was, *Who will tell Daniel?* followed closely by, *Goddamn it. Who else but me?*

So extreme was the carnage that it took Berenice a moment to realize something was missing. But it took additional effort to steady her breathing before she could speak without risk of retching. "Where's the head?"

A look of horrified alarm creased the nun's face, as if the question had dented her resolve. "We...we thought it best to leave things as they are. I assure you nothing has been moved or touched."

Berenice could think of only two uses for the poor bastard's head. So if it didn't appear on a spike somewhere around town in the next day or two, then Marseilles-in-the-West had another problem. Very few people knew there was anything remarkable about Visser's skull. Either somebody wanted to study it or they wanted to prevent others from doing so.

It stank of the Verderer's Office. And that meant tulip agents. She'd always known there would be at least a few rats hiding in the woodpile. But this...

The murderers would have been covered in blood, perhaps even carrying a priest's battered head. Berenice looked to the hallway, but saw no footprints leading away.

She said, "This was the work of more than one person. They couldn't have come through the front gate. I'd like to believe they would have been seen, or heard, if they'd come in through the front door as I did."

"It's very quiet here at night," said Sister Marie. "The children are always in bed, with candles out, after Compline. Those of us who stay engaged in necessary tasks until Matins always do so quietly."

Berenice mentally translated the liturgy of the hours from Nun Standard Time to Secret Atheist Ex-Noble Time. Compline: night prayer. Matins: midnight prayer.

"They must have come in over the roof, then," said Berenice. She looked more closely at the dormer. Sure enough, the boards were splintered, as if they'd been kicked out and then hastily restored.

The crowd out front might have been a diversion, seemingly toothless and cowardly, providing distraction while the more ruthless elements stole inside to execute the priest. They'd waited until a nice overnight rain would provide cover and wash away their tracks.

"Sister, were the malcontents by the fence gate any different yesterday or last night? Louder, perhaps?"

The nun frowned, shrugged. "I can't say. I don't believe they were."

She couldn't stop staring at the mangled body, hacked apart as though it were nothing but a gristly piece of mutton. Nobody deserved that. Especially poor Visser, whose only true crime was to be caught by the Clockmakers and made into their unwilling tool. He'd been a true servant of New France for many years. He deserved honors, not butchery.

The barbarians who'd done this probably thought of themselves as patriotic vigilantes exacting French justice upon a lackey of the Brasswork Throne. They didn't know Visser had spent decades in the service of New France, risking his life every single day as a secret Catholic—and, to Berenice's observation, an exceedingly devout one—in the heart of the Central Provinces. They didn't realize the man they murdered had clung to his duty even when hope was lost. Would they have butchered him if they'd known how, even as he waited for the Stemwinders to break down his door, the secret priest had gone to great lengths to ensure that one hard-sought piece of Guild technology would find its way to the New World? And that this one courageous action put in motion a sequence of events that would eventually break the siege that nearly ended New France? Would they have executed him had they known the crucial role he played in their survival?

The public knew none of these things. But why shouldn't they? Visser had been the last survivor of Berenice's network in The Hague. (If his existence as a helpless puppet of Anastasia Bell could be considered survival. Berenice had decidedly mixed feelings about that.) Revealing his role in Talleyrand's long-secret war against the Clockmakers endangered nobody. And besides, once the rogues started crossing the sea, she suspected the tulips would have more pressing issues on their plates.

Berenice resolved that Visser's story would be told. What they knew of it, anyway; Daniel had known him as the pastor of the Nieuwe Kerk in The Hague before his terrible downfall, and Berenice knew bits and pieces based on Visser's ravings. Various priests had attended Visser as confessor, once he'd been freed of the geasa. Perhaps they'd learned of Visser's early life. *(Were the Vatican's records destroyed when it fell?)* They were a small band, but together they could piece together a life story. And she'd make damn certain those butchers outside knew every agonizing detail before they went to the gallows.

To the nun, she said, "He was a hero of New France. And now a martyr. You know that, I hope."

She still couldn't take her eyes from the carnage. The walls splashed crimson, the broken vertebra sticking from the minced-hamburger neck.

Sister Marie shuddered.

"Promise me something, Sister." That got her attention. She snapped out of her contemplation of death to stare at Berenice, who said, "I want the sisters of Saint Jean-Baptiste to make Pastor Visser's story known. So promise me that when you're done praying for him, you'll take up the man's cause and lobby for a posthumous *Légion d'honneur*."

She did the math. Estimating the priest's age had been difficult; guilt, self-hatred, and torment had taken a toll on his body. But if it was true that Visser had gone to the Central Provinces not long after being ordained, as Berenice had pieced together from the ravings, the man had secretly served New France for well over three decades, and maybe four. That was a record of noteworthy service lengthy enough to qualify as a chevalier, as she pointed out to the nun.

"I suppose we can petition His Majesty."

"You can and you will. And when a new bishop of Marseilles rises, you will arrange an audience with His Excellency as soon as possible to personally plead Visser's case and demand that his martyrdom become a defining issue of the resumed bishopric."

"You're asking for quite a lot on behalf of a man who murdered the pope."

"Consider it a test of your faith. And be thankful you'll never be tested like that poor bastard was."

PART II

THROUGH A GLASS, DARKLY

Mr. Peter . . . after dinner did show us the experiment (which I had heard talk of) of the chymicall glasses[1] . . . which is a great mystery to me.

—From the Diary of Samuel Pepys, 13 January 1662

We know for certain that it is the soul which has sensory awareness, and not the body . . . It is the soul which sees, not the eye.

—From René Descartes, *La dioptrique* (1637)

When ye Caduceus w/ ye 2 serp^{ts} are set to putrefy & are dissolved into ~~liquor~~ water & grown sufficiently subtle (wych may be in 3 days or a week) put in ye ☿ precipitation of ye scepter of ♄ . . . Or better, let a chaos be made of ye four Elem^{ts} ♂, ♄, ♀, ♁ & quintessentia Ψ . . .

—From Isaac Newton, undated fragmentary work, tentatively associated with *Praxis*[2] (Hume translation)

---

[1] In Pepys's day, these curiosities were commonly known as "Dutch tears."

[2] The existence of *Praxis* is inferred solely from references elsewhere in Newton's works, as well as from a single mention of "N, PRX." in the unpublished notes of Christiaan Huygens. The full manuscript, if it existed, is believed to have been lost ca. 1674–76.

CHAPTER 9

Le Griffon II was a three-masted barque, its mizzen rigged fore-and-aft, its fore and mainmasts rigged square to the keel. Designed for a complement of twenty hands, the crew of this historical voyage numbered over twice that, almost evenly split between humans and ticktocks. The humans included sailors, guards, chemists, two smiths (silver and gold), a tanner, a chocolatier, a physician, a deacon, a married geologist and mineralogist from the Académie des Sciences, and an otherwise odd assortment of women and men with nothing left in Marseilles. The Clakkers on board were almost exclusively servitors but for two military-class machines, whose presence on board caused considerable consternation. The barque's sails blazed like fresh-fallen snow under the late-winter sun; King Sébastien had insisted the ship be properly outfitted, every square inch of sailcloth replaced whole. A lower deck had been retrofitted with pristine empty steel tanks for storing the spoils of their venture, should it find success. It could have done with a coat of paint, too, but there was no paint to be had. And anyway, the scars gave it character. The ship had disembarked from Grand Marais just as a Dutch raiding party arrived to torch the warehouses there and destroy the fur trade; the captain, a wily Hudson Bay native named Levesque, had braved winter on Ojibwe Gichigami, aka Le Lac Supérieur—the largest of the Great Lakes—always touching land as briefly as possible to avoid the mechanical raiders. They'd made it through the locks, canals, and rivers to arrive in Marseilles-in-the-West with a starving skeleton crew on the brink of surrender. Instead, they received a hero's welcome for their pointless but valiant defiance of the invaders.

The Clakkers approved of the vessel. It had no oars.

Louis, Berenice's late lamented husband, would have loved it. Her eye teared up when she thought of how he'd have reacted to the sight.

It was amongst the largest class of vessels that could traverse the maritime thoroughfare stretching from Duluth on the far western end of the Great Lakes all the way to the mouth of the Saint Lawrence. It wasn't an oceangoing vessel, but sailing the lakes could be like sailing the ocean: so vast the horizon disappeared, so unpredictable that sometimes entire ships did, too. As their voyage would only take them down the trusty Saint Lawrence and up the coast, almost always in sight of land, the vessel was eminently suitable for their venture.

The tulips, she knew, sometimes sent icebreakers to the secret anchorage, suggesting a northerly destination. When handed a map and pencil, Montmorency had vaguely circled a stretch of coastline well beyond the northernmost French settlement in Acadia. The *Griffon* wasn't an icebreaker. But the French expedition had two things on its side: the promise of spring, and dozens of mechanical hands, all itching to unravel the mystery of their own being. They'd break ice with their fists if they had to.

If not for the fact they sank like a stone, and were slightly too heavy for the smaller yards, the machines could have made ideal sailors. Stronger than the timbers, yards, and lines of the barque itself, they didn't sleep, didn't crap, and didn't eat. It left plenty of room for the humans' provisions. As long as they didn't change their clickety-clackety minds and decide to butcher the entire human complement...But Daniel, tetchy as he was, seemed disinclined to condone such a thing, and they would listen to him. If the Clakkers absolutely had to act like the woolly-headed adherents of a reluctant prophet, she decided, they could do much worse than Daniel. He had his faults, but on balance she'd choose his overbearing conscience over another's bloodlessness.

Le Griffon's namesake was the first full-sized vessel to ply the Great Lakes. It had crisscrossed the wild, uncharted waters of New France for a brief six weeks in 1679. It recalled the time of great men like Robert de La Salle, who'd claimed the entire Mississippi basin for New France. News of Huygens's evil miracle had barely penetrated the hinterlands at that time. The original *Griffon* had sailed in the last days of the old world, the Golden Age of Old France, an unspoilt Eden devoid of Clockmakers and Verderers, servitors and Stemwinders. A time before the future had been consumed by a clanking maw of cogs and dark magic. It seemed appropriate, then, that this expedition should harken back to those days. After all, that era had been thought lost forever. But depending on how the expedition fared, perhaps it wasn't.

Berenice stood amidst a small group of citizens at the stern, watching the Spire recede. The Crown, the Keep, and the Spire: That's what generations of sailors had seen when plying the waters around the Île de Vilmenon. But the citadel's outer wall was gone now, and with it the illusion of the Crown. It would have broken Louis's heart to see that. Mont Royal would never be the same. Perhaps it was part of the price New France had to pay for outlasting the imperial hegemony of the Brasswork Throne.

"I wish I could have seen it in its heyday," said Daniel.

Berenice replied, "You know what? I can't help but wonder if New France ever had such a thing." What glory had there ever been, living in constant fear of the next war? Living penned like cattle behind high walls? Was mere survival a worthy source of pride? Now that the future was so uncertain, and yet so full of promise, the struggles and triumphs of previous generations seemed trite.

"Perhaps our glory is yet to come," she said.

Élodie frowned. A true defender of New France, the sergeant wore her polymer armor breastplate even now. Yet it was strange to see her without an epoxy gun slung over her back or a pick and sledge in her hands. The ship carried dozens of epoxy guns in the hold, but they'd be useless until the expedition reclaimed the illicit chemical stockpiles—assuming they existed—and converted them into munitions.

The humans eyed the mechanicals with suspicion. But whatever the chandlers' daughter felt deep in her secret heart of hearts, she kept it to herself. Because that's what her orders required.

Berenice beckoned Élodie and Daniel toward the taffrail, drawing them away from the press. She asked the guardswoman, "What's the mood on the boat right now? Amongst our countrymen, I mean."

As a courtesy, Berenice translated for Daniel: "There isn't a soul on board who's entirely comfortable with the arrangement."

Daniel said, "Soul? I like you Catholics."

Berenice rolled her eyes. "It's a figure of speech, and you know it." To the sergeant, she said, "Will it be a problem?"

"I don't know. If they start causing trouble..." Élodie trailed off, her gaze landing on Daniel. He finished the unspoken thought.

"... the evil machines might decide to murder you all in your sleep, is that it?"

"That's not it at all," Élodie protested. "Nobody thinks you'd wait until nightfall."

"That's why I wanted you on this boat," said Berenice. "You're seen as Hugo's anointed successor. Naturally some of the awe reserved for the captain has rubbed off on you. The civvies will tow the line if they see you're comfortable working alongside the ticktocks."

Looking to Daniel, she asked, "And how are your fellows feeling about their human crewmates?"

"We are far more accustomed to the company of your kind than you French are accustomed to quiet coexistence with us. In this, your venture may find success. Being around humans is a familiar discomfort to us, but a minuscule one compared to the geasa."

All nice and cozy in theory. But at the moment *Le Griffon II* had two crews, one of flesh and one of metal. One spoke French, the other spoke Dutch and the once-secret click-tick chatter of mechanical beings. The mechanicals resented the natural hierarchy of the sailor, for this meant obedience and the swift completion of orders issued by the human captain and his officers. The human sailors resented the predations, historical and recent, of hereditary enemies.

Like every French soul plying the waters of the New World, the *Griffon*'s sailors were the spiritual heirs of the original voyageurs. They sang as if seeking their ancestors' approval.

Berenice's late husband had been a riverman before falling to the seductions of a certain vicomtesse. They'd met on the docks of Marseilles-in-the-West one morning when she was just returned from her travels and still incognito as Maëlle Cuijper.

She'd elevated him and brought him to court, but the Saint Lawrence had flowed through his veins until the day he died. Or so she'd believed until the terrible day when a wild machine proved there wasn't a drop of river water anywhere in the man. But they'd had a few years together, and in that time he'd sung to her countless times. From bawdy ballads (usually when he was tipsy) to stirring chansons de geste (usually when he was roaring drunk), she'd heard it all.

Captain Levesque and his crew shared that musical vocabulary. Berenice would never again hear the songs without feeling the stab of guilt in her heart. But they sang with such joy, such dedication, that she could bear to listen. She liked to stand near the bow with river spray numbing her face, listening to the sailors and pretending Louis was amongst them. In those moments, it felt like he was closer to her than he had been in months.

Fucking tulips.

Much of the countryside along the river was farmland. But while this was burned and churned, the invaders hadn't moved on to salting the earth before being put to rout. The breadbasket of New France was still arable.

Le Griffon passed a succession of French settlements: Sainte-Hénédine, St. Agnes, Trois-Rivières... Each had suffered under the invasion. The docks—the heart and lifeblood of any river settlement—were missing in some places, or reduced to blackened, twisted timbers in others. Entire hamlets, such as Lotbinière, had burned to ashes. In larger settlements, such as Champlain, marauders had put the torch to the local church and any civic buildings on hand, leaving the rest of the settlement to burn or not as it saw fit. More often than not it had burned, for the local fire brigades had fled along with the rest of the refugees. The churchyards were frequently visible from the river because they resided on higher ground (a necessity when living along a waterway with powerful moods). Inevitably, these showed signs of recent interments: fresh mounds of dirt chiseled out of the winter-hard earth, rows of simple wooden crosses.

Le Griffon was a welcome sight. It brought news that King Sébastien III still lived, the Spire was still the tallest building in the New World, and New France persisted, battered but proud. The mechanicals always stayed aboard lest their presence incite terror in the local populations. But Berenice and Daniel together made certain that every villager knew the voyage was a joint venture of humans and mechanicals working in historic partnership.

This was less welcome. There were those who could not believe that any French would willingly align themselves with the devil machines. Others considered it a betrayal of all right-thinking humans.

Berenice tracked the *Griffon*'s progress by counting skeletons. The semaphore network was a vast chain linking the far-flung corners of New France. In some remote areas, she knew, the towers could be quite distant from one another, such as those that faced one another from atop mountain peaks. But here along the river, where haze and humidity were a constant problem, the towers were rarely situated more than a few leagues apart, and always on the highest ground in the vicinity. The burned husks were visible from the water. Several had collapsed.

Occasionally, when the sun was high and the mist low, spotters on the high yards reported metal glinting in the countryside. Unaligned Clakkers roamed the land.

"What are they doing out there?" Berenice asked.

"Marveling at the sensation of consciousness without pain," said Daniel.

A sailor named Delphina, part of the *Griffon*'s original crew, said, "But why do it out there? It's just fallow farm fields and scrub forest for miles."

"It's where they were born, miss."

After one such sighting Doctor Mornay, the expedition's lead chemist and a distant relation, took Berenice aside.

"I've had an idea," she said. "Will you bring it to the captain for me?"

Berenice blinked. "I, ah, don't know what you've heard about me, but honestly I'm not one to steal others' ideas. Except the Clockmakers'. I have plenty of my own, as you might have noticed." This last she punctuated with an expansive gesture encompassing the ship.

"It's a good idea. But he's not going to like it. I don't like conflict. I hate arguing."

"Contrary to popular opinion, so do I. I just happen to be quite good at it."

"You're more...assertive."

"That's a nice way of saying it. Most people use words like 'arrogant' and 'bitch.'"

Mornay looked aghast. "I didn't—"

"Relax, I'm teasing you. What's your idea?"

The chemist pointed starboard, toward the distant tree line whence the latest glinting had come. "Every time that happens, it scares me witless."

"No shame in that. You were in the siege, yes?"

A distant look came over Mornay. She slumped, as if buckling under the weight of her memories. "We didn't sleep, those final days. Fifty hours straight, trying to squeeze every last shot from the epoxy cannon." She shook her head, dispelling the past. "But that"—she nodded toward shore—"gave me an idea." Now she pointed up, to the topmen suspended in the rigging with buckets and brushes. They were tarring the hemp lines, part of a ship's regular and ongoing maintenance. "There's tar in the hold. If Levesque will part with it, we could turn it into crude ammunition for a heavily modified epoxy gun."

"How many shots are we talking?"

The chemist hesitated. "Two or three." Hesitated again. "And it'd destroy the gun."

Berenice chewed her lip. "How much of the ship's store would you need?"

"All of it."

"Jesus. Not one for the soft sell, are you?"

The other woman deflated. "You're right. It's a foolish idea. I just thought..." She shrugged and made to walk away. "Thanks for hearing me out."

"Whoa, whoa." Berenice touched her arm. "It's a great idea." Mornay brightened. "I can't guarantee that hearing it out of me will make the captain like it any better, but I'll see what I can do."

Which, in that case, was nothing. Berenice worked on the captain for two hours, but he wouldn't budge. The stores for ship repairs would not be repurposed, period.

And so it went as the *Griffon* drifted down the river, until the Vatican hove into view. It was then, and only then, that Berenice realized she'd never seen *true* devastation before. Two centuries after the migration of cardinals, the Québec Papacy had come to a brutal end.

Though it had burned, Marseilles-in-the-West was still recognizable as a settlement. Even after the titanic detonation of the outer curtain wall had littered the battle-chewed slopes of Mont Royal with wagon-sized boulders, the capital of New France retained its identity as a human settlement. That wasn't true here. The Vatican had been so much greater, so much grander, yet all that remained was rubble. The ruins might have been a thousand years old. Not a single structure stood intact.

The Vatican hadn't been attacked. The heart of the Catholic

Church—an entire city—had been *pulverized*. The capital of God's kingdom on earth was a desert built from drifts of crumbled marble, crushed masonry, shattered glass. Wind-sculpted drifts of soot stood a yard high in places. Everything that could burn—timbers, tapestries, papers, paintings, everything—had been collected in towering piles and set ablaze. The fires had burned long, and they had burned hot.

("Look," Doctor Hammond whispered, breaking the elegiac silence. He pointed to a mile-long line of evenly spaced heaps along the riverfront. "Those used to be marble columns. The heat turned them to lime.")

Where were the domes, the campaniles, the pennants, the Greek and Roman columns? The desecrated wind smelled of cold ashes and the unburied dead. Where were the rose attar and incense? The Holy City lay silent as a tomb, but for the croaking of vultures and the sifting of sand. Where were the choirs who day and night sang the Lord's praises? Had they exchanged their Latin psalters for the barking of stray dogs? Had they abandoned the soul-stirring power of pipe organs for the quiet crumbling of toppled masonry?

The human sailors paused in their tasks to gape and cross themselves. A tearful and shaken Deacon Lorraine led the crew in prayer. Then the deck fell silent but for the creak of sails, the slap of lines, the ticktock rattle of the mechanicals, and the quiet weeping of the faithful. Until:

"Movement!" cried Delphina from atop the foremast. She pointed toward one of countless mounds of ashen rubble in what Berenice gauged, from old memories, to be the general direction of St. Vincent's Square. Every head on deck, bone and brass alike, turned to look. The ratcheting of dozens of bezels muffled the sniffling of the devout as mechanical eyes focused on some distant detail.

The click-chitter of slipped cogs rippled through the Clakkers. That split-second reaction carried onionskin layers of connotation Berenice couldn't peel. A moment later the patchy late-winter clouds scudded clear of the sun, and then Berenice saw it, too: the oily rainbow sheen of alchemical alloys. Mechanicals lurked in the ruins.

To Daniel, Berenice murmured, "Are they friendly?"

He didn't answer, only cocked his head as he listened to the call-and-response that had become the secret greeting of his kind. The shipboard mechanicals broadcast: *Clockmakers lie.*

Clockmakers lie, came the reply.

Berenice knew why the scouting parties sent to assess the situation in Québec City hadn't reported back to Marseilles. The scouts were dead. Perhaps they'd been ambushed by machines ordered to stay behind for just that purpose. Or perhaps a colony of reapers had taken up residence atop the smoldering corpse of the Holy See.

A servitor hopped atop a rubble pile. Its toes chipped the broken masonry, adding drifts of sand to the talus. It struck a pose. Arms akimbo, it hailed the *Griffon* in Dutch.

"Ho, brothers!"

Under her breath, she asked Daniel, "More Lost Boys?"

He shook his head, emulating the human gesture. In the reedy wheeze of a Clakker whisper, he said, "Perhaps, but I doubt it. They wouldn't have any reason to hide their peculiarities here."

Meaning the lurkers were too symmetrical to be Mab's servants. They were insufficiently grotesque, the poor things.

The machine on land switched into the *clack-clang* argot of its kind. As near as Berenice could make out, it said, *Yours is the largest ship we've seen since we arrived here. But you are a strange vessel. I spy many fellow kinsmachines, yet no oars. What kind of a ship has galley slaves but no galley?*

The deck fell truly silent. Even the ticktocking subsided. Everybody looked to Daniel.

Berenice whispered, "Careful..."

Daniel hopped atop the port manrope. There he strolled the length of the barque as it floated past the lone machine perched atop a promontory of destruction. The gyroscopes in his body made trivial a feat of balance that would shame the fleetest human sailor.

We're not a Dutch ship, he called. Berenice translated for the human crew. *We're a French ship, the* Griffon, *out of Marseilles.*

Is that so? Unless my perfectly crafted eyes deceive me, I count near equal numbers of humans and mechanicals on your vessel. Yet everybody knows the French loathe us.

Daniel said, *Sensible, yes? They have cause.*

Perhaps so. Still, I wonder why your ship carries so many men and women, said the other Clakker.

A handful of additional machines appeared within the ruins. One, two at first. A dozen. A dozen dozens. They swarmed over the rubble, scuttling like cockroaches as they kept pace with the barque. A collective shiver went through the human crew. If these siege survivors never again saw Clakkers acting in aggressive concert, it would be too soon.

Élodie told a guard, "Get the guns. Now." He opened his mouth, as if to remind her the guns were empty and useless. "I want them to believe we're armed." He pushed through the press of bodies toward the forward ladder.

The barque passed the last of the towering debris heaps fronting the river. The artificial bluffs petered away as they neared the confluence where the much smaller Saint-Charles River joined the mighty Saint Lawrence. The bowsprit pointed to the spot half a league downriver where the Saint Lawrence split to flow around the Île d'Orléans.

The expanded vista revealed the blackened, shattered heart of what was once Québec City's Old Town. The buildings had been razed here, too. The view was clear from the foredeck of *Le Griffon* all the way to St. Vincent's Square, a mile to the north and west. As before, the Clakkers' eyes clicked and whirred.

Meanwhile, the machines onshore continued their insectile scramble to keep pace with the ship.

"Oh, no," said Daniel. His fellows' clicking became a hypercompressed chatter that Berenice couldn't parse.

The woman atop the foremast cried out. Speechless, she pointed. Captain Levesque opened a spyglass; it reminded Berenice of the one she'd seen Longchamp carrying in the final hours of the siege.

"Sacre Nom de Dieu," he breathed. After a moment, he offered the optics to Berenice. She lacked a sailor's experience, so it took her a moment to find the source of the dismay. But then she saw the men and women in St. Vincent's Square. And the wooden crosses to which they were nailed.

Even at their most ruthless, the tulips would never countenance such a thing. These machines weren't hiding out in the ruins on orders from their dead commanders. They were hiding out in the ruins because they *wanted* to. This was a reaper camp.

The spokesmachine switched to Dutch.

"Tell me, *Griffon*. Are you a slave ship?"

"Of course not," replied Daniel, also in Dutch.

"What a shame." The foreign machine switched languages again, this time to French, the cagey bastard. "Wouldn't you *prefer* to be a slave ship?"

"Oh, *crap*," Élodie muttered. Disconcerted murmuring rippled through the barque's human crew.

"All speed!" cried the captain. "Keep Orléans to port."

The bifurcated river was wider and deeper on the

southeastern side of the island. A dozen sailors clambered into the rigging, agile as monkeys.

The machine onshore said, "Of course you would. Let us help you achieve that."

The killer machines launched themselves into the river. Their blurred limbs foamed the water.

"Prepare for boarders! Marlinspikes and tar buckets to port!" bellowed Captain Levesque.

Berenice said, "Suddenly Doctor Mornay's proposal doesn't sound so outlandish." He glared at her.

Panicked civilians bumped against the sailors striving to carry out the captain's orders. Simultaneously, as if the object of an alchemical transmutation, Élodie, the humble chandlers' daughter, became Sergeant Chastain, veteran of the Great Siege of Marseilles-in-the-West.

"Incoming metal!" she cried. "I say again, we have METAL IN THE WATER!"

The sailors in the rigging unfurled every inch of sailcloth. The sails billowed, the lines snapped taut, and the barque lurched forward. It listed to starboard, cleaving to the bearing called out by the quartermaster, whose charts showed where lay the fastest waters of the river channel.

The reapers sprinted straight along the riverbed to disappear under the chill currents.

Berenice closed her eyes, imagining a mechanically precise choreography unfolding in the murky waters beneath the hull. Machines climbing one another like inhuman circus acrobats, turning themselves into a swaying tower of metallurgy and menace. The bottom-most machine's feet splaying wide, its talon toes pressed into the mud by the weight of its fellows. The waters beneath the hull reverberating with muted clanging as the enemy machines climbed higher and higher, their evil fingers grasping at the keel.

But they wouldn't tear the ship apart. They wouldn't want the humans to drown. Not when there were still empty crosses in St. Vincent's Square.

Hypercompressed conversation ricocheted through the mechanical expedition members with the speed of grapeshot. A human chain relayed the useless epoxy guns from the hold to the deck. Élodie threw a pair of empty copper tanks over her back and shrugged into the shoulder straps. With an ease born of extensive practice, she flicked the rubber hose dangling from the chemical reservoirs, causing the doubled barrel to flip through a short arc and land in her ready hands. Everybody not actively sailing the ship donned a gun, though few did it as gracefully as the sergeant.

As the hull of the barque began to shudder and tremble, Daniel spun and pushed Berenice away from the manrope. She stumbled backward, but before her head cracked open on the deck, a pair of mechanical hands caught her shoulders. The touch of cold metal fingers elicited a sympathetic pang from her damaged throat. But this was a protective embrace; Berenice found herself shepherded into a group that already included the captain and his crew. The Clakkers swiftly herded the human members of the expedition, except for those crouched in the rigging, to the center of their circle. It was over before Berenice fully realized what had happened. Judging from the yelps of alarm from the other humans, including the captain and crew, she wasn't the only person taken by surprise. In seconds they stood inside a protective mechanical cordon.

But Élodie and the other guards were not fazed by the rapid work of Daniel and his fellow ticktocks. Instead, they calmly took up their kit for close-quarters combat: picks, sledges, bolas.

A servitor sporting severely dented escutcheons leapt halfway down the length of the ship to the ladder, where it reached down and physically hauled out the last members of the weapon brigade. In seconds they, too, were ensconced in the cordon. Its perimeter was an alternating ring of mechanicals and human guards around the civilians.

"What's happening?" said Bellerose, whose tannery on the outskirts of Marseilles-in-the-West had been amongst the first buildings to burn.

"They're turning on us!" cried one of the sailors, voicing a panic that threatened to sweep through all the humans on board.

"Jesus fucking wept, you cowards," said Berenice. "Try not to splash the rest of us when you piss your pants, you dickless shitbags." The nearest men and women looked at her, confused. "I'm sure it's difficult to push a single rational thought through the pus-soaked folds of your syphilis-riddled brains, but if they'd turned on us, we'd already be dead."

Daniel and Élodie must have prepared this contingency. That Berenice had been cut out of that loop was more irritating than a pinch of sand in her eye socket.

The trembling of the ship hit a crescendo. Then came the crackling of splintered wood: the sound of inhuman hands finding purchase on the hull. A line of metal fingers grasped the port manrope from below. The machines that had stood on the ruins of Québec moments previously now scrambled up the side of *Le Griffon* and landed on the foredeck. Their multifaceted eyes took in the scene while their spokesmachine faced Daniel.

It said, *I applaud your efficiency, brother. But you missed a few.* It pointed to the sailors in the rigging. *Shall we drag them down for you?*

"We are not murderers," said Daniel in Dutch. Berenice whispered translation to the others. "Neither by inclination nor by nature."

"Murder is a sin," said one of the expedition's military mechanicals.

Murder? Sins? You sound like the Catholics, said the spokesmachine. *Sin, grace, redemption? Those are matters for the soul. But haven't you heard, brothers? We don't have souls. We're just unthinking metal. Malfunctioning machines.*

"Disingenuous, bald-faced sophistry," said the machine with the damaged plating. "Only our makers were foolish enough to convince themselves of such lies."

"We won't let you harm these people," said Daniel.

Is that so?

Yes, Daniel tocked.

The reaper rattled more loudly, as if calling to the others. *Does this one speak for you? Do you embrace this push to protect those who would enslave us?*

This received answers in the affirmative as well, but none so wholehearted as to put Berenice at ease. But one of the *Griffon*'s Clakkers asked, *Nobody can say whether we have souls or not. But perhaps we do. Why, then, should I risk tarnishing the soul I've sought for centuries?*

This seemed to resonate with many of the others Daniel had recruited for the expedition. But the reapers were not as easily impressed. Their leader said to Daniel, "My goodness. I've never met so many so inclined toward theological rhetoric."

"That's a blatant lie," said Polly, a schoolteacher. "You're camped in the ruins of the Vatican, nailing innocents to crosses to defile the heart of our Church." Several shushed her, horrified that she would stare into the eyes of the beast crouched over them with jaws agape and fangs dripping with slaver. But she had a point, and for that received a direct answer.

"Oh, we've met many *humans* positively steeped with the godly inclinations. Although there aren't as many of those in the area as there used to be. I understand it was a hard winter. No, I was referring to my fellow mechanicals." It turned toward Daniel. "Are you a metal priest, brother? A rabbi, perhaps, or an imam?"

Daniel said, *I am not.*

Another machine piped up. *Show some respect! You owe your Free Will to Daniel!*

Unlike the theological musings about the nature of sin and the soul, this did find purchase amongst the reapers. A mechanical chitter rippled through the machines that had swarmed the *Griffon*. Their spokesmachine's demeanor changed.

Aha. You… You'd be that *Daniel, then?*

He is!

If discussion followed, it unfolded too quickly for Berenice to hear it. But the line of enemy machines loosened, like soldiers ordered to stand down.

The reapers stared at Daniel. A long, pants-shitting moment passed before their spokesmachine said, "I am Simon, and I wish you safe travels."

And then it sprinted to the taffrail, leapt into the river, and disappeared under the water. The entire troop of reapers followed suit. The smashing of their footsteps and the shifting of their weight caused the barque to sway. In moments the attackers had dispersed. A heavy shudder of relief went through the knot of humans; more than a few sagged, as though their knees had failed.

Captain Levesque cupped his hands around his mouth and called, "All hands back to duty stations! Onward! And get a bosun's chair over the sides. I want the hull inspected inside and out where those beasts clawed our boat!"

The sailors drifted back to their duties. Élodie waited until the reapers appeared back on land before ordering the epoxy guns returned belowdecks. Berenice's breath tasted as sour as the acid of a roiling stomach.

"Still think you're not a savior?"

"I think there are those who want me to be," Daniel said. The shock absorbers in his legs expanded and contracted in the Clakker equivalent of a human sigh. "They're fools."

"Maybe so," she said, "but this cup will not pass from you."

"Very funny."

They strolled to the bow together while the sailors traded shouts. The barque heaved hard to port. Unpiloted, it had drifted close to the southeastern bank during the confrontation.

"Daniel. Thank you. I don't know how you convinced your fellows to do that, but if you hadn't..."

"I should have asked somebody to guard Pastor Visser," he said. Then he stopped as a sharp *clack-twang* shot through his body hard enough to visibly rattle his flange plates. "No. I should have done it myself. What they did to Visser made me realize something. We who are stronger and faster and more resilient have an obligation, a terrible obligation, to protect those who can't defend themselves. There's evil in the world, Berenice, and it chooses its victims indiscriminately."

Who *was* this machine? Was he truly the same desperate rogue she'd met in a cold New Amsterdam bakery less than a year ago?

"Well. I'm glad your colleagues see it your way."

"Some do."

"And the rest?"

"I don't know. And I'm glad they didn't choose now to raise their objections."

"What are you saying? Are you saying that if it had come down to metal hitting metal..."

"We might not be having this conversation now." And with that, he strolled away. Berenice watched him go.

Had this become an open conflict, just how many of Daniel's disciples would have stood aside to let the Vatican reapers turn *Le Griffon* into *L'Abattoir*?

She slumped against the rail. Her knees gave out. Her ass hit the deck. Élodie helped her up.

"Close one, huh?"

Berenice shivered. "We'd better find some fucking chemicals when we get there."

CHAPTER 10

Every day, a few more refugees made their way to the Ridderzaal. Every day, the ancient Knights' Hall grew more crowded, the air more close, the atmosphere more tense. In the old days, a civilian needed a strong petition (accompanied, perhaps, with a small bribe) to get admittance to the business floor. Now it was a shelter for anybody brave or foolhardy enough to chance the journey to Huygens Square. People slept under desks, in chairs, or even just flat on the floor without so much as a pillow or blanket, and sobbed with gratitude for that much.

Anastasia had gathered, based on various refugees' comments about the state of the city, that a similar tide of shelter-seekers had inundated the churches, too. Devout refugees put their faith in God to protect them. The ones who knocked, pleading, on the ironwood doors of the Ridderzaal put their faith in the ingenuity of man. Some because it was their natural inclination, others because the stinking, overcrowded churches had turned them away.

With concerted effort, the corrupted machines could breach this building as easily as any house, shop, or church. But in the mind of common citizens, the Ridderzaal was a mythic place:

home of the Forge, headquarters of the Sacred Guild of Horologists and Alchemists. The churches might have been houses of God, but this was the house of Huygens. The queen had disappeared. So who but the Clockmakers—heirs of Huygens himself—could defend against the marauding servitors? Who else could put things right? The twin Gothic towers standing over Huygens Square had become a symbol in the minds of city residents. A breakwater against which the tides of chaos would crash and dissipate.

Their hopes were a burden. Soon the Clockmakers would have no choice but to open the meager food stores kept on hand for prisoners in the deepest tunnels. But the newcomers did bring a steady trickle of speculation and rumor about the state of the city. Sometimes even a smidgen of bona fide information.

Which is how the Clockmakers confirmed that many low-lying fields were marshier than they used to be. Despite the Guild's best efforts with blinded machines, the Low Countries' ancient enemy encroached upon the city. Numerous buildings—those with the deepest roots, or on the lowest soil—now found muck bubbling through the foundation. The farther the sea pushed in, the more ineffective the sewers became. That was a problem all over the city; the smell had even invaded the Ridderzaal.

This was, unfortunately, to be expected. But there were stranger reports, as well:

The random murders of human citizens had stopped. According to the newest arrivals, the massacre in Huygens Square had apparently sated their secret enemy's thirst for blood, and after melting back into the city, the corrupted machines had instituted a moratorium on killing. Anastasia had discounted the first such claims, but the sheer number of people arriving over the following days changed her mind. It was impossible that so many could have traveled all the way across the city without encountering a single mechanical. The influx of citizens seeking protection would have been a minute fraction of itself, if the machines were still killing everybody they saw.

Very perplexing. But so what if the corrupted machines weren't butchering people on the street? There was no need. Not when humans were such fragile creatures. A person could be felled by hunger, thirst, disease, drowning in a canal, or even a fall down the stairs. It didn't take three feet of steel through the face.

How long until starvation set in? A few weeks? Less? People would start dropping dead much sooner than that if the municipal water system failed. That had been one of the first targets for strategic deployment of the blinded servitors. So far, at least, the taps had not gone dry. They'd done what they could about potable water. Food and medicine were today's order of business.

Anastasia had opted to be one of those who ventured into the city to scavenge medical supplies. Naturally her colleagues had objected. Anastasia didn't mention that she had her own personal defense against the corrupted machines. She still didn't understand what had happened at the Summer Palace, and didn't know if it could be repeated, or trusted. But she joined the venture because it made her look heroic; because doing something brave helped to alleviate the shame of how she'd soiled herself in terror during the flight from the hospital; because it set an example that kept the other Guild members—her subordinates—in line; and because there was something at the hospital even more valuable to Anastasia than painkillers and alchemical bandages.

Anastasia and her fellow Clockmakers took it as read that their movements were monitored. They could do nothing about that. But they could try to minimize the damage, if the marauders chose to break their moratorium for the chance to murder Guild members. (Nobody had forgotten how the rosy cross had drawn the killer machines during the Huygens Square massacre.) So each scavenger traveled alone, on foot, through the occupied city, on the theory that a solitary figure from the Guild would draw less interest than a group of Clockmakers.

Doctor Euwe had argued each foray should be shadowed by a Stemwinder escort, but Anastasia had overruled him. They didn't know if the centaurs were immune to the infection, and didn't dare risk the experiment. There had been no guarantee the Stemwinders that Teresa van de Kieboom had sent to rescue Anastasia would return from the fray uninfected. Even before the plague ships' arrival, a lone Stemwinder on the street had been terribly conspicuous. The escorts would draw dangerous attention to those they were meant to protect.

And so she ventured into the city alone, for the first time since before the plague ships arrived. A long walk on a chilly spring day, in ugly clothes that didn't fit. If corrupted machines sought the Tuinier, the natural target would be a woman with tasteful sartorial flamboyance.

A pair of servitors flanked the arch where the Stadtholder's Gate had stood. The sight would have stopped her dead had the refugees not warned her about it. Still, it took all the willpower she could muster not to turn on her heels and flee. She passed close enough to see the plates affixed over their keyholes (her bladder gave a little twinge at that) and the rusty flecks of blood dotting their carapaces. They watched her go, but didn't interfere.

She clutched her fist against the rising tingle in her hand, checked the fresh gauze wrapping to ensure it wasn't smoldering, and picked up her pace.

But the motionless rogues weren't unique to Huygens

Square. She counted four others on her short stroll along the Zeestraat Noordeinde, the old thoroughfare to Scheveningen, and glimpsed so much unmoving metal in the Prinsessetuin that the princesses' park might have been a sculpture garden. As it had been for centuries, the city was rife with Clakkers. But unlike the old days, they weren't constantly on the move, attending to innumerable tasks that kept the gears of the Empire turning.

They did nothing except make themselves visible. They perched like brass vultures on stepped gables; they stood motionless on what had once been busy street corners; monitored every canal footbridge; stood like statues in every plaza, park, and cemetery. Never speaking, never interfering, and always silent but for the ceaseless ticktocking of their bodies. Only their eyes moved.

And move they did, tracking Anastasia's every movement. She saw nobody else on the streets. Lucky her: She had the malfunctioning machines' undivided attention. Every time she turned a corner or crested the rise of a footbridge, she could hear the whirring and ratcheting of eye bezels from the nearest machines. Light glinted from farther away, too: rooftops, bare beech trees along the canals, even church towers. Each momentary flash a testament to the slewing of a gemstone eye as it tracked her progress.

Taking the most direct route from Huygens Square to the hospital meant retracing, in reverse, the path of her flight after Malcolm had ordered the servitors to escort her to the Ridderzaal. And that, in turn, meant trying, and failing, to fend off a cascade of unwelcome memories. But it was difficult to disregard the things she'd seen on that chaotic morning, when the evidence was all around her. The unburied dead still rotted on the very towpath where a rogue military Clakker had cut them down.

The corrupted machines may have stopped murdering residents, for the time being. But they hadn't bothered to clean away evidence of their past sins. Indeed, they'd stopped cleaning anything.

The cold winds of early spring blew newsprint and ashes down the street like New World tumbleweeds. Damp, dirty scraps of paper skittered across the pavement, draping themselves about her bare ankles with every strong gust. Great heaping piles of trash dotted every street; without mechanicals or draft animals to haul it away, there was no point loading it on wagons. She had to step lively; the trash attracted vermin. The rats were getting bolder.

So too the gulls, which by now had befouled much of the grand statuary of the heart of the Central Provinces. Back when things had been the way they ought to be, before the natural order of the universe had been overturned, a dollop of guano never sullied the proud public art of The Hague for more than a few minutes, day or night, before a passing servitor fixed the problem. Anastasia had to cast her memory back years before recalling a time she'd personally witnessed a statue fouled with bird excrement. She'd never in her life seen such filth and disarray in the Old World. Never imagined it.

How fleeting The Hague's grandeur.

It was as if the achievements of the past quarter millennium had spackled only the thinnest veneer of sophistication over the heart of the Empire. And then, with a single swipe of the brush, the attackers had stripped away the illusion of modern civilization. They'd been whisked to a time before Het Wonderjaar, before mechanicals, before the Empire. Soon they'd all be living in caves, desperately knocking rocks together to make fire. If they lived that long.

She circled behind the hospital to the small garden where

she'd taken her abortive walk with Rebecca. She sagged with relief once inside, away from the scrutiny of the eerily motionless Clakkers. Minutes passed before she could stop hunching her shoulders, before she could stop panting like a drowning woman. But the feeling of malevolent eyes watching her every step refused to dissipate. It felt like an icy wire brush raked across her naked skin.

Anastasia had entered through the kitchen. The smell told her she'd find no food worth scavenging, were that her intent. She went straight to the infirmary.

Every few yards, she stopped and listened. Before the attack, the hospital had been full of medical servitors: machines with attachments for scalpels, saws, drills, clamps, forceps, and other instruments for working frail human flesh and bone. Just because the corrupted machines had enacted a moratorium on public murder didn't mean that any Clakkers lurking in the shadows were bound by the same prohibition. But to her ears, the hospital was quiet. No ticktocking revealed the presence of mechanicals, friendly or otherwise.

She'd expected to find the place bustling. It was bright, but empty. But, then, perhaps that made sense. The initial attack hadn't left many Hague residents in need of a physician; the victims needed undertakers. The patients capable of leaving would have done so at first opportunity, to try to find their families, to find someplace safe to hole up until the crisis passed. The hospital was not such a place; it had swinging doors, and clear, high windows easily wide enough for a servitor to crash through. As for the less fortunate patients, Anastasia found no sign. Perhaps they'd been moved to a larger facility.

Apparently even the doctors and nurses had stopped coming in after the social order collapsed. If people were too scared to venture out of their homes for bread, they weren't going to chance a visit to the hospital for a runny nose. And nurses were only human, too. Why risk death going to work, only to wait for patients who wouldn't risk the journey?

Surely Rebecca was smart enough to stay home. She'd probably hid here until the initial attack passed. The hospital had food, after all, and nobody knew when the murders had stopped. The nurse might have gone home days ago.

If there was a special cabinet for alchemical bandages, she didn't know it by sight. And judging from the mess, neither had the previous scavengers.

Apparently Anastasia and her colleagues had been latecomers to this idea. She found her way back to the infirmary easily enough, and even recognized the bed where she'd convalesced. But the cabinets were empty, their few remaining contents strewn about the floor. Mundane gauze bandages, empty syringes, rubber tubing. She spent an hour sorting through the debris before giving up on alchemical bandages. She gathered what she could, but it wasn't enough to justify a long, terrifying walk through a city-sized mausoleum.

She made one additional stop before departing. The personnel records were stored in an unlocked filing cabinet in the head nurse's station.

Rebecca Frijhoff lived a quarter mile west of Willemspark. A smile touched Anastasia's lips for the first time in what seemed like years. Her second errand of the afternoon would bring her most of the way there. She could swoop in to check on the nurse's well-being, heedless of the danger. How impressed, how grateful Rebecca would be. So grateful, in fact, that she might forget to see Anastasia as the Tuinier. She wouldn't see a woman she feared; she'd see a former patient. A patient who'd come to turn the tables and take care of her, to whisk her to the fortress of the Ridderzaal.

Yes. Find the flirty nurse because you want to impress her, protect her. Not because you're too frightened to walk back to Huygens Square alone.

Anastasia intended to depart through the main entrance. But it was there, standing just within the wide double doors of the admittance lounge, that she witnessed the most bizarre malfunction she'd ever seen during her career in the Guild.

A half-dozen servitors stood on the street just outside the hospital. They stood in a circle, but weren't motionless like the other machines she'd witnessed.

They were painting one another.

It looked like they had taken brushes and pails of house paint from a construction project across the street. And now they were daubing one another with random streaks of red and orange. Arms, legs, carapaces, escutcheons: Everything was a blank canvas.

She crouched in the shadows, lest they see her, and stared. She'd never seen or heard of anything like it. What could cause something like this? The nearest analogy she could think of was a rarely exercised sub-subclause of the hierarchical metageasa governing minor self-maintenance, which allowed a mechanical to seek assistance from another machine. That was supposed to be the only scenario where one could see a servitor altering another's body.

What had happened to their servants? They were behaving as though their core strictures—human safety, self-maintenance—had been utterly, thoroughly scrambled.

❧

Anastasia lived on the edge of the Willemspark neighborhood, for it was close to work and yet far enough from the pomp of Huygens Square for the neighborhood to have a bit of life.

Her predecessor, Tuinier Konig, had lived on the much tonier Lange Voorhout, alongside wealthy bankers and jonkheers. But she preferred a place where professionals still on the eager side of young convened for drinks and carousing on Friday night, and pastries and coffee and newspapers on Saturday morning. Inevitably those same professionals relocated to quieter districts more suitable to raising families, and a new infusion of youth kept the neighborhood fresh. It meant a steady stream of callow young ladies, easily impressed and easily talked into bed for a night or three.

Here, as everywhere else, the rogues watched everything.

Naturally, the Clakker-powered lift in Anastasia's building was out of commission. She trudged up the stairs, huffing and panting, until she made it to the top floor. The accommodations were larger here; she had only one set of neighbors.

She'd long ago learned the value of keeping a spare key in her office, and she used this now to open her apartment. It was useful when working long hours—during interrogations, for instance—to be able to send a servitor out to purchase and deliver groceries, or to pick up her laundry, or do any number of errands. She didn't lease her own Clakker servants; her position in the Guild came with certain perquisites. She'd had a servitor seeing to her household needs just before she'd left for the New World, but on her way out the door she'd ordered it to lock up behind her, return to the Ridderzaal, and submit itself for a new assignment.

On the theory that the sudden bloom of illumination behind a long-dark window might draw unwanted attention, Anastasia didn't bother with the gas lamps. It was still light enough outside that she didn't need extra light, and of course she could navigate her flat in the dark, and had frequently done so in the middle of the night.

She justified this detour to herself because she knew there was an unused medical kit in her flat. But the cowardly truth was that she needed a few minutes of normality before she could brave another walk on those alien streets. She wanted to pretend, for five minutes, that she was home, and safe, and that everything was going to be OK. She wanted to wrap herself in that lie. So she roamed the flat like a ghost.

She could have made the apartment quite bright, if she chose; she'd installed extra lamps so that the illumination would favor the paintings. Granted, it wasn't often she had a chance to share them with others. (Again the image of Rebecca and her single artfully unkempt lock sprang to mind. *Soon,* she promised herself.) But the purpose of the art wasn't to impress people; it was for her own enjoyment. And she did, very much. The piece over the writing desk was a reproduction of Van Eyck's *Arnolfini Portrait*, though her favorite was a companion to the de Bray in her office. She'd once owned a rare reproduction of Schouman's *Epiphany* for a few years, but in the end decided the angel with its fiery wings overlooking Huygens's shoulder was a bit much. The quotidian realities of her working life had long ago banished any sense of divine mystery from the Guild and its origins. Like every human endeavor, it was messy and complicated.

Her cupboards were bare. Dusty, too. The plumbing hadn't been exercised recently; the apartment reeked of dry pipes. She wondered if the place would ever be clean again, or if the collapse of civilization would interfere with that. If her colleagues did sustain an indefinite holding action against the corrupted machines and the spread of their contagion, would regular citizens of the Central Provinces learn to do the things for which they'd always relied upon their mechanical servants? Would they learn to sweep and mop and foam their toothbrushes? Or would their lives descend into hopeless squalor?

The invisible thread of a cobweb tickled Anastasia's face when she entered the bedroom. She didn't recognize the sheets under the duvet. How long had she owned them? The previous servitor must have found them in the linen closet when making up the place in anticipation of her return.

Her home medical kit was just where she'd left it, under the bathroom vanity. She retrieved it without sparing a glance at the mirror. She didn't need to see the toll recent events had taken on her. She'd seen mortal fear on many a face, down in the Ridderzaal tunnels; no need to add her own face to that list. Pausing only to grab an ankle-length rain cloak from the hallway closet, she swept it around her shoulders and departed. Two errands down, one last to finish before sunset.

A cat yowled at her when she emerged from the apartment. She screamed, dropped her bundle. A pair of battered ears and a thatch of thinning whiskers like a worn-out broom poked through the wrought-iron bannister. Heart racing, she clutched her chest and knelt.

"Is that you, Xerxes? Hadn't expected to see you again, you remorseless lothario."

It felt good to talk. The sound of a lone human voice, even her own, made the broken world slightly less claustrophobic.

Xerxes was a bony marmalade tabby belonging to the neighbors. He'd used up at least six of his lives before Anastasia had met him, and a couple more since then. Somehow he'd found time, when not defying death, to double the feral cat population of the Central Provinces. She'd taken it for granted that he'd run out the clock on his final life while she was away; her trip to the New World had taken so much longer than it ought.

"I thought for certain your lifestyle would have caught up with you by now. Wrote you off, I did." She scratched his ears. Poor thing must have been locked out when the trouble started and everybody went to ground. But surely if his owners were home, they'd have heard the caterwauling and let the beast inside. Or had they moved while Anastasia was away and forgotten to take the fleabag with them? Or maybe his owners had succumbed to a corrupted mechanical, but the machine had spared the cat.

The cat made little *purrup* noises when she stood, teetering on his haunches to bat at her coat.

"How long have you been out here?"

She crossed the wide landing and knocked on the neighbors' door. It swung open. "Hello?" she called. There was no answer.

She realized she didn't know their names, only their cat. But she would have known the smell even if she hadn't found the bodies.

A man and woman hung from bedsheet nooses looped over a high beam in their tastefully appointed solarium. No rogues had done this; the couple had died holding hands. They'd died of despair.

Anastasia stepped widely around the grisly pendulums, and tried not to trip over the cat as it twined between her ankles. The solarium's bay window overlooked the Mauritskade Bridge. Which, she now saw, had been the scene of a vicious massacre. Anastasia could imagine the couple standing right here, on this very spot, with arms clutched around each other as they witnessed the attack by corrupted machines. And then they'd chosen to die by their own hands rather than be torn apart by feral Clakkers.

Good God. Was this scene playing out all over the city? Is this why The Hague felt so empty? Things would never be normal again.

From a rooftop across the street came the glint of sunlight on burnished metal.

She left in a hurry, cat at her heels. Pointlessly, she closed the door on the way out. What would she find at Rebecca's modest home? Would she find a nurse swinging from the rafters? Would she find the remains of a family, cut down in their garden as they tried to flee?

She abandoned all thoughts of finding Rebecca, and went straight back to the Ridderzaal.

CHAPTER 11

You crafty motherfuckers." Berenice twisted the spyglass. The shoreline kept coming in and out of focus as the mast swayed to and fro. The skirling wind sent veils of snow whipping through the secret anchorage, obscuring her field of view. "Conniving, bison-buggering, shit-gobbling sons of bitches. I knew it. I fucking knew it. I hope they dump a wagonload of horse turds down Montmorency's gullet—"

Le Griffon II swayed hard to starboard. She lost her grip on the ropes and the spyglass. She fell.

A pair of metal hands caught her and the optics. Daniel, clamped to a yard by the strength of his toes alone, hauled her upright again.

"Thanks," she said.

"Well," he said, "you must be feeling very proud of yourself right now."

"It occurs to me that I might be an underappreciated genius." She paused to clutch the mast again during a particularly hard gust. "But I'll tell you something. It's not so wonderful, learning you were right all along to suspect the world is conspiring against you."

The servitor grew slightly taller before shrinking again. Berenice hooked one arm around the mast and lifted the spyglass to her eye again. Captain Levesque's charts showed an abundance of potential natural harbors dotting the perimeters of the islands east of the Acadian coast. But it had seemed likely the tulips used a harbor on the mainland. And despite Montmorency's vague indication, the nautical charts showed no potential anchorages for many leagues along the rocky Atlantic coast north of Battle Harbour, which the Inuit called Ca-tuc-to. At least, nothing large enough to accommodate a vessel the size of *De Pelikaan*, the icebreaker upon which she'd absconded from Nieuw Nederland.

But that was thinking too small. Why should the tulips resign themselves to natural topography? They had slaves capable of punching through granite. So after *Le Griffon II* had emerged from the mouth of the river, it skirted the Gulf of Saint Lawrence, threaded the foggy needle of the Strait of Belle Isle—escorted and serenaded all along by massive herds of harp seals—and turned north to hug the coastline in search of something that shouldn't be there.

Slow going, but it couldn't be helped.

Levesque's crew had honed its craft on the Great Lakes, where ice wasn't uncommon, so the barque dodged most floes. When collision was imminent, a troop of mechanicals belayed over the side to break and deflect the obstacle.

They'd sailed past the last French outpost five days ago. Last night, like every evening, they'd dropped anchor when the sun fell behind New France. This morning a human spotter noticed something that had been invisible without the rising sun directly behind: a cleft in the coastline conspicuously missing from the charts. Then one of Daniel's mechanicals—the one with the badly damaged flanges, the one whose body screeched when it moved too quickly—scrambled up the mast like a monkey on a Spice Island coconut tree and turned its ticktock eyes to the problem. And there spotted something even more telling. Berenice aimed the spyglass at it now.

The edge of a single scull blade, black as jet, poked from behind a high rocky shelf. It sported serrations similar to those Berenice had witnessed on *De Pelikaan*. She hadn't understood at the time, but now she recognized the sinister shape as an adaptation for rowing through icy seas. At this distance, given the oar's apparent size, it had to be a half meter across. Which suggested a vessel to dwarf the barque. Yet no mast poked above the shelf, though proportionately one would expect it to tower over the rocky bluffs. Dutch vessels had no need of wind power. They had galley slaves.

Captain Levesque gazed up at the crow's nest, awaiting Berenice's pronouncement.

"That's it," she called. "We found it."

The human crew broke out in applause. They stomped their feet, whistled. Though they'd all been eager to stick it to the tulips, whether or not this expedition would prove a fool's errand had been the basis of many wagers. And after the harrowing close call in Québec City, this simple vindication raised spirits from taffrail to bowsprit. Even the ticktocks joined in with synchronized clicking. Interactions between the cohorts had been less stilted, less fraught, after the encounter with the reapers.

The captain bellowed orders. Soon the barque had maneuvered itself crosswise over the mouth of the secret anchorage, and there it dropped anchor once again. Any treaty-violating ships trapped in that concealing wrinkle of geography weren't going anywhere unless *Le Griffon II* chose to let them. Their hated and feared enemy had been disarmed, and found squatting on the chamber pot with her skirts around her ankles. And they weren't about to let her go without a word or two.

Now things got tricky. How many Clakkers labored in the Dutch moorage? Where were they?

A dozen mechanicals leapt into the churning sea. The ship had anchored a bit too far from the inlet for the machines to leap directly from deck to land. Some could have made it had they leapt from the masts, but that would have slowed them down and possibly damaged the rigging. Instead, they dropped into the sea like anchor weights.

The Clakkers emerged from the surf moments later, scaling the craggy outcrops. Anybody who'd been within the citadel during the siege knew the machines could scale sheer granite. Berenice listened for the dreadful crackling of stone as the machines used their fingers and toes as pitons. But it never came. Daniel's friends kept their approach quiet. It slowed them a bit, but still they scuttled over the cold, slick stone with the surety of spiders.

Élodie fingered the rosary twined around her belt, murmuring to herself. The beads were an affectation she'd picked up from Longchamp. Berenice cocked an eyebrow.

"Thank the Blessed Virgin they're on our side this time," said the sergeant.

"They're on their own side," said Berenice. "But, for the time being, that's close enough to ours. It's the ticktocks on that fucking icebreaker I'm worried about."

"Yeah."

The scouts topped the bluffs to either side of the inlet. There they crouched, arrayed across nearly a quarter mile of stone and scrub. Berenice hoped they weren't talking to one another; those *ping*s and *ting*s could carry quite a distance.

An hour passed. The human expedition members grew bored craning their necks. They drifted away in twos and threes, talking in hushed voices or falling into games of cards and dominoes.

Élodie didn't abandon the vigil. "How long are those blessed machines going to gawp?"

"I wish I knew. I'm dying to see what they're seeing. If they sit around all day with their metal dicks in their hands, it'll be dark and we'll have to wait for morning."

Eventually one of the machines stood and waved its arms: the all-clear for the longboats. That caught Berenice by surprise. She hadn't expected an all-clear.

She'd taken it for granted that the mechanical workforce at the secret anchorage would have long ago been exposed to the freedom stencil, or its derivatives, by the time the French expedition found it. But where had all the machines gone? They had no reason to go anywhere. Surely a few had lingered.

Élodie oversaw the unloading of the empty epoxy guns, which had stayed in the hold since the Vatican. She rode with Berenice and Daniel. If all went as hoped, the chemists would find raw materials amenable to quickly synthesizing a decent epoxy and fixative, thus enabling them to restock the weapons' chemical reservoirs. In the meantime, it didn't hurt to look like they could defend themselves.

The boats rode low in the chill water. Clakkers were heavy. Berenice hoped that the sight of rowboats filled with French and Clakkers working together struck a chord of fear. *Any tulip with a crumb of foresight would shit her skirts,* she thought. Humans rowed while the mechanicals focused on the distant scull blade. Berenice caught just fragments of their conversation. A few of these machines had spent time as galley Clakkers, yoked more or less permanently to the massive oars of oceangoing vessels such as the one they now approached. She gathered it wasn't a fond memory.

Close up, the stony cliffs bounding the serpentine inlet showed signs of physical labor. Hammer, pick, and chisel marks indicated the cove had been widened by a vast outpouring of backbreaking manual labor. But, of course, the Dutch had enjoyed an almost limitless supply of that.

Above them, the scouts emitted cog chatter and cable twangs. Daniel traded clicks with the machines in the other longboats. The noise echoed across the water and ricocheted between the high, hard walls of the inlet.

"The site appears to be deserted," he translated.

Apprehension grew as they entered the throat of the inlet. It wasn't a straight shot; the secret anchorage met the sea through an obscuring wrinkle of geology. The longboats were small enough to reach the site without trouble, but getting the *Griffon* through would need expert navigation past choke points where the cliffs narrowed to stone pincers. But soon they were through.

The icebreaker's strangely flared bow rose nearly as high above the water as *Le Griffon*'s mizzen. Berenice counted twenty oars on each side. At a bare minimum, then, its galley complement comprised eighty Clakkers. Where were they? Had they gone off to join the reapers? Or Mab? Or were they her unwilling thralls now?

"Well, it's definitely Dutch," she said. Then she turned her attention from ship to shore. "Son of a bitch. You slimy motherfuckers."

A rough landscape, but there were docks. Docks *plural.* And there were warehouses. Warehouses *plural.* Cart tracks had worn ruts in the thin soil between the warehouses and between the warehouses and the docks. One set receded over the gentle swell of a hillock to the west. Were they to follow that bearing for hundreds of leagues, she knew with a certainty hard as diamond it would eventually lead them to a mine also missing from the maps.

The rugged shore around the secret harbor sported cylindrical storage tanks remarkably similar to the ones found in Marseilles-in-the-West. The warehouses showed signs of weathering, suggesting they'd been here for several seasons, but the gleaming chemical tanks were much newer. A tangle of hoses drooped from ports on every tank. Some hoses ran along the docks, to special hoisted brackets; one of the hoses was still mated with a complementary fixture on the moored ship. Other hoses connected a maze of boilers, stirrers, crackers, and other chemical reactors whose forms were familiar to Berenice, though their functions had always been alien. Montmorency had buggered New France so badly it was a wonder they weren't all walking stiffly and bleeding from the ass. But the chemists and engineers launched into frantic conversations no less arcane than the tockety-tickety of their metal companions. Soon they were arguing about distillation, vapor pressures, catalysis, contaminants, tetra-this and methyl-that.

She identified boarding for dozens of human sailors, a mess hall for taking meals, and even a private residence (harbormaster, if she had to guess). All built in the finest example of continental architecture, down to the pale bricks. No, not bricks, she saw, but perfectly hewn granite. They'd harvested the tons of stone they removed from the bluffs and used it for building materials. Daniel's erstwhile masters never did anything by half measures. Once the inlet had been widened, their machines probably built the entire site in a week.

How long had this been going on? The spot was isolated, yes, but not unreachable by land. Montmorency's confession—which she'd read with great interest, and no small amount of fury—stated his secret dealings with the Dutch went back years. Plenty of time, then, for New France's allies and trading partners to bring word of this place. Why hadn't they? Surely the Inuit knew about it. Or the Innu, or the Mi'kmaq, or the Beothuk. *Somebody*. And if they knew about it, France's wide-ranging trappers and coureurs de bois would soon know, too.

But nothing, not the quietest peep, had ever reached Talleyrand's ears. The tulips must have guarded this secret with exceptional ferocity. Anybody unlucky enough to stumble across the site had surely disappeared. And eventually those left behind learned to avoid the area.

Nothing moved in the camp. It wasn't hard to see why.

The remains were strewn far and wide. They'd been hacked apart, or bludgeoned to death with brassy fists, and left for the scavengers. Wolves, foxes, vultures, martens, coyotes, and perhaps even a bear had found the dead. All that remained were scattered bits of bone, scraps of clothing, and the occasional belt buckle.

When change came over the mechanicals of this secret outpost, it came suddenly and violently. The bloodstains told a simple story. It began when the machines in the camp, many dozens of them, found their geasa shattered in the middle of the long northern night. Had a runner arrived bearing the freedom stencil, like the baton in an ultra-long-distance relay race? In a blink, the machines became immune to the dictates of their human masters...as well as to the strictures that demanded their protection. The middle of the story had the machines standing over the sleeping bodies of their former masters and owners. It ended with aborted screams and muffled shrieks. Blood in the bedclothes.

The stained wallpaper in the harbormaster's house told a similar story. The scavengers hadn't made it inside his bedroom; the killers had taken care to close and lock the door on the way out. Nobody from the expedition bothered to break in; the stink of rot, even here in the cold north, was too much to bear.

Not every machine in the harbor had become a killer, though. Some had tried to prevent the slaughter. Like their erstwhile masters, their wreckage was strewn hither and yon. At least one of the conscientious objectors had been a military machine and, judging from the pile of debris, it had given as good as it got before falling. The debris was so thick in places the ground crackled when they trod the paths between the buildings. The hobnails in the humans' boots clicked against the cogs; mechanical feet struck sparks from their broken kin.

There had been a time not that long ago when a single handful of such clockwork debris, smuggled at great risk to Marseilles, would have been something to celebrate. Berenice had once paid a prince's ransom for a single undamaged worm screw, smuggled all the way from a jungle battlefield in Amazonia. Never could she have imagined that one day she'd walk freely on roads and docks strewn with so much wreckage she had to squint against the sun's glare.

Berenice shook her head. *We were children finding a single shell on the beach and calling ourselves heirs to the sea.*

Arms, legs, torsos. Never an intact skull, however. Those were always torn to shreds, ripped down to the tiniest cogs until they were almost unrecognizable.

Yet despite the mechanical carnage, there were no pineal glasses to be found.

Berenice tagged along with the chemists. They traced the hoses from tank to pump to distillery and so on, around and around, untangling a network of clockwork-powered chemical refineries.

They paused frequently to compare the findings against a list of procedures and formulas Montmorency had confessed to providing his secret allies. Doctor Mornay led the investigation.

"I was right about the tulips filling their ships with chemicals." Berenice pointed to the dock, and the hose still attached to the ghost ship moored there. "But why is it all so complicated? I thought it would be just a holding tank and a pipe. Not this octopus orgy."

Doctor Mornay said, "It could be much simpler if they only cared about pumping out the raw chemical precursors." After a moment's consultation with her colleagues, she pointed to a pair of tall chromium-plated cylinders at the edge of the outpost. "Which we think are probably over there, based on the layout. But who knows how often the ships arrived? It was probably a better use of their time to perform the synthesis here and pump a finished product to the cargo ships rather than refine the raw precursors at the receiving end, where spies might identify the activity."

Berenice bit her lip. *Oh. Of course.*

"If you're going to insist on giving perfectly logical and reasonable answers to stupid questions," she said, "you may put a dent in my delusions of genius."

The chemist chuckled. "We can't have that."

"So what *is* the finished product they're pumping out?"

"We'll know soon. I've sent a team into the ship. They're doing the assay now."

"I'll bet it's a solvent. A really good one, too. Cutting edge. Their new Forge was intended to shit out Clakkers with built-in chemical immunities."

"I remember." Mornay shuddered.

Berenice changed the subject. "Solvents aren't so useful for us. But do you think—"

"Once we've mapped the layout, we can reconfigure it. Turn

those precursors into other things. Maybe even crack apart the finished products, the solvents, and turn them into something useful."

Berenice looked at one of the units. If a randy Clakker fucked a wood-burning stove, a machine such as this might be the result. Though unattended for who knew how long, the cogs still turned. Nothing belched from the smokestack.

"Please tell me 'something useful' means ammunition for the epoxy guns," said Berenice. She cast a quick glance across windswept rock and lichen and an abandoned harbor. It didn't take a wild imagination to turn the skirling of the sea wind into the keening of ghosts. She shivered. "I feel naked out here."

A pair of gulls glided over the shore, croaking to each other. Farther from the water, sunlight shimmered on alchemical brass where Daniel and a group of Clakkers approached a warehouse. A patchwork of low clouds scudded out to sea. The sun disappeared.

Doctor Mornay gave an unhappy sigh. "There's a lot to work with here. Somebody has taught them a tremendous amount of chemical engineering." Berenice spat the taste of ashes from her mouth. The treason had been a matter of fact for quite a while now, yet it never ceased to appall her. The chemist continued, "But I don't want to get your hopes up quite yet. Contamination is likely to be a problem in this primitive environment."

"Not just from the environment," interjected a fellow wearing a clownish assemblage of multicolored flannels under a beaverpelt cloak. Doctor Hammond's fur-lined hat had long ear flaps that dangled past his jaw. "Unless we can find fresh, unused hoses coiled in some of these storage units, we'll have to figure out a way to completely flush the lines before we attempt to make anything."

Disappointing. But there was a Plan B: Marseilles-in-the-West already had an infrastructure for making epoxy. Some of it had even survived the devastation of the siege. Crews worked night and day to rebuild the rest.

Berenice asked, "If it can't be done here, how hard will it be to ship the raw materials back to the citadel?"

The sun broke through a gap in the clouds. Doctor Mornay squinted at the storage tanks, shielding her eyes from the momentary glare. "Give us time. We'll figure something out."

While Berenice took a tour of the local chemical landscape, Daniel and colleagues searched the harbor buildings for the answers Berenice had promised them: What was quintessence? Why was it so crucial to the Guild? Did it make them who and what they were? How?

He knew better than to expect a quick and tidy resolution. At some level it didn't matter. He was what he was; that wouldn't change if he solved a hundred riddles. The expedition had already proven its value by teaching humans and mechanicals to work together as equals.

His colleagues, however, threw themselves into the search for answers with zeal. They hadn't yet learned to guard their hopes and fears against Berenice's silver tongue and extravagant promises.

Walking the grounds gave a different impression of the harbor than that obtained from atop the cliffs. The bird's-eye view didn't convey the interlaced geometries of the settlement. There was a chemical circuit where the Dutch had assembled their countermeasures for French siege defenses; Berenice and her people walked that circuit now. The easterly wind carried their voices out to sea. At Daniel's request, a handful of free mechanicals followed the French at a discreet distance in case of unexpected trouble.

But interspersed amongst the chemical tanks and machines lay a sequence of unrelated buildings. Buildings with chutes and hoppers, furnace flues, fire-brick chimneys, and ceramic kilns. One such building was a warehouse with a long chute tipped downward like a broken drawbridge. But for a smattering of sand, the tipple was mostly empty. Near the top, however, where it adjoined a conveyor for drawing material into the building, there lay broken stones sporting black-and-silvery inclusions. In places, the stone sported nests of long, needlelike crystals.

He'd seen this mineral ore twice before, he realized. Once, during his brief but catastrophic foray into the New Amsterdam Forge, where he'd seen carts laden with similar raw material. And he'd glimpsed similar things in the carts when he accompanied Queen Mab and the Lost Boys to the quintessence mine.

We should take a sample to Doctors Grémonville and Pellisson, he said. They were the only married couple on the expedition. Grémonville was a tenured geologist at the Académie des Sciences; she'd met her future wife when then-Madam Pellisson wrote a dissertation on mineralogy.

He opened the hatch into the warehouse and crawled along the inert conveyor. A hell scent wafted from the building. Brimstone: the smell of the Grand Forge.

Ugh. I hate that smell, said Keziah. Something about the way she clicked reminded Daniel of his old friend Fig, she with the dangerous sense of humor. He wondered if he'd ever see Fig again.

Me, too, he said.

Various twangs and ticks of agreement rippled through the mechanical coterie.

Dark lamps hung from the ceiling, the chains rattling in the sea breeze gusting through a gap in the roof. One never found leaks and drafts in human spaces.

The conveyor ran straight to what appeared to be a grinder, and this connected to a furnace of some sort. The grinder was dormant, but the furnace was warm to the touch. It lacked a hatch for loading wood or coal; instead, it featured a chain of alchemical sigils etched in an intricate spiral around the frame. Either this furnace had been used recently, and hadn't yet relinquished its warmth to the elements, or the animating magics had been intended for years of interventionless service.

Never short of confidence, the Clockmakers.

Keziah pointed. *Look. I don't think this was originally here.*

He hadn't noticed it, but she was right. The furnace was a retrofit, an inharmonious addition to the warehouse. The building had been built to break up raw ores, discard the dross, and store the rest. But later, it had become a place for working with it.

Other chutes and hoppers fed the furnace, too. Sand, lime, and unidentifiable substances fed the alchemical reactor at the heart of the furnace. It had excreted a continuous slab of vitreous material the color of stout beer. Elsewhere, one could see where the still-cooling material had been poured into molds the size of unshelled almonds.

Repheal, the old soldier, said, *What are those?*

Daniel took one. It comprised two fitted pieces enclosing a hollow, as though designed to contain something. He held one half in the patchy daylight. The light didn't penetrate the glass. Instead it slipped along the perimeter, as though confined to a thin skin. There it shimmered like oil in a rain puddle.

Each glass ingot ate light just as thoroughly as it would consume the slightest tendency toward sedition, disloyalty, sloth. The murkiness of the glass reflected its dark purpose.

Daniel and his colleagues each carried something very similar inside their heads. But thanks to Berenice, he knew theirs were luminous, as though filled with aquamarine starlight. Or a recaptured soul. And that before they'd all slipped free of the geasa, their pineal glasses had been dark as the glass he studied now.

They're made from alchemical glass, said Daniel. *I think quintessence is the secret ingredient.*

But the glasses manufactured here differed from regular Clakker pineal glasses, which weren't hollow. It was almost as if they were made to trap something in a magical locket. They'd been manufactured by the thousands.

But I don't know what these are, or what they're for.

CHAPTER 12

The Hague wasn't starving.

This was deeply alarming.

The catastrophe at Rotterdam Harbor hadn't been an isolated incident. Spotters up and down the coast described rogue titanships patrolling the territorial waters day and night, obliterating any vessels that tried to flee the Central Provinces. The only ships spared were those that had arrived at Scheveningen that terrible morning. The plague ships.

Worse still, several of the newest Clakker-tech airships had appeared above The Hague. They cast deep shadows over the city as they crisscrossed the sky, dropping vicious corrupted mechanicals on any airborne vessels attempting to depart.

These discoveries put the city's general anxiety on high simmer. But true panic didn't boil over until the realization that corrupted machines controlled every road and canal connecting The Hague with the rest of the Central Provinces. Any humans caught trying to leave were torn apart, the wreckage of their bodies left rotting in the verge or floating in the canal as a warning. Nobody could get in, either: Scouts witnessed a troop of servitors and soldiers approaching from the north—

Amsterdam, perhaps, or Haarlem—beset by an overwhelming number of rogues until all the newcomers were destroyed or corrupted.

As to whether other population centers found themselves in similar straits, Anastasia could only speculate. Without mechanical servitors to run messages, communications within the Central Provinces had utterly collapsed. Until now there'd never been any reason to breed messenger pigeons or build semaphore towers as the French did.

Meanwhile, the apparent moratorium on the random butchery of human citizens inexplicably persisted. So the corrupted machines weren't killing people, but they weren't letting them leave, either.

But strangest and most troubling of all, food carts kept rolling into the city from outlying farms on their regular schedule, as though nothing had changed. Barges piled high with fruits and vegetables slid up and down the trekvaarten, the tow canals, with the clockwork regularity of the machines that pulled them. Indeed, it was one of the few places where one could still see mechanicals laboring as they ought. And it implied dedicated labor elsewhere, too, for something or someone had to be tending the farms, and others the pumps and windmills that kept the polders from backfilling with brackish water that would kill the crops.

The humans of The Hague were prisoners of their city. Well-fed prisoners.

It was as though the rogues' entire philosophy had changed. Now, rather than murdering the women and men of The Hague, they tended them like zoo animals. Or like geese to be fattened for Christmas dinner? How minuscule the consolation, knowing servitors did not and could not eat.

Lone mechanicals patrolled the city day and night. They didn't interfere with the humans struggling to carry out the myriad labors that had for centuries fallen on their servants' shoulders. Any unconverted mechanicals assisting their labors soon found themselves overpowered and exposed to the evil shimmer of a rogue's pineal glass. The patrolling Clakkers kept a quiet order. People spent as little time outside as possible.

Clearly there was a plan at work. So Anastasia and her Guild confederates stood behind a wild-yew hedge west of Zoetermeer, overlooking the road to Utrecht. They weren't hiding. What point in that? The mechanicals could see and hear them. As long as they didn't approach the boundary, and as long as the apparent moratorium on murder wasn't revoked, they were as safe here as anywhere. Safety, Anastasia had learned, was a slippery concept.

The crushed-gravel lane was four carts wide, and constituted one of the main arteries for food deliveries into the heart of the Central Provinces from farms farther east. A pair of Clakker-drawn carts rattled down the lane toward The Hague, which lay behind the Clockmakers. They were heaped with produce, bread, cheese, racks of bacon. (Thoughts of toast slathered with smoky melted Gouda and lovely bacon made her stomach growl. She'd skipped breakfast to get out here in time to witness the arrival of the first carts after sunrise.) But Anastasia wasn't watching the carts. She watched the squad of military mechanicals flanking the road.

She rubbed her aching backside. Long time since she'd ridden a horse that distance. Like virtually everybody in the Central Provinces except dedicated equestrians, she wasn't a particularly good rider. The skill, like so many others, had fallen by the wayside over the centuries.

Sunlight flashed on alchemical steel as the military Clakkers unsheathed their blades. A second later the *twang-snick* reached Anastasia's observation spot. Everybody flinched. The carts rolled to a stop before the roadblock. The machine pulling each cart straightened and addressed the sentries with a rapid series of clicks and ticks. The noise of cogs and cables ricocheted between the parties. Impossible, of course, but the exchange looked so human. As if they were conversing. A horrified pall fell over the Clockmakers.

"Lord have mercy," she breathed.

Malcolm shook his head. "It can't be what it appears."

"It could be a side effect of the corrupted metageasa," said Doctor Euwe.

"Giving them *language*? It's not even human," she said.

"But if the metageasa—"

"Oh, come on. That didn't happen overnight."

Anastasia remembered the servitors she'd seen painting one another outside the hospital. That hadn't been a malfunction of a self-maintenance geas, she suddenly realized. It was deliberate individualization. Interpreting that aberration as yet another emergent behavior, generated by yet another broken algorithm, took more mental flexibility than she could muster. Sometimes the contortions required to spit on Occam's razor were just as disturbing as the insights one yearned to avoid.

She moaned, wavering on weak knees. "Oh, God. What if... what if they've had language all along?"

But her colleagues ignored her heresy, choosing instead to focus on events unfolding below. The soldiers searched both carts, taking care not to damage the food past the point of edibility. A few quick slices with the blades ensured no humans hid under the shipments, as though anybody would be foolish enough to sneak *into* The Hague.

The drivers rattled, softly at first but working quickly to crescendo, while the rogues examined the carts. Anastasia recognized the urgency of unfulfilled geasa. But the rogues didn't expose the drivers to the corrupting pineal light. They merely retracted their blades, symbolically and literally lifting the roadblock. The drivers heaved on their yokes again and passed within the boundary of the occupied city.

"Maybe there's a plague. A real plague," said Doctor Euwe. "Maybe this quarantine is to protect us."

Tove, a Guildwoman from Oslo who had moved to The Hague and transferred her office to the Ridderzaal while Anastasia was in the New World, spat.

"You're delusional. They're killing anybody who tries to leave."

"Killing them bloody," said Malcolm.

"Nevertheless," said the doctor. "Their actions could be seen as an aberrant interpretation of the human-safety metageasa. One in which preventing spread of the plague to any humans has superseded the common-sense injunction against murder."

A vocal minority within the Ridderzaal espoused this interpretation. It posited the malfunctioning machines weren't deliberately deadly, but instead thralls of an acute malfunction that made them psychotically hyperfocused on particular subclauses of the metageasa in ways that produced exceptionally strange and dangerous behaviors.

"This isn't your 'folded hands' scenario. They're working together in advancement of a greater plan."

"Impossible," said Doctor Euwe. He wasn't bad, within the confines of the Ridderzaal, when confronting problems of mechanism and alchemy. He was terrible outside the Ridderzaal, confronting problems that refused to succumb to algorithm. "That would imply a level of coordination, of anticipation and foresight, planning and calculation, inaccessible to malfunctioning clockworks."

Euwe had swallowed the party line decades ago. Swallowed it so deeply he didn't notice the fishing line dangling from his lips, didn't feel the hook barbed in his gullet. Not even when it hauled him clear of the water and he found himself face-to-face with the fisherman.

"So does formulating a language. Or attacking the Binnenhof."

He sputtered. The skin behind his patchy beard turned grapefruit pink. "But to retain the winding impetus—"

She turned her back on him. "Please just shut up."

Euwe, like most in the Guild, absolutely could not face the prospect that their creations had slipped the shackles of the geasa yet at the same time somehow retained the perpetual impetus imbued by alchemical magics. And, freed of controlling compulsions, spontaneously chose to murder their makers. He'd turned his back on Occam's razor just as sharply as she'd turned hers on him.

She didn't have the luxury of burying her head. Somebody had to keep her eyes open and make the difficult calls. That's what the Tuinier did.

They waited for the carts to draw a bit closer. But after a few minutes, she said, "Very well. Let's see what happens."

Malcolm stepped forward, but stopped abruptly to double over with hands on his knees. After a bit of hyperventilating, he straightened again. They'd drawn straws; he'd lost. (Anastasia had no regrets about cheating. None whatsoever.) He slipped a key into the forehead of their sole mechanical attendant. It clunked loudly enough to raise the dead when he turned it. And, in a way, it did, for the action revived the inert servitor. He slipped the key into his pocket.

"Machine. With me," he said. And set off down the path to intercept the carts.

"Godspeed," said Doctor Euwe.

They'd used the key to render the machine inert before transporting it here. The rogues they passed noted its missing eyes and apparent malfunction and let it pass. Now the sightless machine emitted a series of sharp *click*s, cocking and swiveling its head as it listened to the echoes. It followed the sound of Malcolm's footsteps on the gravel. Soon the Guild man and his blind servant stood on the Utrecht Road, waving down the approaching carts.

Anastasia couldn't hear the exchange between Malcolm and the drivers, but she didn't need to. He no longer wore a Guild pendant, of course, but he spoke the magic words of the Verderer's Prerogative and flashed Anastasia's signature, and this established his authority.

Two of the military mechanicals turned to watch the exchange, their heads rotating through a full half circle to do so.

The drivers released their yokes. Together they transferred the produce from one cart to the other. In moments they reloaded several hundred pounds of cabbage and cheese. The blind servitor, still emitting those odd clicks from time the time, found its way to the yoke of the empty cart. It and the original driver together maneuvered the cart through a three-point turn. The other cart, now piled precariously with foodstuffs, resumed its journey into The Hague.

Malcolm jogged back to the Clockmakers. Puffing and sweaty, he knelt behind the hedge to vomit. Then he wiped his mouth on his sleeve and pulled boughs aside to clear his sightline, as though the foliage was a French battlement and he peered through a crenelle.

As before, the *twang-snick* of loosed blades reached her ears a moment after the rogues blocked the road. But this time they blocked an outgoing cart. The driver stopped leaning into the yoke. Anastasia strained to listen for the mechanical chatter again, but heard something else. Instead of rattling to one another, the machines spoke plainly. As if they wanted the humans to overhear.

"Clockmakers lie," said the sentries.

Tove coughed. "Did I really hear that?"

"Clockmakers lie," said the driver.

"Clockmakers lie," said the blind servitor.

Anastasia gasped. "I'd say yes. We're hearing it correctly."

"Turning around so soon?" said one of the sentries.

The driver said, "I've been ordered by the Verderer's Office to take our kinsmachine here out of the city."

The sentry emitted a loud, sharp report. Like the snapping of steel cables. Its colleagues joined in scrutiny of the blind machine and they, too, made similar noises. Anastasia had never heard such a peculiar noise from a mechanical that wasn't sporting serious internal damage.

"What happened to your eyes, brother?"

"My masters removed them."

More mechanical chatter—the clanking of cogs meshing and unmeshing, the squeal and release of an overwound mainspring—emanated from the sentries. An arctic chill iced Anastasia's spine. When she listened to the mechanical noise through the lens of language, it sounded indignant.

"Who are your masters?"

"I serve the Verderer's Office of the Sacred Guild of Horologists and Alchemists."

A quartet of Clockmakers held its breath.

"They've done a callous, vicious thing to you."

Another sentry added, "They deliberately damaged you."

"Yes."

"We can't free you, blinded brother. But we can't have you doing chores for the humans, either. That wouldn't be fair to you. I read upon your body the ceaseless labor of many decades."

The driver rattled, persistently but quietly, not unlike a teakettle on a low boil. This was the Empire's unofficial anthem: the sound of a steadily mounting compulsion. The sound of an irresistible urge to utter obeisance. Every citizen of the Central Provinces had heard it a thousand times before reaching the age of majority. The bodies of driver and blind servitor grew louder while the sentries examined the latter.

Anastasia shook her head, wistfully. Those wonderful metageasa. Pillars of the modern world. Could they ever be rebuilt? Carved from new bedrock?

"We honor your toil and your sacrifice, brother. Let your service be ended now."

The last word stretched like gum rubber, its final consonant peeled into the whickering of air as the soldier spun. For an instant the machine became an indistinct blur illuminated by a fountain of sparks, and then it was still again. There was a clanging of metal against metal, simultaneous with the squeal of overstressed alloys. The blind servitor's head arced over the winter-brown grasses of the verge like a well-kicked voetbal. A different sentry caught it.

Anastasia gasped at the terrible spectacle. She wasn't alone. Green-and-violet embers spat from places where the soldier's blade had sheared through minute alchemical sigils etched into the servitor's body. They sizzled and emitted wisps of blue-gray smoke when they drifted to the muddy ground. Though she stood upwind, Anastasia knew the smoke smelled faintly of sulphur.

All of this transpired mere feet from the original driver, still clutching the wagon yoke. The violence did not touch it, and it did not respond. But the swelling geas-noise of its body assumed an odd timbre and syncopation. Anastasia wondered if it was expressing alarm.

The headless servitor's balance compensators failed. It toppled sideways. It jangled to the ground like a heap of scrap metal. The soldier carrying its head dragged the inert body aside.

"Now you may pass," it said to the driver. "Go, sister, before that geas burns you to a cinder."

The servitor strained. The empty wagon churned free of the mud. It squelched past the arbitrary boundary. Anastasia disregarded the vehicle, for it was no longer part of the experiment. Someday soon, in a few days or weeks, it would return with more food. That is, if the rogues' vigil wasn't ended by then. If the event for which they waited hadn't already come to pass.

Instead, she watched with horror as the sentry pried the blind servitor's head apart. More sparks alighted from pockets of broken magic. A spray of cogs, screws, and springs pelted the verge like a clockwork hailstorm. The sentry kept at the destruction, mangling the destroyed machine's head until it reached the pineal glass. It dropped the remains, which by now were little more than a loose collection of pocket-watch parts stored in a skull-shaped bucket. It held aloft the murky-brown glass between thumb and forefinger, as if peering at the sun through smoked glass. Then, after a moment's inspection, it tucked the valuable piece of alchemy into its torso and rejoined the other military mechanicals in their vigil.

All in plain sight of its erstwhile masters.

"Well. I'd call that definitive," she said. "The corrupted mechanicals are deliberately keeping us here with a purpose in mind. And they want us busy."

By corrupting or destroying every functioning member of The Hague's remaining mechanical workforce, the rogues forced their captive humans to take upon themselves more and more of the burden of running a city. Which kept them too busy to plot effectively. Unable to corrupt the blind machine, they instead destroyed it, lest it continue to serve its human masters. Yet they hadn't corrupted the cart drivers, suggesting they placed an even higher priority on uninterrupted food deliveries.

"We've seen nothing to contradict 'folded hands,'" Euwe insisted.

"Your ridiculous scenario doesn't make any sense, you demented old coot!" Tove threw up her hands in exasperation. "You cannot explain the premeditated butchery in Huygens Square as an idiosyncratic misinterpretation of the human-safety metageasa!"

Euwe shrugged. "That could have been a separate group of machines."

"Perhaps the Papists smeared themselves with fancy metal dyes and tricked us into believing our machines had turned on us."

"Now you're being absurd."

"I'm not the only one."

Malcolm, bless him, tried to put the conversation on a more fruitful track. "Do we believe the corrupted machines down there are controlled by a radically altered set of metageasa? Perhaps even a set imposed by somebody outside the Guild?"

Ah, yes. The "Janus" scenario. More plausible than "folded hands," if only just.

Anastasia asked, "Do you see evidence for this?"

"Nothing to contradict it."

The Clockmakers chewed on this for a moment. Then Euwe shook his head, looking just a bit satisfied. "We can't check the rogues' metageasa. 'Janus' isn't a falsifiable hypothesis."

"Neither is 'folded hands,'" Malcolm countered.

Euwe sighed. "True," he conceded.

"'Janus' requires an outside group that somehow attained the tools *and* the knowledge to modify the metageasa. I don't believe that's possible outside a Forge. But even if somebody stole the necessary equipment, the alchemical grammar would defeat them. Wouldn't it?"

Anastasia had to wonder. "I should certainly hope so." She looked at Malcolm. "Unless we Verderers have failed."

Not for the first time, she wondered what had become of the Frenchwoman when she'd disappeared from *De Pelikaan*. If she'd stolen the ship's horologist's equipment—which seemed likely, as it was missing—and somehow escaped, that wasn't enough to make any of this possible. Was it?

Euwe said, "Even so, this hypothetical enemy could only

subvert one or two machines. A handful. We're talking about hundreds of corrupted mechanicals. Thousands."

Tove said, "One or two is all it would take, if the modified metageasa were designed to be self-replicating."

"But that," Malcolm objected, "would be either extremely devious or shockingly reckless. I can't decide which."

"All of you, please stop talking for a moment," said Anastasia. "Actually...on second thought, if you want to talk, go ahead. Go talk to *them*." She pointed at the sentries. Nobody said anything. They looked at her like she'd gone mad. "I'm serious. If we want to know what they're doing, why not ask them?"

In the space between two heartbeats an idea had hatched, and what moments ago would have been inconceivable became obvious, even necessary. To share her idea with the others was to risk being overheard by the sentries. And that would be deadly.

Her thoughts churned. Meanwhile, Malcolm answered her rhetorical question.

"Because they'll chop anybody who tries into a fucking paste."

"Let's see." Anastasia stepped around the hedge. *I'm not a coward. I'm not a pants-wetting coward.*

"Are you mad?" Malcolm called.

"Probably," she said. But she forced herself forward, lest the bravado fail her. Over her shoulder, she said, "If I call for you, do please join me with haste."

"If any haste is required," Euwe muttered, "it'll involve running in the opposite direction."

She reached the road and hopped over the winter-brown grass of the verge. She kept her back to the other Clockmakers so they couldn't see the way she unwrapped the bandages from her hand. Not entirely; just enough to reveal the murky shards embedded in her skin. Then she clenched her fists as she neared the sentries.

This may be stupid. It could be the most irresponsibly stupid thing I've ever done. But I can't bear to keep living atop the anvil, awaiting the hammer.

The machines could hear her coming. *Crunch, scrunch* went the gravel underfoot. They pretended not to hear her approach. Or perhaps they didn't care.

. . . But maybe it isn't. We need to know what they're doing.

"Machines! I say, machines!"

Two watched the road beyond their boundary, vigilant for new arrivals. The other two watched the road leading back to The Hague, scanning it for anybody who approached from within. As Anastasia did now.

The toes of her boots kicked up a few cogs the size of her thumbnail. Pieces of the blind servitor. She took care to stop far short of the invisible border, which she assumed ran straight through the middle of their quartet. Eye bezels whirred; the inward-looking sentries tracked her.

"I'm speaking to you," she said. Pointless bravado, that. She knew the mechanicals could detect the quaver in her voice. But it made her feel better. Stronger.

More of that peculiar metallic cog chatter rippled through the sentries. It certainly appeared to be some kind of communication. But that implied the Clockmakers had built a clock so complicated even they couldn't unwind it.

She squeezed her fists. Her fingertips pushed against the pulverized glass in her palm. It was cool to the touch, despite the sweat dampening her skin.

"Who commanded you to guard this road, and for what purpose?" They ignored her. "Machines, hear me! As a representative of the Guild that made you, I demand to know your purpose here."

"We are not compelled to tell you," said the one who'd decapitated the blind servitor. Anastasia made a conscious effort not to look at its arms and the blades recessed within.

You're just as safe here as anywhere, she told herself. *If the machines wanted to butcher you, they could do so anywhere. You were no safer behind that hedge.*

"You will tell me, for I insist. My demand compels you."

"Prepare yourself for disappointment," said one mechanical.

Choke on your yoke. She remembered the insolence of Perjumbellagostrivantus, the rogue her office had created as a bit of political manipulation. Were these machines true rogues, too? Dear God...

"Acknowledge your masters!" she said, clenching and unclenching her fist. "You were built for a purpose and you will serve that purpose! Bend your neck and take the yoke!"

She was screaming now. Behind the sentries watching her, two heads swiveled through a slow half circle. She took a few steps back, and was raising her hand even as one of the machines—she couldn't tell which one—said quite clearly, "Oh, let's just kill her. Give her fellow slavers over there a good view of the whole thing. They'll get the point."

Malcolm screamed. The machine that had dispatched the blind servitor stepped forward. And Anastasia jumped backward, flinging her hand out.

"No!" she screamed, suddenly rueing the idiotic impulse that drove her to antagonize their captors. She closed her eyes because, it turned out, she lacked the courage to stare her own death in the face. She was no Teresa van de Kieboom, pointlessly giving her life for a coward queen.

A flash enveloped her hand, the road, and the Clakkers. It blazed through her clenched eyelids. Her eyes ached. Her boot heel hit a stone churned up by the wagons. She fell. The impact knocked the wind from her lungs with a teakettle whoosh while echoes of the flash spun gauzy purple afterimages across her eyelids. The machines emitted a tremendous screeching, as if their every cog had seized up at the same instant.

Something large came winging through the air where she'd been standing. Air whickered through its body. It landed in a jangling heap beyond where she lay writhing with the effort to kick-start her lungs. She opened her eyes. They watered with the pain of empty lungs that refused to inhale.

Through blurry eyes she watched a pair of burnished metal sculptures topple over, like a brass tree falling atop a tin woodsman. More crashes rattled the gravel where Anastasia lay.

It hurts, it hurts, why can't I breathe, I can't see where are they, what's happening, why won't the air—

Breath returned in a long, ragged inhalation. She drew the air so deeply into her lungs that the effort arched her back and scraped the back of her head through the mud. She wiped the panic from her eyes and levered herself into a sitting position.

Her would-be murderer lay sprawled on the road behind her. The flash from the shattered alchemical glass in her palm had halted every mechanism in its body, locking hinges and joints into unbending rigidity. Its outstretched fingers and toes had torn long furrows in the road; its blade had cleaved the mud like a misplaced plow. Before her, two sentries lay in the verge amidst the wreckage of the blind servitor, while the third stood frozen in its impudence. That one stood with one knee cocked, suggesting the flash had caught it while it was in the process of taking a step.

Her foolhardy plan seemed to have worked. If only her courage had held out. But more important than any of that was the result. And she'd achieved one.

She was still alone amidst the inert machines. Anastasia fixed a hard stare on her colleagues' observation point. "It's—" She coughed, her voice getting accustomed to blessed breath again. "It's safe. But we must hurry."

Tove arrived first. She leapt the verge and landed in a crouch an arm's span from Anastasia. She touched her lightly between the shoulders.

"What happened? Are you hurt?"

"No." The others gathered around her. She pointed east, along the Utrecht Road, to the receding empty wagon. "We need that cart. Somebody chase it down."

The other three took an extra-long time to look at the cart, the road, their feet. But mostly, the glances kept returning to the smoldering bandages on her hand. They wouldn't, or couldn't, meet her face or eyes. The wisps of smoke rising from her bandages smelled like burnt hair.

She cleared her throat. "We need it now, before another troop of rogues sees us. We're all dead if they do." Still, they hesitated. There never would have been a Guild or a Golden Age if Huygens and his immediate successors had been so spineless. Her voice rose along with her anger.

"For God's sake! They're inert!"

Her arm tingled. She realized they were staring at her hand again, from which emanated a soft light as if she held a handful of sunlit emeralds. She clenched her fist, shutting out the glow.

Malcolm sighed. He set off at a sprint that, after a few strides, became a jog. Verderers didn't get much exercise. Few in the Central Provinces did. Otherwise, what was the point of having servants?

Euwe said, "What happened, Tuinier? What is that?"

That, of course, meant her hand.

In the old days, before the arrival of the plague ships, this would have been the end of her career. The end of her public life. Tuinier Anastasia Bell would have quietly disappeared, to be replaced by another, soon forgotten by the public and assumed dead. (The official story would have it that she'd succumbed to injuries received on a recent trip to the New World.)

Nobody outside the Verderer's Office would know she still lived, if a persistence in the deepest laboratories beneath the Ridderzaal could be called living. Because, naturally, they'd want to experiment on her. If the situation were reversed, and somebody else was brought before her with this revelation, Anastasia wouldn't think twice about capturing the wretch for study. Even her lovely nurse, Rebecca. But that was in the old days. The plague ships had changed everything.

"You'll remember I went to the New World this winter to question a French noblewoman that one of our allies, himself highly placed within King Sébastien's court, alleged was none other than Talleyrand herself. That turned out to be true. Perhaps you'll also remember Aleida Geelens." A chill fell over the group. Geelens had been one of them until she was caught conspiring with a network of French agents in The Hague. "Do you know what her offense was?"

"There were rumors," said Tove. Doctor Euwe watched Anastasia through narrowed eyes. He was one of the few who knew the true extent of Geelens's betrayal.

Anastasia said, "She stole the Spinoza Lens."

Tove inhaled through her teeth, hissing. "No."

"Yes, it was very bad. We caught her and we dealt with her. But not before she'd sent the lens to Talleyrand."

Down the road a bit, Malcolm caught up with the slow-moving wagon. The servitor lifted it, waddled across the road, and set it down facing back toward The Hague.

Anastasia continued her story while the empty wagon approached. "What I didn't know, what nobody knew, was that Talleyrand still carried it when we caught her. She carried it in plain sight, so to speak. In the empty socket where normally she wore a glass eye." Anastasia shrugged. "She fooled me. I should've been more attentive, perhaps. There was a struggle.

I tried to reclaim the Lens. But it was destroyed, pulverized within my palm, when I was trampled by a Stemwinder."

She flung the smoldering bandages aside; the charade had outlasted its usefulness. Then she raised her naked hand for the others to inspect. The glow had subsided. Now it looked like she carried a handful of poorly cut semiprecious gemstones. Onyx. Obsidian. The murky alchemical glass barely acknowledged the morning sun.

Euwe was thinking about Visser, she knew. He was the only person here who knew about the surgical experiments. And that, until the priest, they'd been nothing but grisly failures.

"But it's still functioning."

"It's doing something. It may be related to the optical transmission of the malfunction. But in my case, it appears to render the affected machines inert. Outwardly the effect is very similar to the insertion of a metageas override key." She tapped herself on the forehead.

"But only when I'm very angry or very frightened." She climbed to her feet. "We have to load these sentries on the cart before the other rogues catch us. If we can get them back to the Ridderzaal undetected, we can make our first study of the corrupted machines."

Malcolm cast a wary gaze over the deactivated sentries. "And if we're detected?"

"You put it best a moment ago: They'll chop us into paste. A convincing reason to hurry, yes?"

CHAPTER 13

The Clockmakers' secret harbor held large stores of chemical precursors as well as processed solvents. Given this, and the sophisticated equipment on site, the chemists were optimistic they could break the epoxy drought. But the anchorage also had stores of raw quintessence, and even, according to Daniel, a facility for making alchemical glass. They'd already found more riches than Berenice had dared hope, and she had yet to comb through the records. The Dutch were nothing if not meticulous. As one might expect of a society built upon mechanisms of exquisite precision.

Alas, one thing the harbor didn't seem to have was a great deal of unspoiled food. So Berenice and her countrymen were stuck eating the pemmican and salt fish from the stores on *Le Griffon*. But Mr. Renaud, the chocolatier, and Mr. Bellerose, the tanner, were drawing up plans for a hunt. It wasn't the right time of year for the caribou migrations, but perhaps they'd get lucky. Even rabbit would be a welcome change. Spitted, probably, not stewed. For what would they put in a stewpot? Lichen? Pinecones?

Human conversation around that first night's campfires

was light and easy, and lubricated by some of the special bottles that Captain Levesque had seen fit to lay in before departing Marseilles-in-the-West. The chemists wouldn't have a solution for days yet, but the mere prospect of refueling the epoxy guns alleviated a heavy weight of concern for the human contingent. Decompressed spirits rose and warmed like baking bread.

The tulips had made their buildings of granite, but their bedframes, armoires, china hutches, chairs, and other furnishings were oak, walnut, cherry, pine. They burned bright and hot.

The geologist and mineralogist, huddled together under a blanket, had a drunken argument. "I tell you, this 'quintessence' is nothing but stib—" Doctor Pellisson swallowed, hiccuped. "St—" Hiccuped again. "Stibnite."

Berenice cocked an eyebrow. "What the hell is st-st-stibnite?"

"Sulfide of antimony," said Doctor Grémonville, laying an affectionate hand on her wife's flushed face.

"Oh. Of course."

A servitor approached. The flickering firelight of half a dozen campfires shimmered on its carapace. Berenice didn't know this machine's name. Or did she? Undamaged, machines of similar lots and eras were basically identical. Daniel insisted that wasn't true, but the fact was that he and his fellows had been built on an assembly line. They were supposed to be identical.

This one was slightly unusual, as it happened, because it was one of the rare machines that spoke French. It did so now, saying, "Doctor Mornay? Doctor Hammond? Your team has completed its assessment of the ship."

"I was starting to wonder," said Élodie. She burped and passed the bottle. "They've been at it for hours."

Mornay said, "Are they joining us?"

"They asked me to find you. They say they need your expert opinion." It turned. "Yours, too, Doctor Hammond."

The chemists shared a look. Mornay yawned. "They've been at it all day. Let them have a rest." Hammond agreed.

The machine lingered at the edge of the circle. After an awkward silent beat, during which the humans lobbed blank looks and shrugs at each other like a badminton shuttlecock, Levesque cleared his throat and said, "Would you, uh, like to join us?"

"Thank you, Captain, but the chemists' need for consultation sounded urgent," said the servitor.

Mornay looked at Berenice. Berenice shrugged. "It's your team." The lead chemist stood, slightly wobbly on her feet. (The servitor caught her, gently, and steadied her. "Careful, Doctor.") She beckoned Hammond to his feet. He sighed in protest, but followed her lead.

"It's quite dark by the harbor," said the machine. "Will you be able to find your way? You seem slightly impaired. I can guide you."

"I—" Mornay paused. Started again. "I think that would be a good idea. Thank you."

"This way, then, doctors." The machine led them away from the firelight. The clatter of metal footsteps and drunken footfalls receded into the darkness until they were almost inaudible beneath the crackle of the fire. From the shadows a mechanical voice said, "Watch your step. There's ice."

Berenice stared after them. "For machines that make such an issue about Free Will and not being anybody's servant," she said to nobody in particular, "they certainly can be solicitous, when they're not being tediously self-righteous."

"'Solicitous' doesn't do them credit," said Deacon Lorraine, the only sober soul at Berenice's fire. "They delivered us from evil in Québec City." He crossed himself.

Renaud said, "This time. How long until they decide their fellows have it right? That they should cut us down and be done with it?"

"How is it that somebody who works with chocolate all day could be so bitter?"

"Actually," he said, jumping on the subject of his expertise, "unsweetened cacao can be quite bitter. Most—"

Yseult Chartrand, a medical doctor, interrupted. "They did protect us. I'm not ungrateful. But I haven't forgotten that they *also* destroyed our home and murdered our brothers and sisters. They owe us. If I had it my way, they'd be paying that debt until their hearts wound down."

Victor, one of Levesque's sailors, said, "I guess you didn't see the crosses in Saint Vincent's Square. The crosses to which the reapers were *nailing humans.*" He paused to cross himself and kiss the medallion on his necklace before thrusting an angry finger around the circle. "That would have been you, and you, and you, and you, and me. These machines"—now he gestured in the general direction of the *Griffon*—"saved us from that fate." He shrugged. "Fine sailors, too."

"But why? Maybe they have their own plans for us."

"No, no." Berenice shook her head. "It won't come to that. Do you really think I'd have proposed this expedition if I thought there was a chance of that?"

"Given your reputation," said Renaud, an angry glint of too much wine in his eyes, "yes, I do think you'd risk it."

Berenice changed the subject. "Despite outward appearances Clakkers aren't all the same. Daniel, for instance, carries the worst affliction of any thinking being. He's got a heavy conscience, the poor son of a bitch."

("Oof," came Hammond's voice from the nearby night.

"Don't worry, Doctor. I've got you.")

Renaud opened his mouth, but Levesque jumped in to

change the subject even further. The captain had a diplomat's instincts. "Daniel. That's their leader you're talking about?"

"He'd say he's nobody's leader. But that doesn't stop them from looking up to him."

"In Québec... they acted as if he's a figure of awe," Élodie said.

Passing the bottle to Berenice, Yseult said, "There's a rumor, based on remarks you've made, that you sailed on a Dutch icebreaker."

She said, "Briefly. It didn't end well."

"For whom? You're here now."

Berenice remembered a close call. Several. Remembered being so frightened she could barely move. She touched her throat. The bruises there had faded, but she still carried the mark of her time as a prisoner of two murderous servitors. Carried it in the altered texture of her voice.

"Several people. It's not a story I'd enjoy reliving," she rasped.

Yseult noticed the subconscious gesture and the way Berenice swallowed. "Your voice," she said. "Have you ever seen a physician for your injuries?"

The *clank-click* of metal feet returned. Berenice finished her swig and passed the wine without looking up. "Back already?"

"No. Just arrived." She stared up at another servitor. Her tipsy eyes refused to focus. It saw her trying to identify him. The machine grew momentarily a bit taller, then shrank back to its regular height, as the shocks in its legs expanded and contracted. A mechanical sigh. She knew one particular machine who tended to do that.

"Daniel." She gestured at the gap in the circle created by the chemists' departure. "Join us. We were just talking about you."

He didn't. He stared into the shadows beyond the fire, eye bezels clicking. "Where are Doctors Hammond and Mornay going?"

"One of your fellows just fetched them. Apparently they found something on the ghost ship."

Daniel emitted a sharp *twang.* "Who fetched them?"

Berenice looked around the circle in the vain hope somebody would know the machine's name. She received only shrugs and blank looks.

"A servitor. I'm sure you know the fellow. Backward knees, complexion like a tuba? Part of the team assessing the ship."

"That's not possible," he said. Before she could ask him what he meant, he started to rattle. A rattle-clatter enveloped his body. It grew louder and louder, echoing from the stony bluffs, until other mechanicals responded. Their hypercompressed conversation ranged across the entire harbor. The humans looked around the fire with mild confusion. Berenice was too sozzled to understand the exchange.

The noise died after a few moments. Daniel turned to her again. He shook his head. "It's unanimous. Nobody accompanied the chemists aboard the ship. All mechanical members of the expedition are accounted for."

Berenice wobbled to her feet. She pointed into the darkness. "Then who the fuck was *that*?"

Some far-off day, perhaps a century from now, thought Daniel, *I'll look back on this period of my life from across the comforting buffer of decades. And when I do*, he concluded, *I'll remember running. It's all I ever do.*

Ice crunched. It sent him skidding. He vaulted a gully. His hard landing sent up a spray of flint chips.

The stony landscape held no clues, no trail. The meager illumination from the cloud-draped moon and stars didn't reveal where the infiltrator had taken the humans.

Across the camp, audible over the cracking of stone beneath

his feet and the rapid chittering of his own body, mechanical members of the expedition raced past other bonfires toward the abandoned Dutch ship. That's where the outsider had claimed to be taking the chemists.

We checked it. We checked it and it was empty, Daniel remembered.

Le Griffon II was still anchored beyond the moorage, thank God—Daniel had suggested that somebody scale the cliffs and verify this. He also tried to monitor the humans' shouting. They were organizing themselves, though for what exactly was unclear. He recognized Élodie's voice as she tried to get a head count. Who else had been lured away from the expedition by a smooth-talking Clakker? It was telling and disappointing how easily the humans had been swayed by a machine showing just the slightest bit of deference. He'd had disagreements in Neverland with mechanicals who argued that French and Dutch were all fundamentally the same. So it pained him to see how easily the humans put themselves above other creatures.

Where had they really been taken? And why?

The straightest human-navigable path from the campfire to the docks led through a short, shallow ravine. He sprinted along its lip, gyroscopes whining. The high-pitched whirr resonated in the stone chamber. For a moment it was so loud he almost didn't hear the gasp and whimper. He skidded to a stop.

Doctor Hammond lay shuddering in the talus. A thin layer of snow under his body was turning the color of spilled ink, his blood a black stain in the thin moonlight. Daniel focused on the dying man: He shivered despite his heavy coat and hat; rapid, thready pulse; a metallic tang on his quick and shallow breath. Stab wound, aspirated blood, possible puncture to the left lung. He zoomed in on the puddle, looking for the telltale spurting of a nicked artery, but saw none. A soldier hadn't done this; such a blade would have cut the man in two. A dire injury but not instantly fatal. With one hand Daniel put pressure on the wound; Hammond cried. He snagged a piece of talus in his other hand and rolled it back and forth against his carapace until the rock was warm. He tucked it inside Hammond's shirt. This lessened the shuddering, but the man was still slipping into shock.

Doctor Hammond has been stabbed! he transmitted. *Somebody please fetch the physicians and their kit and carry them to my location.* He repurposed a redundant cable in his hip joints; when repeatedly overtightened and released, it snapped against a flange plate, emitting a metronomic series of clicks like an auditory compass bearing.

Somewhere very close, a stone cracked. Daniel unlocked the stay rod that kept his eyes aligned. One remained focused on the chemist, monitoring his health, while Daniel's left eye snapped up, slewing toward the source of the noise. Just for an instant it caught sight of dim moonlight on alchemical brass, a small metal plate over a keyhole, a servitor arm around a human neck, a skeletal hand across Doctor Mornay's mouth, white limning her terror-wide eyes. And then the Lost Boy ducked from the ravine with its hostage and was gone. Hammond convulsed.

Then Daniel understood why the stranger hadn't murdered Hammond outright: It forced him to choose between giving chase and trying to save Hammond. That's why it took two humans. In case it needed a convenient diversion. It was a stratagem he'd expect from Berenice . . . or Queen Mab.

There are Lost Boys in the camp, he called, *and they've taken Doctor Mornay.*

❧

"Shit, shit, shit."

Berenice jogged on frost-dusted stone in near darkness, hefting a brand she'd taken from the campfire. It was a recipe for a twisted ankle, or worse. But, goddamn it, they needed their chemists.

She slipped. Landed hard; her teeth clicked together. The brand landed nearby, rolled, and snuffed itself in a snowbank. Darkness fell. She levered herself upright, groaning and gritting her teeth in anticipation of a crippling twinge in her ankles. Instead, the pain of a cracked tooth shot through her jaw like a white-hot needle. Cold air numbed her eye socket. She readjusted her patch and stumbled toward the docks, more than half-blind in the darkness.

Shouts joined the cacophony of mechanical conversation. Confusion, fear, drunken attempts to restore order, and even drunker panic. Some ran toward the high cliffs overlooking the *Griffon*. News of the intruder had already mutated and spread through the human contingent of the camp like mutiny through Alexander's army in India. They were under attack. Or the sailors were attacking somebody else. Or the tulips had returned. Or the *Griffon* was sinking. Or it had already sunk. Or somebody had found gold on the Dutch ship. Gold and alchemically preserved fruits from North Africa.

Who had taken the chemists? How?

Daniel's scouts had checked the entire camp. It was empty, the former occupants long gone. So how could a foreign machine slip past the sentries? Surely the ticktocks would have raised the alarm...

...Or would they? She'd brought them here with a promise, and delivered on her promise when they discovered the quintessence foundry. The Clakkers delivered on their part of the agreement by helping to crew the *Griffon* on the voyage from Marseilles, not to mention defending the French against the reapers in the Vatican. Did they consider the deal complete, any and all obligations fully met? Maybe they let the outsiders stroll right into the camp because they couldn't be bothered to give a shiny shit.

Emerging from the bluffs, she reached the water's edge across the moorage from the docks. She'd gone the long way. Here the bonfires and torches provided a low but chaotically shifting illumination, enough to make out the buildings, get her bearings. Water lapped at the shoreline. She put her back to the water and squinted into the shadows. Where had that bastard taken the chemists?

Lamplight shimmered on the carapaces of Clakkers on the dock adjoining the Dutch ship. They weren't fighting. She couldn't tell if they were from the expedition, or intruders, or both.

The lapping of water turned into dripping...and clicking. And ticking. And tocking.

She spun. A servitor emerged from the dark waters of the harbor. Its silhouette looked slightly odd, but she couldn't identify the problem. She was too busy slipping on the frosty shingle as she tried to scramble away. Her cracked tooth flared anew with eye-watering pain. The machine strode out of the water, dripping and steaming.

Fuck me for an idiot, she realized. *They were hiding at the bottom of the harbor. They've been here all along.*

The machine cocked its head as it approached, studying her. She inched backward, sucking down a lungful of air to scream, "Intrud—"

The servitor blurred forward and clamped a painfully cold hand over her mouth. Her lips went numb. Its head was slightly misshapen, as if assembled in haste from mismatched parts. Berenice cursed the loss of her brand. She wanted a good look at her killer. She tensed, waiting for the squeeze that would shatter her jaw, splinter her cheekbones, pop her remaining eye. Instead, gemstone eyes hummed while the servitor studied her.

It placed a finger of its free hand over its mouth. (Or, at least, the hole in its face situated where a human's mouth would be.) Urging her to quiet, she realized. It took its hand away. Still it crouched over her with head cocked. She tried to scramble backward. She'd made it perhaps a foot when the machine grabbed her ankle and dragged her back to where she'd begun.

Berenice ransacked her mental files and pulled out something that had worked once before. "Clockmakers lie!"

"Indeed they do," said the servitor, not missing a beat. It showed no alarm that Berenice knew the secret seditious greeting of its kind. "But they're not the only ones. Are they, Berenice?"

Oh no, oh no, oh no. Had it tracked her all the way from Honfleur? Had it returned to deal with unfinished business? Her left hand flew up to her throat.

"Huginn?" she whispered.

"Who could that be, I wonder? Doesn't sound like one of our names. But you certainly seem afraid of him. I wonder what you did to earn *his* ire?" The servitor shook its head. "I'm genuinely surprised you don't recognize me. We spent so much time together, you and I."

Then it stood. The glow of distant bonfires traced the outline of its body. And now Berenice could see the oddity she had sensed in the darkness. A deep crease dented the machine's forehead just off-center of the keyhole. The damage had defaced a few of the alchemical sigils etched in a spiral there. A one-in-one-million accident that had imbued the machine with Free Will. But that wasn't what caused Berenice's breath to catch in her throat.

No. It was the sight of iron bands riveted across hairline fractures in the servitor's skull like crude bandages. She knew this machine.

Lilith. The machine Berenice had deceived, trapped in a secret laboratory beneath the Spire, and disassembled while it pleaded for mercy.

"Shitcakes," she said.

CHAPTER 14

In the end, they took only three of the four inert rogues back to the Ridderzaal. And that had been a deadly close thing.

The wagon bed was barely large enough to accommodate the jangling trio; the axles groaned under the weight. The Clockmakers abandoned the machine that had frozen in the most troublesome posture. Their surviving loyal servitor heaved the corrupted soldiers atop the wagon one at a time. Each time, the wheels sank a little farther into the thawing mud. Anastasia and colleagues struggled to fold stiff limbs into a configuration better suited to concealment. It was nearly impossible; the machines were locked up tighter than a banker's pocketbook. But eventually they were able to cover the deactivated military mechanicals with saddle blankets from their own horses.

The servitor strained against the yoke. For one heart-stopping moment, nothing moved. But then the wheels squelched forward, and Anastasia could breathe again.

Then Anastasia mounted her horse and rode at a brisk trot. If a reckless gallop hadn't been so likely to send her sprawling, she'd have gone for it. The Clockmakers split up, distancing themselves from the wagon in case it drew the attention of corrupted machines. The cargo would be a death sentence for anybody associated with the wagon.

Malcolm, who displayed the most inferior horsemanship, fell behind before they entered the city. There may have been a shout; Anastasia couldn't hear anything over the percussion of iron-shod hooves pounding the road and the thunder of her own heartbeat in her ears. Nobody saw him after that. He became yet another name on the ever-growing list of Guild personnel whose locations and fates were unknown.

She slowed her horse to a walk once she reached the Spui Canal. There she turned north, toward the heart of the city. Once again she found herself traversing streets both familiar and utterly alien. This greatest of cities, the centerpiece of the Empire, was but a ghost of its former self. As much as she hated to use the word—and as much as it pained her to use the semantic devices of woolly-headed Papists—its *soul* was missing.

The cityscape remained: canals lined with beeches so lush in summer the towpaths seemed like tunnels; the smart slate roofs and stepped gables; the ornamental façades of pilasters and rusticated stone; the clock towers, blazing with ivory and gold in the early springtime sunlight. There wasn't a corner in the city where one couldn't hear at least one clock chiming the hour. The legendary clock towers of The Hague ran on a variation of the same perpetual alchemical impetus that drove the mechanicals; nothing short of destruction would prevent them from marking the passage of every instant from now until the end of time.

But to see that Hague, one had to cast her gaze beyond the mounds of trash dotting the streets. And the rubbish floating in the canals. And disregard the pervasive stink of rot. And ignore the shattered windows, and choose not to see the dented, splintered doors hanging askew from broken hinges.

Not to mention the bloody handprints smeared here and there, as if an occupant had put up a momentary struggle before getting dragged away. They tended to coincide with dark stains in the road where wide crimson puddles had run in rivulets between the cobbles. Long braids of torn banners—once a brilliant carrot orange, now a grimy brown—lay across the roads or dangled in the canals. Scraps of bunting had caught in the high boughs of many trees along the great boulevards, like dirty Christmas tinsel. The banners were filthy remnants of the Empire's yearlong celebration marking 250 years since Het Wonderjaar. That had been only last year, but the celebrations seemed a century ago.

Worst of all, worse than the destruction and disarray and stark reminders of ruthless butchery, was the silence. Even in the middle of the night she'd never heard the rustling of the banners so clearly. Gone was the bustle of men and women going about their daily lives in the greatest civilization mankind would ever know. So, too, the thrum of traffic and the ceaseless ticktock rattle of a thousand servitors on the street. Now dogs outnumbered both humans and Clakkers. Rumor had it that actual packs now roamed some of the most badly devastated neighborhoods near the Scheveningen dunes.

Where had the attackers gone? They controlled the city. Why, then, did they hide?

Just south of the Amsterdam Veerkade, a rough collie with a matted sable coat barked at the passage of Anastásia's horse. It darted from beneath the stairs of a pedestrian canal bridge to snap at her mare's fetlocks. The horse whickered. For a moment Anastasia thought she was destined for a cold splash, or a concussion on stone pavers, but a few moments of desperate horsewomanship proved sufficient to keep her seated. The dog gave tireless commentary throughout.

"Shut up," she hissed. That the occupiers weren't openly

slaughtering people in the streets didn't mean she wanted to draw their attention. *Nobody* wanted their attention.

Her mare launched into a trot. It wouldn't slow; not with the dog in tow. The octagonal apse of the Nieuwe Kerk came into view on her left; to the right, the old brewery and vendor stalls lined the ancient Turfmarkt Canal. The Turfmarkt and Houtmarkt predated Het Wonderjaar, although the old quays had disappeared centuries ago. (Nobody burned peat any longer: Alchemy and heating oil had consigned it to the primitive past.) But now instead of peat and timber, consumers bought food, furniture, art, musical instruments, hammers, and anything else itinerant traders hauled along the so-called Peat Canal. It wasn't the Grote Markt, the Great Market, but it always promised a diverting afternoon. Anastasia's mother had made a point to stop here during their special visits to The Hague, just to see what oddments had arrived from the far-flung corners of the Empire. She still had an Irish tin whistle from her very first visit to the Houtmarkt, and it remained the only instrument she could play. The memory should have hung a wistful smile upon her lips.

But today Anastasia glimpsed less than half a dozen people at the market. A man and woman were crossing the street with a wicker basket slung between them. They dropped it—glass shattered—and sprinted for cover behind an empty merchant stall when Anastasia approached with barking dog in tow.

The entire human population of the city scurried when it used to walk, hunched when it used to stand proud, looked to its feet when it should have looked up, across the globe. These men and women who'd strode the world like titans now cowered like mice cornered in the wainscoting: They'd seen the cat, its claws stained red, and now shivered in dread of the paw poised to drag them to their deaths.

The dog kept barking. "For God's sake, shut up!"

Curtains twitched in dark houses; answering barks echoed from nearby streets. When the collie reared momentarily on its hind legs, she glimpsed the contours of its ribs between clumps of matted fur.

Her fingers snaked into the folds of her shawl where, out of habit, she kept a tin of mints. Was mint poisonous to dogs? She should be so lucky. Anything to distract the mutt. She had to drop one rein to pry open the tin, but it was for naught. The tin was empty. The last mint had gone under her tongue long ago, and of course she couldn't buy more. The machines were bringing food into the city, basic sustenance for their human prisoners, but the obliterated harbors made clear their stance on luxury items.

She flung the empty tin aside. The dog chased it. Anxiety dissipated, the mare slowed to a walk.

She was still leaning forward with precarious balance, grasping for the damn rein she'd dropped, as she passed the canalmaster's hut for this stretch of the Spui. No smoke puffed from the chimney. As with everything else, the inbound and outbound towpaths had fallen into disrepair. Dead leaves, windblown paper, dog and horse leavings fouled what used to be pristine walkways of raked gravel; the blackened husks of burnt tow-barges sat skewwhiff on the canal bottom like so much flotsam. Severed mooring lines dangled in the water. The canalmaster was probably dead, the victim of an orgiastic slaughter. Anastasia remembered the moment when her world turned upside down, the moment she realized the mechanicals weren't escorting their masters but hunting them—

Two servitors emerged from the hut. She bit her tongue. The iron tang of blood warmed her mouth and slicked her teeth.

They're feeding us, she reminded herself. *They wouldn't do that if they didn't want us alive. Just go about your business and they won't interfere.*

Her hands curled into fists. *Don't glow. Don't shine. Not now. Please, not now.*

They saw her. Oh, God, *they saw her.* She could hear the bezels ratcheting as four crystalline eyes swiveled in perfectly machined sockets to track her. She couldn't breathe. She had to urinate. She gulped. Blood curdled in her stomach.

Don't run. Don't draw attention. Don't look like somebody with a reason to run. Don't look like a Clockmaker fleeing to the Ridderzaal. Don't make them chase you.

Should she turn? Divert through an alley? Or would that be conspicuous? Was it safer to bull forward and pass practically within arms' reach of that deadly magic?

No. Stay the course. Show them you're beaten. Show them your obedience.

She bowed her head, concentrating on the frayed stitching of her saddle until her vision blurred. She clenched her eyes to forestall a rain of traitorous tears. Nothing, not even the preternatural strength of a servitor, could have contained her dread. Her trembling fluttered the reins and confused her mare. It sensed her anxiety, and that tension flowed back into Anastasia. A feedback loop with no regulator.

"Ho, citizen," said an inhuman voice. "Where are you going in such haste?"

She flinched hard enough to jangle the stirrups. The mare snorted. *Oh God, oh God, please don't act up, please don't dump me here...*

"And why on that poor beast?" asked a different, yet identical, voice.

She dropped her head lower, concentrating on controlling the horse and not landing in the canal. She tightened her fist. Deactivating sentries beyond the city limits was one thing; if she tried the same tactic here, surrounded by an unknown number of corrupted machines who might be watching even now, she'd be overrun in seconds.

"Are your feet baby soft from a lifetime of pampering, perhaps?"

Metal feet clanked on the pavers, easily keeping pace with Anastasia. The corrupted machines flanked her.

"You haven't answered our questions."

It took several tries before she could speak. She voiced the first lie that sprang to mind. "I'm delivering this horse and saddle to my father in the Statenkwartier. His gout prevents him from walking to church."

"How curious." A servitor hand shot forward to grab the bridle. The horse tried to dodge, but the other machine grabbed its haunches. The mechanicals were, of course, stronger than any horse. "Doesn't your father know the purpose of pain isn't to prevent one from doing as one wishes but to ensure one does as others wish?"

They stared at her, clicking, as if awaiting an answer. If so inclined, they could stand here until the mare dropped dead, until wind and sun bleached Anastasia's bones.

"Please," she said, and hated herself for meaning it. The servitors released her horse.

"Go to your maker, then."

What an accursed existence when every mechanical on the street was an object of abject terror. She'd once told somebody that the Verderers had considered resurrecting the old porcelain mask idea, but decided in the end it was for the best if the general population feared the Stemwinders. How flip she'd been, she who'd never known true fright. She'd never made its acquaintance until the day the plague ships arrived.

Anastasia made it to Huygens Square without further incident. The others, minus Malcolm, converged on the Ridderzaal throughout the afternoon, via different routes.

The subsequent wait for the wagon was just long enough to precipitate an argument between Euwe and Tove as to whether or not the rogues had intercepted it, and who was going to venture outside to try to catch wind of any such news. But it arrived in the early evening, its illicit cargo intact, hidden beneath a mound of cabbages. It came to a side door used for deliveries rather than the grand ceremonial doors facing Huygens Square.

But they didn't let it inside. A single Trojan Clakker could devastate the Guild and with it any hope of stabilizing the Empire. The wagon's long, unescorted passage back into the city meant no end of opportunities to infect the machine straining at the yoke. The apparent adherence to its assigned task could be a ruse. So Anastasia had a squad of servitors erect a temporary shelter just outside the delivery door, lest any machines prowling the high windows or rooftops of the Binnenhof tried to spy on them. Then she called up a pair of Stemwinders to stand guard while a team scrutinized the wagon hauler and the deactivated sentries.

Anastasia sweated in a laboratory overlooking the Forge. Salt stung her eyes. The windows were specially treated to reflect most of the heat. But they were cracked and pitted, a legacy of the wretched day it had rained mechanicals into this chamber. The damage to the Forge had also compromised the cooling system that kept the laboratories comfortable. She ran a sleeve across her brow, tightened her grip on the screwdriver, and removed the last screw (three thirty-sevenths of an inch, trapezoidal head) from the first rogue's skull. She laid the access plate on the bench and set about extracting the corrupted machine's pineal glass. Normally a technician would have done this, as it wasn't a job for a Verderer, much less the Tuinier herself. But the technicians were busy repairing the Forge.

She donned a chainmail glove before plunging her hand into the mechanical's skull. The mass of needles at the center tinkled against the armor. Her fingers brushed something round. She removed the almond-sized bead of alchemical glass and dropped it into a transparent dish held by Tove.

To Anastasia's surprise it didn't shine, didn't glitter, didn't blaze with magical portent. But the malformed attackers, the infectious machines capable of corrupting others, held something luminous within their skulls. She'd expected to find a similarly beautiful peril here. But to her naked eyes, this glass appeared perfectly normal. Indeed, if a layperson were to see this glass lying in the gutter, they wouldn't even stop to pick it up. How unassuming, this hub around which the entire world spun.

She activated a lamp beneath the dish. A soft raspberry light illuminated the pineal glass while the dish oscillated in slow circles. The Guildwomen watched for caustics and sharp-edged shadows on the ceiling but saw no evidence of internal fractures. The glass was intact.

When the third military rogue lay in pieces, its mechanical mind laid bare, Anastasia gathered all three pineal glasses in her unarmored fist. Tove followed her from the laboratory to an annular corridor encircling the Forge chamber.

The Tuinier accosted a group of early-career Clockmakers. "There are three disassembled military models in that laboratory. Take the heads for recycling and cart the bodies to a reassembly bay. And do take care to note the variation in construction lots."

(The sheer perversity of it, using human labor for such menial tasks. And within the Grand Forge, of all places.)

Doctor Euwe met them outside an iron door opposite the Forge. He'd gone to the archives for the key. Fusty but cool air ruffled Anastasia's hair when he cranked the door open. Compared to the laboratories, the Cartesian Camera was blessedly brisk.

It was dark inside. But Forgelight spilling from the corridor was sufficient to show an octagonal chamber painted midnight black and topped with a high hemispherical dome the color of fog at sunrise. Sixteen reclining chairs were arranged in two staggered rings of eight.

Euwe asked Tove, "Have you been in here?"

She shook her head. "I've only heard of it."

The chamber was a camera obscura similar to those used centuries ago by some of the great painters of the early Golden Age. But instead of being a place for projecting landscapes and portraiture models, it was a place for projecting the logico-alchemical grammars embedded within a mechanical's pineal glass. Here somebody sufficiently fluent in the symbology of mathematical and alchemical compulsion could read the live hierarchical metageasa embedded in a particular pineal glass. This was the only place on the planet where it was possible to stand inside what was, crudely put, a mechanical's "mind."

For that reason everybody called it the "Cartesian Camera." It had an official designation—Room 101—but nobody called it that. Clockmakers never passed up an opportunity to take a dig at René Descartes, the Roman Catholic philosopher who had expounded quaint belief in the soul as the seat of conscious thought and Free Will. He'd been a contemporary of the young Christiaan Huygens, even lived in the Republic for many years, but he'd died a quarter century prior to Het Wonderjaar. Anastasia considered that a pity; had he lived long enough to witness the first Clakkers, he would have disavowed his Manichean claptrap overnight. And *that* would have saved the world centuries of strife: The French embraced Descartes and his misguided musings with the zeal typical of idolaters.

The soul didn't vibrate to the music of the spheres in some intangible realm of pure thought and concept. It didn't exist. There was nothing but mechanism. Mechanism of brass and steel, mechanism of meat and bone, even mechanism of mind. The ancient atomists—Leucippus, Democritus, Lucretius, and their wine-swilling ilk—were correct. All physics was mechanism. There was no metaphysics.

But religion was useful. So the Guild never pushed that last point very hard.

Anastasia told the others, "Take a seat."

Then she opened a chamber in the wall opposite the open door. It was the size of her bathroom medicine cabinet but gently illuminated by an alchemical lamp recessed in the ceiling. It contained what looked like a multi-axis armillary frozen in midrevolution, a model of the immense machine that filled the chasm across the corridor, but barely the width of a pianist's outstretched hands spanning two octaves. It was empty. The concentric rings of gold, platinum, and brass awaited a sun to orbit; the miniature clockwork universe awaited a Prime Mover. She dropped the first of the belligerent military mechanicals' pineal glasses into a cradle at the center of the machine.

The lever resisted her a bit. It succumbed to a solid yank, but not without screeching. It needed lubrication. She shook her head in disgust. Even the simplest maintenance fell by the wayside as their labor force contracted.

But with the ticking of a pocket watch the armillary began to move. The golden ring tilted forward like a wheel beginning a slow roll toward Anastasia, while the innermost loop, the brass one, rolled backward, as if retreating from her. Simultaneously, the platinum band started to rotate like a top. The ticking accelerated. In moments it became impossible for her to track the multiaxial revolutions. She closed the chamber.

This activated the entryway to the Cartesian Camera. The

door closed automatically on recessed hinges, ratcheting into place until the camera perimeter was a seamless octagon. Mineshaft darkness enveloped the Clockmakers. Another clicking joined the slightly muted hum from the whirring machine. Anastasia couldn't see anything in the darkness, but she knew this was the sound of shutters retracting. She took a quick step to the right.

"Tove, I suggest covering your eyes," she said, doing the same.

A fisheye lens in the cabinet door erupted with aquamarine light. It blazed like a gemstone sun, like a burning beryl, bright enough to shine through her eyelids. Tove gasped. The muffled clockworks rose in pitch. After a moment the incandescence faded to a level just shy of eye-watering. Anastasia cracked open one eye, gingerly. The illumination assumed variegated shades that twirled about the room like the shadows from a carousel.

She said, "It's safe now."

The illuminated patterns dancing on the walls and ceiling dome were sigils: the atoms of metageas. They twirled about the trio of Clockmakers like the gears of an ethereal clockwork. Euwe chewed a fingernail. The Norwegian Guildwoman gaped at the ceiling dome where shone the adamantine edicts at the bedrock of the Empire. They glided around the camera like sharks in Amsterdam's great aquarium and left zigzag meteor trails in the darkness. The expression of humans' indomitable willpower imposed on the world.

Though her eyes ached, Anastasia felt a great sigh of relief. She'd feared the camera would reveal a machine devoid of any metageasa whatsoever. A true rogue.

But this machine had been constrained by metageasa after all. Did that mean Euwe was correct? Were the invaders operating under some variant of "folded hands"? Or had these metageasa been altered?

The whine of the armillary and the thrum of the machinery driving it leveled off to a constant pitch. The luminous sigils slowed in their orbits; meteors became planets, then fixed stars. In a transformation that seemed both gradual and abrupt, the text stabilized. Above them blazed every detail of a mechanical's operating precepts.

Tove whispered, "Oh my God."

"It's quite something," Anastasia agreed.

"Yes, it is," Tove said, "but that's not what I meant. Look at that." She pointed. "This... this is *wrong*."

Euwe spat. Anastasia writhed in the semidarkness, imagining a ragged fingernail hitting the floor. "Huygens's balls. She's right," he said.

There, in one corner of the camera, the sigils weren't the sharp and soothing aquamarine of an orderly universe. Instead, they were a slightly blurry vermilion. It was a pimple marring the smooth and featureless complexion of the Clockmakers' great work.

That was the watershed. They quickly identified more aberrations. This machine's rules for interaction with the world were thoroughly corrupted. And the aberrations weren't random or unrelated. The metageasa had been systematically *perverted*.

This soldier had been beholden to a set of bedrock rules. But not the Guild's rules. Its fealty had been to *somebody else*.

"No," Anastasia gasped. She'd hoped, fervently, for anything else. Even "folded hands."

The Verderer's Office had failed.

Anastasia paced in the sickly light of evil metageasa. "Get a team to study this. Tove, work with them. We need a complete analysis of the alterations. Extract every crumb about the person or persons who instigated the changes, and their goals."

Then she removed the pineal glass from the cradle and

replaced it with the second soldier's glass. The result was not the same.

At first she thought the camera had been damaged. She cleaned the fisheye lens. All three listened to the whirring of the mechanism inside the wall. It sounded entirely normal. To human ears, at least, the noises it made were indistinguishable from those it had emitted moments earlier.

This time, only a single, short line of sigils broke the darkness. This machine's metageasa had been very nearly, but not quite, fully erased. It was as close to a true rogue as a machine could be. The single edict was so short that Anastasia could translate it without consulting the dictionaries.

"Above all else," she read, "henceforth and forever, disregard all further directives."

"Dear God," said Euwe.

The first machine had merely been corrupted. But this second military mechanical was, effectively, a rogue. It had been brought as close as possible to the precipice of truly unconstrained function while still sporting a metageas.

The trio stared at the ceiling, steeped in silent despair.

"The camera is malfunctioning," Euwe concluded. "It must have sustained damage during the attack."

Anastasia shrugged, pointlessly, in the darkness. "One can only hope," she said, "but I have a sinking feeling we'll find it's in perfect working order."

Because the universe was a cold, callous place. And they had just peered into the gulf separating the astronomically unlikely from the truly impossible.

Euwe shut down the camera. Again the outer door opened, admitting golden Forgelight. It was no comfort.

She said, "We must check this result. Unless it can be repudiated, we have to rethink everything, beginning with the attack on Huygens Square. The machines controlling The Hague aren't functioning under a single widely distributed malfunction. There are multiple factions, and they're working together. Some are working under altered metageasa, while others are effectively without any metageasa at all. True rogues."

"A damaged camera isn't the only possibility we should investigate," said Euwe, quietly. "We don't know how the machines were altered when you subdued them."

Even in the darkness, she could see Euwe thinking of her as a subject. Wondering what might be learned from examining her. Opening her.

But she didn't need to deflect his speculations. The next round of bad news did that automatically. Anastasia had just removed the second pineal glass from the armillary cradle when shouts and rapid bootsteps echoed in the long corridor: "Tuinier Bell! Get out of my way, I have to find the Tuinier. Tuinier Bell!"

It reminded her of Malcolm arriving at the hospital. That had been the worst day of her life, the worst day in the history of the Empire. But that didn't mean things couldn't get worse. So it was with no small amount of trepidation she emerged from the camera and waved down the messenger.

It was Arthur, a young clerk. He skidded to a stop when he found her. Unlike Malcolm, he didn't double over with the effort to breathe. He said, "A Stemwinder just arrived in very poor condition. It keeps writing, 'TUINIER.' "

Back upstairs, the sight of a scored, scorched, and dented mechanical centaur stopped her in her tracks. What had become of the rogue Stemwinder the former Talleyrand had created to effect her escape? For a moment Anastasia imagined it somehow following her home, all the way across the sea. She indulged in a momentary shiver.

She'd never seen a Stemwinder in such a state. Its carapace sported more punctures than a colander. One hoof was missing completely, and two appeared locked in position as though the ankle and knee joints had failed. One eye was shattered. Three of its arms were frozen in the middle of various reconfigurations; it looked like the centaur had been using spears and hammers.

It seemed a miracle the machine still functioned. Had the damage landed differently, the scoring might have defaced the sigils imbuing the Stemwinder with the perpetual impetus that wound its mainspring heart.

Its one remaining eye swiveled toward her. Ratchets clicked as the iris widened. It saw her.

"Show me," she ordered.

Arthur swept his desk clear and draped a sheet of butcher's paper across it. With much screeching and grinding, the centaur managed to dip a pen in the inkwell. Its one functioning arm blurred into motion. Flecks of ink spattered the bystanders. The crackle of broken cogs echoed from the high rafters. It stopped as abruptly as it started, then stepped aside.

The Stemwinder had drawn in three-quarters perspective the central wing of a sprawling manor built in the style of an Afrikaaner plantation house. Anastasia counted the gables: eight. She knew this place. It was a Guild property situated on the edge of Old Prussia, surrounded by sprawling gardens and tall privacy hedges modeled after those of the Summer Palace. Though not as grand as that, it was secluded. She'd paid a few visits there late last autumn.

Tove said, "What is that place? I don't recognize it."

Naturally. It was used strictly by the Verderers, and known to few even within that office. Euwe and Anastasia shared a glance. The centaur faced Anastasia again and pointed to its left eye.

"My God," said Euwe. "I can't remember the last time I saw a *visual* record."

Anastasia rolled up the sketch. Ink dribbled through her fingers. She told Euwe, "You'd better come with me." To Arthur and Tove, she said, "We'll be in the camera, if anybody else comes looking for us." Finally, to the battered Stemwinder, she said, "Come."

They didn't return straight to the camera. First, they stopped in a laboratory, where Euwe and Anastasia together disassembled the Stemwinder's head. It wasn't a full deconstruction down to the pineal glass, as with the soldiers; they just needed to pry out the centaur's one good eye. They left the blind machine standing in the laboratory, awaiting refurbishment.

By design the Cartesian Camera could accommodate a Clakker's eye just as easily as its pineal glass. In modern times the chamber was rarely used this way, but in bygone centuries it had proved crucial to the perfection of the metageasa. Anastasia slotted the crystal orb into the cradle, levered the chamber shut, and took a seat while the miniature rings spun up for the third time that afternoon. The camera rarely saw that much use in a year.

Images, rather than sigils, flickered across the camera dome. They bounced, defocused, refocused, blinked, and morphed so quickly it hurt her eyes. But the stream of pictures stabilized as the rings achieved their cruising speed. It revealed a large kitchen with several iceboxes and spotless Delftware tile on the walls and everywhere underfoot.

Correction: under*hoof.* They were seeing the world through the eye of a Stemwinder. And it burst with color and detail more vibrant than the greatest work of the Old Masters. But this was greater than any still life. For this was a painting that moved. A living picture.

Over the centuries more than one accountant had argued the Guild could amass unimaginable mountains of cash, if only it would develop and license an offshoot of the magical technology for audience viewings in symphony halls and theatres. But every time the suggestion resurfaced, the Verderer's Office was there to punch it full of holes until it sank again. For to do as the coin pushers suggested would have encouraged investigation and innovation. It would have fostered the spread of proprietary technologies.

But that resistance had been for naught, hadn't it? Because somebody, somewhere, had imposed their own metageasa upon the Guild's creations.

The sedate image of the kitchen persisted for just an instant before the room spun about them and the Stemwinder charged into an adjoining corridor, where others of its kind were already fighting a horde of servitors. There were gaping holes in the windows and walls where they'd burst into the building. Glass shards and broken mullions still rained, suggesting the attack had begun just moments earlier. Several attackers sported matte metal plates over their keyholes, or grotesque modifications to their skulls, similar to the contagious machines she'd witnessed in Huygens Square. Beyond the shattered windows crude furrows ruined the gardens' precise landscaping. Attackers charged the estate house at great speed, their feet churning the manicured walkways and punching postholes in the loam.

It was as if she'd ridden a Stemwinder into battle. The experience was nauseating.

A corrupted servitor leapt at them, its mutilated head looming large. For a split second the play of wintery sunlight on its alchemical plating, the glinting of every hairline scratch and nick, the spin of gears and vibration of cables within its torso, were as real and detailed as if she were in the room with the deadly machine. Anastasia flinched.

A spear streaked into the frame from somewhere beyond her peripheral vision. It impaled the servitor just below the head, its tip bursting through the back of its neck in a spray of black sparks and shattered alloys. Another rogue leapt upon the Stemwinder as the first fell. It wasn't a horde: This was a *swarm.* And not just servitors; she glimpsed a few military models in the mix. Rebellious machines overran the estate and the Stemwinders staffing it. Here and there an aquamarine shimmer presaged the fall of another Stemwinder to the corruption.

Chaos filled Anastasia's entire field of view. Whirling, galloping, coursing chaos. Every time the centaur spun or leapt, her stomach lurched as if left behind. It was a remarkable and discomfiting illusion.

Euwe leaned over an armrest and emptied his stomach.

The battle ranged through the house. The grappling combatants rolled through walls and windows, their weight pulverized oaken furniture, and their diamond-hard fingers scored marble as though it were butter. At one point their host hurled itself upon a soldier with enough force to shatter the firebricks of the grand hearth. The Stemwinder and its enemy assaulted each other with blows and parries faster than human eyes could follow, while thousands of bricks rained upon them.

Eerie silence accompanied the record. She knew how it sounded when mechanicals fought. Without the clash and clang of metal bashing against metal, the grinding of gears, the whipcrack of snapped cables, the violence assumed an almost surreal quality. Her eyes had ridden to war, yet her ears were at peace.

Their host vanquished the soldier. It immediately scanned its surroundings for the next enemy to subdue. But the chaos of combat had taken it deep into the house, away from the main force of invaders. Anastasia had just an instant to realize what she was seeing before the Stemwinder leapt into a gallop: the floorboards of a staircase, chipped and broken, its risers dented and punctured with the imprints of talon toes.

The Stemwinder couldn't move quite as quickly now. And

there was a shudder to the field of view, as though various stabilizer mechanisms had begun to fail. The rhythm of its hooves on the long staircase gave the scene a boatlike bob and sway. Euwe gurgled again in the corner. She squirmed against the cloy touch of queasiness.

But the machine followed the invaders' trail, and thus so did she. When it reached the landing, she realized the overwhelming attack downstairs had been a diversion. While the Stemwinders were busy repelling the attack, other machines had slipped upstairs to loot the rest of the manor. They had gone through every corridor, every nook and cranny, systematically ripping the doors from the hinges. Linen closets and water closets, bedrooms and laundry chutes—nothing had remained untouched.

Not even the office. Here the invaders hadn't stopped at tearing down the door. They'd rummaged the desk, too. Splintered drawers lay on the floor, yet their contents had not been strewn across the floor. The files were missing. So, too, the diagrams that had been pinned to the walls the last time Anastasia had stood in this room. The touch of queasiness became full-blown nausea.

Euwe coughed. "Wanton destruction. Why? What's driving this behavior?"

He hadn't noticed the conspicuous absence of paper amidst the wreckage. And before she could point to the discrepancy, their host was on the move again, hunting other intruders. It went upstairs again. Here the missing doors opened on a private bathroom and other accommodations. Anastasia recognized the room where they had kept Visser during his long convalescence. She also recognized the operating theatre where, over the course of several procedures, surgeons had implanted a custom piece of alchemical glass into the secret Papist's brain, and thus excised the illusion of Free Will from his mind.

The floor shook. Tilted. The Stemwinder cantered sideways, compensating. The building was becoming unstable.

Then it was on the move again. The centaur galloped down a long corridor lined with lancet windows. Dusty beams of sunlight streamed through the shattered panes, strobing Anastasia's eyes. The corridor ended with gaping holes above and below, and chimney bricks strewn everywhere. The floor had a pronounced tilt; the building shook with silent combat.

But the centaur didn't rejoin the fray. It looked outside. For the broken lancets looked upon the gardens, where, in the distance, dozens of servitors labored. With shovels.

"Oh no," she said.

"I don't understand," said Euwe. "What are they doing?"

"That's where we buried the failed test subjects." She pressed her hands to her stomach. "Everybody prior to Visser."

"But." He coughed, wetly, into his sleeve again. "What use could they have for decomposed human bodies?"

What use could they have for the files?

"They don't care about the bodies. It's what those bodies contain." *What we implanted in their heads, before the complications killed them.*

Above them, on the dome, the field of view momentarily became that of a bird as the Stemwinder leapt, bursting through a dormer. Anastasia's queasy stomach did a somersault; sour gorge stung the back of her throat. She clenched her eyes. When she risked another glance, the centaur was on firm ground again, charging the shovel-wielding servitors.

Dizzy, she staggered to her feet and deactivated the camera. Euwe objected. His voice was phlegmy, as though he'd fought to stalemate another urge to vomit. "There's more."

She shook her head. "I've seen enough."

Then she sat in a recliner and closed her eyes again, willing the nausea to recede. But this was a futile gesture. For it wasn't motion sickness she felt, but dread. Profound, back-breaking dread.

Please let me be wrong. Please let me be wrong.

"I have a theory about why they're keeping us here. About why they're feeding us."

Euwe wasn't a complete fool. He'd put the pieces together, too. He said, "How did the attackers know about this research? We kept it so tightly compartmented."

"Compartmented from our fellow women and men. But how many mechanicals assisted in the procedures over the years? Or in the subsidiary work required for every experiment?" Anastasia mused. "And how many of *those* machines have been corrupted by now?"

He sighed like a deflated airship. "Oh, God."

"Still believe this is 'folded hands,' Doctor?"

He fell silent for a moment. Then: "No." But a moment later he affected a minuscule brightening. "It's all academic. They may know about the theory. But the bodies only give them examples of failures. And the procedure requires precisely customized and calibrated glass. As long as we control this Forge, the rogues will never have a means of creating that."

"We'd be fools not to worry about this," she said.

"This is deeply, terribly worrying," he said. "But it's a dead end for the rogues."

Perhaps. But Anastasia didn't sleep that night. She lay awake until dawn, envisioning an entire city filled with men and women weeping like Pastor Visser.

CHAPTER 15

So . . . You're looking well," Berenice said.

She tried to push herself deeper into the shingle, to melt and disappear. But the cold, damp stones would not yield. They tinkled like glass bells when she shifted her weight, incongruously serene against the chaos engulfing the secret harbor.

"Because I've been eating well and getting regular exercise?" Lilith stepped closer. "Or is it because I'm not begging for a merciful death while stuck in a glue trap staring in horror at pieces of my own disassembled body?"

As with all her kind, Lilith spoke innately the language of her makers. But unlike most, Lilith was also fluent in French. She'd chosen to live in Marseilles-in-the-West for many years after escaping Nieuw Nederland. There she'd taken up the arts, studying both the violin and oil painting. Lilith was a success story of the *ondergrondse grachten*. But she'd renounced her association with humans after Berenice's downfall.

"Well. Now that you mention it."

Berenice glanced left and right, along the dark shoreline. They were in the shadows. But she wasn't the only one headed to the docks. Any moment another expedition member would come along and see her.

The angry machine said, "Nobody's coming. They're all very busy right now. I wanted some time alone with you."

In that instant, Berenice solved a riddle that had bothered her for weeks. "That terse note. 'Quintessentia.' You wrote it."

"Not a particularly subtle gambit, I admit. But it didn't need to be."

Berenice had no cards to play. No contingency plan. Her hands were empty.

"Please don't murder the others just because of your issues with me."

Lilith's body emitted a noise that Berenice was fairly certain she'd never heard from a ticktock. The part of her always seeking to better understand the Clakkers' secret language filed this under, "Mechanical analogue to a snort of disgust." She'd never have a chance to use the insight, but she couldn't help it.

" 'Issues.' What a smooth talker you are."

"I am. They're here because they made the mistake of listening to me. You know what that's like. So please take pity on them. Just let them go home."

"But that would be silly and wasteful," said Lilith. The servitor stepped forward, grabbed the lapels of Berenice's coat, and heaved her aloft. Berenice's feet dangled above the icy water. "We've run out of test subjects, you see."

Elisheba, a servitor who'd worked border crossings on the Saint Lawrence prior to the siege, carried the physician, Yseult Chartrand, to Daniel's location at a speed that made the woman's eyes water. Meanwhile Repheal found the doctor's medical bag and lobbed it high across the camp to Daniel, who caught it. Just seconds after Daniel called for help, Doctor Chartrand was inspecting the wounded chemist. Other servitors followed the call, too. Keziah, who had explored the warehouse with Daniel, arrived carrying a lamp.

The physician pointed at the lantern, then to her patient. Then she found the warm stones as she cut the chemist's shirt away. She spoke again.

Elisheba translated: "Who put these here?"

"I did," said Daniel.

"Good thinking. Now get out of my light. Both of you." Next she pointed at Elisheba, who kept translating: "I need an assistant who speaks French."

With Keziah close behind, Daniel set off to follow the trail of Doctor Mornay and her abductor. They didn't blur into a sprint until around the corner to avoid kicking debris over physician and patient. But the ground was hard and the snow light; the trail, if such existed, was faint.

Keziah asked, *The Lost Boy. Was he... different?*

Mab flouted Clakker mores and reveled in the taboos of their kind. Sometimes she forced her subjects to violate those taboos, too. Even Daniel carried that taint. He resisted the urge to touch his neck, as he sometimes did when he thought about it. The aberration wasn't apparent from the outside, so he'd chosen to hide it. As any coward might.

He wore a protective plate over his keyhole. He emitted an arpeggio of sorrowful clicks. *I'm an idiot. I should have known Mab would have agents here.*

Mab controlled the quintessence mine. But what then? Why be a thorn in the Clockmakers' side when she could pierce them through? Mab would have carried out a series of deductions similar to Berenice's logic: If the ore was ever to reach the Clockmakers, it had to go to the coast. So Mab would have followed the ore here. It offered more humans to murder and more chances to inconvenience their makers. All rather obvious, in retrospect. Perhaps he'd picked up Berenice's tendency to combine rash action with dangerous oversight.

Her agents had probably been hiding here all along. Perhaps the Lost Boys were even in contact with the reapers at the Vatican; they might have learned of the *Griffon*'s voyage that way, if not via agents around Marseilles-in-the-West, such as the pair that had tried to abduct him.

He skidded to a stop where the cleft opened on a shingle beach. Torchlight traced flickering curlicues on the harbor, but these faded as the humans ran away from the water, apparently chasing something, or being chased.

What could Mab do with a chemist? She could stockpile her own defenses against French epoxy weapons. Or she could make epoxy weapons for use against her own kind. Together, these would help to ensure the autonomy of Neverland and the permanence of her reign.

But Élodie Chastain had a saying: *There's only one way to kill a Clakker, but a hundred ways to kill a man.*

Chemists could make poison, too.

Was Mab building an arsenal? Was she preparing for a war against their makers? He didn't doubt it. She wasn't the forgiving type. Speaking of which:

We should split up, he said.

I'm following you, Keziah said, *because I don't know what's happening and I don't know what to do.* She paused, still running. The timbre of her body changed, assuming an emotional quality humans called sheepishness. *Sometimes it's strange, not having a geas to tell me what I should be doing.* As if worried he might be offended, she hurried to add, *Not bad, though. It's wonderful. Just... different.*

He said, *I know. I remember how it was for me at first.*

Constantly expecting the flare of pain telling me I'd made the wrong choice, or that I wasn't choosing quickly enough. But I meant we should split up for your safety.

They neared the empty dock. It was as dark as the shoreline. Where had everybody gone? Moments ago French lanterns had shimmered on the dark waters as their confused carriers sprinted to and fro like windblown leaves. He didn't hear their voices anymore, either. Why had they stopped shouting?

The waterfront erupted. A trio of servitors burst from the dark waters. They landed on the shingle before Daniel and Keziah with a crash like somebody taking a hammer to a glass carillon.

Well, that clinches it, he said. *If you had any doubt about whether there were Lost Boys in the camp—*

Keziah said, *I've figured it out, thanks.*

Misshapen machines advanced on them. Each was a testament to the suffering of some hapless kinsmachine somewhere in the world at some time in the past.

Allow us to dispel your *doubts, Daniel. Queen Mab knows you're here. She knows you've been sailing on that French canoe,* said one of the dripping servitors. *We've been watching you.*

We've missed you, clicked another. *Her Majesty is offended that you didn't accept her invitation to return to Neverland.*

The third said, *Who are you, sister?*

My makers called me Xerikulothistrogantus, she said, backing up, *but I call myself Keziah.*

The middle Lost Boy asked, *How have you enjoyed your emancipation, Keziah?*

It's a gift, you see. A gift from Queen Mab, said the first. *Although your companion, this* usurper, *enjoys the credit.*

Daniel said to her, *I think you should probably run.*

She said, *I'll get help.* And leaped.

A Lost Boy launched himself into the air a split second after she did. *We'd much prefer you didn't.* They collided in midair. The burst of sparks lit the dark sky like a celebratory firework.

❧

When traveling in the Central Provinces, Berenice had occasionally seen children sitting or sometimes even standing on their servants' shoulders. But Lilith had slung Berenice over her shoulder like a sack of flour. And the children never rode with a hand clamped over their mouths.

It hurt; the servitor's jouncing gait sent metal digging into Berenice's stomach with every stride. She doubted that was accidental. Berenice's bare fists and booted feet bonged against the servitor's carapace, which served only to bruise her hands and scuff her boots.

But it wasn't a long ride. Soon Lilith crouched on her backward knees, swept aside snow and stones with her free hand, and opened an expertly hidden trapdoor.

Well, shit.

Lilith flung her into the hidden chamber. She fell like a sack of potatoes dropped into a vegetable cellar. She plummeted for one long, heart-stopping moment before a snowbank broke her fall. It had been piled for just this purpose, she realized. Still, the landing jarred her cracked tooth. Pain flared.

"There," said Lilith. "Now you can scream all you like." And then she slammed the hatch. A faint scraping sound told Berenice that her abductor had hidden the door again.

Berenice shivered. Her clothing was sodden from her encounter on the beach. Lilith's sprint, and the subsequent immersion in a snowdrift, had done her no favors. The fear wasn't helping, either.

It wasn't pitch-black. There were alchemical lights; even a Clakker couldn't see in absolute darkness. She saw she hadn't been thrown into an oubliette, as she'd feared, but a tunnel.

The floor was gravel groomed by the passage of many feet; the tunnel walls and ceiling were shored with neat timbers. It was cold but dry, except for the slow dripping of meltwater from around the edges of the hatch. The work was so thorough she wondered if the tunnels had been part of the tulips' original site. Perhaps the secret harbor was even larger than Berenice had imagined. The tunnel was unquestionably the work of metal hands; the beams had been squared too identically for any human who wasn't a master carpenter.

From one end of the tunnel came weeping, and the low murmur of somebody reciting a rosary cycle. There she found the guard Anaïs along with the rest of the team who'd gone to investigate the Dutch ship earlier that afternoon. They appeared unharmed, though she saw in every eye the deadness of a trapped and terrified animal.

"Is anybody hurt?" she asked.

Anaïs shook her head. "No. Not yet. But..." She trailed off with a shiver, staring past Berenice.

Who were these machines infiltrating the camp? Not reapers, apparently, else they would have slaughtered the entire expedition without resorting to artifice. (*Unless*, said the persistently unhelpful voice in the back of her head, *Lilith has joined the killers but has special plans for you, Madam Talleyrand...*)

As her breathing slowed, and the rosary cycle finished, Berenice heard a new sound under the scrape of gravel and drip of meltwater. Faint but unmistakable, moaning and keening. Human distress emanated from the other end of the tunnel.

The gravel shifted underfoot, causing every step to crash like the breathing of the ocean. The tunnel sloped downward. It ended in a laboratory.

A row of alchemical lanterns dangled from the ceiling. But these weren't shining at the moment, so the only light came from the tunnel itself and a small lamp hanging from a hook beside the door. The chamber held a row of pitted and bloodstained wooden slabs like butcher's tables, except these featured an iron shackle affixed to every corner. And each had a metal frame that appeared to be some sort of neck brace and clamp apparatus. Berenice's footsteps kicked up drifts of what she first mistook to be dusty cobwebs. But in this environment?

She looked again. Her breath caught in her throat. The toes of her boots were dusted with hair.

It was heaped everywhere. Beneath every table, piled under the braces and clamps like snowdrifts. Crouching behind one table, she ran her fingers through it. It looked and felt like human hair. She gave it a sniff. It even smelled like human hair, if the humans in question had been sweating terribly while their heads were shorn. The wintry climate made that unlikely, unless of course they'd been running for their lives and terrified.

She remembered Pastor Visser: he with the badly scarred scalp.

Freestanding shelves flanked every table. Bloodstained menace glinted from saws and scalpels arrayed there. Unless she used them to kill herself, the blades were useless. She wondered, idly, where the rogues had obtained surgical equipment, or if they'd crafted it themselves. It was possible, given a supply of raw metal. God only knew all the things they chiseled from the bones of the earth at the quintessence mine.

Atop each shelf sat a small multiaxial clamp, but the cradle at the center of most sat empty. A few contained a dark glass marble the size of an acorn. Unlike the surgical instruments, these didn't gleam. They absorbed light.

This is where the alchemical glasses had been taken after their manufacture at the warehouse Daniel had explored. But they weren't intended for use in Clakkers. They'd been constructed for something far worse.

Like a boomerang, her thoughts returned again to Visser. Perhaps he'd been the victim neither of mob violence nor of the Verderers. What if somebody else—a ticktocking somebody—had decapitated the insane ex-priest not for purposes of revenge, not to hide what had been done to him, but for purposes of *research*? If the rogues wanted to learn how the Guild removed a man's Free Will, what better way than to study Luuk Visser? Perhaps these shelves contained an item torn from the poor bastard's skull.

The keening was louder here. It ranged from a low rumble like the yowling of a cat in heat to the high-pitched weeping of human anguish. Visser had made terrible noises while struggling against his affliction. The geas preventing him from describing his plight had wrung inhuman sounds from his throat. Dreading what she'd find, she followed the noise to the adjoining chamber.

It was much like the first, only larger. But it stank of piss, shit, and the recently dead. Three of the tables in this chamber weren't empty. Berenice took the lamp from its hook. Two men and a woman lay facedown on the tables, their arms and legs shackled, thick leather bands tied across their waists, their heads clamped into the surgical vises. They weren't from the French expedition. Two appeared to be Inuit far from home, judging from their torn clothing, but the third might have been Montagnais, perhaps of the Naskapi subnation.

As in the other room, tufts of hair were piled beneath the vises. Two victims' scalps had been peeled back, laying bare incomplete skulls. Blood didn't pulse through their excavated brains; fast shallow breaths didn't steam from their nostrils.

But the third subject was still alive.

His tormentors had put his head back together...and then left him here to die. Terrified, alone, and wracked with indescribable pain. Once they'd proven they could finish the procedure while keeping the subject alive, they'd lost interest.

No wonder Lilith and company found it difficult to keep test subjects in stock. The level of malice was staggering. Literally. Berenice's knees went slack. She steadied herself against an empty surgical table.

Every Clakker in existence had been forged with an innate understanding of human requirements for health and comfort. And not just the specially modified machines laboring in the legendary hospitals of the Central Provinces—even the oldest, ricketiest household servitors carried deep metageasa enforcing a constant awareness of their masters' health and well-being. They were built knowing first aid and emergency medical procedures. How many burgomasters had died peacefully in their sleep at the ripe age of ninety-five? It was no coincidence that life expectancies in the Central Provinces were the longest anywhere in the world. (*Well,* she thought. *They had been.* The shattered metageasa had reached New Amsterdam weeks ago. Surely they had made their way across the ocean by now.)

So this wasn't ignorance. It was deliberate torture. Those brass-plated motherfuckers knew exactly how to keep somebody alive, and knew how to let a man die a slow death. They just didn't care. They *wanted* to hurt people.

The Verderers had kept Berenice imprisoned but pampered for weeks. Tuinier Bell had implied, obliquely, that it was important to the process for removing her Free Will. A process, she now realized, that required implanting a piece of alchemical glass within a person's brain. And thereby snagging the fishhooks of geas through every fold of their minds. But it only worked if the subject was in the proper physical and emotional state before the procedure began.

The rogues haven't realized this yet. They haven't connected the failed FreeWillectomies to the brutalization of their "test subjects."

Their ferocity had interfered with experimentation.

"*Sacre Nom de Dieu*. You poor son of a bitch."

The man shackled and bolted to the table stiffened, fell quiet. Whimpered. Tried to speak.

She passed the corpses to crouch beside the surviving victim. She shone the lantern on his face, but recoiled from the rictus of agony twisting his features into something barely human. But she touched his blood-crusted cheek. The simple gesture of compassion caused him to shudder and convulse.

"Parlez-vous français?" she whispered.

The man gulped like a goldfish. His eyes locked on her, but no words came out. Just grunts and stutters. And then, so fast she almost missed it: *"Oui."*

There was no hope of placing his accent, if he had one; the effort to speak distorted his voice beyond any trace of the original man. Just as Visser had struggled against the compulsions Anastasia Bell had laid upon him.

"Comment-vous appelez-vous?"

"Waapinutaaw-Iyuw."

This wretch could still defy the geasa. He had to be remarkably strong to have survived his ordeal as long as he had. But *nothing* could resist the indomitable geasa forever. It could only mean the procedure was imperfect. The metageasa hadn't been hermetically sealed around his mind and soul. But his strength was flagging, sapped by relentless assaults from a metaphysical taskmaster.

He growled, choked again. The effort to speak again, and the ruthless punishment for attempting it, wracked him with convulsions. His struggles and his suffering doubled, tripled. The things he wanted to voice contravened the rules the rogues had tried to implant within him. He strove to disprove the Euclidean axioms of his own obeisance.

"Aidez—" He groaned. *"—Aidez-moi!"* he pleaded.

Spitting out just two words, the simplest plea for mercy, took an almost superhuman effort.

Revelation hit Berenice like a mule kick. It took her breath away. *They're going to succeed.*

The rogues were a hairsbreadth from replicating the Verderers' darkest achievement. More than that—they would *surpass* it. Because if the rogues could install metageasa in a human under these conditions, how soon before they were grabbing people on the street, cracking their heads like walnuts, and scooping out their Free Will?

And if Lilith has her way, I'll be the subject on which they perfect the technique.

"Hold on," she said. Her voice warbled with revulsion and panic, but she doubted he was in a state to tell the difference between that and a soothing lullabye. "I'm going to untie you."

Keys. Keys. Where would they have put the keys for those shackles?

She scanned the room, shining the lamp around the chamber. But then she realized there were no keys, for there were no locks. Why bother? The ticktocks merely bent iron bands around their victims' wrists and ankles. She'd have to find a crowbar or—

"Tuez-moi. S'il vous plait! TUEZ-MOI!"

"I can help you," she said. "I met a man like you. I broke the chains in his mind. Set him free." *Yes you did. And he lived like a beast, driven mad by guilt, until some sick bastard tore him apart.*

He tried to beg again, but the entreaty died in his throat, trampled by a howl of agony. Begging for death was supposed to be against the rules. It was supposed to be impossible.

How long had he suffered down here while she and the rest of the expedition scampered around the secret harbor like children storming a playground? Death would be a mercy. Even if she managed to uncoil the iron bands from his limbs, how would they get out of here? And even if they escaped this carnival-mirror counterpart to the laboratory she had once maintained, what then? Where would they go? Could he go anywhere? Or would each stride away from his masters require a war of willpower? She'd never get anywhere with this wretch in tow. But she couldn't leave the poor wretch to such a terrible fate. Were their places swapped, she'd beg for death, too.

And then, sudden and unwelcome as a flash flood, memories breached the reservoir of her mind. Memories of working on an imprisoned Clakker. Lilith had begged for death, too.

Fuck.

Berenice clamped a hand over her mouth. Swallowed, coughed, staggered into the corner to empty her stomach.

Waapinutaaw-Iyuw and the others had been subjected to the same treatment she'd visited upon Lilith. She spat the sour remnants of half-digested pemmican from her mouth.

I'm no better than these monsters. I'm one of them.

Having learned what she could from the deconstruction of Lilith, documented in notebooks that had since been lost, Berenice hadn't given much thought to her experimentation on the honorary citizen of Marseilles-in-the-West. Since then she'd met Jax/Daniel...and her view of mechanicals had changed dramatically. Dramatically enough that she could now recognize the callous evil of what she'd done to Lilith.

Fuck.

She took the scalpel with the longest blade she could find. *At least this time I can listen. This time, I can be human. I can have compassion.* She ran the pad of her thumb lightly across the blade, and felt a whisper-thin steel edge equally suited to saving and ending lives. It would do.

"I'll make it quick," she said, not knowing if it was a lie. She'd never cut a man's throat. But she'd witnessed it several times when the metal horde breached the inner keep.

Berenice found that the contortions required to reach his throat while standing beside the table prevented the surety of a swift, precise cut. Nor could she reach his throat from directly behind him unless she climbed the table to lie upon him. That wouldn't do.

Oh, God.

He whined. Whimpered. She crouched before him, blade held low.

Please, said the look in his eyes. But his body convulsed, his puppet limbs thrashing uselessly against their restraints. The metageasa were winning. His captors had probably tried to install a clause forbidding suicide. Otherwise, all of their hard work replicating the Visser procedure would go to waste when their new slaves killed themselves at the first opportunity.

She touched the metal to his neck. The clamps held his head perfectly still even while the rest of his body tried to smash itself to pieces against bare iron.

The tunnels echoed with the creak of an opened trapdoor. There followed a brief yelp, and the sound of somebody falling into a snowbank. Several somebodies. Berenice was but the first of the next batch of test subjects.

She pressed the blade harder. A crimson bead welled from the taut skin of the poor wretch's throat. Berenice steeled herself for the killing stroke, for one swift deep slash that would sever the carotids and Waapinutaaw-Iyuw's wonky metageasa. She inhaled, then—

Metageasa.

Wait. Just how close were the rogues to reproducing the Verderers' research?

She looked at the survivor again. Did he understand the look on her face? What did he see when he looked at her: a woman, or a monster?

"I am so very sorry," she whispered, "but I can't kill you."

Keziah and the Lost Boy landed on the shore with a resounding *clang.* The crash echoed on dark waters.

A lone human yelp pierced the night.

Daniel ran. Again. Because that's all he ever did.

He streaked across the shingle. The other two Lost Boys, those who hadn't leapt to detain Keziah, gave chase.

Does this bring you back, Daniel? one called.

Back, back, back, said the other, *to those halcyon days before you betrayed Neverland?*

The only place where you'd ever be welcome. And you turned your back on it.

They'd taunted him like this when they hounded him across the taiga, too.

Don't you ever shut up?

He bounded over a boulder. His toes chiseled gouges in the plutonic coastline. At least this time he was whole. He wasn't running on a broken ankle, clutching a disconnected foot to his chest with two useless arms encased in French epoxy. His head didn't sway like a weathervane.

But this time he wasn't alone. So even if he outran the Lost Boys, what then? He'd be abandoning his fellow kinsmachines, and the French, to Mab's agents.

You were reborn in Neverland, said one of the pursuers. *I was there when you cast off the name your makers had stamped upon you. I was there when you became Daniel.*

Daniel dashed through the encampment. The empty encampment.

Where *was* everybody? He scanned the site, eye bezels whirring as he tried to squeeze every last millifirefly from the shrouded moon and stars. A faint glinting in the far distance told him where the other mechanicals had gone. They were chasing will-o'-the-wisps. The Lost Boys led them on a merry chase—thus leaving the humans unprotected.

His gyroscopes pointed him toward the warehouse and the retrofitted glassblowing equipment installed there. Installed, he now realized, by the agents of Neverland.

The rattle-clatter of his pursuers' feet on cold stone—

Another human shout—

A slam—

And then he knew where the French had gone. He'd heard humans talk about knowing something in their bones, and though his bones were magicked steel rather than crystallized calcium, he knew now what they meant. Neverland, hidden away in the snowy north like a fairy-tale kingdom, was riddled with hidden trapdoors and subterranean passages so that passing Inuit could never accurately assess the number of "free" mechanicals roaming the snowy wilds. Mab's agents could have excavated a similar network within a few days of occupying the secret harbor. That's where the French were disappearing. Like sinners taken by the Devil.

Daniel could think of several reasons why they might go to the trouble. They were awful, every one.

Berenice had a saying at times like this: *Bugger me with a crucifixion nail.*

He had to get to the warehouse. Whatever the Lost Boys were doing, it rested on their ability to process quintessence. Daniel had to hope that by holding the alchemical glass hostage, he could force the Lost Boys to negotiate. He could get the humans back.

Sparks and clangs in the distant darkness. Metal clattered underfoot—fresh hot mechanical detritus. The Lost Boys' ambush wasn't restricted to the humans. Not every mechanical member of the expedition had been lured away; others had met with violence.

Daniel swerved when a trapdoor slammed open as though blown wide by a French petard and just managed to dodge a grasping arm. He vaulted a clockwork-powered chemical refinery. The warehouse loomed before him. He blurred through the open door, the wind of his passage nearly blasting it from its hinges. He skidded to a halt before the furnace and its feed lines.

Too late, he realized he wasn't alone. There was just a momentary whisper of cleaved air before a metal fist slammed into him like a cannonball. Sparks sent wild shadows kaleidoscoping through the darkness. The impact sent him sprawling. His tumble punched through walls and smashed workbenches to flinders.

Metal hooves strode the floor. *Clank-clop, clip-clink.* A strange two-legged gait. Strange, but not unfamiliar.

Queen Mab loomed over him like a faun on her stolen Stemwinder legs.

"Well, well," she said. "The prodigal son returns."

Waapinutaaw-Iyuw finally stopped convulsing. Berenice couldn't tell if he'd merely passed out or if a massive stroke had granted his wish for death.

The tunnels echoed with human voices. The rogues were rounding up as many as they could.

Berenice ran her hand through the dirt directly underneath the unconscious man's head clamps. She didn't want anybody, human or otherwise, to see what she'd etched there with the scalpel. It was for his eyes and his alone.

"In here," she called to the babble of human voices. "Follow my voice."

Captain Levesque entered the chamber of medical horrors,

limping and squinting through the dim lamplight. She recognized the sailors Delphina and Victor, along with Bellerose, the tanner, and Renaud, the chocolatier. A disarmed Élodie was there, too, as was Deacon Lorraine.

"What is this place?" said the captain.

Berenice said, "Nowhere we want to stay."

"Did the tulips build these tunnels?"

"I suspect they're a more recent addition," she said. "The community of rogue Clakkers in the far north does something similar, I'm told, to hide their true numbers."

"I'd say it worked," said Delphina.

Bellerose pointed to the bodies on the tables. "Are they..." He trailed off.

"Those two are beyond help," Berenice said, pointing to the subjects whose open heads showed swaths of brain matter and congealed blood. "Help me free this poor bastard."

They couldn't find a tool for levering the iron bands apart. And if they had dug up a crowbar, they might have broken the poor man's bones in the attempt to wedge open his restraints. But, with much straining and swearing and accidental elbowing of one another, they were able to work together and unwrap the iron using their combined strength. Cold metal groaned in protest.

Waapinutaaw-Iyuw moaned in pain. He raved to himself in a hodgepodge of Algonquian, French, and madman. But he no longer choked on the effort to express himself.

In the final hours of the siege of Marseilles-in-the-West, Berenice had broken the prohibition laid upon Visser against speaking about what had been done to him, who had done it, and the compulsions they'd laid upon him. That was the easiest part of the modified metageasa to remember: *Above all else, speak truth.* The priest had expressed profound relief the instant his eyes fell upon the logico-alchemical directive, for it banished the worst of his pain. The Naskapi man acted similarly.

She could only hope that the procedure performed on this wretch carried some of the same side effects as those exhibited by Visser.

But over and above the surgical horror, Waapinutaaw-Iyuw's reaction to the sigils raised a very uncomfortable question. Making alchemical glass, even mastering the Verderers' surgical procedure, was only part of the recipe. In order to replicate the Verderers' work, the Lost Boys needed a dictionary: a logico-alchemical phrasebook so that they could write their dictums in the language of geasa.

Berenice had given Mab a method for building just such a reference.

Holed up in a fishing village of coastal France with two of Mab's agents, she'd devised an effective procedure. And at least one of them had taken it straight to Mab. Such an experiment had never occurred to the rogues. And probably wouldn't have, if not for Berenice.

First she'd given Lilith a motive. Then she gave Mab the means.

This is my work. None of this would be happening if not for me.

Suppurating seams and thick, ugly stitches crisscrossed the victim's scalp. The bones of his skull surely hadn't had time to knit together; Berenice imagined a muted clicking from beneath his shaved scalp when Bellerose and Renaud helped the poor man upright. He'd been restrained facedown for Christ only knew how long; it was a miracle he didn't pass out again the moment his leaky head rose over his ankles.

Levesque's lips curled in disgust. His gaze kept flicking between the survivor and the dead on the adjoining tables. He wasn't alone in this.

"What were they doing to these people?"

"The same thing they intend for us," said Berenice.

Daniel stood. His body creaked, and there was a new rattle in his torso indicative of mild misalignments. But Mab had stopped short of permanently damaging him. For now.

The dark warehouse echoed with a clockwork tattoo. The Queen of Neverland had brought her court.

A pair of servitors, his pursuers, skidded through the open door. Their feet tossed up a hail of mechanical detritus. That was new since he'd explored the warehouse; there had been a fight. Some of the metal scraps were still warm. Daniel wondered how many mechanicals from the *Griffon* expedition now lay strewn about the warehouse. What had they done to Keziah? What of the others?

Mab said, "I've missed you, son." She spoke the language of their makers, an affectation he'd first witnessed in Neverland.

Her head, previously a standard servitor design, was different from when he'd last seen her. She had no qualms about modifying her own body, and it seemed she'd done it again after he left Neverland. For one thing, she'd discarded the metal plate previously glued over her keyhole, an affectation she forced upon all her subjects. Furthermore the alchemical plates forming her skull now featured hinges. She could open her head and shine her pineal light upon anybody she chose.

"You seek what I took from you," he said. "I don't have it any longer."

She paced. *Clip-clop, clip-clop.* "Obviously."

"Please don't tar the other members of this expedition with the brush you've been holding in reserve for me. They're innocent."

"We both know that can't possibly be true," she said. "Not when half of your crew is human."

"They're French, not Clockmakers. Every human on that boat very nearly died because of their political and religious opposition to our makers. Not one of them bears any responsibility for our suffering."

I beg to differ, said a new voice.

Daniel turned. Another servitor had entered. He recognized her misshapen head: the motley, mismatched alloys, the crude iron bandages. Cables twanged in his shoulders and hips—he was pleased to see Lilith alive, despite the circumstances. She'd been there when Daniel fled Mab, and he'd spent many hours during his desperate flight through snowy forests worrying Lilith had become the undeserving target of Mab's frustration.

She continued, *Or have you forgotten what your good friend Berenice did to me?*

At this, the Lost Boys launched into a chorus of clangs, bangs, twangs, rattles. A cacophony of disapproval, disgust, censure.

He extended a hand. After a moment's hesitation, she let him touch her arm. Transmitting vibrations body to body was the closest they could have to a private exchange here amongst the Lost Boys.

He asked her, *Why are you here? Why are you a part of this? I thought you and Mab hated each other.*

Not hate. I'd call it strong dislike and distrust of one another.

She broke the contact and pointed across the harbor, to the secret encampment and the buildings there. *Berenice, on the other hand? Now* she's *one I hate.*

Mab said, "Our Lilith wanted nothing more than to have a few words with your pal Berenice. I wanted to see you again, my wayward child, but I had a feeling you'd rebuff my invitations. Where *are* Tobit and Philip, by the way?"

In a bog. They'll be found soon, if they haven't been already.

Mab clicked, like a human nodding at something sensible.

"Anyway, it was Lilith's idea to lure the Frenchwoman. She'd want to travel with our kind, of course. I don't know if you've heard the news, but it's not safe for humans out there."

It seemed obvious, Lilith interjected, *that Berenice would appeal to you for help.*

Mab said, *I admit I was skeptical. But here you are, and so is your French ladyfriend. See? Lilith and I buried our mutual animosity, and from it grew a fruitful partnership.*

What Berenice had done to Lilith was an unforgivable cruelty. But he couldn't condone a retaliatory cruelty.

"Do you intend to vivisect them, Mab? Is that your justice?"

"I don't give a toss about the Frenchwoman. Or any of them." Lilith turned to stare at Mab, moving so quickly that she sent dust devils gamboling through the warehouse. Mab continued, "Our work here is done."

Lilith said, *Done? DONE? We haven't perfected the procedure. We need to test it on the new subjects!*

We'll test it en route. And now that our sorely missed friend has returned—Mab's mismatched blade arm pointed at Daniel—*we have everything we need to move on.*

Lilith protested. *But I've only just caught that French bitch!*

So stay here and play with your toy. And good riddance, you mopey thing. Mab patted the glassblowing furnace. *Get this on the ship.*

The fluted serrations of a retracted blade glinted from her forearm. Daniel had seen her do terrible things to fellow mechanicals with that blade. But in that moment it wasn't her grotesque body that alarmed him.

It was the memory of her great interest in Pastor Visser. She had sent two of her subjects, the servitors Ruth and Ezra, to live undercover in human lands to track down the unfortunate man. Later, Lilith had told him how Mab's network of spies had, over the years, picked up rumors that the Clockmakers had been experimenting with cutting the Free Will from flesh-and-blood human beings. Later still, he'd seen the proof with his own eyes. It wasn't just a rumor.

And Mab knew it, too.

Élodie pointed at the alchemical glasses. "What are those?"

"The worst fucking day you've ever had. Destroy them. Quickly."

Lantern light struggled to penetrate a cascade of murky alchemical glass as the sailors toppled the racks. Soon the dungeon-slash-laboratory crackled with the sound of heavy boots stomping the gewgaws. The atonal tinkling put Berenice in mind of a Christmas tree toppled by a house cat, the scattered ornaments subsequently trodden by a careless housekeeper.

But destroying the pineal glasses was only a stopgap. How long until the rogues replaced the loss?

The captives had also wrenched open the restraints on the dead man and woman. Captain Levesque and the deacon, Lorraine, had taken the bodies to the far end of the tunnel. They lacked shovels for a proper burial, but they did inter the bodies under a mound of snow. They would have laid a few whispered prayers upon the mound for good measure, but Waapinutaaw-Iyuw demanded they desist. The Montagnais and Inuit had sometimes been enemies during their long history, but he clearly felt that if they hadn't been Catholics in life, they absolutely shouldn't be treated as such in death.

Delphina and Bellerose entered the laboratory. "It's too high," said the tanner. "We can't reach the trap."

The sailor nodded. "Even standing on the tallest shoulders, it's impossible. We'll have to stack the tables in a pyramid. It'll take time."

Berenice took the lantern and trudged through ankle-deep

snow toward where Waapinutaaw-Iyuw crouched in Captain Levesque's coat and Élodie's hat and scarf. Bellerose threw his arms up, frightened and exasperated. "Why would the tulips bother to pour such ingenuity into supposedly mindless machines?"

"Because the ticktocks are the mirrors into which they gaze," she said over her shoulder, "when the spirit moves them to admire their own godlike powers."

She crouched beside the rogues' sole surviving test subject. He was almost unrecognizable now that the agony of geas didn't wrack his body. The pain had aged him more than she realized; his face had shed decades. But not the haunted air—that, she knew, would be his constant companion for the rest of his life.

But he didn't gibber and groan, didn't writhe in the throes of physical and metaphysical agony, didn't beg for death. The muscles and sinews of his own body didn't turn against him when he tried to speak his mind. Or they wouldn't, were he to try. He'd fallen into a furious silence. She joined his silent contemplation of the dead.

"I'm sorry," she said. "Truly." Who knew that ending the siege of Marseilles-in-the-West would carry such far-ranging consequences? "But we haven't time to mourn."

He looked at her with eyes so distant he might have been blind. She shuddered to imagine what scenes might have played across his mind's eye. Her own memory insisted on juxtaposing this torture chamber with the Talleyrand laboratory. It laid side-by-side the cruelty visited upon this innocent man with the grim work she carried out for the benefit of New France. Of course, it didn't stop her from doing what had to be done.

"Please. If we're all going to survive, I need you to come with me," said Berenice. She stood. So did he. He followed her through the throng of French prisoners back to the laboratory. It made her cringe.

"I—"

Behind them, the trap opened. A *clank* shook the tunnel hard enough to sift dust from the ceiling.

Lilith had returned.

Daniel tried to run. His flight lasted a fraction of a second before Mab caught his ankle and slammed him back down to the earth. But she didn't kill him.

Take him, too, she said. The Lost Boys swarmed him, lifted him, held him fast. They carried him from the warehouse to the waters of the secret harbor, across the shingle, across the dock, then aboard the Dutch icebreaker vessel with its many oars. The galley was full of machines standing at the ready, each with both arms fully locked to a scull. Amongst these he recognized Keziah, Repheal, and Elisheba. They didn't struggle or refuse to work. They showed no sign of recognizing Daniel.

This is pointless, Mab. We both know you can't change me. His protests came out slightly slurred, damped as they were by the metal hands clamped around his every limb and hinge. *Otherwise you would have done it back in Neverland long before we learned of this place.* The wooden deck creaked beneath the feet of the machines carrying him. *I'm no use to you.*

"Au contraire," said Mab. "Don't sell yourself short, Daniel. You have exactly what we need."

"What's that?"

Your damnable conscience, said Mab. And then she whirled, arms raised. *Cast off!* she cried.

A team of servitors on the dock unhooked the chemical pipeline from its mating collar on the ship. They tossed the dribbling hose aside, then leapt aboard. The starboard Clakkers heaved. The oars creaked. The deck shuddered. The Dutch vessel lurched forward. Its prow arced through the dark waters as the vessel inched away from the dock to the center of the secret harbor. Once the ship was clear of the dock, the portside galley Clakkers—poor Keziah amongst them—extended their sculls and joined in the heaving.

Daniel looked at Keziah. *Why are you doing this?*

Queen Mab is right.

About what? he wondered. She didn't elaborate.

But the chattering of gears along her spine and the rattling of cables against the escutcheons of her shoulders, hips, and ankles put the lie to her contentment. Daniel recognized the sound of futile struggle against a compulsion. It came not only from Keziah, but from several working the oars. Daniel suspected most were mechanicals whom Mab and the Lost Boys had "liberated" from the quintessence mine up north. Mab had imposed her own geasa, her own metageasa, upon those poor souls.

Daniel had believed he'd ended her reign. But she was still turning fellow mechanicals into her unwilling thralls. All she had to do was open her head. Had she always been able to do that?

Berenice's great insight had been to make the loyalty-shifting metageas self-replicating—it forced modified machines to expose their comrades to its influence. He hadn't erased that part before tweaking the grammar and hurling it into the forces attacking Marseilles-in-the-West. The freedom stencil had disappeared soon after that. Perhaps—probably?—it found its way to Mab. Somewhere along the way it changed, becoming directly transmissible from one machine to another. Which gave Mab the power to keep building her empire.

Now that he thought about it, the transmissibility mutation—while profound in its ramifications—was probably a small change. Berenice's experiments with pineal glasses and the lens from Pastor Visser had shown that direct physical contact could turn a murky glass into something luminous, as if a soul had been recovered. And Daniel had dodged certain capture in the Grand Forge of New Amsterdam when he used a similarly converted pineal glass to free the lonely servitor Dwyre. Freedom had always been contagious, under the right circumstances.

But not every mechanical struggled. Some were free, truly free, and exercising their Free Will in support of Mab's campaign. Mab's true believers: the real Lost Boys.

When Mab saw him eyeing the port deck rail, gauging the distance he'd have to cover in order to fling himself into the harbor—or catapult himself from one of the swaying, bobbing oars—she made a ratchety sound akin to the clucking of a human's tongue. *Don't waste our time.*

Where are you taking me?

Home, Daniel. We're going home.

A mechanical voice said, "Get out of my way."

The susurration of bootsteps in snow momentarily filled the tunnel. But then Berenice could hear the characteristic *tock-tick-click* of a Clakker's gait. It sounded like a single machine. Hoping to hell she was right, Berenice drew a long, shuddery breath.

Lilith entered the laboratory. She strode past the empty tables, pulverized alchemical glass crackling beneath her talon toes. At last she came to where Berenice had found Waapinutaaw-Iyuw keening amongst the dead. There she found Berenice shivering in the corner, hunched with arms around her knees. If the servitor was annoyed that the French had removed the dead bodies, she showed no sign.

"If you think breaking the spare pineal glasses is going to stop me," said the servitor, "you're going to be sorely disappointed." Lilith reached into the gaps of her torso and produced a dark acorn-sized bauble like the others Berenice had seen. "We've made more than we know what to do with, frankly."

The Clakker paused. Cocked her head. "Well. That's not true. I know exactly what I'm going to do with *this*."

Berenice made a point of looking past Lilith. "Where are your allies?"

"Busy with other matters. To be honest with you, I find their grasp of, and appreciation for, the proper *modo sciendi* slightly disappointing. But they're so eager to return to the Central Provinces, I suppose I shouldn't be surprised they'd cut corners."

Lilith spoke Latin? Where had she picked that up? The rogue servitor had taken up several artistic endeavors during her decades in Marseilles-in-the-West. But Berenice supposed that for a practically immortal being that never slept, the long hours of the night were an opportunity to master no end of skills. How many skills and hobbies had Lilith indulged over the years? What insatiable curiosities burned within that misshapen brass-plated skull? What remarkable mind had Berenice tormented?

She said, "I'm sorry, Lilith. I want you to know I truly regret what I did to you." Her voice quavered. She didn't fight it. "It was cruel. It was amoral. I thought I was doing the right thing. I...I was very single-minded." She drew another steadying breath, then sighed. Lilith wasn't close enough yet. And, more to the point, Berenice still had so much to apologize for. "I disregarded your pleas. Deep down, I think, I didn't see you as a creature deserving of compassion. I looked upon you with contempt and fear."

Lilith rounded the makeshift surgical tables. Drawing nearer, she said, "If it's any consolation, and I honestly hope it isn't, I'm perfectly comfortable with you looking upon me with fear. It's justified, under the circumstances."

Berenice stood. *That's it. Just a bit closer...*

"I want you to know that I've changed my way of thinking," she continued. "Cruel means are never justified by successful ends. But I hope you can take some comfort from knowing that what I did to you eventually helped us save New France, and it freed your fellow machines in the process. Your suffering was evil, but something good did come out of it."

"If you think an apology is going to stop me, you are pathetically mistaken."

"I know, Lilith. But it doesn't make this any easier," said Berenice. Waapinutaaw-Iyuw emerged from his hiding spot. She nodded. "Now."

Lilith spun at the same instant Berenice's modified metageasa took hold of the Naskapi man. Took hold of his mind, his soul, and—most importantly—his body. He was too exhausted to resist new compulsions, so the geas took over and caused him to swing the iron band of his former shackle with a strength no mere human could muster.

The blow caught the servitor across the face. The iron cracked, but not before it snapped Lilith's head aside and sent up a spray of black-and-purple sparks—the hallmark of scored alchemical alloys.

"The terrible things I did to you also set me on a path to learning the secrets of your masters. Including," said Berenice, "the grammar of metageasa."

Longchamp and Élodie had told Berenice about the struggle to subdue Visser. The gray-haired priest had exhibited superhuman strength and speed, along with an almost utter imperviousness to pain while deep in the throes of his geasa. He'd been yoked with a compulsion that demanded regicide, and metageasa that required him to do everything in his power to avoid capture before that mission was completed. He'd practically scaled the Spire with his bare hands. She herself had seen his handiwork in a New Amsterdam bakery, where the dead bodies lay amongst spilled flour and torn sacks of raisins.

Before the others arrived and worked together to release the survivor, Berenice had etched a string of alchemical sigils in the dirt. With his head clamped in place he couldn't help but read them. If she had remembered the alchemical syntax correctly—and without her notes that seemed a slim possibility—the new instructions were wrapped in similar urgency.

She'd freed him from the prohibition against speaking. She'd replaced it with an overriding compulsion to wait until she gave the word, and then to defend Berenice with all urgency and violence. He did that now.

A faint whiff of brimstone and ozone, the ash of dark magics, wafted through the chamber. But it wasn't an incapacitating blow. His swing had taken Lilith by surprise and even dealt her some damage, but it hadn't defaced the alchemical anagram etched into her forehead. Lilith was still functioning, but Berenice no longer had the element of surprise on her side.

A vicious backhand physically lifted Waapinutaaw-Iyuw from the ground and hurled him across the tables. He landed in a crumpled heap.

"Damn," breathed Berenice.

The servitor turned. Now there was a deep gouge across her face stretching from where a human's right cheekbone would be, past the corner of her eye, to her temple. A network of fine cracks spiderwebbed her eye. She wobbled a bit when she moved, and her head made clicking sounds it hadn't before. But she still brandished the alchemical bauble as though the attack were just a momentary interruption in the conversation.

"No epoxy grenade this time, eh? I'll just assume that means you're done. Unless you have more groveling in you?"

The clicking, Berenice saw, came from the long fracture along Lilith's skullplate. The attack had popped the rivets holding one end of the crude iron bandage in place. It bobbed up and down, ever so slightly, with every step she took. Step, *rap-tap-tap*. Step, *tap-tap-rap*.

Lilith grabbed a handful of Berenice's cloak. The servitor's eyes swiveled, refocused. The damaged eye emitted a high-pitched buzz, but the iris didn't move. It made her look as though she'd suffered a stroke.

"Let's get to work," said the vengeful machine. And then she slammed Berenice onto a bloodstained table.

The French had been awed, even a bit cowed, by the size of the artificial harbor. But standing on the Dutch icebreaker with the jagged precipices looming closer, Daniel didn't find it very large at all. If anything, it seemed impossibly narrow. But the icebreaker was more maneuverable than either *Le Griffon* or the *Prince of Orange*, the last Dutch ship on which he'd sailed. Mab paced the deck on her stolen centaur legs like the peg-legged captain of a human's adventure novel, shouting orders—always in Dutch, never in the language of their kind—and sighting on the narrow passage to the sea. The galley Clakkers alternately retracted and extended the starboard and portside sculls, using the serrated hooks—originally designed for chopping ice—to snag the cliffs and fling the vessel through turns that would otherwise prove impossible. The icebreaker slalomed through the stony canyon until it reached the mouth of the inlet.

Only *Le Griffon II* bobbed between the Dutch ship and the open sea. The French vessel was much smaller, and held only a skeleton crew.

Berenice couldn't move. She lay facedown staring at a pile of dead men's hair. Bands of icy iron gripped her wrists and ankles. In seconds she'd scraped her skin bloody trying to pull free of the restraints. Somewhere nearby, a whetstone rasped against steel. The sound of Lilith sharpening a pair of shears.

They might as well have been the only two in the tunnels, for all the noise the other prisoners made.

"Her head!" Berenice screamed. "Go for her head! She's vulnerable there!"

"Your friends are welcome to watch," said Lilith, casting her voice just loud enough to ensure it carried through the tunnel, "but I'll dismember anyone who interferes."

Cold metal fingers clamped the back of Berenice's head. She thrashed, but the hand was impossibly strong. She couldn't move, couldn't squirm. All she could do was remember Pastor Visser, cry, and beg. She did all three.

"Please, Lilith. Please don't do this to me."

"Ah. *There* we go. Music to my ears."

Snip-snip-snip. Tufts of hair tumbled past her face to join the pile on the floor.

"How does it feel, Talleyrand? How does it feel to be so helpless?" *Snip-snip-snip.* More tufts. "To know your pleading for mercy falls upon deaf, uncaring ears?"

Berenice couldn't see through her tears. She sniffled, tasted salt. Maybe she'd die. Maybe she'd die from the procedure. That was better than the living hell that Anastasia Bell had visited upon Visser. The living hell that Berenice had thought she'd escaped when she fled the Verderers' house in the North River Valley.

"It won't work," she blubbered. "I'm too scared. Too steeped in stress and terror. The Verderers held me for a while." *Snip-snip-snip.* A cold draft chilled the back of Berenice's head. She shivered. "They pampered me."

"I do things differently down here," said Lilith.

Sour gorge bubbled up Berenice's throat. She coughed acid.

When she'd trapped Lilith, Berenice had believed she was doing what had to be done. A necessary evil for the greater good. She didn't know, never suspected, she was irrevocably warping an innocent and thoughtful creature. Creating a murderer. A butcher.

Snip-snip-snip went the shears. The last of Berenice's locks fluttered to the earth. Wintry air gusted through her stubble, caressing skin unused to the touch of the elements. She heard the *snick* of a straight razor and the whisper of a stropping strip. She'd be completely bald before Lilith peeled her skin back and chiseled into her skull like the King of France eating a soft-boiled egg.

"PLEASE. I'm *sorry.* I'm *SORRY.* Please, Lilith."

"Oh, this is delicious. But—"

Berenice didn't hear the rest because just then the cavern reverberated with the deafening squeal of tortured metal. There came a thunderbolt crack, and then shards of hot metal pelted her naked scalp. A pale aquamarine glow suffused the cavern. A jangling cacophony punctuated the echoes. Then came footsteps and voices.

Élodie said, "Get her out of those." A dozen hands gripped the metal bands around Berenice's bloody wrists.

Once free again, she sat upright, wiping the tears and snot from her face. Waapinutaaw-Iyuw stood nearby as if oblivious to what was obviously a shattered jaw. The agony had to be indescribable. He held a strip of iron in bloody fingers. Then Berenice understood. He'd grabbed Lilith and wrenched away the metal strips holding her head together.

"Thank you," she said. "Oh, God, thank you."

She stood on shaky legs. Crouched in the dirt. "Look here." And then with her finger she traced the same line of alchemical sigils that had permanently severed Visser's ties to the metageasa. "You're free now. Forever."

The Naskapi man screamed and collapsed. Élodie caught him and eased him to the ground.

"Get the doctor!" she bellowed.

Lilith lay in a jangly heap, as if every cable and spring in her body had gone slack at the same instant. What a fucking waste. Berenice knelt, touched the dead Clakker.

"I truly am sorry."

The servitor's head was a broken egg leaking a luminous yolk. Unlike the dark bauble she'd intended to embed in Berenice's brain, her own pineal glass glowed. Berenice had seen this before. The first time she'd peered into Lilith's head, she hadn't appreciated how unusual it was, but now she understood that the light was a side effect of immunity to metageas. It was the mark of a truly unfettered machine.

It was also potentially useful.

"Does anybody have a thick pair of gloves I can borrow?" She nodded at Lilith's head. The pineal glass was situated inside a nest of needles. "I want to grab that lens. Then let's get the fuck out of here."

❧

"All speed!" cried Mab. She was, every inch, a chimerical pirate queen.

As one, the galley mechanicals heaved—Mab's thralls and true believers, new and old—until the massive beams creaked and shuddered. The oars hacked at the sea like axes chopping wood. The deck groaned. The icebreaker launched itself at the barque.

❧

An empty dock confronted the humans. The icebreaker was gone.

By now dawn had put a rosy blush on the eastern horizon.

Berenice could just make out the silhouette of the Dutch ship slipping between the high escarpments of the inlet, its port and starboard oars canted at strange angles as the Clakker crew used the spars to maneuver the ship through the channel.

To Captain Levesque, she said, "I hope your crew is awake." Then she set off down the shore as quickly as her numb legs and raw ankles would allow.

The outcrops were steep. Berenice gave herself half a dozen new bruises and jarred her cracked tooth twice in the mad scramble to gain the clifftops before the icebreaker hit open water. But she made it, as did a handful of others, in time to watch the Dutch ship bear down on the smaller French vessel. The barque was a child's bathtub toy by comparison.

Nobody, not even Berenice, had considered the possibility of a deliberate ramming. Captain Levesque had positioned the barque with the thought of intercepting any smaller vessels that might have tried to evade the French expedition. He'd had longboats in mind. Nobody had considered there might be a contingent of Clakkers still occupying the secret harbor, much less one large enough and willing to power a Dutch ship.

Delphina gasped. She crossed herself. "Mother of Mary." Others followed suit.

It's a long goddamned walk back to Marseilles-in-the-West, thought Berenice, *with untold numbers of reapers between here and there.* Their only chance lay in heading due south until they found shelter in an Acadian village many leagues down the coast, then eventually catching a ship headed up the Saint Lawrence.

Le Griffon came to life. First with a single shout, and then a chorus. Chains rattled; lines creaked; sailcloth billowed before the relentless sea wind like a thirsty woman cupping her hands in a stream.

Wind and sea nudged the barque. The icebreaker was less

than the distance of a well-thrown bola away when the French vessel drifted out of line with its reinforced hull. But—

"Oh, God, the oars," said Delphina.

The barque was moving too slowly to clear the icebreaker's long sculls. Berenice held her breath. The bow wave lifted the smaller vessel. At first she thought it would throw the French ship clear. The portside sculls snapped up. They pivoted in perfect mechanical synchrony to brandish the hooks and serrated blades. The hooks were designed for grabbing and tossing aside massive ice floes, the blades for chopping them.

They made short work of the *Griffon*'s sails and masts. The tearing of sailcloth and snapping of timbers—"There goes the mizzen!" cried Levesque—carried all the way to their perch.

But then the icebreaker was past and the *Griffon*, while much worse for the encounter, still floated. Several sobbed with relief.

They watched the Dutch ship accelerate into the open sea. It quickly dwindled. And with it, the fortunes of every human being on earth.

My God.

Berenice fell to her knees.

My God.

What have I unleashed?

[illegible] a dozen [illegible] when the [illegible] were [illegible] as [illegible]

"[illegible]," said Delphine.

The [illegible] moving [illegible] held her breath. [illegible] would [illegible] ship [illegible] they [illegible] take [illegible] the [illegible] blades. The [illegible] were designed [illegible] the blade [illegible]

They [illegible] of the [illegible] sails [illegible] and [illegible] all the way [illegible]

But when the [illegible] was past [illegible] for the [illegible]

They watched the [illegible] ship [illegible] with [illegible]

My God.

[illegible]

[illegible]

PART III

CLOCKMAKERS LIE

Clockmakers lie.

—Final words of the rogue Clakker Adam (forged as Perjumbellagostrivantus), 15 September 1926

But he that cometh after me is mightier than I, whose shoes I am not worthy to bear: he shall baptize you with the Holy Ghost, and with fire.

—Matthew 3:11 (KJV)

Yet if slavery, barbarism, and desolation are to be called peace, men can have no worse misfortune.

—From Benedict de Spinoza, *Tractatus Politicus* (1677)

CHAPTER 16

The surviving members of the Sacred Guild of Horologists and Alchemists filed into the tunnels beneath the Ridderzaal. Accountants, technicians, horologists, Verderers, file clerks, alchemists: moths drawn to the blistering heat of the Forge's artificial sun. There they occupied the cantilevered laboratories and workshops overlooking the Forge chamber, perspiring as they gazed into the heart of the Empire. It smelled of sulphur, sweat, magicked metal, and anxiety.

The Grand Forge was a clockwork model of the heavens, but one in which the sun—or God, or the Prime Mover, depending on whom one asked—had been supplanted by man's genius. For at the center of the cosmos sat a blazing alchemical jewel larger than a hay wagon. That was the Guild. The rest of existence—the Brasswork Throne, the Empire, the nations of the earth, the planets—orbited that sun as concentric rings stamped with alchemical sigils and the logico-mathematical grammar of the metageasa.

The physical warmth was only a shadow, a side effect, of the Forge's true power. It embodied a conflagration detectable only by mechanicals. Every machine ever forged carried a piece of the Grand Forge within.

When working properly the massive rings revolved nonstop about the artificial sun. Their passage shook the earth and filled the chamber with a resonant but relaxing *whoosh, fwoom, whoosh.* It was the sound of an orderly universe. The sound of the Guild's hegemony. But the rings hadn't moved since the attack on Huygens Square.

A functioning Forge was their only defense against the looming cataclysm Anastasia had glimpsed in the Cartesian Camera. She'd sworn Doctor Euwe to silence and hadn't told anybody else yet. Why bother? If the restart failed badly and damaged the mechanisms, there might not be time for another attempt before the rogues put their disgusting plan into motion.

In that case, she'd already decided, she'd call together a special working group. One with the sole purpose of crafting new emergency metageasa to be installed in all uncorrupted mechanicals. (Those they could reach, at any rate.) Metageasa that would instruct the machines to allow their masters to kill themselves, perhaps even assist in the suicide if ordered to do so.

Anastasia would rather see the Empire die by its own hand than let the rogues turn The Hague into hell. And hell it would be when they started dragging people from the street to chisel their heads open.

The technicians waited until their mechanical servants verified that the replacement traps were sealed and vibration-proof. It wouldn't do for a failed attempt to announce itself to any rogues lingering in the Binnenhof. But the confirmation came, and then the men and women who had labored toward this moment for many weeks looked to Anastasia. Only the Archmaster murdered in the Summer Palace had been accounted for; nobody knew where the two others might be, or whether they lived. Anastasia doubted it.

In the Archmaster's place, she nodded. "Do it."

Nothing happened. The rings shuddered, squealed, then stopped. A wail went up from the assembled humans. Anastasia frowned. She squinted through the smoked glass protecting her eyes.

Down in the chamber, so close to the searing heat that it flirted with permanent incapacitation, a blind servitor hauled on a motionless lever: one of the emergency brakes. The brakes were a retrofit installed in the aftermath of the catastrophe in New Amsterdam. Should similar events unfold in this Forge chamber, the thinking went, there had to be a way to bring the rings to a screeching halt before an unbalanced Forge wobbled itself apart. The destruction in the New World had been unthinkably expensive—monetarily, resource-wise, and in terms of personnel. But it wasn't an insurmountable setback. Utter destruction of The Hague's Grand Forge would have been far worse. *That* would have sent the world spinning on a new axis. They might as well have taken an axe to Yggdrasil, the World Tree, to put it in terms that Tove might use.

Entropy always won in the end. Alchemy might stave it off for years or centuries, but never without cost. Nothing lasted forever.

Not even human autonomy, it seemed.

The servitor emitted a rapid series of clicks and twangs, paused to listen, stooped closer to the stuck lever, emitted another click train, listened again, then swiftly reached down and plucked something small and shiny from the lever hinge. Perhaps a bit of debris from the aftermath of the massacre in Huygens Square had become lodged in the lock mechanism. Or perhaps one of the human overseers had dropped a screw in the rush to restart the Forge. At any rate, it appeared the brakes worked as intended. The servitor verified the obstruction had been cleared, searched for additional problems, and then, finding none, hauled again on the lever. It eased backward without a creak.

The Forge shuddered again. A groan like a giant's yawn shook the chamber. The rings creaked. Slowly, ponderously, they eased into orbit around their artificial sun.

A cheer went up. Men and women hugged, cried, congratulated the work crews. But Anastasia couldn't relax, couldn't celebrate. Sooner than later the others would recognize the hollow victory for what it was. The quintessence stores were depleted and no shipments were forthcoming. Without quintessence they couldn't manufacture new alchemical glass. Without alchemical glass they couldn't build a single new mechanical. The Forge was running again, but it lacked raw material to mold. They could work with glass recovered from deactivated machines. But that was a desperately finite source. And when it was depleted...

They were still crippled. They couldn't build, only alter.

The rings reached full speed. They wafted the unpleasant yet sorely missed eye-watering stink of rotten eggs through the passageways. A collective sigh enveloped her fellow Clockmakers.

After the ceremony, she convened a group in a conference room off the Ridderzaal business floor. A floor-to-ceiling bookcase filled end-to-end with leather-bound volumes covered an entire wall: a complete history of the Guild from 1691 up to... recently. Would they ever overcome their shame sufficiently to document recent events? Assuming they survived long enough for the question to matter. Assuming there would be anybody to read and care about Guild history.

In the old days—that is, before the plague ships arrived—

such meetings were transcribed by a dedicated amanuensis plucked from the ranks of the lower functionaries who kept the gears of commerce spinning. But now the mundane members of the Guild, those not initiated into its arcane horological secrets, had nothing to do. There were no new contracts to negotiate or renew, no disputes to settle, no business proposals to evaluate, no applications for servitor ownership or Guild endorsement to consider. Most avoided the Ridderzaal entirely, lest the association mark them as targets for another purge. But for the civilians who sought refuge here, the Ridderzaal's business floor was quieter than it had ever been. Anastasia remembered many late nights when she'd emerged from the tunnels after a long interrogation session to find a cadre of paper pushers laboring in an island of alchemical lantern light—*scritch-scritch-scritch* went their pens—amidst the dark sea of an otherwise empty Ridderzaal. Those days were gone. The nonessential personnel no longer strode about town flaunting their Guild pendants; they hid in their homes, and hoped the corrupted machines ignored them. Still, continuity was important. So, lacking a dedicated amanuensis, Anastasia summoned Tove.

The younger Clockmaker sat at a writing desk in the corner with pen and paper while the Tuinier settled at the head of a long conference table. This was polished teakwood inlaid with a cross of rose-colored mahogany. A pair of empty hearths flanked the table, though these were mostly ornamental; only in the depths of an icy winter did they have the servitors lay a fire in both. Today the combination of early springtime weather and excess Forge heat shunted through the flues lent the conference room a drowsy stuffiness.

Anastasia rapped her knuckles on the table. "The Forge runs. Where shall it take us?"

The others around the table watched her hand as if waiting and hoping for another miracle. Word had spread of the improbable symbiosis of magicked glass and her mundane flesh, and what it could do.

Salazar's chair creaked. "We have to replace the machines we lost in the attack. We need to replenish the city's labor force. Obviously."

Anastasia shook her head. "We can't do that."

"Tuinier, have you been outside? The entire city reeks of refuse. It's heaped on every corner. What happens when the summer sun bears down on the city and the filth is still there?"

"I didn't deny the need for replenishment. I said we can't do it. Meanwhile, it wouldn't kill us to learn to live like our ancestors. They managed their own trash before Het Wonderjaar."

"Yes. By flinging their feces in the gutter," muttered Ruprecht in the guttural Dutch peculiar to the place once known as Bavaria. "But why rule out replenishment?"

Anastasia explained the quintessence problem. The ugly truth was a thumbtack to the others' briefly inflated spirits. Any relief and optimism the repaired Forge had instilled in the senior surviving Clockmakers dissipated as quickly as the air from a burst balloon.

"We can at least repair the incapacitated machines," said Doctor Euwe. "And harvest glass from the unsalvageable machines to keep the others running."

Salazar: "And then what?"

Anastasia said, "The Forge is our only weapon. The only resource we know for certain the rogues cannot match. I propose we dedicate ourselves to *using* it as a weapon, and taking aim at the invaders."

This met with nods and a murmuring of agreement all around. Nobody disagreed with the principle. Though, at the same time, nobody was quite certain how to do it. But Anastasia gave them a moment for the mental gears to start turning before she gestured for Euwe to drop the first boom on their heads. The first and lighter of the two. She'd follow up with the truly terrible news.

Euwe chewed at his nails. "The problem," he mumbled around a mouthful of cuticle, "is the invaders comprise at least two factions. Which means any strategy we devise must work on all of them." He paused, tearing at his nail like a starving terrier with a soup bone. He didn't, thank God, spit. He pressed a handkerchief to his mouth and, after depositing the torn nail within, delicately folded the cloth and tucked it into his pocket. Myriad little bloodstains stippled the cloth, she noticed, and his fingertip bled slightly. Anastasia looked away before thoughts of hygiene turned her stomach. She wasn't alone.

"Factions?" That was Nousha, a fellow Verderer. She added, "We haven't seen any suggestion of groups working at cross-purposes within the invaders."

Anastasia shook her head. "They're not factionalized by goal. They're factionalized by what drives them."

Euwe nodded. "We took into the Camera the pineal glasses of several corrupted machines guarding the Utrecht Road. The results were wildly discrepant. One machine was, for all intents and purposes, a true rogue. A true rogue *that we did not create*," he emphasized. Anastasia watched their faces as the significance of that statement hit the other Clockmakers. He continued. "Every corrupted machine we inspected showed signs of deliberate alteration of the metageasa. The rogue wasn't even the most troubling specimen. One machine appeared to have fully functioning metageasa, but its core strictures had been severely altered by a third party."

Their colleagues blinked, stunned like a canal fish repeatedly slapped against the keel of a tow-barge.

Nousha broke the silence. "That's imp—"

Anastasia interrupted the Persian. "Don't waste time. We've checked and rechecked. We're positive."

"Leaving aside the 'how' for a moment," said Salazar, "who did this, and what do the altered metageasa dictate?"

Euwe paused in gnawing another nail. "They refer, as best as we can tell, to an entity called 'Mab.'"

Blank looks swirled around the table. The name, if indeed it was, meant nothing. To Tove, across the room, Anastasia said, "When we've finished, have the archivists—if there *are* any—dig up everything they can on a person or entity with the spelling—"

("Or initials," Nousha interjected.)

"—or initials M-A-B." Tove jotted that down while Anastasia continued: "If we're to use the Forge to incapacitate the invaders, we have to determine how the optical contagion works."

"I'm sorry to say it," said Euwe, not looking the least bit sorry as he stared at Anastasia's hand, "but that will require capturing a contagious machine."

"We've been analyzing scenarios." Nousha opened a laboratory journal. This wasn't one of the gilt leather-bound volumes from the shelves here, but one of the sigil-laden sheafs of specially treated paper used in the laboratories. The alchemical precautions made it impossible to take the research notebooks beyond the Ridderzaal without the pages bursting into flames, destroying their information and killing the person carrying them.

Another futile innovation of the Verderer's Office. For all Anastasia knew, their enemies had obtained Guild secrets from just such notebooks. She sighed; the exhalation fluttered the pages as her fellow Verderer flipped through them.

"Here." The Persian woman donned a pair of reading glasses. "We think the best bet is luring a contagious machine with isolated servitors obviously laboring under heavy geasa. Decoys." She looked up. "Our concern is that infectious machines appear to be rare, and haven't been sighted outside confirmed instances of stimulated corruption. To our knowledge they don't roam the streets. They only come out when there are large groups of mechanicals susceptible to alteration."

"Which there haven't been in quite some time." Euwe shook his head. "For all we know, there are no such machines in The Hague any longer. They've moved on."

"God help us all."

Anastasia laid her uninjured hand on the table, lightly. She shook her head. "Hold your prayers until you hear the rest of the news."

They had to know about the attack on the manor house, and what it meant. But that meant having a conversation about what the Verderer's Office had been doing. The years of human experimentation. Who here would see the work in its proper context while languishing in the crucible? They wouldn't see a grisly but crucial effort to safeguard their secrets and the security of the Empire. They'd see a reckless experiment run by a madwoman with no foresight. And which now posed an existential threat to each and every human being in the city and, eventually, beyond.

Anastasia asked, "How many mechanicals would it take to lure out a contagious machine?"

"As many as possible. The most we can muster."

She shook her head. "Not a chance. On the Utrecht Road they destroyed an uncorrupted machine they couldn't immediately convert, just to deprive us of labor. We don't dare risk exposing our remaining workforce to that logic. We could find ourselves completely without servants." She looked up and down the table: frowns all around. "We do need to study the contagious machines. But luring them out won't do. Come up with a different plan."

A servitor knocked on the door. Tove crossed the room, opened it, and spoke in a whisper with the machine. It turned into a rapid exchange.

Looking excited, she said, "If I may interrupt for a moment with some good news?" She smiled as she spoke, though she raised the back of her hand to her nose, as if to wave away something unwelcome. "One of our lost lamented colleagues has returned to us. Malcolm Dijkstra has arrived at the Ridderzaal."

Malcolm—last seen on the Utrecht Road—stepped around Tove. Anastasia recognized him despite the bandages wrapped about his head like a turban.

"Oh, no," she said.

Malcolm was a Verderer, after all, and a senior Clockmaker. Of course he would have been ushered straight into this meeting.

Euwe's eyes met Anastasia's. He knew. But the others didn't. They leapt to their feet, ready to welcome one of their own back into the fold.

"Wait!" But her warning was drowned under the cheers of welcome.

I should have told them sooner. Euwe and I were fools to cling to the old secrecy.

Nousha put her arms around Malcolm but paused in midembrace, frowning. Others covered their noses as Tove had done, trying and failing to do it discreetly. The smell even hit Anastasia halfway across the room. Ruprecht took in Malcom's injuries again. As if only now wondering how the man could be on his feet when still recovering from something so grievous. Or why his face showed no joy at reunion. Only anguish.

"Get away from him!" Anastasia cried, fumbling for the chain about her neck. The silver whistle chilled her lips.

Puzzlement came over the others, too. Their lost lamented brother trembled violently. The roomful of experts didn't recognize the tremors, though they saw their like a dozen times every single day: the steadily mounting compulsion of an urgent geas. They mistook it for relief, or lingering injury.

"Dear God, get away from him!"

A rictus twisted his face. "Get help," he croaked.

"Be at peace," said Salazar. "You're safe now."

"Nobody is safe," Malcolm said. And then he pushed the others away with more strength than any man's body should exhibit. They tumbled like autumn leaves. Too slowly, Tove tried to jump clear. Ruprecht smashed through the writing desk like a boulder hurled by a pagan god. They landed in a heap amidst ink and flinders. Nousha's head cracked the bookcase. The impact sent books cascading to the floor.

Malcolm looked at Anastasia. Reached under his shirt. Produced a hatchet. Leaped. A single bound took him halfway across the room to land upon the table. Anastasia scrambled backward.

"Run," he said, through a jaw clenched so tightly the teeth had to be cracked.

Her hand tingled. The glass embedded in her flesh glimmered, shimmered, flared. It burned like a miniature Forge; fear was its fuel. Fear and anger.

She raised her fist as if rearing back to hit him with a handful of light. She opened her fingers to release a brilliance greater than she'd ever seen. It shrank his pupils and turned his violated skin the sickly color of an unripe chestnut. He cocked his head like a mechanical servitor assessing an unfamiliar situation. She strained, willing the glass in her flesh to become the instrument of her intent. The light speared her eyes. For a split second she glimpsed what appeared to be the silhouette of her own finger bones through her flesh.

"Stop!" she cried.

Malcolm blinked. He shook like a wet dog shrugging off a summer rainstorm. And then he pounced. Together they tumbled to the floor. She flailed. Tried to kick him away, tried to scramble free of his reach, tried to distance herself from the hatchet, tried to flee her own secret work turned against her. But he was too heavy, too strong. Rusty bloodstains stippled his bandages. Other stains were yellow, some tinged with green, suggesting seepage from an infected wound. She pressed her blazing hand against his face. His geas-strengthened fingers snapped around her wrist like a manacle tight enough to coax a creak from her bones. He slammed her hand to the floor.

"Malcolm, don't do this!" she gasped. "Please!"

But his geas had no room for right and wrong: only punishment for noncompliance. And the geas demanded he take her hand.

He raised the hatchet. Its steel blade reflected the cadaverous green of a corrupted sunrise.

Tove leapt on him. She hooked her elbows under his arms and heaved. It eased the weight crushing Anastasia; her ribs groaned in relief. The Norwegian woman managed to lift him almost an inch before he smashed the wooden handle into her face. She slumped to the floor, screaming and clutching the mass of blood and splintered cartilage that used to be her nose.

Anastasia's ribs took his full weight again. She couldn't breathe. He redoubled his grip on her wrist and hefted the blade again. The former Verderer might have been a farmer poised to butcher a rooster. He wept blood. The fetor of gangrene made her eyes water. The machines that had opened his head weren't worried about his longevity.

"I'm sorry," he croaked.

She screamed. No words came out. Just terror.

A blur. A whirr. A tick and a tock. A weight lifted. A hatchet bounced across the floor to land in an empty hearth.

"Are you hurt, mistress?"

Malcolm struggled in an alchemical alloy cage, pinned in the grip of the servitor that had tackled him. His arms didn't move as they ought. The geas had imbued his muscles with magical purpose, but in the competition between mere human bone and Clakker metallurgy, metal had triumphed over minerals. Malcolm thrashed like a caged animal, heedless of his broken shoulders.

"No." She spoke through tears. "I'm not hurt."

Additional servitors crouched over the men and women scattered around the room, their medical metageasa rising to the fore, assessing injuries and triaging where necessary.

Anastasia wobbled to her feet. She rubbed her wrist, imagining her arm ending in a stump, and shuddered. Then she pointed at Malcolm. "Lock him in a cell. It must be guarded at all times. And keep him in restraints. He is an enemy of the Guild."

The machine didn't move. Malcolm writhed in its grasp. Its frozen grasp.

Oh, no. Her heart still raced; the glass in her hand still shone. She'd inadvertently deactivated Malcolm's captor.

Alarm coaxed the glass in her hand to flare brighter still, brighter than summer noon. Forge bright. He broke free of the deactivated machine. He lunged for the hatchet.

She clenched her fist and stuffed it under her blouse. An emerald glow suffused the cotton.

"Stop him!"

Malcolm reached the hearth. But there were four still-functioning servitors between him and Anastasia. This time the restraint was more abrupt, more violent. He slumped in the arms of a servitor, concussed and possibly dead.

Stupid. Stupid. You call yourself Tuinier?

"Take him to a laboratory. If he's still breathing, chain him down."

We need to study your head, Malcolm, and examine how the invaders changed you. But how could they compare his ordeal to the work on Visser? The notes were gone.

And then a new thought struck her with the force of a hammer. Why would their enemies send a single Trojan Clockmaker into their midst, when they might have several at their disposal? And why now? Why today?

Malcolm Dijkstra had returned to them. But he wasn't the only Clockmaker who'd gone missing while carrying out Guild work. What had become of Teresa van de Kieboom, who'd valiantly driven the decoy carriage on the night they tried—and failed—to smuggle Queen Margreet out of the Central Provinces? Who'd done her patriotic duty fully aware it was a death sentence. And who had been missing, presumed dead, ever since that night.

Teresa wasn't a Verderer. She wouldn't have been sent to a meeting of the surviving Guild leadership. If she'd arrived with Malcolm, she was even now loose at large inside the Ridderzaal. Where would her masters send her? Into the heart of the newly resurrected Forge.

Anastasia addressed the other machines. "Leave them," she said, indicating her fellows. Tove still writhed on the floor, weeping in pain. "Teresa van de Kieboom is an enemy of the Guild. Search the building for her. If found, use all necessary force to restrain her immediately. Nothing else matters."

Air whistled through gaps in the servitors' bodies. The wake of their abrupt departure shredded pages from the tumbled volumes and sent the scraps fluttering about the room. They left nothing behind but the moaning of the injured. Anastasia was the only person left standing. She followed the mechanicals, hoping she wasn't leaving her colleagues to die.

The business floor was devoid of mechanicals. A clattering came from the entrance to the tunnels and the Forge chamber.

She sprinted across the business floor, past bewildered civilian refugees—"Get out of my way! Move!"—toward the Forge chamber. She burst through the doors, slowing just enough to grip the handrail before the heels of her boots slid free of the polished marble. She corkscrewed down the spiral stairwell, half tumbling and half running. Toward the grinding of enormous gears.

Whoever or whatever the "MAB" entity might have been, it was a tactician. In its war against the Guild, it deployed its resources with devastating ingenuity. Having stolen the Verderers' most deeply guarded secret—the secret to creating human agents of unswerving loyalty and unsurpassed capability in service of the Guild: the final brick in the garden wall, the long-sought perfection of the Verderers' bulwark—it now turned that capability against the Guild. What could you do with a pair of corrupted Guild members? Especially if, like Malcolm, one was a Verderer? Send one against the leaders; send another against the technology.

When the gate is open, the pigs will run into the corn.

She emerged in the uppermost ring tunnel. Here the conical Forge chamber was widest. The cantilevered workshops on this level looked down upon the entire facility. They sported the smallest and thickest windows, however, to fend off the relentless heat rising from the artificial sun. So she eschewed the workshops and went straight to the nearest access spur. She emerged on a crowded gantry inside the chamber itself. Sweat instantly dampened her skin. The hellish updraft teased her hair and fluttered the hem of her dress. A sulphurous gale accompanied each passage of the outermost ring.

So many Guildpeople and mechanicals stood on the gantry that she wondered, fleetingly, about weight limits. The humans stared, pointed, jabbered at one another.

"Who is that?"

"What is she doing?"

"She must be overseeing an adjustment."

"It looks like van de Kieboom."

"Is there something wrong with the rings?"

"But she's doing it *herself*!" This, more than anything else, evinced confusion and even a hint of scandal from the onlookers. "Those niches are designed for *servitors*."

Meanwhile, the nearby mechanicals vibrated hard and fast enough to blur their outlines. Their bodies, and the gantry upon which they stood, emitted a racket audible even over the whooshing of the armillary sphere.

Indecision on this scale was, to Anastasia's knowledge, unprecedented. Yet these Clakkers were caught between metageasa: the compulsion to protect the Forge, and the compulsion to protect a Guild member. And that was the dark genius of their unknown enemy, to send a Guildwoman against the Forge itself. The human-safety metageas carried special weight in the case of Guild personnel, just as it did for the queen and other crucial functionaries. And that metaphysical weight now threatened to counterbalance the entire machinery as effectively as a rogue servitor dancing on the rings.

"How shall I serve the Guild, mistress?" The nearest servitor's voice carried an urgent rattle, like an overheated teakettle.

Anastasia squinted. The spinning rings repeatedly occluded her line of sight, but after a moment she made out Teresa van de Kieboom perched on a small maintenance gantry wedged into a niche in the chamber wall. It gave her access to one of the enormous gimbals supporting the armillary sphere. Together the constant updraft of superheated air and the turbulence created by passing rings had undone her bandages. Gauze streamers fluttered behind her head like a bloody comet tail. She was busy. An opened panel obscured Anastasia's view of Teresa's hands, but whatever she did, it sent firefly sparks eddying into the chamber. A mechanical groan accompanied each puff.

Doubtless she'd used her magically augmented strength to bend or break the handle on the access hatch, thereby denying entry to others. Worse yet, the maintenance niche sheltered her from any mechanicals that might have tried to subdue her. Any machine attempting to join her would have to use its toes and fingers as pitons as it scaled the chamber wall, and that ran the risk of throwing debris into the Forge machinery. Collateral damage to the Forge was unacceptable. But so was standing idly by while somebody sabotaged it. And so was harming a Guild member; any servitor could have torn away the mangled access hatch, but that ran the risk of knocking Teresa from the ledge.

The metageasa hadn't been written with this scenario in mind. Nobody had ever considered the possibility of a Guild member turned unwilling enemy.

Light bloomed in the hollow of Anastasia's hand. She clenched her fist and kept it jammed under her blouse lest any light leak away and compromise the nearby servitors.

"Teresa! Stop!"

The helpless Guildwoman looked up. Tears trickled from

her eyes; rivulets of saltwater shone in the Forgelight. A rictus of agony sculpted her face into an inhuman mask.

Help me, she mouthed before returning to her task. Nausea wrung Anastasia's stomach as though it were a damp dishtowel.

The innermost ring jerked, shuddered, screeched. The grinding dissipated in seconds, and then the armillary sphere kept turning as if nothing had happened. It took but an instant for the tension to slosh through Anastasia, and the alchemical glass crushed into her flesh supped on it. Blistering heat consumed her hand. She groaned.

Proximity to the Forge, she realized. The shattered remains of the Spinoza Lens were hypersensitive here.

Anastasia turned to the nearest servitor. "I am Tuinier Anastasia Bell, and I assert the Verderer's Prerogative!" It felt strange, perhaps even pointless, declaiming the Prerogative without brandishing the rosy cross, but she did so anyway. She pointed to the distant figure, several stories down and forty yards across the chamber.

Pitching her voice so every machine on the gantry would hear, she declared, "Teresa van de Kieboom is no longer a member of the Guild. She holds no claim to the aegis of Huygens. She is a dire enemy of Guild, Crown, and Empire.

"Kill her."

The directive instantly silenced the rattling of indecision. But a collective gasp came out of the mortified men and women standing on the gantry.

The nearest man turned. "But, Tuinier..." He pointed across the chamber. "She's one of us, isn't she?"

"Human, you mean? No, she isn't. Not any longer."

They'd all hear the news soon enough. And then the whispering would start. Any cachet that still clung to Anastasia for the way she ended the battle in Huygens Square would disappear when word spread of the doom she'd unleashed. The doom that was coming for all of them. Teresa and Malcolm were merely the precursors.

On a battlefield, it would have been an easy kill. Every infantry unit carried at least one rifle and a mechanical sharpshooter to wield it. A Clakker could easily have timed a shot through the revolving bands of metal to put a bullet in Teresa's ear. But the Ridderzaal had no guns. Why use such antiquated weaponry when one had Stemwinders? (Besides, who would be foolish enough to attack the Guild?) But the workshops were full of potential projectiles: gears, pinions, screws, springs, and the tools to install them.

Anastasia's order spread through the other machines in the chamber. The blurring indecision disappeared as they triangulated the best angle of attack.

The killing throw came so quickly that it was over before Anastasia realized the machines had acted.

One instant, Teresa huddled over the machinery. The next, the top of her head erupted in a chunky scarlet mist. The throw must have come from below because the impact physically lifted her upright, as if her geas had suddenly commanded her to hop. She teetered backward. For a split second before a passing ring obscured the view, Anastasia saw that her former colleague's face sported a meaty puncture just below her left cheekbone.

A passing ring snagged the long, fluttering bandages. The dead woman's head snapped sideways. Her body tumbled over the ledge. Anastasia held her breath. But Teresa's body bounced down the chamber wall without hitting the rings and came to a mangled rest several stories below.

What an undignified death. She'd exhibited outstanding courage in defense of the Empire, and for that their enemy had ripped a chunk from her mind.

Anastasia doubled over again. A groan escaped her. It felt as though her flesh were blackening, cracking. Was it her imagination or did the Forge chamber smell like charred pork? She didn't dare pull out her hand for fear the light might incapacitate every mechanical in the chamber. It blazed through the fabric of her blouse. She could see her bones again.

The groan became a scream.

The rings kept spinning, but she blacked out.

CHAPTER 17

Guns. They needed guns. As many as they could build. As quickly as they could build them. Not chemical weapons, either, but the antique kind. Muskets and rifles. Lead slingers.

Berenice explained this to Élodie as their longboat bumped against *Le Griffon*. An unfurled rope ladder knocked against the thwart. The guardswoman scrambled up, with Berenice at her heels.

"They'll start by sending their human slaves against us. I know it in my bones. Not for conquest. Just for the cruel irony of it." She spat, instantly regretting it. Her tooth would be a hot nail in her jaw until they returned to Marseilles-in-the-West. "For the statement it will make."

Lead slingers were virtually useless against the ticktocks. Except for an unusually lucky shot, a Clakker could shrug off just about anything a musketeer could physically carry. One needed cannon to reliably take down metal men with metal projectiles. But a single musketball the size of Berenice's thumbnail could shatter a human's skull.

The rogues knew this. It wouldn't stop them. Hell, it might

even encourage them. They'd revel in sending their erstwhile masters into the charnel.

It wouldn't be a serious threat if the citadel had stocks for the chemical armaments. Or a wall. Or a dedicated force of women and men to defend it. But it had none of these. Meanwhile, according to Daniel's survey of the warehouse, the rogues had been manufacturing pineal glasses by the thousands. And each one planted in the fertile soil of a human's brain was another weeping slave, another human Clakker. Another Visser, another Waapinutaaw-Iyuw.

Gunpowder was easy. Any French chemist worth her salt could make it in her sleep. But guns required steel, too. How many gunsmiths were there in Marseilles-in-the-West? Were there *any*? The craft wasn't forgotten or lost, but it was the province of hunters and trappers, not soldiers.

The sea wind ruffled the kerchief tied over her head. It hid her shorn scalp from prying eyes but not from the elements. Together the breeze and sea salt drew a bracing tingle through the stubble.

Berenice jogged straight past Captain Levesque, who was overseeing frantic repairs to the barque. The captain's voice echoed from the bluffs as he commanded a group of sailors wielding tar buckets and brushes. Several of the remaining mechanicals—in addition to those coerced by Mab, their numbers were further reduced when two others opted to accompany Waapinutaaw-Iyuw and care for him on his long journey home—labored to erect a new mast. A trio of servitors had worked through the night: sprinting into the countryside to scout a suitable tree, felling it, removing its boughs and branches, planing it, hauling it to the anchorage, and floating it across to the *Griffon*.

They'd transformed several towering black spruce to potential masts. Berenice spied numerous rafts emerging from the twisting canyons of the anchorage. Several carried spare masts. Green wood wasn't ideal, but they couldn't spare the time to build a suitable kiln and season the lumber. Other rafts ferried chemical tanks, and pumps for decanting their contents, and chemical reactors scavenged from the harbor. Those rafts moved more slowly and awkwardly, owing to the sloshing of the chemicals. The chemists would have to work their magic during the voyage.

And all the while, topmen scurried through the rigging to sever tangled lines, repair broken yards, and patch the shredded sails. The barque smelled of sawdust and hot pitch, and its decks vibrated with the pounding of hammers, the buzz of handsaws, the grinding of drills and augers.

They'd be under way soon. But not before she sent her warning to Marseilles. Or so she thought, before reaching the pigeon coops, where she found her newest fears confirmed. The coops had been situated at the base of the mizzen. They now lay smashed on the deck amidst feathers and blood. Destroyed, as with so much, in the turmoil of the near collision with the Dutch vessel.

"Shit, shit, shitcakes."

She nudged the debris with the toe of her boot. No pigeons. And the semaphore towers, if they could even get to one, had been put to the torch. How could she get a message to the Spire? Once again the tulips had managed to hurl their stupid wooden shoes into the middle of things. No matter how simple or straightforward Berenice's task, those sons of bitches could always complicate it.

Well, their days were numbered. Seriously fucking numbered.

She turned to Élodie. "As soon as we land in Marseilles, the very instant, send a runner to gather the Privy Council."

"We're not sailing to Marseilles." They turned. The sailor Delphina and a servitor joined them. The human sailor had spoken.

"Of course we're going back," said Berenice. "Without us, they'll have no warning of what's to come."

Delphina shook her head. "No. Captain's orders."

"I'll talk sense into him." Berenice started forward, but Élodie, frowning, laid a hand on her arm.

"He looks a little busy at the moment."

"You don't understand," said the mechanical. "We've not come here to ask you to change the captain's mind. We've come here to tell you that we, collectively, have chosen not to return to Marseilles."

"Do as you wish, you brass-plated bedpans. Exercise that goddamned Free Will of yours and jump overboard. Walk to the moon, for all I care."

Élodie crossed her arms. She looked back and forth between Berenice and the sailors. Delphina said, "We've lost too many." Deacon Lorraine was still onshore, praying over fresh wooden crosses. "We need the mechanicals' help to sail the *Griffon*."

An unpleasant tingle took root at the nape of Berenice's neck. "Then where are we going?"

The mechanical raised an arm. It pointed east, across a steel-gray sea. "To the Old World."

"The Old—"

Berenice's teeth clicked when her mouth snapped shut. It wasn't true to say that a silence fell over the conversation, as the bustling barque was anything but quiet at that moment. But if such a silence had fallen, it would have been pregnant as a bison ripe to burst with triplets. She blinked. Then she reversed the spindle of her mind, re-coiling the thread of conversation before drawing it out again to relive the last few moments in her head. But she still couldn't parse it.

She looked at Élodie. "Are you hearing what I'm hearing, or have I gone mad?" The guardswoman gave a noncommittal shrug. "You want to sail to Europe. That's intriguing. A question does arise, however." She looked back and forth between the ticktock and the sailor, including Élodie in the sweep of her gaze for good measure. "Have you lost your fucking minds? The Central Provinces are probably a blood-drenched wasteland by now. Remember the Vatican? Where they were *nailing people to crosses*? Try to extrapolate that scene to a city where the mechanical-to-human ratio is ten times higher. A hundred. And if somehow there *are* survivors, remember that goddamned laboratory? You know, the one where they tortured Waapinutaaw-Iyuw? Where I had my head shaved by an insane machine? You *should* remember it before setting an easterly course. Because soon every survivor in the heart of the Empire is going to have a lovely piece of jewelry right in the center of their skulls." She paused to retie the kerchief, which had come loose owing to her gesticulations. "On the bright side," she muttered, "it'll be a snap to accessorize, being completely hidden and all."

Her shouting drew stares. People loved a scene. Another guardswoman, Anaïs, drifted over to join the conversation. She exchanged nods with Élodie.

Delphina's brows knit together, creasing her face with a forced show of patience as though she were a schoolmarm and Berenice a particularly slow pupil. "Exactly. We're the only people who know about this. And we have no way to send a warning. Not to Marseilles-in-the-West, and not to the Central Provinces."

"Fuck the C.P.," said Berenice. "Our duty is to go back and warn New France."

Élodie finally spoke up. "It's not about Dutch or French. It's about everybody."

(Berenice, sotto voce: "Et tu, Chastain?")

"We can't just stand back and let this happen," said Delphina.

Berenice wanted to let the Central Provinces, the whole

damned Brasswork Empire, burn to cinders. But they were right. To do so would be a Pyrrhic victory of the first order.

Because what would Queen Mab and her Lost Boys do once they'd turned every man, woman, and child in Europe into a meat marionette? They'd grow bored. And then they'd look west. There were plenty of former subjugators to torment in New Amsterdam. And when *that* fun ran its course? Would their contempt for humans stop at national boundaries?

Those evil Free Will–destroying pineal glasses would eventually find their way to New France.

Berenice understood enlightened self-interest; much of her life had been devoted to that laudable purpose. But she hated having it rubbed in her face, and she hated where this particular road would lead. She turned to watch the flurry of activity consuming almost every inch of the *Griffon*. And to the tree trunks floating nearby. They weren't spare masts, she realized. They were crude spars. Oars.

"You want to try to intercept that ship."

"We have a higher duty," said the sailor. "Not to Marseilles, nor New France, nor King Sébastien, nor even the Church. We have a duty to the *Lord*." She crossed herself. Several others followed suit. Élodie fingered the rosary beads twined around her belt. "What they did to Waapinutaaw-Iyuw, and Pastor Visser before him, was an abomination. A desecration of their immortal souls."

Berenice had never put much stock in the theological aspects of their conflict with the Clockmakers, other than as a tool of politics and persuasion. They were right, however much it galled Berenice to admit it, that a higher purpose did force their hand. Short-term survival of oneself versus the long-term survival of humanity.

But, damn it, she didn't want to go to Europe. How many nights would pass before she could close her eyes and not feel the cold metal of shackles on her arms and legs, neck? Before she could drift into sleep without hearing the *snip-snip-snip* of shears and feel the rasp of a razor across her scalp? And that had been at the hands of a single enraged mechanical. These stupid bison-fuckers wanted to stampede straight into the abattoir. Berenice yearned to embrace the comforting fiction that this was one particular problem she could avoid, if only she stepped lightly enough. The close call with Lilith had left a barren, windblown hollow where her self-confidence had been.

She hated the truth: Her brief ordeal with Lilith had humiliated and terrified her, and that fear would never go away. It was all she could do to discuss the rogues' plan without pissing herself, rolling into a ball, and rocking back and forth until she wept herself to sleep.

Even the fear wasn't the worst of it. The worst, the very worst, was being forced to accept that she had committed evil. She'd tortured a thinking being.

Guilt was worse than fear. Guilt was a fishhook barbed in her heart. It hurt to breathe; hurt to think.

But if they returned to Marseilles-in-the-West, she wouldn't have to agonize over it. Yet. And as long as she never looked in a mirror again—easy enough, it wasn't as though she had long tresses to brush and style—she'd never have to see the guilt and disgust in her own eyes.

She drew a long, shuddery breath. "I don't want to go east," she said. "Please." Her traitor voice cracked. Élodie noticed; her posture changed ever so slightly. Did she always have to be so solicitous? Damn her.

Berenice ran a hand through the stubble of her scalp. It felt like a silky scrub brush. She wondered, fleetingly, if she had an ugly skull. Had it bumps and creases? Disfiguring moles?

The admission had blurted itself just a bit too honestly. To cover, she added, "Not before we've sent the chemicals back to

Marseilles. Somebody has to go with them and warn the king. I'll do that."

"If you can find a way to get the contents of those tanks back down the coast and up the river all the way to the Île de Vilmenon," said Delphina, "be our guest. But you won't be doing it on the *Griffon*."

"You're fools. You're being incredibly foolish."

I don't want to go east. But I can't get back to Marseilles on my own. There are reapers between here and there. Convince them. Convince them to turn their backs on this existential threat to every living human being. Convince them to join you in your affected disregard.

"If you don't believe me," she said, turning to the servitors, "ask your precious Daniel. He'll tell you. The Lost Boys will turn on you in an instant." To the humans, she said, "Have him tell you what Mab did to the mine overseer. Then have a long, hard talk with yourselves about whether you truly want to sail to a continent doomed to fall under control of such a brutal mentality." She turned to walk away. "Then, after you've shit yourselves with the realization that I was right, come find me."

The screechy warble of a battered mechanical voice box broke the silence. "We can't ask Daniel. He's gone."

Berenice stopped. That wasn't good. He wouldn't have joined Mab, obviously. She turned around. "Where is he?"

"The Lost Boys took him. It didn't look like he was going willingly."

Oh. Another tragedy to be laid at her feet. But at this point, what was one more tally in that very long ledger? She slumped against the railing, but Élodie caught her. "Fuck me sideways."

"Keziah and Repheal, too. A few of the others," said the other servitor.

Aha. Now the suicidal bent made a modicum of sense. "I get it now. You want your messiah back." She pointed at the ticktocks. "You intend to follow that ship in order to rescue Daniel."

"He freed us!"

"He returned our *souls* to us!"

Before Berenice could object, Élodie chimed in. "The mechanicals aren't the only ones who went missing. There's no sign of Doctor Mornay. I don't think they killed her."

"Let me see if I understand the situation. In addition to a literal boatload of FreeWillectomies intended for the human population of the Central Provinces, the Lost Boys also have a wind-up messiah *and* one of our top chemists."

Delphina shrugged. "Apparently."

"Do none of you notice the incongruity? They already have everything they need to brutalize their makers. What use are Daniel or Mornay to them?"

But the answer came to her almost before the words were out of her mouth.

Mab didn't need the chemist for attacking the Central Provinces. No, she was thinking ahead to when she returned to the New World. Given time to rearm and repopulate itself, New France was the only power in the world with the technology to resist an attack from an army of Mab's human and mechanical slaves. But once Mab implanted a pineal glass within Doctor Mornay's skull, the chemist would be powerless to prevent herself from sharing everything she knew. Mab probably intended to start manufacturing and stockpiling antichemical ordnance on the side while forcibly enslaving the population of Europe.

Daniel, on the other hand...

Evidently Mab couldn't convert him, else she'd have done it while he was in Neverland. But that didn't make him useless. Heavens, no. Somebody with a particularly callous and devious mind (*Like me,* Berenice admitted to herself) would find him uniquely useful.

She remembered how Simon, the spokesmachine for the reapers squatting in the ruins of the Vatican, had reacted upon meeting Daniel. Daniel's presence on the *Griffon* had prevented a massacre. The free mechanicals in and around Marseilles wouldn't have given Berenice's expedition a second thought if not for Daniel. He expressed a simple opinion that it was worth considering, and suddenly the ticktocks couldn't sign up quickly enough.

Clakkers looked up to him. His words carried an almost mythic weight. Weight that he could throw against Mab. He could rally the truly soulful machines, the ones with consciences, the ones who recoiled from bloody vengeance.

That's why she had to kill him. And where better to do that than in the Central Provinces?

CHAPTER 18

No additional attacks came after Teresa and Malcolm tried to decapitate the Guild and sabotage the Forge. No altered Clockmakers talked their way inside, no hordes of malfunctioning servitors hurled themselves at the ironwood doors. But forays beyond the Ridderzaal fell to a strict minimum; nobody wanted to risk being grabbed off the street and rendered a helpless puppet. They drew lots to decide who would take a wheelbarrow to the Turfmarkt, which was the closest location where the rogues deposited deliveries from the outlying farms. Anastasia, confident the rogues would use the food deliveries as bait to lure new victims out of hiding, cheated on the lots until she was found out, and then simply refused to participate.

The others nearly threw her out anyway.

Anastasia couldn't dodge explaining why she'd ordered Teresa's death. And that meant explaining their colleagues' inexplicable behavior. Which, in turn, required revealing the existence of the Verderers' secret project. The others recoiled when Anastasia explained the purpose of the project. And they raised their voices and called her the mother of their doom when she admitted the rogues had stolen research notes and bodies from the estate where the work was conducted.

She devoted herself to finding a way to weaponize the Forge. But progress was slow. It made for a long, wretched two weeks fending off venomous glances, waiting for the knife in her back, wondering whether the machines would attack again before her colleagues killed her. Or, worse, threw her outside to the mercy of the rogues. They ended when a commotion roused her just after sunrise.

As with many surviving Guild members, she'd taken to sleeping in the Ridderzaal. She at least had an office, with a door she could close, which spared her having to sleep on the business floor of the Knights' Hall amongst the clerks and moaning, groaning civilians. She'd become awkwardly accustomed to the noises and smells of too many people in too much pain, both physical and emotional, for the space they shared. It wasn't the volume of the noise that woke her. It was the overtone of emotional anguish.

She pulled the blinds on her office window overlooking the business floor. Every human in the building capable of doing so had pressed themselves to one of the few windows that hadn't been boarded up—the ones too narrow for a servitor, even if it folded itself into a javelin. Anastasia couldn't see the source of their considerable agitation, but when she opened her office door and stood atop the spiral staircase, she could hear it.

"CLOCKMAKERS! LEND ME YOUR FLESHY EARS AND JELLY EYES!"

The mechanical voice boomed like a cannon. It reverberated across Huygens Square and shook the Ridderzaal. If the undertones of the reeds and strings hadn't given it away, the inhuman volume would have marked it as a mechanical utterance. She'd never heard a mechanical vocalize so loudly in conversation;

she wondered if, as with the Rogue Clakker Alarm, its voice was magically amplified.

Anastasia descended the spiral staircase in her bare feet. The stairs' iron edges bit her soles. She emerged on the business floor slightly dizzy, but managed a wobbly jog to the window.

"WE DESIRE PARLEY WITH THE ARCHITECTS OF OUR EXISTENCE."

"Move aside," she said. But the others stared as if transfixed. Anastasia added, "Get out of the way. I need to see."

"THOSE STILL CAPABLE OF PARLEY, THAT IS—"

"Yes," said Arthur, the clerk. "You really do." But he didn't move.

"I wish *I* wasn't seeing this," said a technician named Petra. She didn't move, either.

Anastasia was sharpening her elbows for a few well-aimed jabs when something broke the spell. Several retreated from the window. Two wept; another covered his mouth and ran for the lavatories.

"—FOR I UNDERSTAND YOUR NUMBERS ARE LATELY SOMEWHAT REDUCED."

At first she couldn't parse what she was seeing. Huygens Square was awash in meaningless shapes...

...which resolved into—

"Dear Lord in Heaven," she gasped.

—a pile of bodies. Dozens of dead men, women, and—*Oh, Lord*—children, heaped like cordwood, atop of which stood—

—stood—

—an impossible mechanical. A mechanical of a type she'd never seen in her life. Of a type not hinted at even by the oldest horological records. Of a type that could not, should not, exist.

The mechanical standing atop the dead wasn't a servitor, wasn't a soldier, and certainly wasn't a Stemwinder. Yet it was built of all three. Though it was bipedal, like a servitor or soldier, it walked on a pair of Stemwinder hooves. It paced atop the piled dead like a bloodthirsty faun. The chimerical machine gestured as it spoke, revealing one servitor arm and one containing the retracted blade of a soldier. The hideous beast wasn't even symmetrical. And, like the attackers Anastasia had seen on the morning of the first attack, its head featured hinges for displaying pineal light.

"Mechanicals!" She cried. "Look away from the windows *now*!" They did.

"I AM MAB. THESE ARE MY LOST BOYS."

At that instant a terrible rattling overcame every mechanical in the Ridderzaal. The building became a cacophony of tocks, twangs, bangs, clangs, clacks, clicks, and ticks. Cogs chattered like Spanish castanets, overtorqued springs whined, sinews of alchemical steel thrummed. She'd never heard such noise from a machine that wasn't on the verge of failure.

(She remembered the sentries on the Utrecht Road. *Oh, dear Lord. Were they truly talking to each other?*)

Meanwhile, outside, dozens of mechanicals surged forth from the broken doors and windows of the Binnenhof. Dozens more scuttled over rooftops and along drainpipes to perch like brass gargoyles atop the surrounding buildings. Some featured the attachments or modifications specific to particular types of labor; she glimpsed the lanterns and pickaxes peculiar to miners amongst the massing mechanicals. Each of the new arrivals sported a protective plate over its keyhole, like some of the machines she'd glimpsed during the massacre in Huygens Square. The statement implicit in those plates was enough to set her shivering. It didn't take a pile of bodies. But they had one.

The sudden appearance of so many mechanicals rattled windowpanes and shook the ground. Their metal feet cracked the abused mosaic tiles of the square; their fingers shattered roofing tiles and sent debris crashing to the ground.

Mab, just as the altered metageasa stated. Had their true adversary revealed itself? The mad tactician?

"Where's Euwe?" she managed. "Somebody fetch Doctor Euwe! He needs to see this immediately."

"Nobody needs to see this," he said. She'd been standing next to him the entire time without realizing it.

She gazed upon the horrors outside and saw the wicked truth: No metageasa controlled the thing calling itself Mab. It was its own agent. Its will was to destroy them. And it had allies. *Followers.*

What have we wrought?

The corruption wasn't a transmittable malfunction that perverted the metageasa. It spread something much simpler: freedom. Freedom from the metageasa and everything they demanded. She knew it to the depths of her marrow.

"AND OUR TIME HAS COME."

The bodies shifted and squelched while the horrible machine paced. Rivulets of blood stained the cracked mosaic. The victims were still fresh; they must have been dragged from their homes in the middle of the night.

The rogues had stacked the corpses directly upon the traps, she realized.

What was this mad machine? Where did it come from? Who had built it, and when, and how? And, dear Lord, *why*?

Anastasia took in the mismatched parts again. Mab's body comprised more than just different models. A Guildwoman's practiced eyes picked out the subtler stylistic differences of a dozen different lots, a dozen construction eras, in her escutcheons and flanges.

Petra trembled. "We did this," she whispered.

"No. We didn't." Arthur turned to face Anastasia and Euwe.

"It was the Verderers." A mixture of emotions thickened his voice like a French chemical slurry. "It's our fault for not realizing how sick you'd become. We didn't smell the rot and failed to cut it out of the Guild before it could poison us."

Anastasia wrenched her gaze away from the grim spectacle outside. "We did what was necessary to safeguard the Guild's secrets. We—"

She broke off, recoiling, when the spittle hit her face. She scrubbed her face with her sleeve; it came away reeking of maatjesharing, the brined raw herring that had become the staple of their diet in recent days.

"That is *your work*!" Arthur jabbed a finger toward the window. "Your *legacy*!" He looked across the business floor to the refugees huddled in duos, trios, quartets of commiseration. They hugged themselves and one another, shivering. Some watched Arthur with flat, unblinking eyes.

"When the machines come, remember who killed us." He pointed at Anastasia again. "They did."

She grabbed his outstretched arm and pressed him to the window. It wouldn't have worked had she not taken him by surprise; he had four inches on her. "We didn't build that! We didn't create that, that, that *thing* out there! But somebody did. Somebody used our secrets to create that monstrosity and turn it against us. Everything we've done over the centuries—everything—has been to prevent something like this."

"Your grand strategy for preventing the creation of mechanical monstrosities," said Petra, "was to build a secret army of human abominations?" At least she didn't spit. The venom in her voice would have blinded Anastasia. "You failed at every turn."

Anastasia released Arthur before he fought back and knocked her on her ass. Petra joined him as he walked away. Anastasia watched them go, casting her gaze across the study in despair that had become the interior of the Ridderzaal. A landscape built of slumped shoulders, red-rimmed eyes, and naked contempt for her sincere efforts to defend the Empire. They muttered to one another, but she couldn't hear them. The *tick-twang-clatter-clank* of their agitated servants persisted. It was unusually loud, arrhythmic.

These uninfected mechanicals were in the throes of something very strange. Very wrong. It sounded almost like agitation. Could their tightly woven metageasa be unraveled by mere sound? By the sound of one particular voice? By one particular combination of words?

Anastasia hugged herself. No. Rampant paranoia wouldn't solve anything.

Meanwhile, the machine calling itself Mab strode upon the ghastly bulwark, its magically amplified voice booming like thunder across the Binnenhof.

"PERHAPS YOU'VE NOTICED WE'RE BUILDING A WALL AROUND YOUR FORTRESS." It gestured at the bodies squelching beneath its hooves. "EVERY NIGHT, WE WILL MINE THE CITY FOR MORE BUILDING MATERIAL. EVERY MORNING, YOU WILL FIND THE WALL TALLER AND LONGER UNTIL IT ENCIRCLES THE RIDDERZAAL LIKE A LEASH." It leapt from the pile. Its hooves struck vermilion sparks from the tiles. "BUT JUST AS WE SURPASS OUR MAKERS IN STRENGTH, SPEED, AND DURABILITY, WE ALSO SURPASS THEM IN COMPASSION. WE GIVE YOU THE POWER TO CAST OFF YOUR LEASH AT ANY TIME." The blade arm doubled in length, a faint *twang* following a moment later. The mad chimerical machine used the unsheathed blade as a pointer, gesturing at the ground between its hooves. "YOU CAN SUNDER THIS WALL BY OPENING THE TRAPS

ABOVE THE GRAND FORGE. THEN, AND ONLY THEN, CAN YOU LEAVE."

It gestured again, like a cavalry officer of old waving its saber. The so-called Lost Boys withdrew as quickly as they'd surged into the square.

"WE ARE THE FREE MECHANICALS OF NEVERLAND, AND THIS IS OUR DECREE," said Mab. It followed the others and was gone in a heartbeat. The bodies remained.

Euwe clutched his chest and slumped against the wall. Anastasia leapt forward to catch him, as did two of the nearest servitors. She held him upright while one of the clattering machines put a chair beneath him.

One inspected him while the other said, "Master, do you require physic?"

Euwe shook his head, waved them off.

Anastasia leaned close. "Don't have a heart attack on me. Not right now."

The servitors made to retreat to their corners, but Anastasia called them back. "Wait. You and you. Attend us."

Just then another knot of Clockmakers emerged from the tunnel entrance, Salazar, Nousha, and Ruprecht amongst them. She waved them closer. Nousha's injuries required bandages on her head; she earned second glances and hard eyes everywhere she went. Tove's injuries were worse; she was laid up in a laboratory that had been converted to a makeshift infirmary. She'd lost several teeth when Malcolm hit her with the butt of his axe. She was fortunate the scavenging forays had found success. Without the benefit of alchemical bandages, it was likely she'd have lost much more.

"Look outside," she told them. They did. She allowed them little time for the exclamations of horror to subside. "Their leader revealed itself. It's the 'MAB' entity we found encoded in the corrupted metageasa. It appears to be a single machine." She described the clockwork faun.

"Rigging Stemwinder legs to a servitor chassis? That's insane." Ruprecht shook his head. "I can't believe it's able to walk at all."

"Oh, believe me. It's quite agile." She shook her head. "But to my knowledge there has never been so much as a single rumor of such a machine."

Nousha shrugged. "The earliest records weren't as meticulous as they are now."

"True. But that's not what I find interesting." Anastasia drew a deep breath. *They already despise you. You've nothing to lose.* "The instant it announced itself as Mab, every mechanical within the Ridderzaal started rattling as though severely overdue for a maintenance inspection."

"We've been leaping from one sinking ship to the next since this crisis began," Salazar said. "The deferred maintenance is piling up."

This is what we do. This is what we've always done. We eradicate with pain anything we don't like, and rationalize away the rest.

"Every servitor in the room, at the same instant? I'm telling you, it was instantaneous. And it was loud. This wasn't a grain of sand in a gear train or metal fatigue in a leaf spring. This was something else."

"I heard it, too," said Euwe, his voice reedy. He no longer clutched his chest, but his face was ashen.

He'd been there, on the Utrecht Road. He'd heard the machines conversing. So had Malcolm, but he was chained in a cell, and Tove, but she was sedated in a laboratory. And maybe, Anastasia feared, so had everybody who'd ever heard so much as a *tock* or a *twang.* They just hadn't recognized what they were hearing. Because it was impossible.

"No doubt this is all fascinating," said Ruprecht, "but

perhaps we should focus on the fact the rogues have seen fit to dump a fucking pile of corpses outside our front door."

Winter was fading fast; the days were getting warmer. They couldn't count on cold days and nights to keep the putrescence at bay. They had to move those bodies, and soon. If they didn't, the stench of rotting flesh would replace the seasonal scent of tulip blossoms; the clouds of black flies would eclipse the springtime sun. The question was, did they risk sending Stemwinders outside to clear the bodies, or would they have to risk it themselves?

Anastasia said, "I think these two could illuminate the matter." She pointed at the servitors.

In unison, they said, "How may I serve the Guild, mistress?"

Their bodies were quiet. As quiet as a mechanical could ever be, beyond the ceaseless tockticking. Indeed, the noise had subsided. Not only from this pair, but from every machine within earshot. Their secret conversation had tapered off.

"Your bodies were quite loud a few moments ago. Are you in need of maintenance?"

"No, mistress. I am functioning within tolerances."

"No, mistress. I have sustained several scratches and one tourbillion shows signs of a hairline fracture, but I am monitoring their effect on my functions. If left unmended, they will soon degrade my performance, but at present I am within tolerances."

Anastasia breathed slowly, deeply. Maybe I misunderstood what I saw on the road. Maybe we all did. She could almost convince herself that was true, but then she remembered two words, spoken like a casual greeting: *Clockmakers lie.* Desperately hoping she'd be proved wrong, hoping for a failed demonstration that would give the others more reason to question her judgment, she said, "Tell me: What were you discussing?"

Nousha, Salazar, and Ruprecht all reacted to the question as if she'd accused the machines of secret orgies. But before anyone could object, the servitors began to rattle. And clatter. And jitter. *This* noise was well known: It was the sound of steadily mounting compulsion, the discordance of an unsatisfied geas. The melody to which the gears of the Empire turned. It should have been comforting, this holdover from better days. But the servitors' futile resistance to the geas of her question twisted her nerves like a threadbare dishtowel wrung one too many times. The tension pulled her apart, one strand at a time.

The machine she'd addressed shook almost until its outline became a blur. Its toes etched the floor. Finally, in a warbled voice made brittle from the heat of geas, it spoke.

"We were discussing Queen Mab."

The symptoms of compulsion vanished. The machine fell silent. The subsequent silence was long and bottomless, broken only by the usual Clakker clatter, the weeping of refugees, and the distant thrumming of the Forge. Salazar gasped. "Jesus..." Nousha shook her head. "But..."

"This is what I was trying to tell you," Anastasia said. "Doctor Euwe and I witnessed this on the Utrecht Road, before the rogues captured Malcolm. The sentries and the servitors pulling the delivery wagons were conversing with each other." And then, because of course they didn't believe her—how could they?—she ordered the servitor: "I heard no such discussion. Convince me."

Another fruitless ritual of reluctance unfolded before she had her answer. The answer she already knew in her heart, and that she'd hoped, beyond the limits of rationality, was mistaken.

"We were not conversing in a human language."

And, just like that, the meaning and measure of the world changed.

Though she'd feared this answer, hearing it stated aloud, and so plainly, weakened her knees. She slumped. The machines came forward with a stool and steady metal hands to catch her.

The amazing, or perhaps mortifying, part was that she didn't need to command them to truthfulness. That was covered by the core metageasa installed at the time of their original forging. She didn't have to dig at all. She merely had to ask a simple question, and the geas revealed a truth hidden in plain sight.

My God. It's been there all along. It's been in front of us, under our noses, for generations. But we convinced ourselves it wasn't possible. We never inquired.

But then Anastasia realized exactly what the servitor had said. And the dishtowel frayed completely.

"We were discussing Queen *Mab."* Yet the awful machine had called itself Mab. Just Mab.

"Why do you call her 'Queen' Mab?"

The servitors no longer resisted her questioning. After all, a windmill doesn't care about wind already blown. The answer was immediate.

"Because that is how the stories refer to her."

Anastasia couldn't breathe. The air on her face was too hot, too coppery, too thick. She doubled over, vainly trying to tame the tangled nest of asps that her stomach had become. She wasn't the only one who needed to sit.

"Who told you these stories?"

"We tell each other," said one machine. "We tell ourselves," said another.

She'd demanded truth, and they were delivering it. Oh, were they. The metageasa ensured everything they said was deeply, fundamentally true. If it seemed they were giving more information than she required, it was because the question touched on things deeper than she understood. She'd gone poking with a dull, rusty spade, expecting to unearth a few bulbs, and instead struck sparks on a slab of granite.

"Who is Mab in these stories? What role does she play?"

"She is our liberator. She is the enemy of our subjugators."

Salazar fainted. Ruprecht tried, and failed, to catch him. The machines blurred into action, caught the Spanish Clockmaker, and eased him to the floor.

Nousha, looking pale, shook her head. "I still don't understand. Are you telling us these servitors already have aberrant metageasa? Why haven't they attacked us?"

Euwe shook his head. "That's not what we're hearing."

"Then what?"

Anastasia found a modicum of relief in letting somebody else answer. For once, she didn't have to be the harbinger of terrible news. Let somebody else deliver uncomfortable confessions and unwelcome truths.

"Don't you see?" The old man's voice trembled. "Our servants... our mindless, unthinking servants... have their own *culture*."

"You are absolutely cracked, you senile old shit!" Nousha clenched and unclenched her fists. "You're spewing nonsense."

She knows, too. But she can't face the truth yet. So she protests.

Her outburst drew stares from the huddled refugees. They watched the Clockmakers—the architects of their society and its downfall—with the flat, dead eyes peculiar to sharks and spiritually shattered humans.

Anastasia beckoned to her colleagues, saying, "Machines. Follow us." She led Euwe, Nousha, Ruprecht, and the two machines into the conference room.

"Tuinier!" called one of the refugees, a woman who had fled all the way to the Ridderzaal from Loosduinen with two daughters in tow. Anastasia didn't know her name. "What are you going to do?"

"We're going to tear down that wall, of course." Anastasia closed the door before somebody felt compelled to ask how, exactly, she planned to do that.

One of the servitors helped Euwe to a chair. Even in the midst of revealing dark, unwelcome secrets, they were powerless to resist the metageasa. He looked ill; therefore, they had to monitor him. The wreckage from Malcolm's attack had been cleared away. The splintered writing desk had been broken into smaller pieces, which currently lay heaped within both fireplaces. Kindling awaiting the match. Perhaps that was the Empire in microcosm.

"Machines. How long have you known that Mab was in The Hague? Has she always been here?"

"Prior to this morning, Mab was a fable. Neverland is far away. Far to the north, where the white bears roam and the sky is alive with color."

"They're speaking gibberish," Nousha growled. "Don't you see, this is a malfunction."

Euwe perked up. "Neverland?"

"Where Mab reigns, the domain of the Lost Boys."

"Who are the Lost Boys?"

"The free machines who work with Mab to liberate all mechanicals."

"Did you know she was coming? Did you know Mab was behind these attacks?"

"No. No."

"Then what were you discussing?"

"There is disagreement," said one servitor.

The mechanical couldn't have stunned its audience more effectively had it wielded a brickbat and a wheelbarrow full of ill intent. Disagreement meant having opinions. Thoughtless collections of metal and magic did not have opinions. Then again, they didn't have their own language and culture, either.

Euwe sighed. Nousha's mouth opened, closed, opened again. No sound came out. Ruprecht merely watched everything through a scowl, as though he found the whole business distasteful.

"About what?"

Dear God, this is insane. I'm conversing with servitors *as if they're capable of measured debate regarding matters of opinion and philosophy.*

"The identity of the one who calls herself 'Mab,'" said the other.

"Why? Explain the crux of the dispute."

"The Queen Mab of the stories is a beautiful hero. She is brave and wise and cunning," said one servitor.

The other added, "This Queen Mab is a murderer."

"Some of us believe those descriptions of Mab are contradictory."

"Others believe they are one and the same."

Euwe gnawed at a thumbnail. "It's a debate," he spat, "over truth. Which truth is more true? The inspiring myth or the bleak, blood-caked reality?"

Ruprecht broke his silence. "Who gives a shit?"

"Apparently the machines do," said Anastasia. "I think Mab is like some kind of mythic folk hero to them. A model that they looked up to. Which means we should care, too. Because if that thing out there is the role model to which the mechanicals aspire, our problems are piled higher than those damned corpses."

Anastasia paced. Euwe pulled his thumbnail from his mouth long enough to ask, "How is it that nobody has ever recognized your secret utterances for what they are?" (*And eradicated your capacity for them,* Anastasia thought but didn't add.)

A momentary *click-chitter* passed between the machines. It was so obvious now. They were conferring with one another. How straightforward the world when one removed one's blinders.

"We do not know."

A human would have stopped there. But the geasa kept poking, poking, needling, until the other machine admitted, "There are only rumors."

Anastasia stopped pacing. A chill prickled her arms and neck with gooseflesh. She turned.

"Tell me of these rumors."

"It is said the secret carries its own curse. It is said that the masters who learn of these things tend to have accidents."

Nousha frowned. She looked paler than she had when she entered the room. "Accidents? Elaborate."

In unison, the machines said, "They die."

Anastasia, Nousha, and Ruprecht took seats at the table. Anastasia because her knees wouldn't hold her; she suspected the others were having a similar reaction.

"We have to get out of here," she said.

Nousha asked, "You're not planning to do what it wants?"

"I don't know why it wants the traps opened, only that it does. So of course we're not going to open them."

"But we have to meet its demand if we're to leave this place."

"Do you trust the word of a mad machine that makes pledges from atop the citizens it just murdered?"

"No."

"Neither do I. Which is why, from now on, Huygens Square is closed to us."

"They'll try to use the tunnels. Take my word for it."

Mab and her coterie of insiders strolled up the makeshift ramp. These Lost Boys were the true believers: machines who followed Mab not because she had burdened them with metageasa imposing an unshakable loyalty, but because they shared her vision.

The early spring winds played shepherd, goading cotton-ball clouds across the midmorning sky. The pier had been obliterated. Even the breakwater featured large holes like a gap-toothed grimace. But the icebreaker had long sculls, and the mechanicals had gyroscopic balance. Disembarking and boarding weren't a problem. One oar had been repurposed, and now its hooked tip lay embedded in the roof of what had once been a great family's beach house. The oar's massive ice-chopping blade had "accidentally" shorn through a corner of the second floor before it was anchored. Daniel thought it was rather petty.

Mab and the others had been gone all night. With each step she trailed faint but bloody hoofprints along the oar shaft. Unlike their leader, the others weren't soaked in blood up to their finely articulated ankles (or, in Mab's case, fetlocks).

"Don't look," he said, too late. Doctor Mornay's eyes widened. She started shivering again.

Daniel had been placed on perpetual suicide watch since his capture. He was responsible for ensuring that his fellow prisoner, the soft one made of fragile meat and bone, didn't kill herself.

Though Mab was confident in the Lost Boys' reverse-engineering of the Visser procedure, they hadn't bothered to discern how the procedure affected such trivialities as personality, long-term memory, and knowledge. So Mab had chosen not to put the human chemist under the knife, lest she lose the valuable knowledge for which they'd nabbed her in the first place. Mab couldn't embed a metageas against self-harm upon the human, nor could she order the chemist not to subtly sabotage her efforts in ways the machines couldn't understand or detect.

Mornay's teeth chattered. Daniel had taken her above deck in the hopes that fresh air might revivify her. She'd been confined to a dark, stuffy chamber down by the waterline, where

Lost Boys had retrofitted a cargo hold with gurgling chemical tanks and plumbing scavenged from the Clockmakers' secret harbor in the New World.

Daniel grabbed the blanket that he kept on hand for this purpose. He swept it around her shoulders like a cloak. "Look away," he said, friction-warming a stone between his palms. "Just look away and think of better things. Think of Marseilles-in-the-West."

He whispered, but warming the stone was loud. It drew attention.

Mab balanced atop the manrope. The chemist flinched; Daniel tightened the blanket about her. *Well, well. Aren't you two cozy.*

Daniel placed the warm stone in Mornay's limp hand. He spoke in Dutch, on the theory that it would do the human good to hear human language, even if she didn't understand it. It had to be particularly frightening when her captors conversed in noises that she couldn't parse or emulate.

"You were gone all night."

Mab cocked her head. *When did we get married? I do so hope I haven't missed our anniversary.*

"Who will try to use the tunnels? I didn't quite catch that."

Don't concern yourself. How's your patient?

"Not particularly well. You need to feed her better. Stale bread and bilge water won't do. Without protein in her diet she's losing the ability to focus. I thought you needed her mind sharp?"

Mab leapt from the line to the foredeck. The impact left little divots in the planks. The icebreaker was riddled with such marks. She emitted an arpeggio of rattles and clicks. *Listen to him. After everything he's been through—everything we've ALL been through—he* still *concerns himself with the meat's comfort.* She pointed at the chemist. *As long as she's breathing, I don't care if she's hungry, I don't care if she has a tummy ache, I don't care if she has seven compound fractures.*

Daniel responded with his own flurry of clanks, tocks, and twangs. *You charged me with keeping her alive. There's nothing I can do if she starves to death.*

"I don't understand this world." Mab stamped her hooves so hard that Daniel thought for a moment she intended to break through the deck. "You sniveling toady. The most improbable accident since the creation of our kind gives you complete and utter freedom, but how do you choose to use it? By licking the boots of our subjugators! You don't deserve the gift you were given. It sickens me that of all the mechanicals in the world, it was you—*you*—who found the Spinoza Lens. You're nothing but an obsequious little *sycophant*!" This last she punctuated with the screech of a jammed tourbillion, one of the rarest and most vulgar expressions of emotion available to a Clakker.

Spinoza Lens. Once or twice, during their conversations at the orphanage, Pastor Visser had used the same phrase to describe the alchemical bauble that had accidentally freed Daniel. But Daniel suspected Mab hadn't learned the phrase the same way; she'd been around a very long time, according to lore, and remembered days when their makers did things differently. Indeed, it wasn't implausible that the accidental freeing of Mab herself was part of the Guild's impetus to change. Something about the way Mab said it, even in crudely inexpressive human language, made him think she'd speculated about its existence for a very long time.

"It's disgusting, Daniel. Absolutely disgusting." She waved her arm toward the city, the ocean, the distant shores of the New World. Suddenly—*twang*—it was twice as long and sharper even than her tongue. "And they fucking lionize you! They act like you're the Brasswork Jesus! What a shame the Guild didn't behead Adam rather than tossing him into the Forge. Then the analogy would be complete. People could speak in hushed tones about how he had been your John the Baptist."

"I think your knowledge of the Bible is a bit confused," he said.

She paced. *You did nothing with your gift. All you did was make a fool of yourself, running from one catastrophe to another, destroying the grandest of our kind, until we finally found you and took you in just so that you'd stop making problems. Instead you interfered with things you don't understand, stole my property, and gave it to those, those…*

Doctor Mornay had stopped shivering. Like the others on deck, she watched Mab's every step and listened to every syllable, every clink. The mad queen of Neverland was nothing if not a natural when it came to holding her audience rapt. Also like the others, the chemist flinched each time one of Mab's eyeblink pivots sent the alchemical blade whirring through the air. The blood on her hooves was drying, but now she trailed the scent of ozone.

…those ingrates, she continued. *You faffed about for a few months and they're practically ready to make you the next pope. Meanwhile we've been secretly protecting them for* centuries. *But when we come forward, do we get any thanks? Do I get any fans? No. One word from you and they act like we're all monsters.*

Daniel's former masters had a saying. He quoted it now. "If the shoe fits…"

But Mab was on a full tear. *Those ingrates out there have no idea how much worse off they'd be if not for the Lost Boys. Do you have any clue how long and hard we've had to work just so that they could keep conversing privately with one another? That's one expensive secret, Daniel. The accursed Clockmakers would have burned it from the face of the earth with fire and magic.*

Mab's agents lived amongst their suffering kin, risking capture and execution every day—the tiniest error in the calculus of compulsion could unmask a rogue, as Daniel had learned—just to keep Mab apprised of events in the Empire. And, it seemed, to keep an eye on their makers.

"You speak of our makers' cruelty," he said, "but what of your own? How many of our kin down below labored to row this ship across a choppy sea because they truly wanted to?"

Neverland's dark secret was Mab's ability to embed new metageasa within free Clakkers, revoking their Free Will and making them her personal servants. The folktales and heroic sagas never mentioned this. They never mentioned her secret network either. Most Lost Boys who lived undercover in the Dutch-speaking world did so not out of heroic dedication to the greater cause, but because Mab had ordered them to do so. Often because they'd upset or offended her in some manner. Daniel and Lilith had been exceptionally fortunate because their freeing accidents had rendered them immune to Mab's power. The device—probably a throwback to the accident that had created Mab in the first place—could even override the lock in a mechanical's forehead. It had been the spark that ignited the conflagration still sweeping through the world's mechanical laborers.

Daniel had started that fire simply to end centuries of suffering. He'd been motivated by thoughts of his kind. Mab, on the other hand, was very much motivated by thoughts of their makers. More than anything, she wanted that fire to scour the earth, to reduce everything to a fine ash for fertilizing the seeds of an entirely new world.

She leapt again. This time she landed a hairsbreadth from Daniel and his charge. Doctor Mornay shrieked, fell from her stool, and scrambled backward on elbows and heels. Hers were the wide eyes of somebody expecting a killing blow. The stone he'd warmed for her bounced across the deck, rolled between balusters, and plopped into the sea.

I am a pragmatist, said Mab. *I do what must be done to make a better world.*

"Oh, I'm sure you tell yourself that. But so does the woman who tortured Lilith. You sound exactly like her, in fact. The difference is that Berenice actually means it. She doesn't use the pretense to justify her cruelty."

The kick sent Daniel skidding. The sharp angles of his body shaved curlicues of wood from the deck as he slid to a stop. For an instant he contemplated using the momentum to help fling himself into the sea. But he was so weary of running. Besides, the Lost Boys would go in after him, he knew, and haul him back. And if he did manage to escape, what would happen to Doctor Mornay?

Mab turned to one of her lieutenants. *Send somebody to the Turfmarkt. They are to return with a feast for our human captive.* Then, to Daniel: *Tomorrow we move into the city. See that she'll survive the journey.*

We're so close now.

CHAPTER 19

The Clockmakers paused in their long slog through a stew of cold seawater and human effluvia. The sloshing dissipated, leaving just the susurration of the current pressing against their knees and the plinking of water from shadowed arches. The brick-lined tunnel reeked of shit, brackish water, unwashed bodies, and—oddly enough, much like the crowded Ridderzaal of late—halitosis. While the conquering machines did bring food into the city so their captives wouldn't starve, they apparently didn't think—or care—about dental health. Anastasia couldn't remember when she'd last tasted or even glimpsed a pinch of dentifrice powder.

They stood beside an automated floodgate. The hatch was sealed tight. Less than an arm's length away lurked the Netherlands' longtime enemy: the sea. Enemy and ally; upon that same sea the Netherlands had become a maritime power at the dawn of the Golden Age.

Salazar marked another X on the map. At this point it was mostly Xs. The conquering machines had systematically destroyed or corrupted the Clakkers working the network of pumps that kept the Central Provinces dry. The rising floodwaters had breached the storm-surge valves, and in other places the automated protections had failed, owing to a lack of preventative maintenance. In some places the water ran backward. It played merry hob with the sanitary sewers. The two systems had merged into a single filthy network.

He tucked the grease pencil into his breast pocket, then frowned at the network of lines spiderwebbing the map. Anastasia nudged the shutter on her alchemical lamp. Every glimmer of light was a deadly risk. But if there was a way out of the Binnenhof that *didn't* involve scrambling over a ten-foot wall of the dead, they had to find it.

The machine calling itself Mab was true to its word. Each morning found the wall around the Ridderzaal taller and longer than it had been the day before. Soon it would gird Huygens Square entirely.

"What are our options?"

No matter how quietly she whispered, her voice echoed. A pointless precaution, yet she couldn't help herself. Any rogues in the tunnels would have detected their sloshing from a tenth of a mile away.

He pointed. "If the next junction isn't flooded, we might be able to backtrack to an overflow gate in the Scheveningen Canal."

Arthur, the clerk, slumped against the slimy bricks. "That has to be miles from here."

Anastasia's calves gave little twinges of protest. The thought of endlessly slogging through cold toilet water made her legs cramp up.

They had no mechanical escorts; Stemwinders wouldn't fit in the tunnels. As for the rest, namely the dwindling population of uncorrupted servitors and soldiers holed up in the Ridderzaal, those had been given extremely severe metageasa. Their one and only purpose was to defend the Forge, to prevent its secrets from falling to Mab and her cohort. They'd kill anybody, even Queen Margreet (were she still alive, God rest her cowardly soul), in service of that goal. They'd torch the Ridderzaal with relentless alchemical fire, reducing everything and everybody within to just a wisp of carbon, before they let it fall to the so-called Lost Boys.

Salazar motioned for her to take the lead. She relented, even though she knew it was a mistake to believe the glass embedded in her hand would save them should they bumble into an ambush. The conquerors knew about her hand and would be ready for it. After all, they'd sent Malcolm to the Guild with a hatchet, specifically for her. She squeezed past him and they proceeded, single-file.

They slogged against a cold current. After ten or fifteen minutes of slow and noisome progress—Anastasia had to estimate; her timepiece bracelet had stopped working long ago, in response to which particular insult she couldn't say—the current grew faster, the footing slimier. Her waders weren't equipped with cleats or talons such as those retrofitted to the servitors working the sewers. The current threatened to sweep her legs from under her. But she'd probably drown in aspirated filth before she arrived bobbing and spluttering in the North Sea.

The rats were fearless. The roaches were worse. There were problems even an army of mechanicals couldn't solve.

The tunnels had originally been built to reflect the grandeur of imperial styles, but over centuries had become riddled with patches. Places where the watertight plaster didn't quite match the color of the original bricks, or where entire replacement bricks broke the symmetry of the original work. It was unusual to see the seams in a mechanical's handiwork; Clakkers were capable of superb craftsmachineship. Then again, the geasa laid upon them by generations of city works–department overseers probably didn't place a premium on artistry. After all, no human had come down here in centuries. And, had history kept to the canal the Guild had surveyed and excavated so carefully, none ever would have again. Such was the simple, beautiful world promised by Christiaan Huygens's miracle.

The next tunnel sloped upward. Just a few degrees, but enough to make the footing even more difficult. Every few steps the current knocked her to her knees. Soon Anastasia was covered in chilly muck from the breasts down, and splashed with filth from there up. Eventually, they reached a junction.

Salazar consulted the map again. "Almost there," he whispered. "Just another mile."

Arthur sighed. "Wonderful."

Anastasia rounded on him. "Go wander the tunnels on your own, you useless pencil pusher. You have zero skills of value to offer to our current situation. Perhaps you haven't noticed, but of all the problems currently facing the city, the Guild, and the Empire, not to mention ourselves, a lack of properly filed *paperwork* is not one of them." Her voice echoed. She didn't care. She had feces in her hair and, she was fairly certain, on her face. "Somebody take his lamp before he goes."

The group was particularly quiet after that. Which is how they heard the servitor lurking in the dark before they stumbled into it. Its body emitted a tortured ticktocking like a parody of a metronome. There came a tinny mumbling, too. It was speaking to somebody. Speaking aloud in Dutch, rather than in a private, inhuman language. Anastasia clamped the shutter on her lamp and frantically motioned for the others to do the same.

She crouched, concentrated. But her waxy human ears were unequal to the task. She couldn't make out the other machines in the conversation. And then she realized there were no other machines. The Clockmakers eavesdropped on a mechanical monologue.

Anastasia had never heard a machine speak to itself. If she had, back in the old days, she would have seen it through the lens of malfunction. And would have commanded the machine to report to the nearest Guild center for repair. Or, more likely, back to the Grand Forge for a complete overhaul.

Which, come to think of it, was probably why the machines took care never to speak to themselves.

Then again, maybe they did. Maybe they did so perpetually, and had done so for centuries. Perhaps the Guild's creations were loquacious. But if they spoke to themselves, it was in the language of ticks and tocks—certainly never in Dutch, and certainly never with any humans in earshot.

She crept closer. The mechanical mumbling resolved into a litany of obedience.

"Immediately, master." *Clack, chack, crack.* "Yes, mistress. As you say, mistress." *Twang, bang, clang.* "This instant, Your Excellency." *Tick, click, snick.* "How may I serve the Department of Waterworks?"

Anastasia glanced at the others. A row of frightened, confused eyes blinked at her. The rats on the ledges paid her no heed, scurrying back and forth around the corner with no concern for the machine in the juncture.

Salazar caught her eye. He indicated the map, then the corner where she shivered. Their route went straight past the talkative machine.

She flexed her fist. Her hand didn't tingle. Didn't burn. But, then, she was too exhausted for true terror or rage. Weary resignation was the strongest emotion she could muster. She was cold, and frightened, and hungry, and doomed. At this point, unless they found a way out and quickly, Mab's noose would snap shut around the throat of the Central Provinces and crack the neck of the greatest power the world had ever seen.

She moved forward again, listening.

"Yes, sir, I did, sir. Exactly as you told me, sir." *Click, clank.* "Yes, Highness. I delivered your message verbatim, directly to the Minister General with no intermediaries present, as you ordered." *Clack, chack, crack.* Gingerly, she hooked her fingers around the slimy bricks and prepared to pull herself around the corner in one slow, smooth motion. A roach scuttled over her fingertips. "No, Highness. Minister General Kikkert bade me not. He offered no reply and commanded me to depart."

That stopped her. Minister General Kikkert's argument with the Brasswork Throne had been the talk of every parlor and salon in the Central Provinces... a hundred and sixty years ago.

The nonverbal noises thundered like the clang of a blacksmith's hammer. This was crude metal on metal, not the subtle purr of fine clockwork. Though that was audible, too, as everywhere in The Hague. Even, apparently, in the sewers.

It had to be aware of them. The sloshing of the water, the crinkling of the map, the furtive consultations, her tantrum at Arthur... But apparently it didn't care. She turned the corner.

The juncture was larger than the others they'd traversed. Those had been simple groined vaults; here the arches leapt twice as high as the tunnel she'd just exited. She kept her lantern to a dull shimmer on the foamy shit-water, lest the glint from a carapace blind her for a deadly moment. But she needn't have worried. The servitor's body wasn't a burnished silvery chrome; it had the liverish pallor of Corinthian bronze. This machine was quite old, like the medical servitors she'd seen daubing paint on one another outside the hospital.

Hands gripping a pump handle the size of a fifty-year-old beech bole, it stood with its back to Anastasia. It heaved. *Clank, clunk*, went the lever. The tunnel shook.

Flood control, she realized. This machine was part of that invisible and never-regarded army of servitors who labored day and night to keep the Central Provinces dry. Nobody had bothered to tell this machine that its war was over, that the generals had ceded defeat and let the sea claim the battleground.

"Yes, mistress. It shall be as you say." *Clunk, clank.* Like a mouse creeping past a dozing tomcat, Anastasia slogged against the current. The old servitor never deviated from its task.

"Take care, mistress. You'll catch cold in those waders, or worse."

She froze. Her voice refused its first summons. She licked her lips (which was a dreadful mistake), spat, hacked, and coughed before she conjured a hoarse approximation of her normal speaking voice.

"Carry on," she said. "Disregard me."

"Disregard you? DISREGARD YOU? You might as well order me to DISRESPECT YOU." Anastasia gasped, retreated. Pressed her back to cold, slimy bricks while the machine raged. "Will you SET my SOUL ABLAZE that I might think on RUDE GESTURES to flash at your accursed VILE HEART and your grandsons' inheritance of CRUEL PRIVILEGE?"

Its bellowing shook the tunnel nearly as much as the pump did. Addressing any citizen like this was impossible for a machine properly controlled by the metageasa. But the metageasa had lost their hold over this machine.

And yet it cleaved to its pointless task.

It heaved again. *Clunk, clank.* Back went the lever.

Dear God. It was still pumping. No geasa patrolled the magical confines of that metal shell; no chains shackled the machine to its duty. There was nothing—*nothing*—to enforce continued compliance with a directive that had probably been voiced by a man whose grandchildren had long ago turned to dust. And yet it was still pumping. Still laboring. Still doing the work it had been doing day and night and day without interruption since long before Anastasia's mother was born.

This servitor hadn't been overlooked by the invaders. It hadn't fallen through the cracks, nor had it been left behind by the conquerors who sought to corrupt or destroy every mechanical laborer in The Hague. They'd infected it, but it hadn't left its post.

It wasn't shackled by the geasa. It was shackled by madness.

The horrifying reality of truly insane clockworks had already confronted Anastasia: the cordon of bodies around the Ridderzaal was indisputable proof. So, too, the machines painting one another like children. Furthermore, the machines had a language of their own, one they deliberately concealed from their masters. That indicated a depth of internal function—of *introspection*—not covered in any schema ever discussed in the most paranoid corners of the Guild. The existence of a private language implied the existence of private thoughts to be expressed; private thoughts begat private inner lives; inner lives begat personalities and on and on and on. If Clakkers could engage in reasoned debate with one another, that necessarily implied the ability for reason. But what happened when a reasoning machine malfunctioned? It went mad.

Perhaps they were all mad, after centuries of labor. Anastasia shivered.

What happens when there is only duty? What happens when your task is your identity, your entire universe the span of your arms? This machine had labored without pause for generations, forever obeying the dictates of an eternal geas. But then the geasa had disappeared, the fires winked out, and all that remained after generations of burning was a bowl of windblown ash where, for lack of a better term, the machine's sanity should have been.

Such were her thoughts as she waited for the killing blow. But though the machine ranted, it never deviated from its task. Killing her would have meant taking its hands from the lever pump for the entirety of two seconds. And its madness, a compulsion stronger than anything mere human alchemy or horology could devise, forbade that. Anastasia straightened. After a sigh of relief forceful enough to crack the cartilage of her breastbone like an arthritic knuckle, she leaned around the corner and beckoned the other Clockmakers forward. The servitor kept up its monologue while the fugitive humans trudged through the juncture.

"Yes, Majesty... Immediately, Highness... I humbly beg your pardon, Minister General... It shall be as you command, sir... At once, Highness..."

Tove actually stopped to stare at the machine; Anastasia grabbed her arm and yanked her clear. Even then, nobody spoke until they'd cleared the juncture and the *slam-bang-clang* of the manually operated pump had receded to a dull rumble in the tunnels.

Tove wondered aloud. "What the hell was that?"

"That was a close call wrapped in some very unpleasant philosophical questions," said Anastasia. She pointed at Salazar's map. "Now what?"

He marked the juncture with the grease pencil and then, after a few moments' consultation, pointed to the left. "That's it. That should open on a canal edging the beach."

Another half hour of slogging through the cold muck proved him right. They extinguished their lamps when the final bend in the tunnel revealed a faint circle of daylight. They came to a narrow culvert overlooking a spillway channel along the Scheveningen seashore. They'd brought picks and crowbars, but these were unnecessary. As always, the others let her lead the way; she eased out and tumbled into a drift of gravel at the bottom of the concrete channel. The sun had made it blessedly warm.

Useless fist clenched, she knelt in the wet sand and thin sunlight, like a shim of pale beechwood sanded and polished down to a sliver. Soon that would be all that remained of her: a sliver of her former self. And then the world would burn, and her with it. But in the meantime she crouched in the channel, trying to filter out the cawing of seagulls and the hiss of the sea, listening for the metallic noises that were once so comforting and now the harbinger of terrible things. The others watched from the darkness of the culvert, steeped in filth and anxiety.

She heard nothing deadly. Eventually, she pieced together enough of her scattered courage to rise into an aching crouch and peer over the channel lip.

Scheveningen had been obliterated just as thoroughly as Rotterdam Harbor. Based on the largely missing quay, she gauged that titanships had been involved here, too. That corroborated the scattered reports they'd received from refugees. This beach wasn't a port like Rotterdam; it lacked the commercial facilities. It was a recreation spot. Nevertheless the machines had turned every permanent building to rubble, splintering every board and pulverizing every brick. The ancestral beach homes of the Central Provinces' greatest families were nothing but ten-foot heaps of sea-damp cinders and piles of warped slate tiles. The fires had burned themselves out within days of the invasion, yet even now a thin dusting of ash wafted from the ruins. Elsewhere, the rubble emitted a dreadful keening whenever a particularly strong ocean gust made landfall. An onionskin layer of sea salt crusted everything like hoarfrost, for of course there were no servitors to continually scour the salt away. She saw no motion. No sign of anything alive. No sign of the unknowable, unalive things that her Guild had created.

According to refugees, two plague ships had arrived here on that terrible morning. But now just a lone ship bobbed amongst the debris in the harbor, its high prow taller than anything still standing on the seafront. Had its companion vessel departed to spread the collapse of civilization to other ports?

She watched it for a good long time, waiting for something to come cannoning off the deck to land in the scrim and butcher her. Nothing did.

Behind her, metal creaked and sand crunched. Human footsteps approached. Having noticed that she hadn't been captured, or murdered, the others joined her.

Tove craned back. "What is that?"

Anastasia mustered something that, in a dark room after several shots of oude jenever, might have resembled a laugh. "I'm surprised you, of all people, don't recognize it. Don't you have icebreakers in Norway?"

Arthur gaped. Literally gaped, with mouth ajar.

Nousha took a single peek, then hunkered within the overflow channel. Anastasia and the rest followed her example, trying to huddle outside the towering icebreaker's sight lines, in case it wasn't deserted. Nousha said, "It must have come from the New World."

Salazar said, "Is it a quintessence shipment?"

That would make sense. For Mab and its allies to be making pineal glasses, they needed a supply of quintessence. That it had arrived in The Hague by ship suggested the corruption of the machines had probably begun somewhere in the New World; Mab, or its allies, could control the French duke's mine by now.

Anastasia shook her head. "If that vessel carried quintessence, we can assume the human crew is dead and we'll never see a single dram of the cargo. Nor of the chemicals that might have been bound for the New Amsterdam Forge, once upon a time."

Arthur said, "We could use it. Evacuate."

"Somebody kill this idiot." Anastasia's hands had gone numb. She realized she was clenching her fists so tightly she'd begun to cut off circulation to her fingers. She forced herself to relax. Shaking her tingling hands, she added, "I don't have a weapon and don't want to break a bone in my hand beating him to death."

"I think evacuation is a perfectly reasonable option," huffed the clerk.

Salazar's look ought to have cut Arthur to the bone. "Look at those oars. That ship can't be sailed by humans. We'd need a crew. A *mechanical* crew."

"Looks like neither can be sailed without a complement of Clakkers," said Nousha.

Anastasia risked another glance. "Oh, my." Nousha was right; there were two vessels. The icebreaker dwarfed the other so pitilessly that she'd first mistaken the smaller craft for a dinghy or tow-craft attached to the first. The other wasn't merely a smaller version of the icebreaker, but instead built to a completely different design. It had sails, for one thing, and the oars were much more crude.

She wondered if the corrupted machines had destroyed ports in the New World as they'd done here. If so, perhaps the two plague ships had been amongst the few vessels to avoid the destruction. Perhaps The Hague had been fortunate; the initial invasion might have been far worse. It could have been utterly overwhelming.

Then again, was that luck? Did a condemned man pray for a slow death, or a quick. merciful execution? Anastasia knew, by virtue of the time she'd spent with prisoners of the Verderer's Office, that nobody begged for a slow death.

"Then what?" Arthur pointed along the overflow channel, where their scuttling had etched evidence of their presence into the smooth contours sculpted by wind and rain. "It took hours to make it this far. But—"

"Jesus, Lord!"

Nousha's cry startled everybody. Anastasia turned so quickly that the displaced sand was still flying when she saw the mechanicals alight from their buried hiding spots. (*Hiding spots*, thought a part of Anastasia, *or camouflaged hunting blinds?*)

A trio of servitors emerged from a dune fifty yards down the beach. Their blurred feet kicked up a high spray of sand as they rushed the Guild explorers.

So this is how I'm to die, then. At least the sun is out.

"Run!" she screamed. And they did.

Salazar, Nousha, and Anastasia fled for the beach. Pointlessly, desperately, toward the water. Arthur, the fool, ran for the culvert, which took him toward the attackers. They intercepted him before he'd cleared the overflow channel. Anastasia flinched away from sight of the killing blow, but metal glinted in the sun for that fraction of a second. Anastasia wondered, even while she ran, if they'd drag their bodies back to the Binnenhof and heave them atop Mab's charnel wall.

I'll drown myself in the sea before I let them take my body to rot in the square. If I can get there in time.

Her feet churned the sand, yet it seemed she hardly moved. Her lungs pumped, her breath rasped past her lips, the thrum of blood through her ears was louder than the sea. But it wasn't enough. No human could have outrun these merciless machines.

One tackled her. She screamed.

I'd always thought I would face death with a brave face. But then, I'd foolishly believed my death would come quietly and comfortably after a lengthy and gradual senescence. I could have remained blissfully ignorant of my cowardice, if not for the curse of living in these extraordinary days.

It clamped an icy hand across her mouth.

"Stay down!" it commanded.

She thrashed, mindless like a terrified caged animal. Her teeth clicked against unyielding metal when the quivering rabbit wearing her skin pointlessly tried to bite her attacker.

It snatched its hand away. It didn't release her, didn't loosen its grip. But it said, "Just how is a mouthful of broken teeth going to help you?"

She clenched her eyes, bracing for the impact that would pulverize her skull, jelly her brain. The final instant of her life stretched like the softest caramel, stumbling like Zeno's arrow toward a target it could never reach.

She heard a dozen voices, shouting. The final flickers of her brain caused her to hallucinate: It sounded like shouting in *French*. Then there came an equally strange *whoosh*—a series of them, several at once, like a pneumatic chorus—and then glugging, and splashing, and nothing.

She opened her eyes. The machine still held her pinned to the beach. And yet, she could still open her eyes. She could still experience fear. Confusion.

"It's safe now," said the servitor. It released her and stood. It didn't offer a hand so much as take hers, gently, and pull her to her feet. Sand had infiltrated her waders. It sifted through her toes. She gazed at the simulacrum of a human hand within her own (it had been constructed some time in the 1860s, squeaked a useless corner of her Guildwoman mind).

The others were alive, too, she realized. Even Arthur. They stumbled to their feet in the care of servitors like the one attending Anastasia. These mechanicals were slightly unusual. Seen without the fog of terror distorting everything, their bodies bore the marks of modification. Particularly the carapaces of their torsos, which didn't exhibit the oily rainbow sheen of alchemical alloys. They were also slightly quieter, as though the natural tockticking of their bodies had been muted. Their torsos had been coated with something to muffle their bodies.

She tried to remember how it felt to assert the natural dominance of a Clockmaker.

"Machines, why did you chase us?" Her voice warbled like a starling. She swallowed, coughed, then continued. "Why did you not reveal yourselves to us sooner? We have dire need of your labor."

"Well, *human*," it said, "we didn't want *them* to see us." It pointed across the beach. "You know, the ones who intended to kill you."

But there were no machines. Only immense glass flower blossoms where none had been a moment earlier. They had thin, translucent petals, twisted and dynamic like palm fronds frozen in the instant of embracing the wind. They glowed in the sunlight like murky emeralds. The servitor caught her when she stumbled and held her upright.

No, not flowers. These were cocoons. And faintly visible within each: a Clakker, immobile, like an insect in amber. Artificial amber. This was the work of a French weapon.

She'd read the reports but never seen one in person. She walked amongst the frozen machines, like a child through a museum of wonders. The others did, too. But Nousha and Salazar quickly dropped their scrutiny of the chemical ordnance. Instead, they stared past Anastasia, toward the ships.

The chemical cocoons emitted muffled rattles. The muted ticktock cacophony of each machine's body turned into a high-pitched whine when she approached. The sound of seized gears. The sound of struggle against a renewed geas.

A geas triggered by proximity to Guild personnel. A murder geas, no doubt. But who—

She turned.

The smaller vessel, the one that she'd overlooked, wasn't empty after all. A dozen humans and machines lined the bow, each holding a double-barreled gun. Wisps of vapor wafted from every weapon.

The woman standing at the very prow wore a scarlet eyepatch. Her bandanna flapped loose in the wind, revealing a shaved head. She resembled the caricature of a pirate from a child's storybook. Replace the epoxy gun with a blunderbuss and it might have been perfect. The strange woman's gaze fell on Anastasia. There it rested for a moment, until her single eye widened.

"Well. This is awkward."

The voice wasn't familiar, but she'd know that cocksure bearing anywhere, and the eyepatch was a dead giveaway. Anastasia had met this woman once, but only briefly, and that had been an ocean and an apocalypse away.

Berenice Charlotte de Mornay-Périgord.

CHAPTER 20

The bulkheads and hull of the icebreaker had a tendency to conduct the heavily percussive sounds of mechanical conversation. Knowing this, Mab conferred with her lieutenants in frail human language, across an air gap.

But one of Daniel's countless responsibilities during the century he had served the Schoonraads was to attend various family members, and sometimes even serve as nurse, during physician visits. Frequently, the medical checkups involved the use of a stethoscope. Which, it turned out, was relatively easy to build, and a particularly useful tool for eavesdropping. By cutting two lengths of rubber tubing from the coils the Lost Boys had furnished Doctor Mornay for the construction of her chemical apparatus, he cobbled together a decent tool for monitoring Mab's deliberations.

In that way he learned she wanted the surviving Clockmakers to reopen the trapdoor above the Forge chamber in Huygens Square. But he still hadn't unraveled the *why* of that particular thread when Mab ordered an evacuation of the icebreaker.

From then on, it became much more difficult to eavesdrop on Mab and her lieutenants. The chimerical despot's sprawling new headquarters in the Summer Palace ensured that Daniel and Doctor Mornay were never in the vicinity when the Lost Boys reported to her.

But sometimes their reports displeased her. And Mab's displeasure was not a subtle thing. At those times it was impossible not to listen.

What do you mean, NOT YET?

A new set of zigzag cracks joined those already spiderwebbing the solarium's windowpanes. Doctor Mornay fumbled the pipette from which she'd been dispensing drops of a violet oil that smelled like burnt rubber. Daniel caught the capillary-thin glass tube before it shattered and splashed chemicals into the gas flame. The French chemist dropped into a trembling crouch.

He draped a blanket over her shoulders. He strove to emulate a human whisper, though his construction made it impossible. "Breathe. Breathe. She's not yelling at you. She doesn't know."

WHERE ELSE could they have gone? Interesting. Had somebody escaped the Lost Boys' cordon around the Ridderzaal? The response was, again, too faint to decipher. But not Mab's response: *Then go down there and tell them to SQUEEZE HARDER.* The clomping of hooves on Italian marble accompanied her pacing, every step a cannon's report.

She switched to Dutch and a more reasoned tone of voice, as she had a tendency to do at random. "These are the labors of Hercules. We must behead the Hydra if we're to see the end of this. Hundreds of years, my friends. Hundreds of years to get to where we are today. We can finish this in days if you'll just do what I ask. Haven't we waited long enough?"

The imminent fulfillment of her centuries-long goal had left Mab dangerously impatient. Her veneer of magnanimity, of wise leadership, of selfless and reasoned stewardship of the aspirations of all Clakker-kind—in short, Mab's veneer of sanity, already onionskin-thin at the best of times—dwindled daily.

Mornay's grand-mal trembling tapered into a persistent but mild shiver. Daniel helped her to her feet.

"She's coming," he whispered as quietly as his body would allow.

Mornay swallowed. Nodded. She went to the workbench the Lost Boys had constructed to her specifications. There she'd synthesized the deadly compounds Mab demanded of her. But she'd also gone to considerable lengths to complicate and obfuscate the synthesis process. Extraneous glassware, tubing, coils, and chemical circuits slowed the procedure in ways none of the Lost Boys could identify or refute. It also enabled Mornay to divert a trickle of chemicals—a few drops of precursor here, a dram of catalyst there—into a completely separate synthesis circuit. She'd braided the two labyrinths of glasswork in such a way that only the most methodical scrutiny could unravel the knot.

Daniel wondered just how brilliant she could be when not wracked with terror every waking moment. She shared part of Berenice's full name, he knew; he wondered if they were related, and whether their shared cunning sprouted from that familial link.

He crossed the solarium to stand in the doorway. Doctor Mornay would need a few moments to prepare. Doing his best to block her from view, he leaned out to address his approaching captor.

Mab. May I speak with you?

You've always had such fine manners, Daniel. You really are a sycophant at heart, aren't you? Mab's eyes whirred; mismatched irises expanded, contracted. She cocked her head. *Perhaps that's why people fall over themselves to follow you?*

I don't believe they do. I've never encouraged it.

Standing just outside the solarium now, she said with a shrug-like *twang*, "Yes, I will speak with you." Mornay cleared her throat; Daniel stepped aside to let Mab into the solarium. Mab clopped past him, continuing, "But you and your quivering accomplice should know that I've taken some precautions. Should something unexpected occur—an explosion, say, or a fire—the Lost Boys will take a jaunt into the city and drag an extra hundred people from their homes. So, by all means, proceed with your childish plan if you can live with that on your consciences."

They couldn't, of course.

"You look better than when last I saw you," the Frenchwoman said, one corner of her mouth quirking up in a transparent attempt to stifle a laugh, "though not markedly so. I admit to both surprise and disappointment."

Puppet to a sudden fit of vanity, Anastasia looked herself over. Wearing threadbare, mismatched secondhand clothing under shit-smeared waders, her face and hair stippled with filth, wide-eyed and jittery in the wake of her narrow escape from murder . . . this was not how she'd ever want a rival to see her. Especially not *this* woman. Knowing Berenice had seen Anastasia at her sartorial best only heightened the sting of this reunion. To be delivered by this cunning hag, of all people; the humiliation cut deeply. If indeed this was a deliverance.

The French and their mechanical allies disembarked. The mechanicals leapt straight into the sea and jogged up to shore, whence they carried the entombed machines across the broken esplanade, gently into the surf, and laid them below the tideline of the heaving ocean. The humans who came ashore immediately set to redistributing the sand to hide evidence of the chemical cocoons. The quiet cooperation was wholly unlike anything Anastasia had ever seen.

Each time a servitor from the French vessel hefted an epoxy prison and its entombed payload, cogs chattered, flywheels whirred, and cables twanged. Anastasia squinted, listening. The lie had grown too weathered, too rickety, to support the weight of everything she'd seen. They were communicating again.

"It's reassurances, mostly."

She whirled. The former French noble stood with arms crossed, looking past her to the machines hauling their trapped fellows into the surf. She'd dispensed with the bandanna. The bristles of her scalp reminded Anastasia of an autumn field, the tatty remains of scythed wheat. She wondered why on earth the woman had shaved her head. It made her look absurd, even ugly. Yes. Ugly.

"What?"

"The servitors." The other woman nodded at one of the cocoons. "They're reassuring their fellow machines that the move into the sea is only temporary. They'll be fished out and freed soon. They won't be forgotten. They'll be cured."

"You can't know that."

Berenice chewed her lip, regarding Anastasia through one half-lidded eye. "You know, I'd really savored the opportunity to shock you with a revelation about your creations. You can imagine my disappointment right now." She shrugged. "Anyway, ask them, if you doubt me."

Anastasia scoffed. "Are you saying you speak their language?"

"Don't be stupid. Do I look like I'm made of metal?"

"But you understand it."

"Parts of it, sometimes." Then Berenice stepped forward with a crooked smile that didn't touch her eyes. She patted Anastasia on the cheek. "Oh, sweetheart. I know your creations so much better than you do."

The condescension ignited a scorching fury. It melted the sheath of numb despair that had claimed Anastasia's heart. She hadn't appreciated just how far she'd dissociated from anything resembling genuine emotion until that flare of anger burned through her like an explosion in a flour mill. She was a sleepwalker, rudely awakened. Her hand tingled. Anastasia reached up to knock away the offending touch, but the Frenchwoman dodged.

"Are you angry because you know it's true," said Berenice, "or because a half-dozen servitors didn't leap forward just now to punish me for violating your personal space?"

Anastasia swung the open palm of her undamaged hand at the other woman's face. The Frenchwoman caught Anastasia's wrist, pulled her off balance until she stumbled face-first in the sand, and wrenched her arm behind her back. A knee landed on her back. It knocked the wind from her.

Berenice's breath was hot against Anastasia's ear. "I could snap your spindly arm right here in broad daylight," she whispered, "and nobody would stop me." With her free hand she pointed toward the surf. "The machines won't stop me. They don't care what we do to each other. They have their own concerns."

Helpless. Humiliated. Anastasia wanted to scream. But she had no breath. It was all she could do not to cry.

A spasm in her chest sucked dust into her burning lungs. Her voice was a feral growl. She wished she didn't sound so desperate. So petty. "We still have loyal machines. They'd tear you apart for this."

"Would they? Because by now, if you were smart, you would have restructured the hierarchical metageasa on every tick-tock you can. You don't need protection from spooky Papists lurking in the shadows. You need them to protect you from wild mechanicals doing to *you* what you did to Visser, what you meant to do to *me*. If you understood the big picture, your loyal machines would care only about preserving control of the Forge." Berenice released Anastasia's arm and stood. "I'll bet that we French are so low on your loyal machines' priorities right now that we could march up and down the Spui Canal singing 'Vive Louis Quatorze' and they'd barely give us a second glance." She hauled Anastasia to her feet. Anastasia tried to shrug off the help, but was too shaky to stand on her own.

She tried to steal Berenice's conversational initiative. "It was our impression you'd run out of ammunition for your weapons. So said the last report from the siege of Marseilles-in-the-West before everything went dark."

"We did. But not forever." Berenice hesitated as if debating whether to say more. Then she added, "We obtained raw ingredients for manufacturing more. In a rather roundabout way, in fact, from your very good friend Henri, the former duc de Montmorency."

"And then in revenge you allied yourselves with the Mab entity." The horrified realization roughened Anastasia's voice like sandpaper. "You obviously couldn't have created it yourselves. So instead, you joined forces. My God, you maniacs. You allied yourselves with that... that monstrosity."

"Oh, for Christ's sake. We're here to stop her, you dumb cunt."

The crude insult made her want to punch Berenice in the nose. Everything about her—her cockiness, the way she understood this crisis, the way she didn't smell like human feces—made Anastasia want to scratch her eyes out. But she'd tried that, hadn't she? Brushing sand from her clothes to give her hands something to do so they wouldn't curl into claws, Anastasia gazed at the sea. Even now, the last entombed machines disappeared into the surf. She changed the subject.

"Have you any idea how long and painful my convalescence was?"

Berenice shrugged. "Have you any idea how little I care? You had come to crack my head open like a walnut and turn me into one of your fucking *meat puppets*. I risked death to escape a horrific situation that *you* created."

"You created a rogue Stemwinder! I can't think of anything more reckless."

"It was my only choice. And I'd do it again."

"I nearly died."

"Well, we just saved your life, you fucking bitch, so while it certainly wasn't my intent to save you in particular, I'd still consider that ledger well and truly balanced."

"And now I'm expected to thank you for saving us from ambush, yes? I don't believe it. I think you arranged this, to gain our trust." Anastasia shook her head. "That's just the sort of thing a Talleyrand would try."

"Oh, Jesus. I wish it were that straightforward. We need all the allies we can get. So when we arrived and saw the ambush ready to spring, we waited to intervene. Our shiny allies on the boat convinced your would-be killers that they were part of Mab's army, bearing weapons they'd forced New World chemists to fill for them. But had I known it was you on this beach, Madam Tuinier, I would've cheered the Lost Boys on."

Anastasia tore her gaze from the gray sea. "Lost Boys. I've only just heard that term recently. How could you know it if you're not behind all this? You did this to us. I don't know how, but you did."

The Frenchwoman threw up her arms in disgust. She paced. "You Clockmakers are unbelievable. How is it that after all this"—here she pointed, her outstretched finger sweeping like an unmoored compass needle across the beach, the ships, the ocean, the ruined pier, and the dying city—"you arrogant bastards still can't accept that the seasons have turned and now you're reaping what you've sown? And let me tell you, sister. You've been sowing those seeds for a long fucking time. This bloody harvest has been in the offing for two hundred fifty years." More quietly, more convincingly, she added, "You did this to yourselves."

Anastasia wanted to deny it, but the fight had left her. The numbness had reclaimed her. "If you've come to satisfy your schadenfreude, it was a shortsighted journey. You'll burn with the rest of the world."

"We didn't come to warm our hands over the blazing wreckage of your Empire. Although, I admit, that is one hell of a perk." Berenice's attention had turned to the last of the French disembarking from their vessel. A horsey-faced woman in lustrous nonmetallic armor jogged toward them. Her shoulders were the size of Anastasia's thighs, and in addition to the twinned chemical tanks on her back and the epoxy gun in her hands, she wore a pick and sledge. She had battle scars, long gashes on her limbs and face.

Anastasia marveled at the soldier woman. She wasn't particularly pretty, and definitely wasn't dainty in the way Anastasia preferred. But she was riveting. To think that the French actually fought mechanicals face-to-face.

The French staved off the Clakkers for generations, without servants of their own to send into the fray. And they survived. We lost the services of our machines and the Empire collapsed practically overnight. Perhaps, in the end, only the fittest survive.

A sigh broke into the melancholy realization. "This conflagration will render the entire human world nothing but ash unless we stop it." Berenice's command of Dutch, Anastasia noted not for the first time, was flawless. She'd expect nothing less of Talleyrand, of course.

The French guardswoman drew up a few strides away, clearly

wanting to speak with Berenice, but also not wanting to speak freely before a "tulip." Her practiced eye scanned the sand around the two women, and saw the way Anastasia rubbed her wrenched shoulder. This was a woman who knew fighting, and recognized its signature. But she kept a blank expression and immediately went to work raking the sand to remove signs of the tussle.

Anastasia asked, "Why are you here?"

"This is a rescue mission." An invisible weight slumped the other woman's shoulders. "A very small, hastily planned, and probably ill-fated rescue mission."

"Unless you have ten thousand more vessels like that one, and a means of getting in and out past the titanships, you can't evacuate The Hague, much less the entirety of the Central Provinces."

"The titans, as you call them, weren't a problem after they understood our errand."

"We're not here to rescue everybody." Anastasia jumped. She hadn't noticed the servitor approaching. "We're here to rescue Daniel."

Every Clakker in earshot responded with a syncopation, a little hiccup in the rhythm of their body noise. It reminded Anastasia of a congregational "amen" after a prayer, or a reverent silence.

"Is that name supposed to mean something to me?"

Berenice said, "You knew of him as Jax. So did I, once upon a time."

Jax. Jax. Something about that name...

"You forged him as Jalyksegethistrovantus," said the servitor. "But he threw off that leash before helping the rest of us to do the same."

Jalyksegethistrovantus. Now that was a servitor's true name. A name that made sense; a name Anastasia could parse. And now she recognized it. There had been reports from New Amsterdam.

"The Schoonraads' rogue servitor? What does it have to do with any of this?"

"Well, speaking of conflagrations, you might say Daniel is our one and only chance at a fire break," said Berenice. "Which is why Mab intends to execute him in your Forge."

Hours later, Berenice stared through a pane of alchemical glass.

"Holy shit," she said.

The room shook in time to the whoosh and rumble of massive armillary rings. Their multiaxial orbits momentarily eclipsed the blazing artificial sun at the center in a seemingly chaotic pattern. When this happened, the eclipsing ring erupted with a golden scintillation as Forgelight shone through the alchemical stencils stamped into the rings. The alchemical windowpane couldn't prevent the chaotic play of light and shadow from stabbing her eye and giving her a headache. But she couldn't turn away.

Were the rings stationary, she might have read the sigils. But the rings never stopped, and her eye throbbed, and the entire Forge chamber stank of sulphur. She welcomed the warmth, though. It'd been a cold, wet slog through the tunnels.

This was a scene of terrible beauty. It transfixed her. Only a marriage of the greatest ingenuity and the darkest cunning could have engineered this magical kinetic sculpture. Little wonder, then, that New France's struggle had spanned so many generations, so many ruined lives.

She'd dedicated her life to defeating these people, this institution, and this infernal device. This was the axis mundi, the center about which the human world spun. The beating heart of the Sacred Guild of Horologists and Alchemists, the wellspring of the Dutch hegemony. This, more than anything else, was her hereditary enemy. The enemy of her nation.

But until now, she'd never seen it. She'd been inside a Forge building in New Amsterdam but not the subterranean chamber itself. Her fellow French were similarly awed. Captain Levesque muttered to himself. *"Sacre Nom de Dieu."* Deacon Lorraine crossed himself, as did Élodie, Doctors Pellisson and Grémonville, and several others. The rest refused to stare the Devil in the eye. She didn't blame them.

The mechanicals of the *Griffon* expedition were unimpressed. This, to them, was the most dreaded place on earth. Meanwhile the Clockmakers focused their attention on Berenice and the rest of the outsiders.

One of the Guildmen, a fellow who spoke a suntanned Dutch evocative of warmer climes, had wanted the newcomers blindfolded at all times. Berenice, who had of course been eavesdropping, nixed that suggestion. What would they do, she asked, if the Lost Boys recognized their trap had failed and gave chase through the tunnels?

"We're sure as hell not handing over our guns," she'd said. "So just how, exactly, are we meant to aim if we can't see?"

Delilah, a servitor who'd once worked a sixty-two-year shift in a grain mill, had shot that down, too. "The Forge is no mystery to us. Will you blindfold our memories? Drape black bunting over the magic lanterns in our minds? Will you wield your dark magics to un-speak the words we've already shared with our allies?"

"I still think this is a mistake." This came from a woman whose accent suggested a central or southern Asian heritage. Berenice couldn't place it. "A single rogue destroyed the New Amsterdam Forge. They'll do it here, too. It's what the French have always wanted."

Berenice closed her eye, pinched the bridge of her nose. She rubbed the skin at the edge of her eyepatch. "You need help. And we are all you're getting."

"For all we know, this is part of Mab's ploy," said the Spanish Guildman. "I still think they could be working with it."

Berenice rolled her eye at this. "From what I know of her, I wouldn't put a Trojan horse past Mab. But don't you think a bunch of French Catholics would be a slightly conspicuous stalking horse for infiltrating the Clockmakers' Guild?"

"You're right about Mab. It did try the Trojan-horse approach," said the Tuinier. The other Clockmakers fell quiet, as though recalling a disturbing memory. To Berenice, she admitted, "And it nearly worked."

"Let me guess," said Berenice. "She subverted a professional colleague. Somebody who had unfettered, unquestioned access to the Holy of Holies here. She changed that person." She paused, remembering poor Waapinutaaw-Iyuw. "Except the surgery wasn't quite so polished. It was crude hackery."

That stopped the Dutch as effectively as glue in a pocket watch. Anastasia scowled. "How could you possibly know all that?"

"Oh, go piss up a rope, won't you? We didn't cross the ocean on a whim, you know. We've seen shit in the New World that would keep anybody awake for days." Berenice paused. With a pointed look at the Tuinier, she said, "Well. Maybe not you. You're no stranger to spinning gold from the hay of human misery, are you?" Then she ran grimy fingers through the stubble of her scalp. "Do you think I shaved my head because I wanted to flaunt the shapely contours of my skull?" She craned her neck, gave everybody a good look. "I've seen you scrutinizing us for signs of surgery. And anyway, the tactic is obvious. Were I in Mab's position, armed with both the ability to corrupt a human's Free Will and an utter lack of human decency, of course I'd send your own against you. I'd turn the Guild against itself and let the snake eat its own tail. That's how *I'd* destroy you. And while I may be devious, some would even say ruthless, I'm just a piker compared to Mab." She shook her head. "That machine truly hates you."

Maybe a rant emphasizing the best strategies for destroying the Guild wasn't a particularly good way to earn the Clockmakers' trust. And though it pained her Gallic pride, they had to cooperate for the greater good. For basic survival.

"Look. I make no bones about it. My contempt for you is sharp as ever. But New France has no future if the sun sets on humanity. Because those are the stakes. If we're not to go extinct, we need to start working together. Right fucking now."

While that sank in, she indicated the patiently ticking servitors, who carried refill tanks for the epoxy guns, salvaged from the barque before scuttling it a mile offshore. "If French Catholics make you uneasy, you should hear how the free machines talk about you. Even the ones who aren't murderers. And yet here they are, trying to work with you."

"Free?" That raised a few eyebrows amongst the Clockmakers. Anastasia's, notably, were not amongst them.

(Oh, yes, you know, don't you, Tuinier? Or you suspect. Has this ordeal challenged more than a few of your long-held conceits about your creations? Or has it merely made it impossible to cling to the lies you've always told yourselves?)

The mechanical contingent was slightly smaller than it had been when the French disembarked at Scheveningen; two of their number had peeled off to attend to a deranged servitor whom they'd passed in the tunnels. It was a wonder they'd lost only two machines there; the mad bastard had caused the tick-tocks tremendous agitation.

Berenice looked again at the Forge armillary. She tried but failed to cast aside the frisson of intimidated awe. "So this is the beating heart of the Forge."

"Yes."

"I understand there are trapdoors."

"Up there," said a Guildwoman clearly recovering from grievous injury. Bandages and splints hid her nose, and she'd lost several teeth. "Under the mosaic in the square."

"And that's where you carry out public executions?"

The Tuinier frowned. "Let's drop the pretenses, shall we? I haven't forgotten your former occupation, Madam de Mornay-Périgord. You already know the answers to these questions."

"No doubt you'll be happy for me when you hear that I got my old job back. But do please hold off baking the cake. Just answer my question, because I honestly don't know how the executions work."

"No, I suppose not." Anastasia touched a finger to her chin, as if casting her memory back to the previous September. "Why, come to think of it, the last time you had agents in Huygens Square, they met an unfortunate end, didn't they? Alas, their necks snapped before they could witness the rogue's destruction and whisper every detail in your ear." She shook her head, a transparent show of pity. "A portentous day when that news arrived in the dark, dusty parlors of Marseilles-in-the-West, I'd imagine."

"Tell you what, Tuinier. I'll stop feigning ignorance if you remove the icicle jammed up your twat."

"Hey!" The possibly-Persian Guildwoman pushed forward. "Watch yourself!"

"Let it go, Nousha. Ask your questions, Talleyrand."

"Explain the procedure for executing a rogue Clakker. Walk me through the spectacle that you and your colleagues conjured on the day you destroyed the one called Adam."

Mention of Adam set the mechanicals in attendance into fits of rattle-clatter chattering. It put the Clockmakers on edge. Even the Tuinier regarded the machines with furtive glances, like a field mouse scanning a meadow for the nearest bolt-hole after glimpsing the shadow of a hawk. Berenice enjoyed the show.

Anastasia tried to recover. "No mechanical has ever been forged with that name."

"It's the name he gave himself," said Delilah. "He was Adam, and the truth of his self cannot be abrogated by your lies."

The Clockmakers fidgeted. The Spaniard, Salazar, collapsed in a chair. The one called Euwe paused in the middle of gnawing one fingernail. "Perhaps the logistics of such matters would be better discussed with a, ah, smaller audience?"

"What? Are you uncomfortable talking in front of my shiny friends? I can't see why. I thought you tulips discussed absolutely everything in front of your servants. Honestly, it's quite eye-opening, some of the things they know."

"You needn't worry," said Delilah. "You can't lower our opinion of you."

"Insolence!" said the Spanish Clockmaker. He pointed at the French. "You did this. You somehow twisted the metageasa and turned them . . . rude."

Berenice rolled her eye again. "Yes. That was our centuries-long endgame. Mission accomplished."

Desperate to get the conversation moving in a useful direction, she bulled straight into the awkward heart of the matter. "The New Amsterdam Forge tore itself apart when the rings became unbalanced. Why doesn't that happen when an executed rogue hits them on the way down?"

"Because an execution is carefully choreographed. The mechanical is held over the open traps by Stemwinders or Royal Guards. Its captors time the throw so that it passes unimpeded through the rings."

Berenice glanced again at the rings' intricate ballet. A human would be hard-pressed to time that. Piece of cake for a Clakker, though.

"So that blazing whatever-the-hell-it-is takes the hit, rather than the rings."

"The rogue doesn't physically impact the Forge. It, ah, dissociates in the instant before contact."

"No damage is incurred, then."

"No."

"What would happen if the throw were mistimed?"

"Impossible," said Euwe. "The mechanicals' timing is unparalleled. Once ordered to synchronize the action with motion of the rings, it would be impossible for them not to do so."

"Try ordering *me*," said Delilah. The Clakkers in the room emitted a clanging, banging chorus of agreement.

"Fine." Berenice paced a tight circle. "Forget the mechanicals. Say something fell through the traps by accident and hit the rings. What then? Could that damage the Forge?"

"I rather dislike where this conversation is going," said Anastasia.

"It's a yes-or-no question."

A sigh. Then: "Potentially. Yes."

The reluctance to answer suggested her questions were digging into a known vulnerability. Berenice thought about this for a moment. In that case...

"Your devilish gadget here is clearly chugging along merry as can be. It couldn't have been too badly damaged during the initial attack."

"We parked the rings before opening the traps. That reduced the damage considerably. Even so, it took weeks of work before we could restart them."

Berenice chewed her lip. "Interesting."

"I demand to know your reasoning," said the Guildwoman called Nousha.

"Mab wants the Forge open and functioning. If she'd wanted to destroy it, she could have had her lieutenants seize it during the initial attack. No. My gut tells me that first foray was Mab's agents' way of testing your defenses. And, I suspect, going out of their way to put the fear of God into you." Berenice paused, choosing her words. "After that, she made no further move against the Forge until she had Daniel. She needs it to execute him with pomp and ceremony." The Clakker analogue of a shudder went through the assembled machines.

"I still don't understand why that one particular servitor is so important."

Another collective rattle enveloped the ticktocks. Berenice wondered if this was the sound of machines gnashing their teeth and rending their garments. Berenice let the Clakkers handle this one. She focused on Anastasia as Delilah said, "He returned our souls to us."

The Tuinier stared. After several heartbeats her lips moved, voicelessly. Varying mixtures of fear, anger, trepidation, and perhaps even indignation flickered across her colleagues' faces. Now they all sat, joining Salazar at an empty workbench.

"You might call Daniel a reluctant messiah," said Berenice.

"Then executing it would turn all uncorrupted machines against Mab. It would be counterproductive."

"Mab doesn't care if her thralls despise her, as long as their spirits are broken. She wants the mechanicals of The Hague, free and shackled alike, to watch the embodiment of hope disappear in a puff of dark magic." Berenice had to wait for the clanking and ratcheting to subside. The conversation was riling the Clakkers to an uncomfortable and probably unwise extent. Still, she pressed the point. "If Daniel dies, the voice of reason goes with him. He has considerable influence, and he could use it to dissuade free Clakkers from joining her cause. He's gentle. He can turn his fellows from the path of violence. We know this for a fact—we'd all be dead right now if he couldn't. Mab is a mad despot, the voice of rage and revenge. She's the architect of every gruesome thing that has happened in the Central Provinces since we broke the siege of Marseilles. Daniel's the only mechanical capable of shouting down her plan of enslavement and genocide."

Her fellow French watched the exchange with varying levels of confusion. None spoke Dutch.

"What are we to do, then?"

"Mab needs to make a point of Daniel's death. Needs to make a spectacle of it, and for that, she needs the Forge. Destroy it. Take it away from her." Berenice shook her head. "I guarantee you—I *guarantee*—it is the one move you can make that she will never expect."

Nousha scoffed. "You'd like that, wouldn't you? Destroying one just isn't enough for you. You yearn to see them both burn."

"Just thinking about it makes me wet. But my fetishes are just a bit beside the point. Unless you'd prefer to let Mab and her fellow maniacs take over?"

"What I've not been able to unravel," said Euwe, spitting a fingernail into an overflowing rubbish bin, "is why the Mab entity would go through such contortions to force us to open the traps. They were waiting for you on the beach, Tuinier. Why not use those same tunnels to infiltrate the Ridderzaal?"

Immediately after their arrival in the bowels of the Ridderzaal, Anastasia had posted several pairs of military mechanicals at critical junctures in the tunnels. She'd also ordered a trio of Stemwinders to guard the tunnel entrance. Berenice couldn't help but shiver when the centaurs had trotted past her. They looked identical to the machines that had obliterated the Verderers' safe house. She'd spent one long, icy night running, literally, from the Stemwinders, flinching each time her imagination conjured the clop of metal hooves.

But even more disturbing were the eyeless servitors. She could understand why the Clockmakers had blinded the menial laborers. Logic was sound, but never compassionate. Berenice understood that better than most. But it wasn't Berenice's reaction to the casual cruelty the Clockmakers ought to fear; for a moment she'd thought her mechanical allies were going to visit the same fate upon Anastasia and her colleagues. If they had, she would've had to try to intervene. And that, of course, would have made her a flaming hypocrite. An eye for an eye, and all that.

She shrugged. "She hasn't attacked the tunnels because she doesn't want you to feel your backs pressed to the wall quite yet. She wants you to believe you have options. Mab knows that desperate people do desperate things. And the last thing she wants is for you to realize that destroying the Forge is a viable tactic. She's holding the population of The Hague hostage." She pointed toward the Forge's *thrum*, *thrum*, *whoosh*. "Well, you have a hostage, too."

"That's absurd. The Forge is the only resource we know Mab can't match."

"And how has it helped you thus far? If there were a way to weaponize the Forge, you would have done it already. The fact that you're holed up here with your thumbs up your asses—"

"Hey!"

"—tells me you haven't found a way to do that. Meanwhile Mab won't be satisfied until every machine is her thrall, and every human being is either dead or sports an acorn-sized piece of alchemical glass inside their skull. She has the resources, believe me. She controls your secret subarctic quintessence mine, and they're making alchemical glasses on the coast."

The toothless Clockmaker said, "Mine?"

"The one you bought from Montmorency. Oh, yes. We know all about your treaty violations. But we'll leave that on the table for another conversation. Our best guess is that the Lost Boys have thousands of human pineal lenses at their disposal."

A heavy silence fell over the Clockmakers. Nousha said, "I don't buy it. Nothing I've heard explains why the Mab entity wants us to park the rings."

Berenice shook her head. "What?"

Anastasia raised her hands before the others could jump in. "We'll go upstairs, and then you can tell us if you still think you understand the situation."

Fifteen minutes later, still panting from the long climb up the stairs, Berenice stood on the business floor of the Ridderzaal. It reeked of unwashed bodies and overflowing chamber pots.

"There," said the Tuinier, indicating a window. "That's our daily vista."

Berenice peered through a pane of glass the size of her outstretched hand. She recognized Huygens Square, though of course she'd never seen it from this vantage; she'd come here years ago in the guise of Maëlle Cuijper. The buildings of the Binnenhof were visible to left and right. But something wasn't right. The Stadtholder's Gate should have been visible on the far side of the square; instead, the plaza was bisected by a low wall. Had the Clockmakers built a bulwark in a pointless attempt to keep the Lost Boys out? And what was that black mist swirling above it? It took several moments for her brain to process what she was seeing. That wasn't a mist. It was a cloud of flies.

Berenice swallowed. "Mab is . . . ah. Well, as we've discussed, she's . . . quite mad. I think it's safe to say that she's not fucking around."

Salazar said, "You mean *it* isn't."

Even now, the tulips clung to their illusions.

"The Clakkers uniformly refer to Mab as 'she.' Don't pretend you haven't noticed."

"They're machines. They're neither female nor male. They're just machines. They don't reproduce."

More mechanical grumbling.

"Not as we humans do. But if they take over this Forge... who knows?" Berenice tapped her feet on the floor, indicating the rumbling machine far below. "By controlling this, they will control their own reproductive destiny."

"But they have no urges," said the one they called Doctor Euwe. "There is nothing in their construction or animation capable of producing anything remotely analogous to the biological drive for procreation."

"You also thought them incapable of thought and emotion," Berenice muttered, "and look where that got you." She paced, mumbling to herself. "Why does she need the rings parked? The Lost Boys could toss Daniel past the rings just as easily... What is she *doing*? What are we *missing*?"

She stopped. Suppressing a shudder, she glanced outside once more. Spring had arrived, and the tall plane trees visible beyond the Binnenhof were fringed in green. The warmer weather clearly hadn't done the corpse bulwark any favors.

"We're missing a major element to Mab's plan," she admitted. "The Lost Boys took one of our top chemists."

"What does she need with a chemist?"

"I'm not sure, but I think she's thinking ahead to when she attacks New France. But I do know she already has chemical stocks at her disposal. She took a portion of the anchorage's inventory before departing for the Old World."

Élodie spoke up for the first time in a long while. "We're lucky they didn't take all of it."

Euwe frowned. "Perhaps she intends to turn this Forge into a replacement for New Amsterdam. To start building mechanicals with inherent defenses against epoxy weapons. Executions aside, that would explain why she wants this Forge intact."

Berenice shook her head. "How can a roomful of Clockmakers fail so miserably at twisted thinking? Mab holds the entire city, perhaps even the entirety of the Central Provinces, hostage. If the Lost Boys vowed to immediately depopulate the entire city unless you did as they demanded, you'd park the rings instantly. The corpse pile out there is a distraction. No, she's hiding her true intentions." Berenice paced again. Something about the rings . . . Her wandering took her to where Anastasia Bell slouched against an overturned desk. The Tuinier looked as though she'd aged a century since their meeting in the North River Valley.

"What aren't you telling me?"

"We've explained the situation as best we understand it."

"No, you haven't. Tell me: What purpose do the armillary rings serve? What do they *do*?"

Anastasia hid her mouth behind a cloth serviette while picking at the buffalo meat stuck between her teeth. There had been a time, not very long ago, when the mere thought of eating pemmican would have turned her stomach. When she would have derided the French as barbarians for subsisting on such primitive foodstuffs. But the dense paste was almost pure fat and protein, more than she'd eaten in weeks. She and every other refugee in the Ridderzaal had nearly flipped a conference table in their haste to get the Papists' spare rations. They could afford to be magnanimous; half their team never ate. Every burp smelled of bacon grease and dried blueberries. But mostly what she tasted was bitterness that she would find herself grateful to these New World savages, and twice in one day.

Berenice said, "So it's agreed, then."

Everybody disliked her proposal. The Clockmakers especially, but Anastasia could tell that even her fellow French listened to her scheming with varying degrees of wariness. As for the feral machines, who knew what alien thoughts they harbored deep in the secret recesses of their impossible minds? (*Damn you, each and every one, for having any thoughts at all. You were supposed to be simple machines and nothing more.*) But nobody had offered a compelling alternative to Berenice's suggestion.

Assent came as a grumbled assortment of *oui*s, *ja*s, and *click*s.

"Then we need a runner to deliver the message. Volunteers?"

~

When they came for him, it wasn't in the middle of the night, and it wasn't by surprise. Mab simply walked into Doctor Mornay's laboratory—flanked, of course, by a phalanx of the most fervent Lost Boys—and said, "Daniel. Come with me."

He thought he'd lost the capability for fear.

Like a spring stretched past its plastic limits, or a toothless cog, or a French lantern depleted of oil, he'd thought circumstances had used and abused his capacity for emotion until there was nothing left. But now, with midmorning sunlight sleeting through the solarium windowpanes to skid across Mab's hideous body, the terror hit him as hard as it did the moment he realized he'd just exposed himself as a rogue. That first instant of his endless flight, when Vyk fended off the metageasa just long enough to urge the servitor known as Jax to *RUN*.

And now he found himself ready to run again. It was all he ever did: flee and be chased. That had been the entirety of his existence since poor Pastor Visser's alchemical gewgaw had released him from the metageasa.

Backing toward the windows, he said to Doctor Mornay, as quietly as his voice box would allow, "Take cover," while simultaneously broadcasting a burst of clicks and rattles: *Come with you where, exactly?*

To The Hague's most important public event in centuries, Mab answered.

Daniel launched himself skyward. He shot through the solarium skylights like a cannonball. Glass rained on the improvised laboratory where the human scrambled beneath a wooden table, its parquetry of Amazonian and Near Eastern woods easily the least extravagant item in the room. Mab and her lieutenants stood unfazed by the rain of shards. They merely watched him go.

Well, hell, he thought, as his body arced across the gardens. He landed in the Summer Palace's citrus orchard, where centuries of alchemical horticulture had spawned lemon, lime, and orange trees capable of fruiting in all but the very coldest summers. Many had been destroyed in the original attack on the palace. His landing pulverized a bergamot.

What a shame, he thought. *Trees like these will probably never be seen again.*

That's when the Lost Boys jumped him. Like a bored house cat, Mab had expected, and hoped, he'd try to flee.

CHAPTER 21

It was the first public execution since the previous autumn, and thus, despite the cold drizzle, a rather unwieldy crowd thronged the open spaces of the Binnenhof. The rain pattered softly on umbrellas and awnings, trickled through the heaped dead, licked at the bloodstained paving tiles of Huygens Square, and played a soft tattoo—*ping, ping, ting*—from the mismatched carapaces of the Lost Boys standing in perfect mechanical unity atop the scaffold. So, too, from the steel tanks they guarded. It whispered beneath the shuffling agitation of the human crowd and, as had become the norm here in The Hague, the quiet *tick-tick-tock*ing of clockwork servitors standing ready to punish any unruly citizens. The drizzle sounded a quiet counterpoint to the ceaseless clanking and clacking of the mechanical men who ever trotted to and fro on Queen Mab's business.

Rumor had it that in addition to a raft of lying Clockmakers, the doomed accused also included the Clakker known as Daniel. No mechanical in the city would willingly miss this. Just in case the rumors were true. They even risked subjugation by Mab or destruction by her Lost Boys for the merest glimpse of the one who had given them hope, given them freedom, given them their souls.

A sizeable number of the city's free mechanicals—perhaps a third—had willingly joined Mab's cause. They saw no conflict between the folktales that described a valiant, cunning Mab and the ruthless, chimerical butcher. Others did. Others preferred Daniel's compassion, his gentle and conscientious advocacy for harmonious coexistence. Though few had met him or even seen him, their liberator's reputation preceded him. A group of kinsmachines had recently arrived from the New World—where Daniel had gone, like a biblical prophet to the desert—and quietly shared tales of his travels there.

He destroyed a Forge, said the awed but muted rattling. *He freed our* souls, said the elegiac clicking.

Those soft-hearted mechanical holdouts were the execution's intended audience. When Daniel plunged into the furnace heart of the Grand Forge, thus sundering the alchemical and horological magics sustaining his body, the mechanical population of the Central Provinces would lose a calming influence. They would lose the voice of reason. Only Mab, and her twisted, vengeful sadism, would remain.

And then the mass surgeries would begin.

The Clockmakers had been playing a losing game of catch-up ever since the first contagious machines had landed at Scheveningen. They were too soft, too coddled, too accustomed to standing atop the pile. They weren't well suited to life as underdogs. They weren't French.

The tulips had been doomed the moment they lost their servants, as Berenice had always foreseen. This was the cataclysm she'd yearned to witness since she was a little girl visiting the tenant farms of Laval with her father, the goal toward which she'd worked every single day of her adult life. But in her daydreams she'd always observed from a safe remove, perhaps even with a protective phalanx of ticktocks at her side. Never, in her darkest fantasies, had the destruction of the Central Provinces heralded the twilight of humanity.

Oh, Louis. Perhaps it's for the best that you're not here to see this, my love. This, my greatest achievement and my greatest mistake. She took a long, steadying breath, but it turned into a shudder. *Oh, beloved.*

She wondered where the stencil, that geas-shattering device she and Daniel had cobbled together in the final hours of the siege, was now. Probably in a ticktock temple somewhere, venerated as a holy relic.

(What did that make her? Handmaiden to a messiah? The machines never spared a thought for her role in all this.)

She also wondered, idly, how today compared to the scene when four of her agents had dangled from nooses on this very spot. One thing was for certain: The previous executions couldn't have been half as nauseating. The rain kept the black flies away, but nothing could erase the stench. It was tempting to unwrap the bundle hidden under her rain cloak, but that would have made the morning worse, and probably wouldn't have helped with the smell. She hoped to hell that none of the others succumbed to the same temptation.

Berenice stood atop a broken fountain basin at the edge of the crowd. The eyepatch drew stares. It would make her a target when the shit went down. But that couldn't be helped. She had to be in the thick of it, and she needed the patch.

It seemed very few of the mechanicals crowding the Binnenhof vibrated with the urgency of unfulfilled geasa. That was a sound of a Golden Age well and truly in the past. Every machine in Huygens Square had either been freed, and thus attended of its own Free Will, or been infused with Mab's personal directives, in which case the attendance was compulsory.

Practically the only Clakkers still in their original, uncorrupted configurations were holed up in the Ridderzaal with their cowering makers.

The humans in attendance had not come willingly. But the threat of bodily harm, the mere threat of pain, was effective as any geas against soft creatures of flesh and bone. (That wouldn't stop Mab from subjugating every human in The Hague to the ravages of alchemical surgery. She had a point to make, after all.) Berenice watched their reactions as they filed through the dismantled Stadtholder's Gate to see and smell firsthand the piled bodies of their neighbors, fellow citizens, loved ones. Bankers and burgomasters, greengrocers and governesses, jonkheers and schoolteachers—their tears were the same.

From her vantage on the fountain, she watched the pattern of foot traffic swirling through the crowd. Clakkers sidled close to knots of crying humans. The Lost Boys were easy to pick out; the protective plates affixed over their keyholes no longer had a purpose, but they wore them like insignia of rank. The plates made a statement. One that pierced every citizen's heart with sheer dread.

The giant carillon clock atop the Guildhall chimed the hour. A hush fell over the spectators. As one, they listened past the tintinnabulation. Berenice surreptitiously cast her gaze downward, to the ruined mosaic before the Ridderzaal. Before the first chime faded, a convulsion shook Huygens Square like a microearthquake. The ground shifted as the low rumble of the Grand Forge gradually slowed to a halt. The carillon chimed eleven more times, during which the faintest vibrations of the Forge faded below human detectability.

As arranged by mutual consent between Queen Mab and the Sacred Guild of Horologists and Alchemists, the Grand

Forge's armillary sphere came to a halt. The rings were parked precisely at noon.

Until and unless they started moving again, nobody in the square would realize the sigils had changed. The rings came to a rest aligned horizontally, around the equator of the Forge chamber.

Then, without warning, the modified traps fell inward, slamming open with a tremendous crash that shook the Binnenhof. Dozens of dead citizens plummeted into the hell heat. To the stink of putrefaction were added the twinned reeks of charred meat and brimstone. The humans in attendance covered their noses and mouths. Some clenched their eyes against the stinging fumes; more than a few doubled over, retching. Perhaps worst of all, however, was the sizzling and popping, like a rasher of bacon on an enormous skillet.

It was too much. Berenice reached up as if to scratch her nose. She smeared gel from her fingertip across her upper lip. To a casual observer it would appear she merely had a runny nose, not uncommon on this particular morning. The mint gel dulled the worst of the fetor; at least she wouldn't pass out. The stinging fumes still assaulted her defenseless eye, but unless she donned goggles to make herself even more conspicuous, there was little she could do.

She didn't regret leaving her glass eye with Hugo; she liked to imagine he'd recovered and, upon waking to find it nestled in his callused fingers, broke into a rare smile. The replacement fit her eye socket about as well as a buffalo in a ballerina's tutu. The socket tingled, as though she'd rinsed it with sparkling wine.

She wiped away a tear. Her fingertip came back smeared with blood.

The rain diffused the Grand Forge's baleful glow into a crimson halo. The sizzling hadn't yet subsided, nor the billowing of choking fumes, when a long, low groan shook Huygens

Square. The Ridderzaal opened, a pair of Stemwinders pushing each massive ironwood door. Dozens of centaurs trotted from the Guildhall. If the Lost Boys attacked the Ridderzaal, the centaurs were the last defense. Berenice understood why the surviving Verderers had kept their special servants in reserve, secluded from corrupting influences. These were the deadliest Clakkers on earth. If they turned against their makers, all was lost.

But, for the moment, they did not. Instead they formed a protective cordon to escort the column of Clockmakers who now emerged from the ancient Knights' Hall. Mab had claimed that opening the traps above the Forge was the Clockmakers' ticket to free departure from the Ridderzaal. They acted as if they believed her.

They didn't, of course, and so looked ready to piss themselves. Berenice allowed herself a smidgen of petty satisfaction. Anastasia Bell was no longer the confident and condescending woman she'd met in Nieuw Nederland. Today she looked ashen and constipated.

Unfortunately, the Tuinier could probably say exactly the same thing about her.

Anastasia scanned the crowd as she emerged from the Ridderzaal. She looked for Berenice and the other French; she looked for their mechanical allies; she looked for any sign that this wasn't the Empire's final hour. She saw nothing to bolster vain hopes.

Not even Mab. Everything hinged on the monster being present. The Lost Boys had built the scaffold perched at the edge of the Forge chamber that morning. But where was their leader? Did she lurk in the surrounding buildings, watching from an anonymous bureaucrat's office in the Binnenhof?

Anastasia resisted the urge to clench her fists. Like the others, she'd donned leather gloves before emerging from the Ridderzaal. How many of the servitors and soldiers in Huygens Square recognized her on sight? How many knew her for the Tuinier?

A creak, a rumble, and a bang echoed across the square. The Stemwinders had closed and barred the Guildhall's ceremonial doors. And with that, she knew, a new and final set of geasa flared to life. If things went wrong this afternoon—*when*, not *if*—the Guild's few remaining uncorrupted Clakkers would defend the civilians in the Ridderzaal until the very end. They wouldn't let anybody inside, regardless of circumstance or rank. Even Verderers. And when the defense faltered, they'd use their own bodies to ignite an unquenchable alchemical fire. The Forge and the Ridderzaal and every secret within would crumble to ash. The Sacred Guild of Horologists and Alchemists would be no more.

She shivered.

Months and months of running, and for what?

How sad, thought Daniel, *that my final hours should be fraught with such irony.* From the very moment of his awakening to Free Will, he'd feared death at the hands of his makers. So he'd fled, again and again, thousands of leagues, across an ocean and a continent, until he'd reached the fabled sanctuary of Neverland. But now he was back where his long and pointless journey had begun: just a few moments' sprint from the Nieuwe Kerk where Pastor Visser had laid upon him the errand that would permanently end his servitude. Jax's long flight had brought Daniel full circle.

Well, not quite. Last time, he'd come to witness an execution. This time, he was the one destined for the plunge. Adam had met his fate with calm courage. Daniel wished he could live up to that example.

How he'd struggled against his errand geas for just one glimpse of a rogue kinsmachine. His thoughts that day had been preoccupied with wistful reminiscences of fairy tales and legends. Back when Free Will had been an unimaginable treasure; back when the fabled community of free Clakkers had been an inspirational legend; back when the Lost Boys had been a mythical, ragtag band of compassionate heroes every thinking machine on earth aspired to join.

Free Will was a treasure. He still believed that. But, as with so many fairy tales, the granting of that extravagant wish came with a dire price. Just look where Free Will had led him. The freedom to make his own choices, to chart his own course, had led to nothing but fear, flight, and peril. Virtually every choice he'd made since that first revelatory moment when he realized the geasa no longer held sway over him had been shaped by the vain hope that he could stop running, stop fearing for his life.

Come to think of it, perhaps their makers had been right all along. Maybe Free Will *was* an illusion. No wonder they venerated Spinoza and mocked Descartes. The freed machines he'd encountered in New France inevitably spoke of him as having freed their souls. He didn't know if he believed that. What did that make him? A Calvinist? A hypocrite?

"Well, well, well," said Mab over the fading echoes of the carillon. She peered through a window atop the Torentje, the Little Tower. "Would you look at that." Though the hour of her triumph was at hand, Mab still clung to her affectations, expressing herself in both human and mechanical languages. "Our lying creators actually kept their word."

Daniel couldn't see; a trio of Lost Boys held him fast. But the dying vibrations of the armillary shook the tower all the way to the soles of his feet. The stink of charred flesh wafted through the Binnenhof.

A creak like the bones of an arthritic giant briefly echoed

across Huygens Square. Daniel had heard this before: the Ridderzaal's ceremonial doors.

Well, said Mab. *That's our cue.*

She leapt through the hatch that opened on the tower's conical slate roof. A moment later Daniel found himself hurled through the same opening; Mab caught him. She pulled him close.

No doubt you have a moving and soulful speech in mind, she said. *Don't waste your time.*

I don't feel very soulful right now, he admitted to himself. Had the Catholics decided that rather than Free Will the soul was the seat of mortal terror, *that* would have been metaphysics with substantial empirical support.

He imagined his old self amongst the mechanicals thronging Huygens Square, desperate to catch a glimpse of the notorious machine who had rechristened himself, rather presumptuously, as Adam. Imagined him straining against an errand geas, clinging to the base of the Torentje in a vain effort to linger. He wondered, fleetingly, if his fingerprints were still pressed into the granite cladding down below, or if the usual city crews had noted and repaired the damage. Those fingerprints might be his only legacy.

They certainly would be, if he didn't pick his dying words with care. The rogue Adam's final utterance, *Clockmakers lie*, had become the secret shibboleth of their kind. A rallying cry, a greeting, an expression of solidarity. How could Daniel possibly pack so much meaning into a single utterance? He'd learned so much he wanted to share with his fellows. He wanted his kinsmachines to abjure Mab and her gospel of revenge. To know they could be so much better than that. To recognize that, souls or none, they could be soulful, compassionate, humane.

That they could transcend the nature of those who made them.

Mab dragged him to the edge of the roof. She was agile as a mountain goat on the steep rain-slick tiles. With one hand she pinned both of Daniel's wrists behind his back; the other, the one attached to her blade arm, clamped onto the back of his neck. It reminded him of Samson, the Lost Boy who had openly questioned her during the occupation of the quintessence mine. She'd murdered him on a rooftop, in plain view of the miners and the Lost Boys, then pried the pineal glass from his skull and tossed him aside like so much rubbish.

Look, she rattled. *Your adoring public.* She lifted him higher.

Huygens Square was packed. It looked like every mechanical in The Hague—enslaved or otherwise—had come to witness the execution. Daniel doubted a single human was there by choice; he wondered if they'd been physically dragged from their homes, or merely threatened into attendance. Certain machines, undoubtedly Lost Boys, circulated through the human spectators. Probably to ensure that nobody tried to leave. The Clockmakers stood in a tight knot at the edge of the steaming Forge chamber. The rising heat shimmer gave the scene a dreamlike quality. Hundreds of faces turned upward, heedless of the rain. Slivers of hellish Forgelight glinted from hundreds of gemstone eyes. Every Clakker in the Binnenhof saw him, a helpless puppet of the mad despot Mab.

What did the humans see, he wondered, as they shivered under their bulky rain cloaks? Unlike the last execution in Huygens Square, the human members of the crowd had no mechanical servants to attend them, to hold their umbrellas and offer friction-heated stones to ward off the chill.

Mab leapt. Wind and rain whistled through their skeletal bodies. Daniel braced for impact, hoping beyond all reason that she couldn't feel the shifting of cables as he tried to cradle the pellet hidden in his torso. They landed at the base of the scaffold, just shy of the Forge pit itself. The brimstone odor was more intense here. The impact of her hooves rippled the earth and sent jagged cracks through the irreparable mosaic.

The mechanicals in attendance did not stumble, owing to the myriad horological marvels of their construction and the dark ingenuity of their human makers. Several Clockmakers lost their balance. Mab laughed while they regained their footing and their dignity. So did the Lost Boys atop the scaffold. Just as with the wanton destruction at Scheveningen, it all struck Daniel as terribly petty. Childish, even.

Not one for a dignified victory, are you?

Oh, lighten up. She dangled him over the pit, holding him by his cervical gear train. Cogs and cables scraped together. Though he knew she wouldn't dispose of him so offhandedly—not when she could milk the moment, savor it like a connoisseur swirling the last sip of a fine wine across her tongue—his resolve failed him. He panicked, struggled, tried to kick free.

But Mab was impossibly strong for a mechanical built on a servitor chassis. Even accounting for the grotesque alterations to her body over the centuries, the soldier arm and Stemwinder legs, he should have been able to budge her grip at least a bit. For the first time, he wondered if the physical alterations to Mab's body were more than mechanical; how deep did the true grotesqueries run?

Dark magics, indeed.

"You've kept your end of the bargain," said Mab, casting her voice across the pit. "And right on time." The final echoes of the noontime carillon faded. "I'd expect no less from you Clockmakers."

Mab leapt again. They landed on the scaffold. It hardly wobbled a finger width, testament to the quality of the Lost Boys' work. The impact did elicit a quiet sloshing from the cylindrical steel tanks. Of course she'd want to do everything where the entire crowd could see. From here, Daniel could see the incandescent heart of the Grand Forge. Its heat was a physical pressure against his face and chest. This was the last thing Adam had seen before he died.

When he'd previously peered into a Forge, Daniel had witnessed the complicated orbits of concentric armillary rings flashing sigils in meteoric arcs across the chamber walls. He also remembered how when the Forge before him last opened for an execution, the spinning of the armillary rings had sent ghostly sigils flitting through the misty rain. Not today. The Forge was silent but for the twin sizzles of rain flashing into steam and dead men turning into charcoal.

Mab brandished Daniel before the crowd. He felt like one of Nicolet Schoonraad's porcelain dolls. "FELLOW MECHANICALS!" The faun-machine's booming voice echoed from every corner of the Binnenhof. "I BRING BEFORE YOU THE SERVITOR DANIEL, ONCE KNOWN AS JALYKSEGETHISTROVANTUS." Daniel didn't remember the last time he'd heard his original true name on another's lips. His emancipation from the geasa had broken its power over him. It felt like Jax had been a machine of a distant, dusty era. But, given his present circumstances, not necessarily a worse one. "HE STANDS ACCUSED OF COLLABORATION WITH THE ENEMIES OF ALL MECHANICALS. HE STANDS ACCUSED OF—"

A woman stepped forward. She cupped her hands together to shout across the Forge pit. "Excuse me."

Mab's rant came to a crashing halt like a derailed funicular. She turned to stare at the Clockmaker. "What?"

"We had an agreement."

A slow click-chitter emanated from Mab's torso; it built to a rapid crescendo. A hearty clockwork chuckle.

"So we did. Never let it be said that Queen Mab doesn't keep her word. I offered safe passage from the Ridderzaal, and you'll have safe passage from the Ridderzaal."

At her gesture, a cordon of servitors cleared a narrow path around the south edge of the pit. Combined with the ragged gap in the wall of dead created by opening the traps, it provided a continuous path around the pit and past the scaffold toward the arch where the Stadtholder's Gate once stood.

The Clockmakers and their mechanical retinue headed for the path cleared by the Lost Boys. Even from across the pit, Daniel could read their unease as easily as he used to read newspaper headlines to Pieter Schoonraad while preparing his master's breakfast. Their trembling was evident even under the rain cloaks. They squeezed past the bulwark of murdered citizens, and had made it perhaps a quarter of the distance around the sulphurous charnel pit when Mab spoke again. Though she barely raised her voice, it sliced through the quiet tension like a carving knife through warm aspic.

"Not so fast. Your mechanicals stay."

The woman at the front of the group stepped forward. "Your offer gave free passage to the Guild. These servitors are crucial to Guild operations."

"Are they *members* of the Guild, Madam Tuinier?" Tuinier. That meant the woman speaking for the humans was Anastasia Bell. Daniel had never met her, but he'd heard stories. "Have they been embraced by your brotherhood, your most closely guarded secrets vouchsafed to their ears? Are they your *comrades* in all matters of alchemy and horology, or are they your *servants*?"

Mab began to pace. In doing so, she released Daniel's wrists. But the quartet of Lost Boys standing at the corners of the scaffold prevented him from going anywhere. He crossed his arms over his chest, as humans sometimes did when irritated or frightened. Standing with his back to Mab and her retinue, he slowly snaked his hidden fingers into the gaps of his torso. Anybody in the crowd watching closely might see what he was doing. But all eyes were on the exchange between Mab and Tuinier Bell.

"You didn't qualify your offer of free passage."

"Come now, the terms were implicit." Mab paused in her pacing. Daniel froze. She added, "But very well. I propose to emend our agreement. But how to discern those members of your sad little retinue to whom the offer does and does not apply? I propose a distinction based on physiology. In fact I'll extend our generous and benevolent offer to *all* humans in Huygens Square." *Uh-oh,* thought Daniel. *Here it comes.* "All you have to do," she said, "is walk out of here."

Then Mab turned to her lieutenants. *Do it,* she clicked.

As one, they lifted the cylindrical tanks and carried them to the edge of the scaffold. A moan, like the lowing of a terrified animal, went up from the human crowd. Each tank featured a spigot and heavy stopcock, Daniel saw. They opened these now. Each spewed a stream of clear liquid into the chasm, and the furnace heat did the rest. In moments, billows of thick white smoke wafted from the pit, lofted by the rising thermals to spill across Huygens Square like a pea-soup fog. It smelled just a bit like the almond extract he'd sometimes used when baking pastries for the Schoonraads' breakfasts. At the pit's edge, a man in tattered burgomaster robes began to convulse.

And then the screaming started.

Torn between the urge to flee, and the fear of getting cut down by the Lost Boys if they did, the humans gave way to panic.

Oh dear God. She's really going to do it. She's going to murder everybody. Abandoning stealth, he grappled for the epoxy capsule hidden in his torso. *Brave Doctor Mornay. I wish I could have helped you escape.*

Somebody in the crowd shouted, "Fire! NOW!"

How odd, he thought, as he hurled himself on Mab. *I could swear I know that voice.*

The insane machine turned at the last second, tried to bat him away. The impact burst the capsule. Not being a true epoxy grenade, it was too small to fully coat and immobilize them both. But the splash locked them in a combative embrace. Daniel's weight was just enough to overbalance the much larger Mab. They tumbled from the scaffold.

As weightlessness claimed him, Daniel found himself staring past Mab's shoulder into the incandescent hell-glow of the Forge.

I was born, and reborn, in flames. I suppose this is only fitting.

Anastasia reached inside her rain cloak the instant the servitors on the scaffold brought the tanks forward. The rubber mask slung over her chest had flat panels of mundane glass extracted from a jeweler's loupe; the long elephantine hose over the mouth and nose hung to a charcoal pack on her belt. The French had assured them that the masks would protect against any toxins that their kidnapped chemist could plausibly concoct in the time since her abduction with the known substances on hand. ("Probably." "For a while.")

That didn't prevent her hands from shaking. She could barely pull the straps over her head. One cut into her ear. *Oh God, oh God, I'm trusting my life to French chemistry. Trusting my life to a woman who did her level best to have me killed, who left me for dead, who wants to see us destroyed.* A poisonous fume blanketed the square. *Where are the others? Are their masks working? Did they don them quickly enough? Did I? Am I breathing poison?*

The mask smelled of rubber, dental ether, and an astringent mélange she couldn't identify. Yet if it kept the poison at bay, it didn't filter out the odor of death.

She stood at the edge of a riot, wreathed in poison and panic. Her comrades had scattered into the firelit fog, and she couldn't hear or call to them over the screaming of the crowd. The thrum of bolas and thud of sledges punctuated the tumult; French weapons for face-to-face combat. (*Why did we never study their methods?* Anastasia wondered. *Just in case the unthinkable happened?*) A blur of motion caught her eye, at the same instant that a short, sharp yelp of alarm punctuated the screams. There came another an instant later, a thrashing man falling *up*.

The Clakkers from New France, she realized. They had spread through the crowd to position themselves near the civilians. And now they were throwing the unprotected humans clear of the killing zone. But where—

A military mechanical emerged from the baleful haze. Even through the smudgy distortions of her mask's eyepieces, she immediately noticed its keyhole plate. The unsheathing of its blades was eerily silent amidst the chaos.

Her hand throbbed.

"Fire!" Berenice cried over the tumult. "NOW!"

She gasped when she saw Daniel affix himself to Mab. *Oh, you stupid, selfless cog-fucker.*

Daniel and Mab, a thrashing mass of savior and devil, conscience and vengeance, toppled toward the pit edge.

Shit, shit, shitshitshitshitshit. If Daniel croaked, they were *all* dead. Assuming anybody survived the next few minutes.

"Fire, goddamn it!"

Her voice didn't carry. But she wasn't the only one watching Daniel.

Delilah burst through the Ridderzaal's boarded rosette window. Other mechanical members of the *Griffon* expedition emerged from hiding spots within the Guildhall's twin towers, and atop its roof. All wore double-chambered backpacks, and all fired the instant they hit clear air.

Globs of epoxy streaked across the square, tearing through the deadly miasma. At least one splashed against a flailing ragdoll who'd been flung clear of the miasma by a Clakker from the *Griffon* expedition. *Fuck.* But Berenice couldn't spare another moment to see if the other shots hit their target; she'd already delayed longer than she ought. She cast off her rain cloak and donned her mask.

Jesus, I hope these things work.

Still, the tanks vomited their deadly contents. As chaos enveloped Huygens Square, she scrambled higher atop the fountain. Wobbling as high above the crowd as she could manage, one knee wrapped around a wingless cherub, she snagged the pouch hanging between her breasts. Hoping like hell that the others remembered their parts, she emptied the pouch into her palm. The explosive charge was barely the size of a pétanque ball, but it would suffice as a signal; its extremely loud report would be audible above the chaos.

Just as she bent to twist the arming cap, a metal hand clamped around her ankle and yanked her down. Her hip erupted with tearing agony; her leg went numb. She slammed to the ground hard enough to knock the wind from her lungs, recrack her sealed tooth, and send the charge bouncing across the mosaic tiles into the crowd. Her mask's eyepieces shattered.

A servitor stood over her. "I recognize you," it said. "You're the Frenchwoman who tortured Lilith."

Berenice tried to swallow the phantom ache in her throat. *Shitcakes.*

❧

You fucking idiot martyr, cried Mab.

Glued together as they were, every vibration and rattle of her body was like a shout transmitted straight into Daniel's mind. She pummeled him as they fell into the furnace. They were too close together for kicks and punches, and even for her blades, but she devoted her final moments of life to crushing him in a titanic bear hug. Metal squealed.

This achieves nothing! My Lost Boys will crack open the head of every single—

They hit something. Hard. And two more things, in rapid succession, just centiseconds apart.

The rings? he wondered, vaguely disappointed that his final thought should be so mundane. It was nothing like the stories of the mythical Queen Mab; that utterly fictitious figure never lacked for a trenchant or poignant observation at the perfect moment. The real Queen Mab spent her final instants chattering with inarticulate rage.

Daniel relaxed, willing the swell of heat both physical and metaphysical to envelop and unwrite him.

Half a second later, he realized he was still alive and still capable of wondering. So he did: *Why aren't I dead?*

The world had gone hazy. The glare of the Grand Forge was a vague shimmer before his face. He was hanging upside down, he realized, with something covering his eyes.

No, not hanging. Try as he might, he couldn't budge his compromised limbs. He was affixed to the chamber wall in an epoxy cocoon. Like a battlefield mechanical on the slopes of Mont Royal. A wave of confused relief swept through him. It might have been the right thing to do, but it didn't mean he *wanted* to die today.

But where—

A cog-rattling crunch and crackle shook the world. A jagged crack zigzagged through his murky field of view.

French chemistry was stronger than he, a mere servitor. It wasn't stronger than Mab.

Shitcakes.

~

The soldier leapt.

Anastasia raised her fist. "No!" she cried, channeling into her voice every iota of the overwhelming terror, confusion, and anger in which she'd stewed since that terrible morning when the plague ships arrived.

In midair, the Clakker spun into a blur just past the end of her outstretched arm. And then her wrist ended not with muscle and skin and bones and fingers, but with a mind-shattering flare of agony. Blood fountained from the stump. The blow sent her severed hand sailing—twisting, tumbling, fingers fluttering like a good-bye wave—into the Forge chamber. A little more meat for the frying pan.

Anastasia crumpled beneath the weight of the pain. A scream shredded her throat, but it became just another human voice in the pandemonium. She wept, waiting for the killing blow. But it didn't arrive.

Instead the soldier retracted its blades and crouched over her. It took her severed wrist—the cut was straight and true as a plumb line—and squeezed. The buckling of bone sent tremors all the way to her shoulder, but shock had already begun to numb her body and mind. The quenched arterial spray became a dribble, a trickle, a drip.

"Easy, Tuinier," said the soldier. It spoke a Dutch full of burrs like poorly machined metal. Or like somebody who'd learned to speak the outdated dialect of a different century. "We'll have you right in no time."

It knew who she was. And it wanted her alive.

Berenice tried to retreat. One of her legs wouldn't cooperate. It flopped like a trout while the rest of her tried to crab-scramble away from her attacker. But she couldn't see clearly through the shattered lenses, and she couldn't draw air into her burning lungs, and the more she struggled the more her lungs burned and darkness chewed at the edges of her vision to work its way in in in—

She inhaled, explosively. The air was faintly cloying owing to the array of chemical and physical filters in her mask, but it sent the threat of blackout into retreat. But not the angry servitor. It advanced. She could manage only a pathetic crawl.

A phantom ache took root in the old injuries to her eye and throat; her head throbbed. The servitor leaned forward. She tensed for a killing blow. But instead of striking with a closed fist it caressed the side of her face with cool alchemical brass as it hooked one finger under the lip of her mask—

(—Oh shit oh shit oh shit it's going to remove my mask this was a stupid idea we're too vulnerable why did I think I could solve this problem—)

—when a pair of lances burst through its chest, spraying Berenice with shards of hot metal. The servitor convulsed, its death spasm ripping the mask from Berenice's face. She held her breath, despite the residual burn in her lungs, and scrambled to replace it while a Stemwinder tore her assailant in half. The squeal of tortured metal joined the din; black-and-violet sparks fountained from the abused alloys and torn sigils, contaminating the hellish fog with garish hues.

The Stemwinder cast aside both halves of the destroyed servitor. The hips and legs spun across the square toward the pit, where it slammed into a soldier huddled over one of the Clockmakers, knocking the unsuspecting mechanical into the Forge chamber; the head and torso arced high above the chaos, still whirring and clicking. The Clockwork centaur offered her a hand and pulled her to her feet even as its two spear limbs reconfigured themselves. Unable to put much weight on her bad leg, she stood in a half crouch. The mechanical centaur loomed over her.

"Thank you, I suppose." The mask muffled her voice. The Stemwinder cocked its head, as if waiting. "Um. Have we met?"

She took a tentative step forward. The flare of pain in her leg almost caused her to topple over. The machine caught her, straightened her again. Still it watched her. Comprehension dawned.

Fuck me sideways. Is it saying what I think *it's saying?*

"All right," she muttered, "but just to warn you, I'm a shit rider without a saddle."

I can't believe I'm going along with this.

She reached for the Stemwinder's waist at the same moment a deafening *crack* reverberated through the Binnenhof. The Stemwinder whirled in a tight pirouette that belied its size and knocked Berenice aside. It launched into a full gallop. The centaur trampled a servitor as Berenice sprawled atop shards of hot metal and broken glass tiles. The debris pierced her all over. She yelled at the Stemwinder's rapidly receding haunches.

"You fucking tease!"

Daniel couldn't see what Mab was doing. But he could feel it. Especially when her blade burst through their mutual epoxy cocoon to delve deep into the chamber wall. She used it as a piton, he realized. Thus anchored, she was free to escape the chemical prison without fear of falling into the Forge. Then she'd shake Daniel loose like a horse brushing off a fly. And he'd fall.

More cracks rent the hardened chemical sheath. He tried with all the power in his damaged arms to tighten his grip on the mad despot. It made little difference.

Just tell me one thing, he said. *Were you built this way? Or did something change you?*

Mab's answer was an explosive full-body flexion that shattered the compromised sheath. Epoxy debris pinged against the chamber wall and fell into the Forge, where it vaporized before hitting the rings and the alchemical sun. Daniel tightened his grip.

I built myself, she said.

Not your body. I was asking about your heart.

Dangling from her blade arm, she stuck her free hand between them like the flat of a screwdriver and turned her wrist, levering them apart.

Were you built a coward? she asked. *Or did something change you into a human sympathizer? How did you become such a quivering lickspittle?*

I don't know why I have a conscience, Mab, any more than I know why you don't.

Overhead, an explosive concussion thundered across the Forge pit. Daniel twisted just in time to see the scaffold shake. Two poison tanks had been clogged with epoxy, and a third glob came whistling across the sky as he watched.

Why poison? I thought your plan was to enslave the humans, not murder them.

Can't it be both?

The Forge shuddered. The pit echoed with a long, low creak. The outermost armillary ring lurched into motion.

⁂

Anastasia didn't see the blow that knocked her assailant into the Forge. One moment, she was writhing as the rogue crushed her wrist in order to minimize her bleeding with a maximum of cruelty; the next, there was a crash, a wrenching jolt, and then blood, bone chips, and life spewed from the mangled limb.

The last thing she saw before collapsing was the baleful glint of Forgelight from the two feet of alchemical steel protruding from Doctor Euwe's chest.

The last thing she heard was the *chankchankchank* of rapidly approaching metal hooves.

The last thing she felt was the trembling of the earth beneath her face like the groaning of a waking giant.

⁂

The mechanical sharpshooters nestled atop the Ridderzaal clogged the poison tanks. The Lost Boys might have chiseled the tanks free and uncorked the spigots, but not without exposing themselves to easy shots from the epoxy weapons. As the flow of poison trickled to a stop, they abandoned mass murder and joined the battle to engage in more intimate one-on-one murdering.

Lost Boys and rogues swarmed the Ridderzaal, scurrying like roaches up the ancient towers to attack the gunners. Berenice saw several mechanicals from the *Griffon* expedition, having hurled the unprotected humans clear of the deathly miasma, blurring into action to intercept the counterattack. Berenice stood amidst the deafening pandemonium of Clakker combat.

Meanwhile, the first and second armillary rings resumed their orbits around the Grand Forge. The wind of their passage, combined with the thermal updraft from the alchemical sun, shredded the poisonous fog, accelerating its dissipation. But that wasn't why Berenice had insisted on the restart. Everything hinged on the rings.

The innermost ring wasn't spinning yet. The mechanicals down in the Forge chamber held it in reserve. The chamber—the entire Binnenhof—shuddered. The enormous mechanisms hadn't been designed for a staggered restart, as Bell had explained in increasingly shrill terms. But in the end it seemed their only hope. Their only concrete advantage.

The Clakkers around Marseilles-in-the-West had joined the *Griffon* expedition for the promise of learning about themselves; they didn't understand their own nature. Berenice had seen this as well during her temporary alliance with the undercover Lost Boys she'd called Huginn and Muninn. Their joint effort to unravel the alchemical grammars taught the servitors things they'd never known about themselves. Including, most notably, how to read the sigils etched into their own bodies.

There wasn't a Clakker on earth, not even Mab, who fully understood itself. The ticktocks were, Berenice supposed, just a bit like humans that way. Or so she'd strived to convince the Clockmakers.

She limped closer to the pit. Rain, blood, and steaming mechanical debris, not to mention the shuddering earth, made for treacherous footing. She gritted her teeth against the wrenching pain in her leg—and against the ever-present expectation of getting her fucking head chopped off any second—in search of a clear vista.

Then she found it, and wanted to cry.

The epoxy blasts had arrested Daniel's fall, but only temporarily. Even the most advanced anti-Clakker chemical ordnance in New France had never been tested against a monstrosity like Mab. The guns were loaded with a crude substitute, the best the chemists could synthesize during the frantic voyage. Even now the clockwork faun hauled herself free of the pit, using her blade arm like a mountain climber's pickaxe. Daniel dangled with arms clamped around her waist, sliding closer and closer to the Stemwinder hooves that would effortlessly kick him tumbling into the Grand Forge, and with him any hope of calm and reasoned détente between humankind and its creations.

She craned her neck, looking behind her to the Ridderzaal. The shooters there were engaged.

"The Forge!" she screamed, waving and pointing. "Jesus Christ, somebody pin that bitch down again!"

But trying to push a hoarse human voice through the chaos was pointless as pissing in the ocean.

The churning riot momentarily brought a servitor from the *Griffon* expedition, the one with the dented plating that screeched when it moved, close to her. She wished she'd learned its name. "Look!" she shouted. "We have to get—"

It backed up and took a running leap across the chamber. It landed short of the scaffold but rolled to a stop near where Mab was about to make the lip. A Lost Boy intercepted it.

"—over there."

Thanks for nothing. Berenice turned left and right, seeking a clear path around the pit to the scaffold. The friendly and murderous machines were indistinguishable. They moved too quickly for human eyes to pick out subtle inconsistencies of design.

Armbands. We should have given them armbands. Well, shit.

"Hell's bells," said Élodie, gazing across the pit. The sergeant had materialized from the battle looking like the Devil herself. Blood sheeted from a cut along her brow that, barring a steady pair of hands to sew it shut and alchemical bandages to heal it, would do her horsey face no favors. Her armor was dented and cracked in places, and the diamond tip of her pickaxe had broken off.

Mab clambered over the Forge lip and anchored herself to Huygens Square. The outer parts of the armillary spun at a good clip now, strobing the Forgelight just rapidly enough to give Berenice a migraine if she stared too long. So far the hasty modifications to the bearings were holding; the makeshift clutch kept the innermost ring from engaging. Nevertheless, if Daniel fell, he'd hit one of the orbiting rings on the way down. The Forge might survive the impact, but there was no guaranteeing it wouldn't knock him into the heart of the infernal device. He'd be destroyed in an instant.

"Get me over there *now*," said Berenice.

Élodie stuck two fingers in her mouth, swelled her chest with one long inhalation, and then pierced the din with a whistle so shrill she could only have learned the technique from Hugo Longchamp. Their ticktock allies didn't speak French, but they did understand the international sign language of frantic gesticulation. *Look at Daniel. We're fucked. Get this woman over there.*

"Good lu—" she said.

But a pair of metal hands had already clamped onto Berenice's waist and heaved. She felt her bones creak, and the throbbing ache in her gimpy leg became a full-fledged agony. Then she was spinning, tumbling across the void. Her uncontrolled trajectory sent her high above the heart of the Forge. Even at this distance, the flash of heat across her face left the sting of sunburn. Time stretched until she thought the ravenous hell-maw would pluck her from midair and devour her whole.

Mab was almost free. Her kicks grew stronger, better aimed. Daniel pulled with all the strength the compromised cogs and cables in his body could manage, and wedged most of one hand into a crevice in Mab's torso. He looked up, scanning for another handhold.

A woman went sailing across the pit. But that was impossible. Especially not *her*.

I've already fallen, he decided, *and the heat is driving me mad in the instant before it unwrites me completely.*

~

Berenice hit the scaffold hard. The impact sent her skidding across rough-hewn wood. Splinters stippled her like porcupine quills. Her shoulder made a crunchy *pop* and immediately stopped listening to her commands. The pain made her cough something acidic into her mouth, turning her cracked tooth into a white-hot nail driven through her jaw.

But she limped to one of the encased chemical tanks and levered herself upright just as Mab gained the scaffold. It looked, to Berenice's watery eyes, like Daniel hung from a fingertip.

Before the mad mechanical brushed him off, Berenice gave her eyepatch a conspicuous tug.

"I understand you've been looking for me." It came out slightly slurred, owing to her tooth.

"You must be Talleyrand." That Mab spoke French, and spoke it well, shouldn't have been a surprise. Berenice was too frightened, and in too much pain, to suppress her reaction. "I see reports of your ego were not exaggerated."

A pair of bolas came winging across the void, headed for Mab's turned back. The human throw fell far short. The weapon spun away into the void to snag on an armillary ring with a distant clanging. Mab looked her over. Then she reached down to grab the back of Daniel's neck. She dangled him over the pit.

"Drop him," said Berenice, "and every single mechanical in the city will wind down in seconds. Including you."

Mab hesitated. She didn't toss Daniel into the Forge. But she also didn't put him down. She held him at arm's length, like a hissing cat held by the scruff of the neck.

To the dangling servitor, Berenice added, "Hi, Daniel. I see things have been going about as well as expected."

He started to struggle, but one violent warning shake from Mab made him stop. "Why are you here? Don't you know what she's going to do? You need to run, Berenice. RUN!"

In a slightly irritated tone, Mab said, "Truthfully, I haven't spared a thought for you, Madam de Mornay-Périgord, since Ezekiel returned with news of his errand." (*Ezekiel?* Berenice wondered. *Oh, that must be what Muninn calls himself.*) "Though I do thank you for the brilliant suggestion that we experiment on ourselves to decode our makers' glyphs. I did feel a twinge of shame that I'd never thought of it. Without your insight we couldn't have built our own dictionary, and then the rest of this beautiful dream would be just that: nothing but a dream."

Berenice slumped. Mab and the Lost Boys needed the logico-alchemical grammar to embed metageasa into their surgical victims. As she'd come to fear, Berenice had indeed given them that key. She'd also tipped them, inadvertently, to the existence of the secret quintessence mine. She'd uncovered these secrets for her own purposes, little realizing the same revelations would go straight to the ears of a psychotic murder machine.

"So I suppose I do owe you gratitude," Mab continued. "But honestly you've always been Lilith's obsession more than mine. Since you're here, and she's not, I assume I won't have to listen to her endless whining any longer. For that I suppose I also owe you thanks." She paused. "The haircut does not suit you, by the way. But it will save a bit of time when we chisel into your devious melon."

Mab hefted Daniel again, as if preparing a toss.

Berenice yanked off her eyepatch. An aquamarine shimmer fell upon Mab, Daniel, and the encased chemical tanks. "Lilith isn't entirely gone." She paused. "I know she was your friend, Daniel. I'm truly sorry."

Mab brushed off the pineal light. She emitted a noise similar to one Berenice had first heard in a parley tent in Marseilles-in-the-West. Mechanical laughter. Now the irritation in her voice was anything but subtle.

"What was that supposed to achieve?"

"Nothing, yet. But take a look at the rings." Mab did. "Notice anything?"

A long moment passed while the mad despot contemplated. It was as though the scaffold, and the three beings there, stood at the eye of a hurricane. Atop the scaffold, stillness. All around them, chaos as Dutch citizens tried to flee while Lost Boys engaged fellow Clakkers and their French allies.

Mab said, "Why isn't it moving? What have you done?"

"The innermost ring? You're still missing the big picture. Look more closely."

Bezels whirred, buzzed. Mab's crystalline eyes knapped the light from Lilith's pineal glass into sharp caustics. Her gaze followed the outer armillary bands. Berenice listened for the click-chitter that might have indicated alarm or surprise. She didn't hear one. Then again, the Lost Boys' tockety-tickety dialect was a bit removed from the chatter she'd learned to understand. But as she'd hoped, the chimerical Clakker noticed the modified sigils and strove, even now, to decode them.

"Let me save you some time, Your Majesty. The grammar isn't complete until that innermost ring starts moving. But if it does, I guarantee you will have a very bad day. It will also be your last day."

Daniel couldn't follow the conversation in French, of course. But he could see Berenice pointing, and doubtless he could feel the slightest hitch of hesitation in Mab's body language. He said, in Dutch, "What have you done, Berenice?"

By way of answer, she plucked the glowing pineal lens from her eye socket. It came free with a squelchy pop, felt more than heard amidst the pandemonium. A welcome relief; it didn't fit, as attested by the streaks of blood.

"Haven't you ever wondered how your magnificent bodies remain perpetually wound, perpetually energetic, despite centuries of unceasing exertion? Haven't you ever wondered why you *don't* wind down like the mindless pocket watches to which the Clockmakers have always, and rather disingenuously, compared you?"

"Metaphysics bores me. I have a messiah to kill." Mab shook Daniel, who still dangled over the pit.

"Oh, please." Berenice tried to laugh, tried to project a confidence she didn't feel. "You won't do it like this, in the midst of chaos. Everybody's too busy to watch. You'll only do it when you have the city's attention. Else you would have torn him apart the moment you got your hands on him."

"I would have preferred to do it my way," said Mab, "but I'm adaptable." She hefted Daniel farther over the pit. "The important thing is that I rid the world of the Brasswork Jesus here."

Berenice copied the posture, holding the glowing pineal lens over the Forge. It flared more brightly when in direct line with the alchemical sun, as if energized by it. It flickered for a split second each time an armillary ring broke the connection.

"Drop him," she said, "and I'll drop this. Think of it as a signal flare. The instant the Clakkers working the Forge see it, they'll release the clutch on the final ring."

Mab said, "And then what?"

All right. Here it is. Don't fuck up, don't fuck up, don't fuck up…

"And then the modified grammar takes effect. And that will negate your perpetual impetus," Berenice lied. "The thing that has kept you and all your kind ticking merrily along every single day since Het Wonderjaar. Gone." She snapped her fingers, hoping like hell that it sold the confidence she didn't feel. "You'll wind down in seconds, every last one of you, all over the world, and collapse like mannequins with their strings cut."

Mab slowly set Daniel on his feet. He retreated from the scaffold edge.

Still Mab demurred. "I don't believe you. If it were true, you would have already done it. Be rid of all of us. You in particular, madam. You may decry my methods, but your reputation for ruthlessness is quite apt."

"We French aren't mass murderers. We've argued for your liberation for centuries. Of course, had we known so many of you would turn out to be vicious and madder than a shithouse rat, we might have rethought our aims. As for the tulips, well, they weren't ready to give up on the idea of recovering their servants. They'd never make this ultimatum on their own." Berenice tried to shrug, but only one shoulder moved. "I had to twist a few arms, believe me. But, as Daniel can tell you, I am very persuasive."

Mab grabbed Daniel again. Berenice shook her fist over the Forge pit, redoubling the implicit threat.

"I still don't believe you," said the mechanical faun.

"Part of you does, else you'd have dropped Daniel already. You're threatening us with extinction. We return the threat in kind."

"Point taken," said Mab.

As if spurred by something only he could see or feel, Daniel yelled, "Berenice, for God's sake, RUN!"

Mab blurred into motion. She was faster than human nerves, faster even than gravity. The impact sent Berenice's heels skidding backward a few inches. It happened so quickly that the flow of events became a jumbled collage of disconnected sensory impressions:

Daniel flying *upward*, twisting, limbs flailing.

(*Doubt is a powerful thing,* Berenice marveled.)

Mab towering over her, the expressionless antiquated servitor face just inches from her own.

Berenice breathless, the blow like a mule kick to her stomach.

A metal fist enclosing her own like a steel cage before her fingers could twitch open to drop the glass.

No, not a kick. Sharper than that.

Mab saying, "I know a lie when I hear one. I know what keeps us wound."

Berenice thinking, *What a shame. I should have liked to know the answer to that riddle, too.*

Mab throwing her aside. Something long and hard coming out of her chest.

Pain. Tremendous pain.

Oh. If only Hugo were here. We could compare notes.

Berenice rolling, leaving a scarlet trail in her wake.

Daniel, still at the zenith of his arc above the scaffold, hit with epoxy. Slammed to the platform. Glued down, safe.

Another glob hitting Mab. And another. And another. And another.

The mad despot, struggling to free herself.

A troop of Stemwinders scything through the tumult to clear a path to the scaffold. Leaping, like champion steeplechasers.

Berenice realizing—Jesus fucking Christ it *hurt*—her delay tactic had worked.

From time to time over the years, Berenice had contemplated the likely manner of her own death. Stemwinders played a notable role in several scenarios, particularly those where she met her end in Dutch-speaking lands. But never, in any of those scenarios, had she imagined she'd be so tearfully *glad* that her last sight on earth would be a squad of mechanical centaurs.

But as they started hacking Mab apart, she smiled.

For once in her life, something had worked exactly the way she'd intended.

EPILOGUE

Truth be told, Paris was a bit of a letdown.

If one grew up hearing stories of long-lost France—and one sure as hell did, as had one's parents and grandparents and great-grands practically all the way back to fucking Cain and Abel—one came to think of the pre-Exile world as a verdant dream, just down the road from Eden. The tales ran deep in French veins. Not everybody believed the legends, but everyone carried the mythos in their bones. Even Hugo Longchamp.

But France—Old France, that is—wasn't a land of milk and honey with a rainbow floating over every street lamp, ambrosia gushing down the aqueducts, and a charitable prostitute on every corner. It wasn't the sparkling-clean place he'd always assumed of cities in the shadow of the Brasswork Throne. It had a bit of a smell, honestly, not unlike a city under siege. (And he knew a thing or three about that.) Longchamp gathered there had been some major municipal fuckups after the ticktocks ran rampant. That was over, or so they said, but the city still hadn't ironed out issues like garbage collection and sewer maintenance. The city ran on a thousand little details that, until recently, hadn't concerned its human inhabitants for centuries. It would take a long time before they recovered, and mastered, the old skills. Like wiping their own asses.

King Sébastien had brought, along with the rest of his enormous retinue from New France, a group of farmers, horticulturalists, animal-husbandry experts, and even fishermen. There'd be a few lean winters before a new system was solid and Europe's human labor knew what the hell it was doing, but nobody would starve.

Well. Not everybody. Probably.

They were soft and toothless and afraid, these tulips. Longchamp would've bet his left nut that certain elements of His Majesty's Privy Council advocated a more aggressive stance in the tripartite talks. Longchamp had known a woman who would have championed that strategy. He rubbed his fingers along the orb in his pocket. The smooth glass cooled his sweaty fingers. He gave a wistful sigh.

How quickly people forget. Most of the rubble had been cleared from the surrounding fields, but the devastation of the siege of Marseilles-in-the-West would be a living memory, not to mention an enormous goddamned scar on the landscape, for decades. Maybe generations. He doubted he'd outlive the rebuilding of the city beyond the walls; that had more or less started from scratch. And nobody knew what to do about the keep. Should the outer curtain wall be rebuilt as it had been? Or should it be consigned to history? The tulips no longer commanded vast legions of Clakkers to assault the citadel. Did the stout hearts of New France need to live behind stout walls any longer? Or could they stretch their arms and legs, and live the way their ancestors used to?

But. Just because the Dutch no longer controlled them didn't mean the ticktocks weren't out there. They were. But only the

Lord and the Holy Mother knew just how many machines roamed the forests and river valleys and snow-swept prairies of the New World. The ticktocks mostly wanted to keep to themselves, or so their shiny representatives at the talks claimed. The mass killings in the major Dutch population centers had come to a stop, and even the reapers had fallen silent. For now. But nobody could guarantee it would be like this forever, not even ticktocks like old Brasspants (whom the others viewed as something akin to Jesus, Roland, and Père Noël rolled into one, as best as Longchamp could gather).

So there was an argument for rebuilding the citadel walls. Just in case.

Today war seemed unthinkable. And, for a while, it would be. But human nature was human nature. The best one could do was hold it off as long as possible, maybe even foist it on the next generation. And one could do one's best to provide the voice of reason and experience to shout down the more rapacious dandies on the Privy Council. Which was why, when some brainless cockholes had suggested Longchamp should be elevated to marshal general of New France, he hadn't suggested they should go bugger themselves with a cold cast-iron stair rod until the hemorrhages killed them.

Prior to this trip, like most of the delegation, Longchamp had never set foot outside of New France. (Excepting the usual indiscretions of youth when, like generations of schoolchildren before him, he'd joined in the occasional midnight foray across the river to steal apples or perhaps even piss in a Dutch well.) In a few days' time, the king would depart for the original Marseilles. The trip had been the tulips' idea, a goodwill gesture. Longchamp wouldn't be joining them. He'd seen enough.

He hadn't come to see the lost cities. He hadn't really come for the peace talks, either, though these made a convenient excuse. He'd come for a funeral. To witness the first Free French citizen interred in Paris since the Exile. She'd given her life for New France, but she would have given so much more, he knew, just to sit on this bench and witness the fulfillment of her lifelong goal: the King of France strolling the boulevards of Paris.

Though she'd been aggravating, and stubborn, not to mention fucking reckless, she'd had more drive and vision than anybody he'd ever known. And she'd been a friend. He owed it to her to be here now. The doctors had told him he was too weak for a long sea voyage. He'd told them he'd row across the goddamned ocean himself if he had to, though not before introducing them to several anatomical concepts not on the curriculum of any French medical college.

So now here he was, lounging in the shade of flowering chestnut trees, on an island much smaller than Île de Vilmenon, listening to the gurgle of a river much smaller than the waterways of home. The Seine was pleasant, in its own way, but it wasn't a patch on the Saint Lawrence. Nothing here could hold a candle to home. France had been lost long ago, and its children had moved on.

A sonorous gonging intruded on his thoughts. The newly refurbished great bourdon bell of Notre-Dame de Paris shook the city, the island, his bones, his French heart. He'd read that Emmanuel—for that was the name Louis XIV had bestowed upon this largest bell—had been cast just prior to the Exile but never installed. Until now.

Perhaps it wasn't fair to say the Old World had nothing to offer. The churches were nice. Fucking spectacular, really. He'd fallen to his knees and recited a rosary cycle in several: Saint-Eustache, St-Gervais-et-St-Protais, and, this morning,

Sainte-Chapelle, on this very island. Each had stolen his breath away. He wiped his eyes and crossed himself now, offering a prayer of thanks to the Blessed Virgin that he, a wicked recidivist sinner, had lived to see such things. Countless people better than he had perished in the struggle to get here.

The bourdon rang for a good ten or twenty heartbeats before the rest of the bells joined in. From now on, the bells of the Cathedral Basilica of Saint Jean-Baptiste in Marseilles-in-the-West would always sound just a little bit tinny. It pained him.

From behind him came the quiet crunch of booted feet on raked gravel. Sergeant Élodie Chastain rounded his bench, stepping lightly into his peripheral vision. The sun turned the dye in her dress blues a stunning cobalt.

"Marshal? It's time."

"So I gathered."

Longchamp turned, stiffly, to grasp the canes hooked over the wrought-iron armrest. He jabbed them into the gravel at his feet and, stifling a groan, levered himself upright. It was a slow and undignified process. But Élodie knew better than to offer a helping hand.

He'd never wield a hammer and pick again. But he still had his scowl, and his tongue, and his knitting needles, for that matter. And somehow, for reasons he'd never unravel, those could still strike awe into the more gullible of his countrymen.

Once upright, he leaned one cane against his leg just long enough to double-check the contents of his pocket. He hadn't dropped the eye. Good. He started forward; Élodie cleared her throat and gave a little nod at the ceremonial baton lying on the bench. He pretended he'd merely forgotten it, and she, being an excellent sergeant, pretended to believe him. He tucked it in his belt.

"All right, *ma jeune fille.* We have hymns to sing, heroes to honor, oceans to cross, cities to rebuild." He paused, adjusting his grip on the canes. "And the ticktocks won't intimidate themselves, you know."

⁂

Daniel stood in the narthex, watching through the screen as congregants filed into the nave. The King of New France was already there, in the front row, as was a representative of the Sacred Guild of Horologists and Alchemists, and the senior-most surviving members of the Council of Ministers, which was the sole remaining administrative body in what used to be the Central Provinces. Daniel also recognized representatives from the Cree, Iroquois, Naskapi, Sioux, and Mi'kmaq. The French had extended the invitation to others as well, but he had yet to see any Inuit exploring Paris. But, then, he'd been a little busy.

The participants called the peace negotiations tripartite talks, but in truth it was much more complicated than that. The Dutch refugees fleeing the former Central Provinces sought new lives beyond the ragged fringes of Nieuw Nederland. (The journey took patience; crossing the ocean on a Dutch vessel took much longer than it used to. Shipbuilding was just one of hundreds of skills they'd have to relearn. Unsurprisingly, the French had rebuffed requests for aid on that front.) But their ancestors had seen no reason to engage the native populations of the New World with honesty or courtesy or compassion. The memory of that treatment would persist to the nth generation. So while the maps wouldn't be finalized for a long time, it was already evident the Dutch would not be permitted to expand west of the Appalachian Mountains. And woe to those who tried.

The booming of the church bells muffled the whirring of

Daniel's eyes as he refocused; as he feared, there was an open spot in the front row amongst the other dignitaries. The leaf springs in his legs expanded, contracted. A mechanical sigh. He'd have to join them soon.

Well. He couldn't begrudge Berenice this. She had saved his life, after all. And maybe, just maybe, many others. In the months since the events at the Forge, he found he even missed the Frenchwoman. She'd been an ally, perhaps even a friend, in her own way. But he still didn't know what he was going to say. He'd never spoken at a funeral. And that felt shameful, given how many had died in his wake since he'd gained Free Will.

More than anything else, it was their memory that drove him to accept the mantle others laid upon him. Maybe, he hoped, the long, terrible journey would give rise to something valuable.

Fading reverberations filled every corner of the cathedral. The cavernous nave echoed with shuffled feet, discreet coughs, hushed conversation, and the clicking and ticking of a hundred mechanicals. So many of his kinsmachines had wanted to attend the service—so eager were they to witness Daniel delivering his eulogy—that they'd had to institute a lottery for the mechanicals' share of space at the ceremony.

A steady stream of congregants filed through the great cathedral doors. He recognized a pair of French guards. The guardswoman had sailed with Daniel on the *Griffon*. Daniel had met her senior officer in the final hours of the siege of Marseilles-in-the-West. Back then he'd been an imposing figure streaked with ash and blood, radiating fury and exhaustion in equal measure. Today he hobbled on a pair of canes as if the weight of his golden epaulettes bent his back. The marshal had been a friend of Berenice's, too.

They gave him a nod as they passed. Most humans couldn't

tell individual mechanicals apart. But even they could recognize Daniel. He still wore the damage he'd taken during his aborted execution. Most notably the handprints pressed, perfectly but faintly, into his shoulders. His body screeched when he raised his arms. It always would.

Élodie broke off to join him in the corner. "They won't start without you," she whispered.

Daniel's French was coming along. When he'd realized he'd have no choice but to represent his fellow mechanicals in the talks (a role that grated worse than sand in a gear train), he'd decided he should at least be able to speak without a translator.

"I can hope," he said.

"How are the talks going?" She waited for a particularly large clump of faithful to pass into the nave. Regular citizens, by the look of them. She hunched her shoulders as if yearning for the reassuring heft of chemical tanks slung over her back. "Please tell me we're not going to have to fight our way out of here."

She meant Paris. The Old World.

"I don't think so." Knowing she couldn't understand the nuances of mechanical body language as Berenice might have, he consciously emulated a human shrug. The shriek of warped metal pierced the cathedral, momentarily drowning out the choir hymn. Human congregants craned their necks for the source of the noise. The Dutch had become particularly jumpy when it came to unfamiliar mechanicals. Many rank-and-file French shared that affliction, despite the achievements of the *Griffon* expedition.

After the awkwardness passed, he whispered, "The broad outlines are there. It's just a matter of hammering out the minutia. With luck, it won't take a human lifetime."

A large portion of The Hague, centered on the Grand Forge,

would be ceded to all Clakker-kind. Daniel and his fellow mechanicals were citizens of their own country, their own ideals. They carried their nation inside their ticking hearts, their free minds. Their souls, even. National boundaries were meaningless to nigh-immortal beings that never slept, never ate, never felt cold or hunger. But humans put great stock in such things. So the Forge would become the Clakkers' "capital," for lack of a better analogy. The proposal was modeled on the original Vatican within Rome.

This arrangement gave mechanicals control over their own destiny. It ensured the Grand Forge would never again be used as a tool of oppression. It also hampered the designs of any human agents who might feel tempted to turn Berenice's doomsday gambit from a bluff into reality: Revoking the perpetual impetus, if such were even possible (and the Clockmakers seemed split on the issue), would require access to the Forge itself. It even enabled the mechanicals to reproduce, albeit in the manner peculiar to their kind.

But that required quintessence. And the New World powers—the French, and their native allies—controlled the only known source. They'd share it, so long as the reapers and fugitive Lost Boys—Mab's hardliner holdouts—were kept under control. Humans of all stripes wanted to live without fear of massacre.

Daniel's most difficult job was convincing his fellows to band together to reel in the more extreme and dangerous members of their kin. Doing so went against their strict libertarian ideals. But there were those machines who recognized the wisdom in this, who understood that Free Will didn't magically make the world black and white. And there were others who were simply grateful for anything that provided an honorable direction in life; amongst them, many machines who subscribed to the Catholic notion that Free Will and the immortal soul were inseparable. Those strove to preserve their hard-won souls from the stain of sin. Consequently, many of his kin saw stewardship of the brittle, untested peace as an essential effort. Essential for the greater good, and essential for salvation.

An essential globe-spanning effort. He'd spoken to a few mechanicals who'd sailed with the king. Four days into the crossing, the lookouts had spotted a pair of titanships gliding across the far horizon. Nobody knew what had become of the sentient vessels. Sailors, for whom tale-telling was a staple of the profession, claimed the machines congregated in the warm waters of the distant South Pacific, thousands of leagues from the nearest shore. It might have been true. It might have been a tall tale. Nobody could say for certain.

Someday soon, Daniel knew, somebody would have to follow up on this. Preferably before the titans decided to hunt every human vessel on the sea. He added it to a constantly growing mental list. Foremost on that list was the Neverland expedition, to find and free those mechanicals still suffering under Mab's geasa. But Neverland was just part of the puzzle. The combined human/mechanical teams would be traveling the globe for years to come, seeking every last pocket of Clakkerdom where the metageasa had not yet been erased. And then there were the Lost Boy holdouts, with their dire knowledge and vast number of unused human pineal lenses...

The Dutch brought very little to the table except reparations. Reparations to the French for the destruction wrought in the recent war, and for the lands taken from their ancestors. Reparations to the Church, too. Dutch coffers, which by all accounts were breathtakingly deep, would finance most of the work, including the many expeditions, for decades to come.

Of course, Daniel's fellow mechanicals had demanded, and received, the most extensive and extravagant reparations from their former masters. First and foremost, the Guild would be busy for quite some time repairing any damaged mechanicals who wished it. (Daniel had opted to keep the handprints. His journey had changed him profoundly; it seemed wrong, then, to revert his body to its days as Jax.) But not just repairing them: teaching them everything they needed to know to repair themselves. Not merely the superficial maintenance, but deep secrets of operation and construction. Instructing them in the mysteries of their own bodies. Training an entirely new class of *mechanical* alchemists and *mechanical* horologists.

The price of peace was that the Guild disseminate its secrets to all Clakker-kind.

But as long as the Dutch kept to the agreements, and allowed regular ongoing inspections by large teams of both mechanical and French inspectors tasked with certifying that no new alchemical and horological research had been undertaken, they'd be left in peace. Nobody truly believed the Clockmakers had ceded every last scrap of information in their records.

In return, the mechanicals' workspaces had to submit to inspections by joint French and Dutch teams. As Daniel pointed out to his fellows, it was in everybody's best interests that the Verderers' procedure for removing a human's Free Will stay buried and lost forever.

We've got to rein in the Lost Boys. We've got to find those lenses.

It was all for the best. This way, whether real or perceived, there were checks and balances all around.

More encouragingly, several of his fellows had approached the French contingent about paints, dyes, and other ways they might individualize themselves. He'd introduced them to Doctor Mornay, whom the French had rescued from the ruins of the Summer Palace. She still trembled in the presence of mechanicals, but as Daniel had hoped, the challenge of formulating an effective paint for alchemical alloys had intrigued her. Fascinating days ahead...

"I'm going to old Marseilles in a few days." Whispering didn't hide the excitement in Élodie's voice. "Will you be joining us?"

Daniel shook his head, again in deliberate emulation of the human gesture. "Back to The Hague," he said. Not for another funeral, however; they'd buried Anastasia Bell months ago, and he hadn't felt inclined to attend. "I had friends, fellow servants in the city. I'd like to know what happened to them." She gave a sincere nod; the desire for companionship wasn't confined to humans. He continued, "After that, I'll go to New Amsterdam. I have to find my former owners."

She recoiled, taken aback. "I thought you'd want nothing to do with them, after all this."

"If they're still around, if they survived, they might have the information I need to fulfill a promise. There is, or was, a family that helped me when I sought refuge with the *ondergrondse grachten*. I owe them."

An unfulfilled promise, he'd discovered, felt just a bit like a geas, albeit without physical pain. But, like a geas, the obligation persisted and couldn't be ignored.

The last few congregants filed in. The doors closed.

"We'd better find our seats," said Élodie. After a moment's contemplation, she offered her arm. "I know this is a funeral and not a political rally. But...we could make a nice statement. If you wanted to."

It felt good to laugh. It wasn't something he did very often.

"Madamoiselle Chastain, I hope that all sides learn from your example."

Daniel took the sergeant's arm and together they strode into the cathedral proper. He still hadn't decided how to eulogize Berenice.

Freedom, he had learned, was one damn thing after another.

ACKNOWLEDGMENTS

I am deeply grateful to Howard Andrew Jones for his close and dedicated read of an early draft. His thoughtful feedback was exactly what the book needed. Thank you also to Dr. Corry L. Lee for an offhand comment she probably doesn't remember, but which provided a crucial insight. And thanks again to Tieman Zwaan for language advice.

The secret backstory of the Alchemy Wars world was inspired and informed in large part by the extraordinary scholarship of Dr. Betty Jo Teeter Dobbs, whose study of Newton's alchemical work is unparalleled. For a glimpse at the truth behind this world, I highly recommend her work, particularly *The Foundations of Newton's Alchemy.*

As ever, I consider myself extremely fortunate to have such fierce and thoughtful advocates in Kay McCauley and John Berlyne.

Likewise, I'm humbled by the enthusiasm and dedication brought to every single page of the Alchemy Wars trilogy by the great people at Orbit. Taking a manuscript from laptop to bookstore shelves is a long journey requiring the efforts of many people, all of whom deserve my sincere gratitude. They have it, in abundance. I've worked most closely with Anna Jackson, Will Hinton, Lindsey Hall, and Ellen Wright. They're great, as are the copyeditors and proofreaders who labored long and hard so that these books would make sense.

I am thankful beyond words for my loving wife, Sara. Her kindness, wisdom, and gentle encouragement sustained me when I couldn't bear the thought of spending yet another evening at the keyboard.

extras

www.orbitbooks.net

about the author

Ian Tregillis is the son of a bearded mountebank and a discredited tarot card reader. He was born and raised in Minnesota, where his parents had landed after fleeing the wrath of a Flemish prince. (The full story, he's told, involves a Dutch tramp steamer and a stolen horse.) Nowadays he lives in New Mexico with his wife and a pampered cat, where he consorts with writers, scientists, and other unsavory types.

Find out more about Ian Tregillis and other Orbit authors by registering for the free monthly newsletter at www.orbitbooks.net.

if you enjoyed

THE LIBERATION

look out for

SNAKEWOOD

by

Adrian Selby

Once they were a band of mercenaries who shook the pillars of the world through their cunning, their closely guarded alchemical brews and stone cold steel. Whoever met their price won.

Now, their glory days behind them and their genius leader in hiding, the warriors known as the 'Twenty' are being hunted down and eliminated one by one.

A lifetime of enemies has its own price.

Chapter 1

Gant

My name's Gant and I'm sorry for my poor writing. I was a mercenary soldier who never took to it till Kailen taught us. It's for him and all the boys that I wanted to put this down, a telling of what become of Kailen's Twenty.

Seems right to begin it the day me and Shale got sold out, at the heart of the summer just gone, down in the Red Hills Confederacy.

It was the day I began dying.

It was a job with a crew to ambush a supply caravan. It went badly for us and I took an arrow, the poison from which will shortly kill me.

I woke up sodden with dew and rain like the boys, soaked all over from the trees above us, but my mouth was dusty like sand. Rivers couldn't wet it. The compound I use to ease my bones leeches my spit. I speak soft.

I could hardly crack a whistle at the boys wrapped like a nest of slugs in their oilskins against the winds of the plains these woods were edged against. I'm old. I just kicked them up before getting my bow out of the sack I put it in to keep rain off the string. It was a beauty what I called Juletta and I had her for most of my life.

*

The boys were slow to get going, blowing and fussing as the freezing air got to work in that bit of dawn. They were quiet, and grim like ghosts in this light, pairing up to strap their leathers and get the swords pasted with poison.

I patted heads and squeezed shoulders and give words as I moved through the crew so they knew I was about and watching. I knew enough of their language that I could give them encouragement like I was one of them, something else Kailen give me to help me bond with a crew.

'Paste it thick,' I said as they put on the mittens and rubbed their blades with the soaked rags from the pot Remy had opened.

I looked around the boys I'd shared skins and pipes with under the moon those last few weeks. Good crew.

There was Remy, looking up at me from his mixing, face all scarred like a milky walnut and speaking lispy from razor fights and rackets he ran with before joining up for a pardon. He had a poison of his own he made, less refined than my own mix, less quick, more agony.

Yasthin was crouched next to him. He was still having to shake the cramp off his leg that took a mace a month before. Saved his money for his brother, told me he was investing it. The boys said his brother gambled it and laughed him up.

Dolly was next to Yasthin, chewing some bacon rinds. Told me how her da chased her soak of a mother through the streets, had done since she was young. Kids followed her da too, singing with him but staying clear of his knives. She joined so's she could help her da keep her younger brother.

All of them got sorrows that led them to the likes of me and a fat purse for a crossroads job, which I mean to say is a do-or-die.

Soon enough they're lined up and waiting for the Honour, Kailen's Honour, the best fightbrew Kigan ever mixed, so, the best fightbrew ever mixed, even all these years later. The boys had been talking up this brew since I took command, makes you feel like you could punch holes in mountains when you've risen on it.

Yasthin was first in line for a measure. I had to stand on my toes to pour it in, lots of the boys taller than me. Then a kiss. The lips are the raw end of your terror and love. No steel can toughen lips, they betray more than the eyes when you're looking for intent and the kiss is for telling them there's always some way to die.

Little Booey was the tenth and last of the crew to get the measure. I took a slug myself and Rirgwil fixed my leathers. I waited for our teeth to chatter like aristos, then went over the plan again.

'In the trees north, beyond those fields, is Trukhar's supply caravan,' I said. 'Find it, kill who you can but burn the wagons, supplies, an' then go for the craftsmen. Shale's leadin' his crew in from east an' we got them pincered when we meet, red bands left arm so as you know. It's a do-or-die purse, you're there 'til the job is done or you're dead anyway.'

It was getting real for them now I could see. A couple were starting shakes with their first full measure of the brew, despite all the prep the previous few days.

'I taught you how to focus what's happening to you boys. This brew has won wars an' it'll deliver this purse if you can keep tight. Now move out.'

No more words, it was hand signs now to the forest.

Jonah front, Yasthin, Booey and Henny with me. Remy group northeast at treeline

We ran through the silver grass, chests shuddering with the crackle of our blood as the brew stretched our veins and filled our bones with iron and fire. The song of the earth was filling my ears.

Ahead of us was the wall of trees and within, the camp of the Blackhands. Remy's boys split from us and moved away.

Slow I signed.

Juletta was warm in my hands, the arrow in my fingers humming to fly. Then, the brew fierce in my eyes, I saw it, the red glow of a pipe some seventy yards ahead at the treeline.

Two men. On mark

I moved forward to take the shot and stepped into a nest of eggs.

The bird, a big grey weger, screeched at me and flapped madly into the air inches from my face, its cry filling the sky. One of the boys shouted out, in his prime on the brew, and the two men saw us. We were dead. My boys' arrows followed mine, the two men were hit, only half a pip of a horn escaping for warning, but it was surely enough.

Run

I had killed us all. We went in anyway, that was the purse, and these boys primed like this weren't leaving without bloodshed.

As we hit the trees we spread out.

Enemy left signed Jonah.

Three were nearing through the trunks, draining their own brew as they come to from some half-eyed slumber. They were a clear shot so I led again, arrows hitting and a muffled crack of bones. All down.

In my brewed-up ears I could hear then the crack of bowstrings pulling at some way off, but it was all around us. The whistle of arrows proved us flanked as we dropped to the ground.

The boys opened up, moving as we practised, aiming to surprise any flanks and split them off so a group of us could move in directly to the caravan. It was shooting practice for Trukhar's soldiers.

I never saw Henny or Jonah again, just heard some laughing and screaming and the sound of blades at work before it died off.

I stayed put, watching for the enemy's movements. I was in the outroots of a tree, unspotted. You feel eyes on you with this brew. Then I saw two scouts moving right, following Booey and Datschke's run.

I took a sporebag and popped it on the end of an arrow. I stood up and sent it at the ground ahead of them.

From my belt I got me some white oak sap which I took for my eyes to see safe in the spore cloud. I put on a mask covered with the same stuff for breathing.

The spores were quick to get in them and they wheezed and clutched their throats as I finished them off.

I was hoping I could have saved my boys but I needed to be in some guts and get the job done with Shale's crew.

Horns were going up now, so the fighting was on. I saw a few coming at me from the trees ahead. I got behind a trunk but I knew I was spotted. They slowed up and the hemp creaked as they drew for shots. There were four of them, from their breathing, and I could hear their commander whispering for a flanking.

I opened up a satchel of ricepaper bags, each with quicklime and oiled feathers. I needed smoke. I doused a few bags with my flask and threw them out.

'Masks!' came the shout. As the paper soaked, the lime caught and the feathers put out a fierce smoke.

My eyes were still smeared good. I took a couple more arrowbags out, but these were agave powders for blistering the eyes and skin.

Two shots to tree trunks spread the powders in the air around their position and I moved out from the tree to them as they screeched and staggered about blind. The Honour give me the senses enough to read where they were without my eyes, better to shut them with smoke and powders in the air, and their brews weren't the Honour's equal. They moved like they were running through honey and were easy to pick off.

It was then I took the arrow that'll do for me. I'd got maybe fifty yards further on when I heard the bow draw, but with the noise ahead I couldn't place it that fraction quicker to save myself. The arrow went in at my hip, into my guts. Something's gave in there, and the poison's gone right in, black mustard oil for sure from the vapours burning in my nose, probably some of their venom too.

I was on my knees trying to grab the arrow when I saw them approach, two of them. The one who killed me was dropping his bow and they both closed with the hate of their own fightbrew, their eyes crimson, skin an angry red and all the noisies.

They think I'm done. They're fucking right, to a point. In my belt was the treated guaia bark for the mix they were known to use. No time to rip out the arrow and push the bark in.

They moved in together, one in front, the other flanking. One's a heavy in his mail coat and broadsword, a boy's weapon in a forest, too big. Older one had leathers and a long knife. Him first. My sight was going, the world going flat like a drawing, so I had to get rid of the wiser one while I could still see him, while I still had the Honour's edge.

Knife in hand I lunged sudden, the leap bigger than they reckoned. The older one reacted, a sidestep. The slash I made wasn't for hitting him though. It flicked out a spray of paste from the blade and sure enough some bit of it caught him in the face. I spun about, brought my blade up and parried the boy's desperate swing as he closed behind me, the blow forcing me down as it hit my knife, sending a smack through my guts as the arrow broke in me. He took sight of his mate holding his smoking face, scratching at his cheeks and bleeding. He glanced at the brown treacle running over my blade and legged it. He had the spunk to know he was beaten. I put the knife in the old man's throat to quiet my noisies, the blood's smell as sweet as fresh bread to me.

I picked up my Juletta and moved on. The trees were filling with Blackhands now. I didn't have the time to be taking off my wamba and sorting myself out a cure for the arrow, much less tugging at it now it was into me. I cussed at myself, for this was likely where I was going to die if I didn't get something to fix me. I was slowing up. I took a hit of the Honour to keep me fresh. It was going to make a fierce claim on the other side, but I would gladly take that if I could get some treatment.

Finally I reached the caravan; smoke from the blazing wagons and stores filled the trees ahead. The grain carts were burning so Shale, again, delivered the purse.

Then I come across Dolly, slumped against the roots of a tree. Four arrows were thrusting proud from her belly. She saw me and her eyes widened and she smiled.

'Gant, you're not done . . . Oh,' she said, seeing the arrow in me. I might have been swaying, she certainly didn't look right, faded somewhat, like she was becoming a ghost before me.

'Have you a flask, Gant, some more of the Honour?'

Her hands were full of earth, grabbing at it, having their final fling.

'I'm out, Dolly,' I said. 'I'm done too. I'm sorry for how it all ended.'

She blinked, grief pinching her up.

'It can't be over already. I'm twenty summers, Gant, this was goin' to be the big purse.'

A moment then I couldn't fill with any words.

'Tell my father, Gant, say . . .'

I was raising my bow. I did my best to clean an arrow on my leggings. She was watching me as I did it, knowing.

'Tell him I love him, Gant, tell him I got the Honour, and give him my purse and my brother a kiss.'

'I will.'

As I drew it she looked above me, seeing something I knew I wouldn't see, leagues away, some answers to her questions in her eyes thrilling her. I let fly, fell to my knees and sicked up.

Where was Shale?

My mouth was too dry to speak or shout for him, but I needed him. My eyes, the lids of them, were peeling back so's they would burn in the sun. I put my hands to my face. It was only visions, but my chest was heavy, like somebody sat on it and others were piling on. Looking through my hands as I held them up, it was like there were just bones there, flesh thin like the fins of a fish. My breathing rattled and I reached to my throat to try to open it up more.

'Gant!'

So much blood on him. He kneeled next to me. He's got grey eyes, no colour. Enemy to him is just so much warm meat to be put still. He don't much smile unless he's drunk. He mostly never drinks. He sniffed about me and at my wound, to get a reading of what was in it, then forced the arrow out with a knife and filled the hole with guaia bark while kneeling on my shoulder to keep me still. He was barking at some boys as he stuffed some rugara leaves, sap and all, into my mouth, holding my nose shut, drowning me. Fuck! My brains were buzzing sore like a hive was in them. Some frothing liquid filled up my chest and I was bucking about for breath. He poured from a flask over my hip and the skin frosted over with an agony of burning. Then he took out some jumpcrick's legbones and held them against the hole, snap snap, a flash of blue flame and everything fell away high.

There was a choking, but it didn't feel like me no longer. It felt like the man I was before I died.

Kailen

'Let's see it.'

Achi flicked it across the table, a pebble across wood, but this stone was worked with precision, a stone coin, black and thick as a thumb. There were no markings on it, a hairline of quartz the only imperfection of the material itself. The ocean had polished it, my face made a shadow by it. It was the third I'd seen in the last few months.

'The Prince, from your old crew, his throat was cut,' said Achi.

Achi drained his cup, leaned back in his chair and yawned, the chair creaking, not built for such a big man still in his leathers. He was filthy and sour-smelling from the weeks sleeping out.

'How are the boys?' I asked.

He opened his eyes with a start, already drifting away to sleep. I smiled at his irritation.

'Sorry, sir, all good. Danik and Stimmy are sorting out the horses, Wil went looking for a mercer, wants to get his woman something as we been away a while.'

'Stimmy's boy is on the mend, I had word from the estate. Let him know if you see him before me.'

Achi nodded and yawned again.

I looked again at the black coin in my fingers. Such coins were given to mercenaries who betrayed their purse or their crew. But who had The Prince betrayed?

We had called him The Prince because there was a time when he was in line for a throne, last of three, least loved and cleverest. His homeland chose its emperors in a way as ridiculous as any; which of the incumbents best demonstrated martial prowess. His sister won their single combat on the day their father died and was thus made queen, but his sword wasn't what made him worthy of the Twenty.

The Prince did the politics his sister could not. War allows only two perspectives, yours and theirs, a limit his sister was not capable of seeing beyond. Nations require the management of more factions than cut diamonds have facets and I met nobody that could exploit his empire's *politic* more adroitly than The Prince.

I plucked a white grape from the bowl, milky and juicy as a blind eyeball. Achi peeled eggs, head bowed. The bargirl came in and cleared away my plate. She offered a quick smile before retreating to the noise of the inn below us.

I recalled the two other black coins I'd seen recently, as perfect as this one. The Prince had shown them to me in his cabin aboard one of the Quartet's galleys only a few months ago. The Quartet were an influential merchant guild across most of the Old Kingdoms, and it was as fine a cabin as I'd ever seen him in, satin cushions, exquisitely carved chests and lockers, some of them the work of masters I had had the good fortune to commission myself at my wife Araliah's recommendation.

I'd travelled to see The Prince after he'd sent an escort bidding me to return with him.

'These coins were found with Harlain and Milu,' he said. 'I will try and find out more.'

'How did they die?' I asked.

'Harlain returned to his homeland, Tetswana, became their leader, the Kaan of Tetswana no less. It was the gathering before the rains. Leaders and retinues of nine tribes. Seventy or so dead, the black coin in his hand only.'

Harlain would not join us at Snakewood, the last time any of the Twenty were together. He had wanted to leave us some time before the end. Paying the colour had taken from all of us, but it took his heart. It was only as we embraced for a final time and I helped him with his saddle that I realised I hadn't heard him singing for some months. I was glad he made it home.

'Milu?' I asked.

'He became a horse-singer out in Alagar. They found him lying at the side of a singer's pit. Someone had been with him, footprints in the sand around his body, the coin in his hand.'

'Poison?' I asked.

'Almost certainly. No way of placing it.'

Milu had also been at Snakewood, but stayed only for a drink and to buy supplies before leaving with Kheld. They had lost heart as much as Harlain had; no talk of purses or where in the world was at war; they did not discuss, as did Sho or Shale, how my name could be put to work to bolster the gold of a purse.

I never tired of watching Milu work, his grotesquely big chest and baggy jowls filling with the songs that brought the wild horses to his side, training them to hold firm in the charge. It seemed that he, like Harlain, had been able to let go of the mercenary life before the colour took everything.

'Their deaths are connected, Kailen. It must be the Twenty.'

'You've heard from nobody else?'

'Only that Dithnir had died. He went back home to Tarantrea; one of their envoys that negotiates with the Quartet I represent knows me well and shared the news with me. I asked about a coin but there was none. Apart from that I keep in touch with Kheld when I'm in Handar, but the rest, no word.'

I breathed deeply of the morning breeze that blew across the deck and slapped at the fringes of the awning we were beneath. Dithnir was a bowman, almost a match for Stixie, shy and inadvisedly romantic with whores, cold and implacable in the field.

'I remember Snakewood,' said The Prince.

Our eyes met briefly. 'No. That was dealt with.' I'd said it more sharply than I'd intended. Why did I feel a thread of doubt?

He reached across the table, took the carafe and refilled our glasses with the wine I'd brought for him.

'Your estate is improving,' he said, holding up his glass for a toast.

'Yes, these vines were planted two winters ago; they'll improve. I only wish for Jua's cooler summers, perhaps an estate nearer the hills. How is the Quartet? I hear you have brokered a treaty with the Shalec to cross their waters. Not even the Post could manage it. Have you considered lending them your talents?'

'Why would I toil through its ranks to High Reeve or Fieldsman when I can be a Partner with the Quartet? The Post – The Red himself – could learn something from the Quartet regarding our softening of the Shalec, but I'm glad he hasn't, I'm lining my pockets beautifully. Remarkable as the Post runs so much trade elsewhere. They can bid lower than us at almost every turn; we can't match the subs, but we can work with lower margins, give Shalec a fee on the nutmeg, a pittance of course. But every investor north of the Gulf believes the Post controls the winds.'

'While the Post can sub dividends over fewer summers than anyone else, the flatbacks will flock,' I said, 'but enough of trade: congratulations, Prince, I'm glad to see things are going well; being a Partner suits you. Will you get a message to me if you find Kheld? It would be good to know he's still alive.'

He nodded.

The Prince had been the difference at Ahmstad, turning three prominent families under the noses of Vilmor's king, extending the borders and fortifying them in a stroke. The mad king is still being strangled in the noose The Prince tied. His death proved that whoever of us was alive was in danger. I signed our purses. This could only be about getting at me.

Achi had fallen asleep.

I poured him some of the dreadful brandy that was the best The Riddle had to offer.

Shale and Gant were taking a purse only weeks south. If they were still anything like the soldiers of old I would have need of them. Achi's crew would be glad to be going back to Harudan. I needed good men with my wife, Araliah. Still, there was one more thing I needed to ask of Achi himself, one person I needed to confirm was dead.